The Ballad of Clay Moore

Eric S. Hoffman

For Dad,
Who told me to keep writing.

Part I

Here Comes the Rain, Baby

Chapter 1

Baxter senses it first.

Ol' bloodhound.

I don't know if he smells something or hears something or what. Call it canine intuition.

We're out walking Dob's Creek at three a.m. No moon. Stars forever. Beautiful night.

I'm strolling through sagebrush, kicking rocks, when suddenly Baxter seizes up.

"What is it, boy?"

Teeth bared. Hackles raised. Something ain't right.

"You smell coyote?"

We've had a pack of prairie wolves roaming around lately. Mean mothers. Best to steer clear.

"Let's turn back."

I point toward home and whistle Bax to follow. Haven't gone five feet when he woofs at me. That burly bloodhound bark. All balls and business.

"All right then."

His lead now. Baxter shuffles across the creek bed and up the other side. I make to follow then I hear it. A noise on the wind. Weak and whiny, like a lightbulb buzz.

"What the hell?"

I ford the shallow creek after my dog. He's stock still for a minute then takes off on a line.

"Go get em, Bax."

Our land is like a fishbowl. A big one. Hills to the east. Mountains to the west. Valley in the middle. God's country.

Home's a quarter mile back on Dob's Creek. Ain't much of a creek, really. "I could piss across that," my Daddy might say. I tried once but came up short.

"Whatcha think, boy?"

The noise is getting louder but we still can't place it. Baxter's huffing scent, spinning this way and that. He gives me a shrug. I light up a smoke.

See we've got a routine, ol' Baxter and I. Round about three I get up and we walk. Sometimes down the creek. Sometimes through the hemlocks. By deed we live on fifty acres, but really the whole damn valley's ours.

Ashley calls it "nocturnal recon." She's an ol' grunt. She sleeps sound while Baxter and I hit the trails. Report back. Gives me time to think and drink in the land. Just me and my dog and that big Wyoming sky.

Tonight started out like any other. Hiking east along Dob's, Baxter sniffing the same rocks he always does. Now we're freewheeling. Walkin' down this buzz.

"The heck is that?"

I ask the night but get no answer. Bax turns toward the house and I'm about to holler when he stops.

We look up.

There!

A hazy blob against the stars.

Some kind of aircraft. Sailing over like a ghost.

I stand there like a dummy, but Baxter sounds off.

"Baxter!" I yell. But just like that it's past us. Flying on south toward Denver or the Springs. Must be military. We've been buzzed before, but never like that.

I watch it drift a bit then lose sight. Just a shadow in the dark. Looking back toward the house I see a light on in the window. Ashley is up. I can picture her in bedclothes, thinking through her drills. Is this an airborne raid? Perimeter assault?

Naw, just an ol' hound dog barking at the sky. She'll have questions though.

I whistle for Baxter and we start toward home. Fifty yards out he pops a squat. In all the excitement, he forgot to shit. I finish my smoke while the dog does his thing. It's about three-thirty and I'm ready to crawl back in with Ash. Maybe she feels frisky. Hell, we're both up.

I'm zoning out, thinking about her tits in my hand, when I hear it again. That buzz. Baxter pinches off and he's at my side. We both

10

look south and dammed if it ain't coming back around. That same black shadow. Humming like an old TV.

"Son of a..."

The bird's lower this time. Few hundred feet, tops. It dips below the skyline and I lose it in the hills.

"Clay!" Ashley calls from the porch. "What's going on?" Baxter answers for me and I keep my eyes on the valley. There's a broad stretch of flatland south of the creek. It's all gophers and shortgrass for a couple of miles.

"What's that sound?" Next to me now. She's quick in them bedclothes.

"Some kind of aircraft. Almost looks like it's trying to land."

We stare across the murk in the moonless night. The buzz drops an octave and then we hear a thump.

"Was that..." Ashley starts but she knows. Smarter woman you won't find.

After the thump comes a low rumble, maybe half a mile out. I squint and strain and then I spot it.

"There!"

Baxter barks and Ashley puts a hand on my shoulder. She sights down my arm and gasps.

It's a plane all right. Black as midnight, but sure as shit. It rolls to a stop in a sea of buffalo grass.

The night goes quiet.

Ashley hands me a gun.

Chapter 2

I hate guns.

Never been my thing.

Now, I know what you're thinking: Ol' country boy, living out in fuck-off Wyoming, must be strapped.

Well I ain't tryin' to be.

Way I see it, if my life depends on putting holes in a man then I ain't lived right. Ashely calls me 'fatalistic'. I just reckon things work out the way they ought to.

Of course, my wife's a different story. Did two tours. Only black girl in her company so you know she's fit to scrap.

"Take it," she says, handing me a bolt-action .22. I follow orders. Ashley packs a 9mm and purple silk pajamas. We set off.

Ashley runs point and I flank half a step behind. Baxter falls in formation as we move quickly down the valley. It's quiet out here. A field mouse scatters and I don't blame him.

About a hundred yards out the aircraft starts to take shape. Long. Sleek. Skinny wings swept back. It's strange in a way I can't put my finger on.

"Not one of ours," Ashley whispers. "Probably a drone. Chinese."

A Chinese drone? Now I love my gal, but she can't eyeball that on a moonless night.

"How'd China get a drone this far?" I whisper back. "NORAD would be so far up her ass..."

Ashley doesn't reply. Beretta trained on the black ahead, she motions me to hang back. Cover her approach. I settle in the grass and take a clean sight down the rifle. She's the one thing I'd probably kill for.

"Baxter, on me." I whisper the command and he camps down like a good boy. I watch my wife stalk forward. Black braids. Round rump. If this don't all go haywire, we could get one in out here. Never had sex in a Chinese drone.

I pull my eyes off her ass and study the plane. It's dark and stealthy. Not like any craft I've ever seen.

"What do you think, Bax? We being invaded?"

Old hound just whimpers. He doesn't know. I pan the barrel of the .22, scanning for threats. I'll have to be quick if it comes to it. Ash could drop a dozen men before I got my safety off.

She nears the plane and starts to circle. Smooth and practiced. I don't see anything and the air's real still. Be careful, Ash.

She completes a circuit and creeps back. Baxter yips hello and I start breathing again.

"Well, it's not a drone." She crouches down next to me. I can smell the rosehip cream she wears every night to bed. "There's a cockpit up front and a hatch on the side. I can get in, but I'll need a boost."

"Get in? You mean inside the plane?" Of course she does. "Maybe we leave this bird alone. Call someone more equipped."

"Call who, Clay?" She looks at me like I'm washed but that ain't fair. It's three a.m. and a bogey just landed in my backyard.

"I don't know," I stammer. "Air Force? Airport? Who else might have lost a plane?"

Ashley just shrugs. "That's no ordinary plane, Boo." Yeah, she calls me Boo. "No flags. No numbers. Not even a damn manufacturer's stamp."

I nod and we lock eyes. Ashley has hard features and a soft complexion. She does most of her talking with her eyes, and I see something in there now. Some demon she tries real hard to keep down.

"I just need a boost," she says again. "Six feet ought to do it."

It's a warm June night but I get goosebumps across my arms. Ashley grabs the rifle and checks the chamber. She hands me the pistol and whistles Baxt to hop to.

"I'll wait here and watch for movement. You and Baxter go get the truck."

Ashley leans close and our lips meet for a kiss. Five seconds. Ten. I taste toothpaste on her breath and feel a nipple beneath her shirt.

"I'll be right here, Boo," she says when we come up for air. Then she hikes up her pants and hunkers down into the brush.

13

Chapter 3

I lost my Pops in '05.

Ol' ranch boss.

Brought me up in West Texas alongside five hundred head.

Daddy was a beef man. His daddy was a beef man. You could say I got Red Angus in my blood.

Pops was also a smoker, and it was cancer finally caught him. I was nineteen when he went, still chasing hooch and trying to get my dick wet. Had me a big ol' skull tattoo like that meant something.

Momma kept things running, but it wasn't in her heart. She married into the life, and with Daddy gone she was fit to retire. Move back east.

She sat me down one day, about six months on. "Clayton, the ranch is yours."

I picked some snot out of my nose and stared at her. "Come again?"

"It's time you took the reins." Mom had tired eyes but a lively smile. Took up smoking after Pops died. Trying to chase him down.

"You know how things go around here," she said. "Javier will help with the stock. Just keep everybody fed. Be a good boss."

Jav was Daddy's number two, and a better 'poke there never was. We employed about a dozen hands. Mostly Mexican. Good folks that got to be family over the years.

Well, there was no use arguing with Mom, and I sure got heady picturing myself a big swinging dick boss. But it's no small thing filling Daddy's boots.

First month on I fucked everything up. Had to call Momma back home.

She was patient. Walked me through the business of things. Time passed and I started hanging. Momma went off again. "Be a good boss, Clay. Stick to what works."

So that's what I did. Bring up the calves. Sell down the lot. Balance the books. Rinse, repeat.

Two years on I was flying high. Looking to hire more help.

One day this black girl walked in. Tall. Strong. Looked like city folk, but I could see in her eyes she'd been around.

"I hear you're hiring hands?" She wore combat boots and her hair was cropped short. Big ass duffel over one shoulder.

"We got need in the hay fields. You know your way around a baler?" It was late summer, and we had acres of fodder to wrap. Shit job, but we started hands at the bottom.

"Not yet, but I once drove a Humvee through a poppy field." Well, that explained the look. Those haunted eyes. We'd hired vets before, and they were good help. Hard working. Usually got along with the Mexicans.

"We can keep you busy here. Where you staying?"

"At the moment? An old Honda. But I'm looking for something indoors."

I'd seen Ashley's type before. Running from something that chased her all the way out west. Ranch work attracts all kinds, but the folks that come from afar are usually looking to escape. Lose themselves in the land.

One morning I caught her patching fence at four a.m. Said she couldn't sleep. Sure enough, some rowdy steer had jacked up a stretch of field wire. Ashley had an eye for what needed done.

Didn't take long she was one of the boys. "*El Toro Negro*" they called her. The Black Bull. I started teaming up with her for field work. Roped her in to help wrangle some pregnant cows.

"These girls like a woman's touch."

Of course, Ashley knew better. I was twenty-two and horny as shit. Hotshot ranch boss looking for love.

Now, it's never good policy to sleep with the help. If Pops knew I was courting staff he'd be on my ass. But a young man needs company. And those winter nights get cold.

One morning we were in the horse barn sipping coffee. It was a habit we'd got up to, share a brew before the early rounds. She was quiet and I could tell she hadn't slept. Had that thousand-yard stare.

Normally I'd let it go. Let the morning breathe. But I was feeling chivalrous, so I went in and patted her on the shoulder. She was wearing blue flannel and a gambler's hat. Converted cowgirl.

15

She turned to me like she wanted to say something, and I gave that shoulder a squeeze. Damn, she was built. Let out a big sigh like she'd been holding it in all night.

"Nightmares," she said.

I nodded and took up her hand. Clayton's here for ya, girl.

She leaned on my shoulder and sighed again. Slipped into a hug. Her hat fell off. We stayed like that a while, just breathing together. When she finally pulled back, I watched her wipe away a tear.

"Thanks." She gave me a vulnerable look.

"Anytime, ma'am." I tipped my hat. Ol' cowboy charm. Ashely smiled and we fell into a kiss. It was soft and sweet until an old bay blew snot in my ear.

"Oh my." Ashley pulled back and pinched me on the rump. "Let's get these horses fed."

I muttered a curse, but my heart was doing rolls. Ashley hefted a bag of feed and winked at me.

Spent the rest of the day with a horseshoe in my pants.

Chapter 4

I fire up the pickup and let it breathe. We only use it once or twice a month, so the girl needs time to get loose. It's Pops' old Chevy we drove up from Texas. Quarter million miles. American made.

Baxter sits in the passenger seat, tongue flappin'. He doesn't know what to make of all this but he's happy to be involved.

I pivot the rearview and catch my own eye. It's wild how much I've grown to look like Pops. All ears and forehead. Three-day beard. I suddenly feel naked without a cowboy hat and fish around back for a dusty Cattleman. Now we're ranging.

When the engine warms, I ease the old truck out of the shed. I can ride the slope along the creek and down into the flatland. Just watch for rocks. I kick up the brights and putter out toward the prairie. Barely see the plane, but I know Ash is camped nearby. I'm coming, girl.

Bax and I jostle as the truck bounces through a rut. Sea of grass isn't all smooth sailing. How could anyone land a plane out here? We're getting close when a shadow steps out of the brush. Commando in pajamas. I'll have to check her for ticks later. Without a word, Ashley hops up in the bed and knocks twice on the roof of the truck. Here we go.

We roll toward the plane and my lamps light 'er up. Matte black. Menacing curves. Looks kind of like a B-1 with the engines tucked up. I pull around the far side and park as best I can beneath the hatch. Goosebumps again. I climb out and wave Bax to follow but he doesn't want to move. Ashley reaches down and pulls me up into the bed.

"You sure about this?" I give a quick hug and Ashley rubs my back to ease my nerves. The dark plane looms above us like a thunderhead.

"Let's try the handle."

Laying down the .22, she climbs on the roof of the truck. I offer a hand but she doesn't need it. Ashley always moves steady. She stands tall and reaches for the latch. Grabs. Twists. Pulls. The door swings open and Ashley lets out a gasp.

"I didn't expect it to be that easy."

I wish it wasn't.

Ashley pulls a strap, and a little ladder drops down. I feel like we're in some old movie, about to board a pirate ship. She looks back at me to steel herself once more.

"You don't have to do this," I say. "We can crawl back into bed. Cuddle 'til sunrise."

"Hand me the nine."

So much for that.

Ashley tucks the handgun into the waistband of her PJ's. Look like she's done it before. Probably has. She takes a deep breath and starts up the ladder. I watch her ass while she climbs hand over hand.

"Be careful, Ash."

Once her feet disappear, I wait a beat then follow. I consider taking the rifle, but I'd probably just shoot myself during the climb.

I hate guns.

I pause halfway up and scan the landscape over my shoulder. From this height the valley is a sea of midnight black. Calm. Quiet. Too fucking so. Shouldn't we have a damn battalion here by now? Black choppers and jackboots telling me to move along?

"You coming?"

Get it together, Clay. I clench my ass and glance up at a dark hand reaching out. Steady and strong. My rock. I grab hold and Ashley hefts me into the cabin. Just like that we're on the plane.

Shit.

It's dark in here and I pull my wife close. I find her lips and some courage. Needed that.

We step into a narrow hall that runs off in both directions. To the front, I see a cockpit full of switches, all lit up like Christmas. A wide windshield overlooks the valley, and I can see my house from here.

To the rear I can't see shit. It's dark and narrow and fuck this plane.

Ashley taps me on the shoulder and points toward the pilot's chair. It's a one-seater, and from behind I can't tell if it's occupied or not. She stalks slowly forward, handgun trained. I have no weapon and no room to operate so I just stand there like an ass. Maybe I should have stayed with Baxter.

18

No movement in the seat, but Ashley keeps the gun steady. She creeps around the right side and gives me one quick glance. Moment of truth. Anybody home?

Ashley lunges forward and levels her gun. "Freeze!"

Better do what she says, buddy.

Her eyes dart around but the gun doesn't waver. "Hands up!" She yells. "Hey!" No response. Ashley kicks something and moves to whip the Beretta. "Can you hear me?" Confused now. She reaches down with her free hand and raps on a helmet or a mask.

"You're trespassing on private property. Identify yourself!" Still nothing. She waves me over and I squeeze around the bulkhead to get in beside the pilot's chair. There's a person there all right. Full spacesuit and flight helmet. This bird must get pretty high.

"Hey, Buddy..." I knock on the visor a few times. "You alive in there?"

The pilot doesn't respond, but something triggers in his suit. Clicks. A beep. Then a slow hiss like air letting out of a balloon. The body lolls toward me and I take a step back.

"Fuck this." Ashley gives me a look and I nod my head. Let's do it. She trains the gun and counts to three. I grab the helmet and yank it off.

We both gasp.

It's a man all right. Unconscious, but breathing. Mid-thirties. Crew cut.

And dammed if he ain't Chinese.

Chapter 5

Now I've got nothing against no Chinese.

Hell, I've got nothing against anyone.

Black, white, brown, red. Folks are what they are. Daddy taught me that.

My first love was a Muslim gal. Egyptian. Her name was Kema and she broke my heart.

Kema lived in a little Arab enclave south of Amarillo. Who knew, right? Her pops ran a restaurant and fixed tires on the side.

One day they rolled up to the ranch and the whole family poured out of this Astrovan. Men, women, children... must have been a dozen folks all up in robes.

Pops and I were standing there in cowboy boots, smelling like shit. Everybody gawked for a minute then this greybeard stepped forward and shook Daddy's hand. He said they were looking for clean meat. *Halal* he called it. Word had got 'round we did right by our stock, and they wanted to perform a sacred slaughter.

Well, Pops was game, and they went off to browse some steers. Left me to entertain the women and kids. I was fifteen and barely knew my ass from a cleft rock. Never met no Muslims before.

One of the young ones toddled over and stared up at me. He was squinting in the sun, so I plopped my Stetson on his head. That got a laugh. Everyone seemed to relax. The kids took turns playing with my hat and they were all pretty fun. Kids usually are.

One point I looked up and caught one of the girls smiling at me. She had a lavender scarf and big smoky eyes. Looked about my age. I gave her my best good-ol'-boy grin and that smile opened up wider. Sure enough I just made a friend.

Kema and her family started rolling through every couple of weeks, and I kept coming up with bullshit to get her alone for a few.

"Did you ever feed a horse before?"

"How about some cactus jam?"

"Wanna see a goat in heat?"

Kema would just laugh and say something in Arab and off we'd go. She was a peach. At first, I didn't think she spoke English, so I'd stammer through some gibberish and wave my hands a lot. She walked on her tiptoes and smiled at everything.

One day I was showing off this jerky I was real proud of and she reached out her hand.

"Can I have a bite?"

She grinned like the Joker and my chin hit the dirt. Kema grabbed the jerky and brushed my fingers real slow. Deliberate. She ripped a hunk with her teeth and put it back in my hand.

"Y'all do raise tasty beef."

I stood there dumbstruck watching her chew. Cleopatra eatin' a cowboy stick. Pretty sure my hat fell off.

After that she was all I could think about. I'd count down days until her crew came back, and each time she showed up prettier than the last. Silky robes. Rainbow scarves. Strappy sandals all laced up. She still followed me through the muck like it was nothin'.

Something just clicked for Kema and I. We came from different worlds, yet we could get together and laugh like old friends. She'd tell me stories about growing up in Egypt. About the heat and the dust and the family farms. Sounded a lot like Texas except they didn't eat pork.

One time I took her across a creek to find some songbirds. Kema liked that. We were huddled in a cypress grove, listening to wren calls, when she leaned in and kissed me on the mouth.

She smelled like jasmine. Tasted like cinnamon and pears.

I ran my hands over her robe and felt nothing underneath. No bra. No corset. Just Kema. She tugged off her headscarf and damn near drowned me in black hair. Allahu Akbar.

When it was over, we laid for a few minutes just holding each other. Kema whispered some Muslim prayer in my ear. I don't know what she said but it was beautiful.

Eventually we brushed ourselves off and made back to the van and everyone was there waiting. Guess we lost track of time. Kema climbed in and Daddy gave me a look that said something was up. He pulled me aside and Kema's pops followed us over to a little oak bench where Daddy liked to smoke.

They both lit up and offered me one. That was new. I took a few drags and tried not to cough. Started feeling dizzy when Dad cut to it.

21

"Son, we noticed you and Kema spend a lot of time together." I watched Kema's father take a serious puff. "We're not mad, but there are some things you need to know."

Kema's dad went on to explain that he took his daughter's courtship seriously. Said he didn't do sneaking around.

"Your father is an honest man," he said to me. "He's been good to our family, and he vouches for you. So that means a lot to me."

I furrowed my brow and glanced sidelong at Daddy. What were they getting at here?

"If you want to continue seeing Kema, you have my blessing to do so as husband and wife."

Now I choked on my cigarette. Coughed up a storm and lost all breath to respond.

"No need to answer now," he said. "Take some time and think on it. Pray on it. Seek your father's counsel."

Pops just sat there stone faced, staring at the tip of his cig.

"I'll put the same offer to Kema, and we'll be back in a few weeks. If you choose to marry my daughter, you can propose to her then."

With that, Kema's dad stubbed out his smoke and shook Pops' hand. He walked back to the van and I stood up to find some air.

"She's a pretty girl, son." Pops called as I walked away. "Lots of pretty girls out there..."

He was right, of course. I was just a fifteen-year-old horndog. Too young to be getting hitched.

I watched the dust settle as the Astrovan pulled away. I pictured Kema in there. Smiling. Glowing. Was she thinking about me? About us? I suddenly wasn't sure about anything. Found myself wrestling feelings I barely knew I had. Better sleep on it.

Woke up the next morning and decided: I'm gonna marry that gal. Shit.

Now you might think I was crazy and maybe I was. I was young and dumb. Probably thinking with my dick. But I'd seen enough to know women like that didn't come around every day. I'd rolled with my share of cowgirls. Never met anyone like Kema.

But what would we do? Where would we live? Would she move to Daddy's ranch? Would I join her with the Arabs? Cook shawarma for her pops?

22

I spent the next two weeks chewing on it and decided I didn't care. It would all work out. Good things usually did. With that girl by my side, whispering in my ear, I'd march to Cairo on a camel's back. I'd stop the world to make her smile.

See, Pops was right about all the pretty girls, but there's more to love than how a lady looks. I craved how Kema made me feel. Delirious. Swept away. I wanted to live in that feeling. When that van rolled back to the ranch, I'd get down on one knee and propose. I couldn't wait. The more I thought about it, the more right it felt.

I told Pops my plan, figuring he'd want to talk me out of it. He tried in his own way.

"Propose, huh?" We were bedding down horses and Dad talked while he worked.

"Yes sir. Next time they come through. This Friday if I've got the schedule right."

"Mmmhmm." Pops unwrapped a hay bale and gave himself a minute to think. I stood tall in my boots.

"Kema's father gave his blessing. Now I'm asking for yours." Daddy stopped and looked at me. Really looked at me. He dusted off his hands and pulled out a cigarette.

"So you've thought this through? Spend your whole life with this girl?"

"Yes sir." I looked him right in the eye. "If this is how they want it, this is what I'll do."

"Those are brave words, son." He blew out a puff of smoke and smiled at me. "You ready to start a family?"

"Hell no." I shook my head. "Not sure I'll ever be ready. But I've seen enough of Kema to know she's legit." I reached out my hand and he passed me the smoke. I took a drag and passed it back. "I feel high when she's around, Dad. I want to feel that forever."

Pops nodded. Eyes distant. "I ever tell you how I met your mom?"

"No sir." I knew they met when she moved out west for school. Mom grew up in Florida and was a fish out of water in Texas. Daddy reeled her in and turned her on to cowboy life.

"I was seventeen years old." Pops lit a fresh cigarette and offered one to me. "Not much riper than you, I suppose. Went to Lubbock for a rodeo." He studied the smoke drifting off his cherry as the memory came back.

"I was in the bleachers, hootin' at a game of Cowboy Poker, when I looked across the pit and saw this pretty thing all in red." He smiled at the memory. "I'm talking red dress, red hat, red boots... dressed to the fucking nines. She was way over there, though. Four or five sections from where I sat. I couldn't stop staring, and somehow across that crowd I caught her eye."

I took a puff and felt the power of that moment. My whole existence. But for a glance across a rodeo pit.

"I'll never forget it. I was admiring her derby hat when she looked right at me. Even smiled a bit, like she caught me at something. I guess she did." Pops hitched up his belt like he was preening himself for mom. "Now I was feeling cocky, so I tipped my Cutter. Ol' cowboy charm, you know? I scanned the bleachers and saw some open seats a section closer. Moseyed over and plopped down and not long later she spotted me."

Pops was caught up now, living in the memory. Ash grew long on the tip of his cig. "Well, that worked once, so I spied some more open seats. Made my way, settled down, found her eyes again." I pictured my dad as a young man, wearing his rodeo best and creeping across the bleachers toward my mom.

"I kept moving like this. Section by section. Inching closer. Every time your momma found me and every time she smiled. Fucking rush. Before long I was in her section with a bunch of sorority girls. They dragged her out I guess and thank God they did."

I realized Momma told me a version of this story before. She said her sisters brought her to a rodeo for some local culture. She liked watching the cowboys but hated the clowns.

"Eventually, a bunch of girls got up to hit the head. I followed at a distance, eyes on that red hat. Your mom was crafty about it. Cut some corners and lost her sisters and next thing you know we were making out behind the chutes."

If Pops was trying to turn me off Kema he wasn't doing a lot of good. He finally ashed his cigarette and brought his focus back to the barn. "The point is, we had fun with it." He leveled his eyes on me. "It was something special with your mom. I never had to question what we found."

I pinched out my cigarette and let the moment breathe. I knew better than to break Dad's chain when he was on one.

"Of course, it didn't hurt she was looking for a young punch like me," he said. "Maybe your Kema is too."

And there it was. I'd brought him around and earned his consent. My heart did a flip, but I got this cold feeling too. Like things were about to get real.

Friday was the big day. The old Astrovan rolled up the road and I was waiting in my best bib and tucker. Had my jeans pressed. Boots shined. Shirt tucked in. I wore a baby blue Cattleman and clutched a bouquet of daisies. This was my moment.

The van parked and Egyptians started piling out. Kema's greybeard dad. The old Muslim priest. I couldn't wait to see Kema. Her smile. Her strut. My palms dripped and my heart hammered in my chest. I stared in rapture at that door until her pops slammed it shut.

Everything stopped.

Where's Kema?

I tried to call out, but my lips wouldn't work. Made to step forward, but my feet wouldn't move.

Where's Kema?

My brain shut off. Couldn't think. Couldn't breathe.

Where's Kema?

Her dad started toward me with a somber look on his face. That's when I knew.

"I'm sorry, son." He sighed and looked back over his shoulder. Toward home, I guess. Toward Kema, wherever she was. Sweat ran into my eyes and the flowers keeled over in my hand.

She wasn't coming.

Why, Kema? Why?

The men went off to kill a cow and I just stood there, feeling dead myself. Eventually I found my feet and stumbled away. Embarrassed. Destroyed. I trekked over to the cypress grove where Kema and I made love. I could swear I smelled jasmine, but of course that was horse shit. Everything was horse shit.

I put my head in my hat and cried.

I spent the next few weeks in a haze. Tried to lose myself in work but it all reminded me of her. I felt cheated. I felt lost. Daddy gave me space for a while, but one night he sat me down on the porch.

"I'm proud of you son."

I turned to stare at him, keeping my face hard.

"What you did took balls. Not your fault you got 'em kicked in."
He patted me on the shoulder. Rare tenderness from the ol' ranch
boss. "If Kema had shown up she'd be a lucky wife."

I started picturing her again and it made my stomach hurt. I could
still smell jasmine and hear that whisper in my ear. I turned away so
Pops wouldn't see me cry.

"Everybody gets their heart broke, son." He sighed and stood and
left me to my pain. "At least now you know you got one."

I never did see Kema again. Her family still came by for beef, but
she stayed away. It was probably for the best.

A few months later I got a letter in the mail. Knew right away who it
was from, but couldn't read it for a week. I stuck it under my pillow
and the paper smelled like jasmine. Seeped into my dreams.

Finally, I went for it. Ripped the damn thing open. Inside was a
prayer:
Oh Allah,
When I lose hope because my plans have come to nothing
Please help me remember
That your love exceeds my disappointments
And your plans are always better than my dreams.

Aw hell, Kema.

I'd been so sure she was The One until she wasn't. Maybe there
was a lesson in all that. I picked myself up and played the field for a
while. Square dances. Hay rolls. Once followed a girl around a rodeo
until she slapped me.

When Ashley finally arrived, it was like meeting an old friend. The
moral of a story I started all those years ago.

Chapter 6

"Son of a bitch."

Ashley gives me a look. Somewhere between *What-the-fuck* and *I-told-you-so*.

I got a million questions running through my head: Who is this guy? Where'd he come from? Does this rule out getting freaky on the plane?

Ash puts on her thinking face and I wait it out. This shit's over my head.

"Must be a spy," she whispers. "A foreign spy in our backyard. This is big, Clay."

Don't need to tell me twice. I'm ready to call the Air Force. Let Uncle Sam sort it out.

"Let's wake him," Ashley says. I groan and look at the sleeping pilot. He looks peaceful and all. Breathing slow. Even snoring a bit.

"Why's he asleep, anyway?"

"Hypoxia is my guess." Ashley starts patting the pilot down with one hand. Never lowers her gun. "Maybe his oxygen failed and he passed out. Plane landed on its own."

"Landed on its own?" I look at Ashley like she's losing it. "In a field? At night? Can they do that?"

"I don't know," she snaps. "Help me out here."

I run my hands over the flight suit and find a handgun strapped to his calf. I hold it up for Ashley.

"Glock 19. Nice piece. Hold on to it for now."

The little pistol feels cold and clunky in my hand. Did I mention I hate guns? Ashley looks around the cockpit and grabs a backpack strapped behind the seat. It's full of water with a little tube for the pilot to drink. I train the Glock on our man and give my wife a thumbs-up.

"Here goes nothing." She twists a cap off the water sack and dumps it over his head. The pilot jerks awake with a gasp. Looks about to flip, but then sees the gun in his face.

"Don't move if you want to live," Ashley says. I raise an eyebrow. Does she expect me to kill this guy?

"You're trespassing on sovereign territory of the United States of America. You are being detained as an unlawful entrant and held under citizen's arrest. Do you understand?"

The pilot doesn't respond. Nothing moves but his eyes.

"You hear me, buddy?" Ashley yells. "Speak English?"

Still nothing.

"Well, he knows what that gun's about. Let's get him off the plane."

We fall into our roles. Ashley jerks the man to his feet, and I cover him with the Glock. He's short. Maybe five-foot-six. He's wearing a black flight suit and athletic shoes. Looks around a lot, but doesn't resist. Ashley sticks her gun in his back and marches him to the open cabin door.

"I'll climb down first," she says. "Then you send the pilot, and I'll cover from below." She leans down to get right in the short man's face. "I think our friend knows better than to try anything. Am I right?"

Again, no response, but a flicker of understanding behind his eyes. Ashley can be persuasive in any language.

She starts climbing down the ladder to the truck below. The airman stands still, but I watch his nervous eyes glance toward the back of the plane.

"What you got back there, buddy?" He twitches uncomfortably. I peek down the hallway but it's too dark to see. I hear Ashley's boots hit the truck bed and she calls up from below.

"Send him down!"

I peer over the edge and admire my wife. She's in a power stance in the back of the pickup. Purple silk pajamas and combat boots. God, I love her.

I give ol' Sully a nudge. "Best get on then. She won't wait all night."

He takes one more furtive glance to the rear then climbs out through the hatch. I watch Ashley stare daggers as he descends. Her gun barrel follows him down.

When the pilot hits the roof of the truck, Baxter goes nuts. He lets out a whoop from inside the cab and the airman nearly tumbles off in surprise.

"Stay right there," Ashley calls. She hops down and opens the truck door and Baxter comes surging out. He runs circles around the pickup, sounding that belly bark of his. The pilot looks around the valley in confusion. Like he doesn't know how he got here.

"Clay, sweep the rest of the plane."

"I think I'm just gonna climb down, Ash." This bird is dark and weird and I want off it.

"Oh, grow a pair," she calls from below. "I got the pilot."

My shoulders droop and I consider climbing down anyway. Not like she's gonna shoot me. But then I see the little Chinese man give another look my way. He's trying to play cool, but he's nervous about something. Something in the back of this plane.

"Come on, Boo!"

Aw hell. I glance around the murky entry. Can't see shit. I fish a lighter from my pocket and it offers just enough light to creep around by.

"Okay, Ash. I'm going."

I say a prayer and start slowly toward the rear. The hallway is cramped and creepy. Made for little airmen, not my six-foot-two self. Eventually it opens into a small chamber, and I see a bedroll and some half-eaten food. Looks like living quarters. On a military jet? For the first time I consider there might be someone else on this plane.

"Anybody home?" I call out and immediately regret it. I hoist the Glock in one hand and my wobbly lighter in the other. The silence hangs and nobody shoots me. I let out a breath and move on.

There's another squat hallway leading toward the back of the plane. As I duck into the narrow corridor the hot lighter burns my thumb.

"Ow! Dammit!"

I drop the Bic and shake out my hand. I pause to take in the dark when I realize it's not completely dark. There's a faint glow coming from somewhere down the hall.

Interesting.

I retrieve the lighter and tiptoe forward. Careful. Quiet. The glow gets brighter with every step.

My adrenaline cranks up and for a moment I think I hear Ashley. Was that her yelling? Probably just Baxter. Another ten steps and the hall opens into a second chamber. That glow is all around me and the room is full of... fish tanks?

What the hell?

I rub my eyes a bit. This is not what I expected. Big glass tanks, maybe fifty gallons each, arranged in rows around the room and filled with shiny rocks.

I lean in to one and feel heat coming off the glass. I don't see any fish. I don't see much of anything. Just these little round stones. Golf ball sized. They're beautiful and colorful and polished up like jewels.

Without really thinking, I lift the lid and dip my hand into warm water. I feel a tingle. Almost a shock. I dunk my arm to the elbow and grab one of the rocks. It's warm and smooth and feels electric in my hand.

Plutonium?

Shit Clay, you dumbass.

My hair stands up and there's a ringing in my ears. Is that Ashley again? I close my eyes and I can almost hear her. Almost...

But the stones are calling me. Like sirens to the shore. Swirling blues and sparkling greens and gosh these things are pretty. Ash would probably love a few.

I reach back in the water and enjoy that warmth again. That tingle. That power. Something tells me this is stupid, but I'm spellbound by these stones. I slip two in each pocket when I hear a crack.

Shit.

Was that a gunshot?

Shit.

I hear another one.

Shit.

I rush back down the hall to the open door of the plane. The truck is still there, but Ashley and the pilot are gone.

Shit.

A third crack to my left. Toward the hills. I squint in the dark and see figures running through the night.

Shit. Shit. Shit.

I scramble down the ladder and into the truck below. I pull the keys from my pocket and feel one of those silky stones. What the hell was I thinking? Leaving Ashley like that?

Another gunshot.

Shiiiiiiiiit.

I turn the engine over and we're rolling. No time to warm her up. Brights on. Pedal down. I bounce across the prairie saying prayers for my wife.

What the hell happened? Did the pilot jump and run? How long was I even up there? It all feels hazy like a dream...

Boom!

The truck shudders and jumps hard to the left. What the fuck was that? Another gunshot?

No... I think I hit a rock. I feel a tire go flat and the wheel gets sluggish in my hands.

Get it together, Clay!

I don't even know where I'm going. My lamps are on but all I see is grass. The dark hills loom like shadows in the distance. This isn't going to work.

I stop the truck and hop out. "Ashley!" I put my ear to the wind. "Baxter!"

I hear a bark. Balls and business. That's my hound.

"Ashley!" I call again. "Ash, are you okay?"

Please be okay.

I put my head down and run. Honing in on Baxter's woofs. "Ashley! I'm coming!"

"Over here!"

I pick up the pace. Galloping through knee-high grass. I can't see shit and it's a wonder I don't fall.

Suddenly I'm on them.

"Ash-" I try to talk but I'm out of breath. "What-?"

She's on her knees atop the little pilot. 9mm pressed into his ear.

"Ashley, what...?" I'm still sucking wind and can't put two words together. I should probably quit smoking.

"Bastard here ran off." She's got the pilot face-down and probably outweighs him by fifty pounds.

"I heard gunshots..."

"Warning shots." She jams the gun against his ear. "And that's the last time you get a warning!" Despite the threat, the man continues to struggle beneath her weight. I can't believe we're out here at four a.m. shaking down a Chinese spy.

"So, what now?"

Ashley contemplates while the pilot squirms. "You find anything on the plane?"

"A bunch of fish tanks. Also, I'm pretty sure-"

Suddenly the pilot starts screaming.

"Noooooo! We have to move! They'll kill us!" He bucks and thrashes under Ashley's weight. She's army strong, but he's making her work.

"Ash!" I move to help hold him down. Baxter barks like crazy and the pilot just keeps screaming. He's frantic and wild and gets an arm free before Ashley cracks his head with the gun.

"Mmph."

Just like that he's out. Limp and snoring. Same way we found him.

"Shit, Ash..." I hate to see a man brained like that, but she did what needed done.

My wife shrugs and hands me the gun. She stands and adjusts her nightclothes, purple silk all muddy at the knees. "He'll be out for a bit. Let's get him in the truck."

"Truck has a flat. I popped a rock chasing after you guys."

"Aw hell, Clay."

"How'd he put the slip on you, anyway?"

Ashley bites her lip and sighs through her nose. She does that when she's annoyed.

"I thought Baxter would keep him from running, but you know how he is." She reaches out a hand and Bax trots over to her feet. "He stood watch for a minute but got distracted. Some rodent in the grass. Let his guard down and the damn pilot jumped off the truck." She squats and scratches the old bloodhound behind his ears. "I ran around to grab him, but he must have rolled underneath. By the time I realized, he had a hundred feet on me going the other way."

That was a ballsy move. Guy must be desperate.

"Bax popped back into gear and eventually chased him down. Flanked him in the tall grass and the little man stumbled."

Baxter lets out a woof and I can tell he's proud. Ol' hound was never one to bite, but he loves the chase.

"So, what now?" I ask. "The truck's flat. The pilot's out..."

Ashley puts on her thinking face. She's smarter than me, so I wait her out.

"First thing is to get him restrained. No more fighting. No running off." She eyeballs the limp pilot in the grass. "Anything in the truck we can use to tie him up?"

"I think there's an old leash in the cab."

"That'll do." She stands and brushes prairie grass out of her hair. Still breathing heavy, I watch her chest rise and fall. "Not the time, Boo." She knows what I'm thinking. It's a scolding, but playful. "Go fetch that leash."

"Yes, Ma'am!" I salute and turn back to the truck. Start off at a jog but my ashy lungs protest.

Aw hell.

I slow to a walk and light up a cigarette. Baxter catches up and I give him a shrug. What a night. The plane. The pilot. The guns. I just wanted to walk my dog and make love to my wife. Don't act like I haven't earned it.

I'm closing in on the truck when I hear something funny. A low whistle on the wind. It reminds me of an old record Dad used to play by Roy Orbison. *Here Comes the Rain, Baby.* Pops used to jam oldies like that and we'd throw a party on the porch. Even Mom would get in on it, strumming air guitar.

I always liked the Orbison track because we'd all whistle along to that bit at the end. I mostly just spit on myself, but Dad could whistle like a motherf-

BOOM!

The world explodes and I'm in the air.

Dizzy. Tumbling. Flopping like a doll.

BOOM!

I hit earth.

I taste metal and blood.

BOOM!

I'm on fire.

I can't see. I can't breathe.

BOOM!

The ground trembles.

BOOM!

I love you, Ashley.

BOOM!

Darkness.

Silence.
I'm dead.

Part II

World War Three

Chapter 7

Everyone goes through runs in life.

High and low. Right and wrong.

At twelve I was a complete piece of shit. Trying it on, I guess. I picked on kids. Fought with friends. Didn't do a damn thing Daddy said.

But then, I've had other times where it all kinda clicked. I found that flow and got my head right for a minute. *Hell, I can do this...*

Then – BOOM! Trouble again.

That's how it goes.

If I've learned anything, it's that those lean years prepare you to embrace what really matters. You gotta go hungry sometimes to appreciate a proper meal.

After my whiff with Kema, I was hard up for a while. Hurt. Despondent. Pissed off. I felt like I lost something I'd never find again. Of course, that was just my naive teenage blood.

Couple years later I found out what it's *really* like to lose. Dad got sick and the whole world changed. You lose someone like that, a part of you dies too. It's like a broken bone that doesn't set right. A lifelong hitch in your step.

We were hauling firewood one afternoon to get a start on winter prep. Javier and I were loading a truck bed while Pops checked the logs for rot.

Suddenly he started coughing.

"Dad, you okay?"

He was hacking and spitting and struggling just to breathe. Jav stepped in with water, but Dad couldn't get it down.

"Get him in the truck!"

We tried but Pops was dead weight. He went slack and started turning blue.

"¡Dios mío!"

We laid him on his back and Javier did CPR. I stood there like a spooked doe, watching Jav try to breathe life into my Dad.

Not like this... I thought. *Don't take him now, on his ass in the mud.*

Somebody listened and Pops came back around. He opened his eyes, but they were all pain and fear.

We got him to a hospital where he laid up for a week. Hated every minute of it. Then came the verdict: Lung cancer. Stage two.

"Just cut it out of me," Daddy said to the doc. "Do what you gotta do."

"It's not that simple." The doctor was a tall, greying man. You could tell he went to school back East but knew his way around a Texan. "Your history of smoking suggests this is just the beginning."

The doc recommended surgery followed by several months of radiation and pills. Pops had a talk with Javier and I about holding down the ranch.

"You're looking at a long winter," he said. "But come spring I'll be back on your butts, don't think I won't."

Then Pops attacked cancer like a rabid coon. Lobbied for "aggressive surgery" and went under the knife that week. After the procedure, the doctor sat Mom and I down to lay it out.

"The surgery went well," he said. "Your husband is strong, but there's a lot of scarring and damaged tissue in his lungs."

Momma took my hand and squared her eyes on doc. "What's your expectation? Long term?"

The doctor nodded and leaned forward. "Lung cancer is a tough ride," he said. "You should all prepare for setbacks, and he's going to have to follow orders." He raised his eyebrows like he knew how hard that would be. "We think we cleared out all the malignant tissue, but he'll need months of radiation to keep tumors from coming back. He also needs to quit smoking."

Mom and I exchanged a look. We both knew he wouldn't stop. Probably sneaking a puff right then in the ICU.

"I'll do what I can," she said. "How long do you think he's got?"

Woo, she was bold. But I guess that's where we were at.

The doc nodded and turned his eyes on me. "With this diagnosis, median survival time is twelve to eighteen months. What I've seen of your father, he's got the fight to go twice that..." He trailed off, letting something hang. Give it to me, doc. "But if Mr. Moore can't kick the smokes, I'm afraid he won't last a year."

39

Damn.

I sat back in my chair. "A year?"

"It's cancer, son." The doc sighed and put his hands together like a prayer. "A lot of it depends on your old man. But a lot of it doesn't."

So that was that. Pops was gonna die. Maybe soon. Mom was real quiet walking out of the hospital that day. She started up the old Chevy and it purred like a kitten. Always made Daddy proud.

We sat in silence for a few minutes then she sighed and took my hand. "My mom had cancer too, you know? Leukemia." I knew of Grandma's fate but not much behind the story.

"You were just a baby," Momma said. "Not three months old when I got the call." She laughed to herself, remembering. "Dad wanted me to come back to Florida, but Mom wouldn't have it. I can still hear them arguing on the phone." She put the truck in gear and started to roll out.

"Truth is, I didn't want to go back. Drive twelve hundred miles... your cranky ass in the back seat." Mom chuckled again, but I could see her fighting tears. "I loved my mother, and she knew that. But I was just a new mom myself." We pulled out of the hospital lot and headed toward the freeway. "You needed me. Your father needed me. I had to put our young family first."

We stopped at a red light. Mom was quiet for a minute and I let the moment breathe. I was always good at that. Eventually the light turned, and she went on.

"So, I asked them to give me time. Just a few weeks. I couldn't drop everything. *Give me a few weeks,* I said. Well..." We hit the freeway ramp and she punched the gas. Merged in tight between two big trucks.

"Well..." she was choking up now. "Dad said she might not have a few weeks. Mom said nothing, so I knew it was the truth." She stared at the road. Tears welling in her eyes. I looked out the window rather than watch my momma cry.

Finally: "I never made it..." Her voice dropped to a whisper. "I didn't go. Not even the funeral." I turned to her now with eyebrows raised. Never heard the story like this. "It's not your fault, Clay." She shook her head. "It sure as shit ain't on you."

I turned back to the window to hide my own creeping tears. Cowbirds kissed the sagebrush while storm clouds grew to the west. This was real shit. Life and death. Real lessons. Real scars.

"You loved her though," I offered. "And she knew that, like you said."

"I did, son." Mom exited the freeway and we turned toward the ranch. "I called her every day. Until she couldn't take the phone anymore."

We drove a few minutes in silence before we hit the main gate. A weathered timber sign spanned the road: *Moore's Ranch.*

Daddy's ranch.

"The point is..." Mom steeled herself as we bounced along the dirt track toward home. "Is that death comes and nobody gets a say. You face it how you choose, but you'll live with that forever. That's the hard part. The part you can't see yet."

I tried to comprehend what she was getting at.

"Your father might have six months, or he might have more. Whatever it comes to, make the most of it." She pulled the truck up to our three-bedroom house and parked out front where Daddy always did. "He's a good man and he loves you." She looked me square in the eye. "When this is over, I want you to hold your head up high."

"Yes, ma'am."

"I want you to know you did your father right."

"Yes, ma'am."

"Don't pity him. Don't coddle him. Just be there with him."

"Yes, ma'am."

"All right then." She nodded. I nodded. Mom shut off the truck. That night we both cried ourselves to sleep.

Daddy came home a few days later, weak as a newborn lamb. Doc said they removed about five percent of his lung, but it cut his stamina in half.

He set up shop in an old poster bed. Mom, Javier, and I kept the ranch running while Pops barked orders. We suffered his tyranny with love.

"Clay! You get that filly dressed for show?"

"Yes sir. Brushed and shod this morning."

"How many milk goats we got up?"

41

"Jav rustled two dozen last week."

Daddy poured his life into that ranch and didn't know much else. It was hard for him to give up control, and even harder to watch us carry on without him.

Those were trying months.

I took Mom's words to heart and tried to cherish what we had left. Problem was, I was still so young and untested. Pops knew it all. I felt tiny in his shadow.

Early on we just played like things were normal, talking about a future we both knew he'd never see. Then around midwinter the tumors came back, and the whole family bunkered down for the worst. I gave up hoping. Pops started smoking again. What did it matter now?

That's when I finally accepted things and tried to find a bit of peace.

Just a bit.

I knew I'd never fill Dad's shoes, but I still had growing left to do. He was an old man. I was a young buck. We were two ends of the same rope.

One spring morning Pops asked me to bring him his horse. It had been months since he'd gone riding and he was keen to saddle up.

"Bring ol' Donnybrook around, would ya son? I feel like ranging today."

Well, I knew that was against doc's orders, but I also knew Pops needed the ride. Old man humped a bed all winter. That's no life for a ranch boss.

So, I helped him up and helped him dress. He was thin and frail and the clothes hung loose. Even his hat didn't sit right. But when we got him on that horse, he looked half a cowboy again. Head held high. Surveying his land. That was the Pops I knew.

"Let's start at the feedlot."

We rode that ranch like Butch and Sundance. Horses on strut. Dicks dragging in the dirt. Pops could barely get out of bed, but he never wavered on ol' Donny. When we hit the maternity pen, he climbed down and joined Javier with a calving heifer named Anne. She'd always been one of Dad's favorites. Said she had wise eyes. I don't know how you see that in a cow, but Daddy did.

"Won't be long now," Jav said.

42

Anne was lying in the grass, away from the herd. I could see something poking out her back end.

"Hey there, friend." Pops eased to a knee and gently stroked her by the ears. Jav and I just watched as he coaxed that old cow through labor. When it was done, we had a baby bull, slick with afterbirth. I helped Pops to his feet while Anne stood to lick her newborn clean.

"That's my girl." He blinked his eyes and pulled his hat real low. "Jav, you take it from here."

Pops and I mounted up and rode back in. I dropped him at the house and I could see that he was tired. So tired. Still, there was color in his face as he shuffled to the door.

"Thanks for the ride, son." He turned to me and tipped his hat. Big ol' smile. Proud ol' man.

"Anytime, Dad." I returned the salute and held my head up high.

Pops died later that night.

Chapter 8

Water.

All I want is water.

My world is dust.

My throat is raw.

I try to move, but everything hurts.

Everything.

It feels like I fell down a mineshaft.

Did I fall down a mineshaft?

I'll just lay here a while. Wait for the angels to come...

Clay!

Pops' voice. Hey Pops.

Clay, get up.

Aww Pops, I think I'm dead.

You ain't dead, son.

You sure, Pops?

You ain't dead.

I can't move.

Try harder.

But it hurts.

You got work to do.

I think I'll just lay here a while.

Work to do...

Sometime later, Ashley comes over and kisses me back to life. She caresses my eyes, my nose, my mouth. Licks the dust clean off. I can breathe again.

"Ashley..." I mutter. "Thank God..."

I creak open an eye. Wish I hadn't. The sky is blood red and that isn't my wife.

"Baxter?"

Old hound's been licking my face. He yelps a greeting but it's not his normal bark. Something's wrong. Everything's wrong.

I try my left arm, but it doesn't work. Right one does. I rub my dog's head.

"You okay, Bax?"

Where are we? What happened?

Memories come flooding back:

The plane. The pilot. A chase. A blast.

Baxter and Ash-

Oh shit...

Ashley!

Time to get up, Clay.

I try my legs. One's folded under while the other's splayed out. I attempt to roll over, but I'm covered in rocks.

WHY AM I COVERED IN ROCKS?

Get up, Clay.

I'm trying. I'm trying.

I find an elbow... then a knee...

My head swims and I lean over and puke.

Are you sure I'm not dead?

Ashley.

Right.

I lift my head and look around.

The whole valley's on fire.

I put my head back down.

Ashley.

That you, Pops?

I taste vomit and blood.

My dog woofs. My ears ring.

My head spins like a top.

Take a breath.

I inhale. It's all ashes and dust.

My eyes burn. My nose bleeds. My left arm doesn't work.

Get a grip, Clay.

ON WHAT?

Take one step at a time.

I'm trying. I'm trying. But I think I just died.

Where's Ashley?

I don't know.

Go find her.

Baxter woofs again.

Okay.

I struggle to my feet.

My left arm is dead. Just hangs there.

Baxter hobbles around with a limp.

What the hell happened?

Ashley.

Right.

I try to get my bearings. We're in the valley. I think? It's all rubble and craters and... where the fuck is my house?

Find Ashley.

Okay.

Focus.

I smell smoke.

Wasn't there a plane...?

Focus. You can do this.

I can do this.

Look around.

The sun is rising over hills to the east. Chaplain Hills, Ashley calls them, because they watch over our valley like clergy. The real name is some Indian word I could never pronounce. All due respect to the Cheyenne.

The sunrise is hitting dust in the air, that's why everything looks red. It's eerie as hell, but fitting since the WHOLE FUCKING VALLEY EXPLODED.

Okay.

So, where's Ashley? I close my eyes and think. Try to remember...

Ashley and Baxter chased down the pilot and she wanted to tie him up. I was walking back to the truck. Would have been heading... north. So, Ashley must be... that way?

I squint vaguely through the dust. Nothing looks familiar. Baxter woofs again.

"What do we do, Bax?"

I could keep heading north and find the creek. A rinse and a drink. God, that sounds nice.

But Ashley's the opposite way.

You know what you have to do.

I take a wobbly step. Then another.

46

Baxter limps to my side and we set off in search of my wife.

Chapter 9

I'm walking in a dream.

Nothing feels real.

Not the land. Not the sky. Just the pain.

The pain feels real.

Bax and I stagger through a broken landscape. Dead grass. Scorched earth. We skirt a crater thirty feet wide. Smells like sulfur and rust.

I call out for my wife, but my voice is weak. Baxter calls too. No response.

Maybe we're doing this wrong.

"Come here, boy." I bring Baxter to my side. "Can you find Ashley? Pick up her scent?" He's a bloodhound, after all.

He looks at me with those honest eyes. Wants to help but doesn't understand. Could he even smell her in this mess? We have to try.

I fumble around my pockets for a scrap of Ashley's scent. Pull out a blue stone.

Oh yeah.

My mind flashes back to the plane. Those fish tanks. Warm and humming. Filled with water and these weird-ass rocks.

I roll it around in my hand. Blue-green swirls. It's beautiful. Like a baby earth. So serene I could live on it...

Baxter woofs and I snap back. Shove the stone in my pocket and remember my goal: something that smells like Ashley.

Try another pocket. Lighter and smokes. That won't do. Dig into my back pocket and strike gold: An old hankie.

Two nights ago (was it?) Ash was getting ready for bed and putting on some cream. Rosehip. Her favorite. She hit a bubble and the tube barfed all over. Boy, was she mad. Wiped the waste on this hankie and handed it to me. I was on my way out and just stuffed it into my jeans.

"What do you think, boy?"

I hold it out for Baxter and he gets excited. Tail starts wagging. Now he knows.

"Go find Momma!"

The old hound woofs and sticks his nose in the dirt. Lifts his head and tastes the wind. He's got something. I try to keep up.

Bloodhounds are amazing. They can tease a week-old trail and track it for miles. Blows my mind. Not just the hound's huffing power, but the fact that we all leave that kind of trace. Some essence off my ass that hangs for *days*. Old hound comes by like, "Yup, that's Clay."

Baxter never had the discipline of a working dog, but tracking Ashley ought to be cake. I say a little prayer and try yelling again.

"Ashley!" My call hangs flat in the quiet morning. Should be all kinds of prairie critters mixing it up, but the valley feels dead. I look down and see half a rabbit. Fight the urge to vomit again.

"Ashley!"

I can't take this. Deliver me, Bax.

And then he does.

Two quick woofs from up ahead. I stumble forward, afraid to look.

A body in the dust. Black braids. Purple silk. Face down.

She's dead.

Oh, God.

My heart goes cold. My nuts drop. My eyes roll up.

I choke on rage and anguish and pain.

Who did this? How could you?

I want to scream at God.

I want to rip the world in half.

I want to pull down the stars and set fire to the sky and-

She moves.

She moves!

"Ashley!"

I drop to my knees and feel my wife for warmth. She's covered in dust and dried blood. I brush her clean and roll her over and she squints at me with big brown eyes.

I weep with joy. Baxter sings. We're a family again.

Ash mumbles something but I can't make it out. I lean in closer and smell rosehip.

"Water..." she moans through dusty lips.

I lean down and kiss her 'cause for now that's all I've got.

Chapter 10

"Bombs," Ashley says, sitting up now. "We were bombed."

She flexes her fingers and cranes her neck. Looks bloody and bruised, but not broken.

"Who? How?" I stammer uselessly while Ash spits in the dirt.

"Think, Clay." She probes a knot on her head and winces in pain. "A plane lands in the night. No markings. Chinese pilot. We confront him and he runs off. Minutes later, someone lights up the valley."

Ashley shuts her eyes and shakes her head. "This is the big one, Boo. World War Three."

Now it's my turn to wince. Goosebumps pop and my legs go numb. World War Three? No way...

Breathe, Clay.

I gather myself and look around the shattered valley. I can't see my house, can't see my truck. Even the plane is gone. Did he fly off while we were unconscious? How long has it been?

"Where's the pilot?"

Ashley sighs and climbs to her feet. "Who cares?" She rocks back and forth on each leg, flexing and testing. Feeling herself out. "He damn near killed us and brought down hell." She spits in the dirt again. "I hope he's dead."

Maybe she's right. Maybe it doesn't matter. Maybe the world is falling apart as we speak.

"Are you hurt?" Ashley asks, looking me up and down. I shrug with one hand because I can't raise the other. "Let me see that." She steps over to examine my shoulder. Waves of pain turn sharp as she probes at the joint.

"Easy! Easy!" I pull away and cradle my arm. It hangs limp and useless.

"I think it's out, Clay. Dislocated." Her eyes meet mine and I know what's coming next. "We need to pop it back in."

I shake my head but she's already coming at me. "I'll make it quick." She reaches out. "Just get it over with." I whimper and twist but it's no use. She's right. I can't drag a dead arm through World War Three. I close my eyes and bite my tongue and submit to my wife's strong hands.

"Just hold still." She grabs my arm and braces to pull. "One, two..."

She jerks and the joint slides home. I feel a burst of blind pain... then relief.

Thank God.

I swing my arm around as the nerves come tingling back.

"Take it easy," Ashley cautions. "The muscles are strained and it can pop back out. You'll have to baby that wing for a while."

I look my wife in the eyes and don't know what to say. I thought she was dead. I thought I was dead. Maybe we *are* dead. Is this heaven or hell?

"Thank you," I whisper. "I thought..."

"I know."

We hug for a while.

Time to move, Clay.

Not now, Pops.

Now's the time, son.

I grumble and step back.

"We need water. You up for a hike to Dob's?"

"Water sounds amazing."

"Can't be more than half a mile..." I scan the smoldering valley. "That way?"

Ashley nods and hikes up her silk bottoms. "Never thought I'd go to war like this," she says. "At least I put my boots on."

"That's my girl."

We start our trek to the creek, but Ashley quickly calls a halt. "Wait," she says, jogging back to where I found her. She scans the ground for a minute and kicks at a few rocks. Finally reaches down and pulls a pistol from the dirt.

She trots back over to me, dusts off the 9mm and checks the clip. "Looks like... nine shots left. What about the rifle?"

I give her a shrug like you're asking the wrong cowboy. "Rifle was in the truck."

She scans the valley and sees no truck.

"Damn."

"The plane's gone too. And our... uh... house."

Ashley scrunches up her face and studies the landscape. Looks like she wants to say something, then just shakes her head. Baxter woofs and I reach down to give him some love.

"What about the Glock?"

I close my eyes to think. Must have dropped it in the blast. I make a show of patting down my waist, then give Ash a sheepish look.

She frowns. "Last time I trust you with the guns."

Works for me.

Now we walk.

Slow and methodical. All three of us hurt.

Baxter shuffles ahead and sniffs at every odd thing. He's got a little limp and I wonder what he thinks of all this.

"What do you suppose he smells?"

Ashley doesn't respond.

"All this earth turned up, probably flipped the whole smellscape. Dredged up old gopher runs."

I watch my hound sniff and snort through the dirt. If not for his bladder, we'd be buried in our bed.

Thanks, Bax.

I look for the house again. It was a good home we had. Quaint and quiet and cozy for three. An open plan with big windows. Little breakfast nook where we played chess.

What the hell happened?

I kick a rock and it almost hits Baxter. Sorry, boy.

Ash gives me a look and I can see she's hurting too. Demons and dark thoughts. Angry and thirsty and sweating through silk pajamas. I guess we're lucky it's June. Winters out here can be windy and fierce. Snow drifts up to your hat. We wouldn't last a-

"What's that?"

A glint to my left. Something shiny in the dust. Ashley sees it too and we veer. Fifty yards... thirty...

It's the truck.

Daddy's truck. Ol' Chevy S-10, mangled and mashed. What a fucking shame.

We stand there a while, just looking it over. Feels like a funeral so I say a silent prayer. Pops loved that truck. I loved that truck. Baxter whimpers around the wreckage like even he wants to cry.

I let out a long sigh.

A good truck. A good valley. A good home. Ruined.

For what?

"War," Ashley says.

Was I thinking out loud?

"You asked me what Baxter smells. He smells war."

I nod and take her hand.

"I know because I've smelled it. Smoke and sulfur and scorched earth." Ashley spits between her feet. "I left that life, Clay. I did my time."

I think back to our first meeting. Ashley's heavy bag and heavy eyes. I know she's still got ghosts.

"We made a home here. We didn't bother anybody..." I look in her eyes and see tears welling up. "What happened, Clay?"

I wish I knew. Or maybe I don't. None of the answers seem good.

Tell her what she needs to hear.

"I guess..." I stammer. "I guess we focus on what we have right now, rather than what we've lost."

She nods as tears cut down dusty cheeks.

"There's an old saying," I offer. "A prayer I once heard..." We bow our heads together.

"Dear lord, when I lose all hope because my plans have come to nothing, please help me remember that your love exceeds my disappointments, and your plans are always better than my dreams."

"Amen," Ashley adds. "Where did you learn that?"

"An old friend who taught me a bit about hurt."

Not bad, son.

Ashley sighs and turns to head toward the creek.

We leave Pops' truck where it lies.

Chapter 11

I've always been fond of Dob's Creek.

It ain't much on the map, just a small spit of water dribbling out of the Chaplains. It takes a slow East-West meander before feeding some fork down the way.

When we bought the land, the creek didn't even have a name. Ashley worked with a surveyor named Dob, and we named the creek in his honor. It's clear and rocky and sings like a warbler.

God's country.

When Ashley and I come up on it it's like an oasis. We've been stumbling through carnage and here Dob's looks untouched. A pair of mourning doves preen along the shore.

"Sweet Jesus."

Before I know it, Ashley's out of her clothes and in the ankle-deep water. Baxter splashes in behind and takes a long, happy drink.

"What are you waiting for, Clay?"

I fumble out of my britches and waddle into the creek. The water feels so good I lay right down. Cleanse me of this dusty nightmare.

"Mind if I join?"

Ashley wades over and lays next to me in the soft sand. Just two naked souls, sloughing off the trauma of World War Three. After a few minutes she reaches over and starts fondling my Johnson. Her hands know just where to go. Just what I like. Before long I'm rock ready and she climbs on. A mourning dove coos and we lose ourselves for a while.

Afterward, we lay together while the current takes my seed downriver. The water is cool and her body is warm. I start to feel human again until Baxter barks a warning.

"Something's coming."

Ashley snaps up like a gunshot. Quick as a cat, she's out of the water and heading for her pistol. Might be those coyotes, but they rarely roam this hour.

"What is it, Bax?"

I struggle to my knees and lean hard on my left side. Fuck! My shoulder pops back out. Whole joint turns to jelly and stings like a snakebite. Ashley stomps off while I cradle a dead arm and a dick in my hand.

Get it together, Clay.

Oh God, Pops is watching.

I'm always watching. Put some pants on.

I stumble nude out of the creek, bare feet slipping on wet rocks. When I reach high ground, I see a bulky black flight suit walking our way. It's the fucking pilot.

He's fifty yards out and limping bad. Coming in slow with both hands above his head. Ashley marches out to meet him and it's quite a sight. She's tall and bare and dripping with creek water. Tits sharp and gun high.

Meanwhile, I stand stupid like a scarecrow. I should go help my wife, but I'd like to get some pants on first. I split the difference by grabbing my cowboy hat and jogging after her. At least I can cover my privates.

"Stop right there."

Ashley barks an order and the pilot stops.

"Keep your hands up and get down on your knees."

Again, he complies but it's a struggle. Looks like a bad knee. He winces as he goes down, but keeps his eyes on the gun.

"I'm going to ask you some questions," Ashley says. "And for every wrong answer, you get shot."

He straightens up but says nothing. Baxter bristles and glares. I crouch behind both with a Cattleman over my junk.

"Who ordered the bombing?"

The pilot just stares. Ashley racks a bullet.

"Last chance. Who blew up our valley?"

He bites his lip and exhales. Knows he's got. There's a brief staredown, then the pilot cracks.

"I can't answer that." He slowly pans his head to the surrounding destruction. "But I can tell you who delivered the ordnance. United States Asset Command. Stationed out of Billings."

Ashley's body goes tense. Every muscle. I can see them all.

"Bullshit," she says. "You're PLA."

"I don't know what you're talking about."

"People's Liberation Army. Chinese Air Force." She shakes her head. "Is this an invasion? Spill it, or you die here."

Now the pilot shakes his head. "Sorry lady, I'm American." He spreads a shit-eating grin. "And you just got bombed by America."

Ashley says nothing. The whole valley goes quiet.

Then the pilot's hand explodes.

"AAAAHHH FUCK!" He drops to the dirt. "You shot me! You bitch!"

"I warned you." Ashley racks another bullet. "Next time it's a gut shot."

"Dammit! I told you the truth!" He sounds weak and pathetic now. All that bravado blown away. "USAC ran the bombing. This isn't what you think!"

I can see Ashley hesitate and she turns to meet my eyes. I offer a shrug that can't possibly help.

"U.S. Asset Command," she asks, turning back to the pilot. "What is that? I've never heard of that."

He sits in the dirt staring at his mangled hand. He's losing blood and probably fighting shock.

"It's just a finger," Ashley says. "You've got nine more and I've got more bullets."

"Fuck you," the pilot points his bloody nub. "You have no idea what you're caught up in." He sweeps his eyes around the valley before squaring them back on Ashley. "This isn't a war. It's a burial."

"What are you talking about?"

"Powerful people," he shakes his head. "With powerful secrets." Now he looks at me and I nearly drop my hat. "Ask your man there what he found on that plane."

Again, Ashley turns my way and gets a one-shoulder shrug. "I don't know babe..." I mumble. "Just some rocks. Like... blue rocks."

Now the pilot laughs and sits up. He rips a scrap off his flight suit and starts to wrap his injured hand. "I can see why you keep this one around, and it ain't for his brains."

I adjust the hat covering my manhood. Can he really see?

"Just do this for me..." He turns back to Ashley with a long leer. His eyes linger where they shouldn't. "If you're gonna screw in the creek again, let me head for those hills on my own. I figure we've got twenty minutes before USAC comes back and kills us all."

56

Ashley narrows her eyes and shuffles over to me. She leans in close and I smell rosehip, gunpowder, and blood. "You believe him?"

I study the defiant airman. Baxter paces a perimeter and the two growl at each other.

"He doesn't sound Chinese," I offer.

Ashley nods her head. "What was he talking about? You found rocks on the plane?"

"I grabbed some..." I gesture back toward the creek. "They're in my pants."

She looks lost in thought. Studies the gun in her hand.

"Asset Command? You buy any of that?"

"I don't know, Boo."

She sighs and gives him one more glare. "Well, either way, we should head for those hills. There's nothing left for us here." She offers the gun, but I don't take it. I don't want it. I've got one good hand and it's covering my junk.

"I'll walk back and get our clothes," she says. "If he tries anything, just kill him."

I beg with my eyes, but it's no use.

"Take it, Clay."

I slowly raise the hat to my head and take the pistol.

"There's the ol' cum gun!" The pilot yells and Ashley rolls her eyes.

I stand there naked in the dust. My arm hangs limp. My dick hangs limp. What a fucking morning.

"Like I said," Ashley calls as she starts back toward the creek. "If he tries anything, just kill him."

Chapter 12

Ten minutes later we're fully clothed and hiking toward the Chaplains. I didn't kill the pilot, and now he sets the pace. Limping bad but pushing hard.

"So, what happened to your leg?" I'm trying to mend fences after Ashley shot his hand. I know she's been through worse, but I'm not used to seeing that kind of violence up close.

"Your damn dog tripped me." The pilot stumbles through a clump of beard grass. "Twisted my knee when I fell."

Baxter barks the bloodhound equivalent of: "I'll fucking do it again."

"Just be glad that's all he did," Ashley warns. She's back in silk pajamas and combat boots. Before we set off, she popped my shoulder in again and rigged my shirt into a sling. We could all probably use a hospital right now.

The pilot huffs and lumbers toward the hills. He keeps looking back with wary eyes. Maybe something really is coming. Maybe he's stringing us out to buy time. We're a quarter mile from the trees and marching hard. The valley is open land, but the adjacent hills are thick with hemlock and fir. It's old-growth forest. God's country.

"Hey what's your name anyway?" Still trying to break some ice with the pilot. "I'm Clay Moore. This is my wife, Ash." He says nothing but scans the horizon again.

"Call me Tuck," he offers after a minute.

"Where you from, Tuck?"

"Enough talk. We need to reach cover."

Just then, Baxter barks and Tuck stops in his tracks. He raises a hand. "Listen."

I cup my ears. Just the nearby babble of Dob's Creek. Maybe a faint cadence on the wind...

"Helicopters," Ashley says. Still got that soldier's ear.

"Are you serious?"

"They're coming." Tuck drops his head and takes off at a run. Baxter and Ashley follow on instinct, but I waver a beat scanning empty sky.

What are we running from?

"Clay!" Ashley yells without turning back. I lurch into a sprint but it's no easy thing. My whole body hurts. Shoulder jolts with every step. I focus on my wife's behind and slowly gain ground.

"We have to reach the trees!"

Tuck lurches with a desperate gallop. The trees are still two hundred yards ahead, but now I hear the thump of rotors over my own breath.

"If they see us, we're dead!"

I don't want to believe him, but Tuck's terror spurs me on. I think back to that whistle I heard as the bombs came down. We're lucky we're not dead already.

I lean into the sprint as we close to a hundred yards. I round on Tuck and glance over. His face is a mask of pain and fear. Baxter nips at his heels while Ashley pulls ahead and shouts commands.

"Bear left!" There's a copse of trees jutting where the creek comes out of the woods. It's our first shot at cover. I peek over my shoulder and see a swarm of helicopters coming from the north. I guess this is really happening.

"Watch the scree!" Tuck and I both skid as we come into a patch of loose gravel. I flail to keep my feet and wait for chain guns to rip us apart.

"Almost there!"

My chest burns. My legs quake. I pump blindly toward the trees.

We gonna make it, Pops?

You have no choice.

I block out everything but the path ahead. Thirty yards. Twenty. Ten. If I don't survive, please watch over my wife and-

"Oomph."

I crash into Ashley with a grunt. She pulls me clear of a stout trunk I almost ran right into. We cower under bobbing pine boughs and try to catch our breath.

"Did they see us?"

"Keep moving." Tuck scrambles deeper into the shade of the pines. We follow thirty yards to the neck of a ravine and there we collapse. Even Baxter's sucking wind.

From here we're hidden but have view of the valley. I watch in awe as some fifteen helicopters descend on our land. Little figures in black jumpsuits pour out before they're even on the ground.

"First thing they'll do is secure the plane," Tuck says between heaves. "Then they'll comb for bodies."

"What do you mean, the plane?"

"I mean what's left of it."

We're all quiet for a minute. I pull a blue stone from my pocket and roll it around in my hand. Tuck massages his knee then stands with a grunt of pain.

"We need to keep moving. When they don't find bodies, they'll start tracking."

He starts wobbling down the ravine, cursing under his breath. I rub my sore shoulder and thank God I don't have to walk on it.

"Maybe we need a minute." I could really go for a cigarette.

"We don't have one." Tuck grumbles and limps off.

Ashley and I hang back. She looks at me with doubtful eyes, still trying to puzzle this all out. I gesture toward the valley.

"USAC?"

"I guess." She squints and frowns. "Those look like Black Hawks. Came in from the North."

"Billings?"

Ashley just shrugs.

I watch Tuck totter down the ravine and out of sight. He's not about to lose Baxter, so I don't mind letting him go. Still, it feels like a decision point here.

"You wonder if we're suddenly on the wrong side?" I squint across the valley. "We could hail them Joes over there, have Tuck in chains within the hour."

"I haven't picked a side yet." Ashley waves the gun as if I need a reminder. "Let me see that stone."

I hand her the rock and watch distant soldiers swarm the wreckage of our house.

"You really think Americans dropped those bombs?"

"I'm sure of it," she says. "The question is, why?"

60

I ponder this for a minute. It's hard to imagine some foreign force in Wyoming unless our whole defense was down. But then who's Tuck flying for? He says he's American, but the Air Force bombed his plane?

I need a cigarette.

I pull one out and light it up. The nicotine speeds my heart and calms my nerves. The smoker's rush.

Ashley reaches over and plucks the butt from my lips. I think she's gonna chide me, but instead she takes a drag. That's a first. She passes it back and holds up the stone.

"You said the plane was full of these? How many do you think?"

"I don't know..." I try to remember. Feels like days ago. "Hundreds, probably. Maybe thousands? All sitting in water."

"Hmmmm."

She's working some angle. I suck on my cig.

"You ever seen a stone like this, Clay?"

I shake my head. "Reminds me of turquoise. Like some Indian craft. But the colors are off, and it feels weird in my hand."

"It's not turquoise..." She squeezes the stone and her eyes get far away. Something dark in there.

"You've seen this stuff before."

"I have."

Ashley grabs the end of my cig and this time stubs it on the ground.

"And I've spent ten years trying to forget."

Chapter 13

By the time we catch up with Tuck, he's crossed the ravine and started back uphill. It's slow going. I propose sticking to the creek, but Tuck and Ashley say the easy line makes us easy to track.

I feel like the odd man out here. Tuck is driving us through hard hills while Ashley chases ghosts. I whistle for Baxter and he trots over to my side.

Keep your head, son. Keep moving.

What is all this, Pops?

You've waded into something, but you'll get through. Stay close to your wife.

She shot a man, Dad. Blew his finger off.

Hell of a shot.

That isn't the point.

I struggle up a steep slope, grabbing branches with my good arm. It's cooler in the shade, but what do we do when night falls? This is coyote country. Not to mention all the bears. I hope we're someplace safe when the sun goes down.

We push hard for another hour, then take a blow. Tuck drops to the ground and rubs his swollen knee. The dress on his hand is soaked with blood. Ashley rips a sleeve off her nightshirt and offers it his way.

"Better give that a fresh wrap."

Tuck says nothing, but takes the scrap of silk. Ash looks even more badass with one bare arm. I give everyone a minute, then pop the question.

"So, what's the plan?"

We've been humping dense woods and I feel thoroughly lost. Moving mostly east, but it's hard to tell.

"The plan," Tuck says through gritted teeth, "Is to stay ahead of USAC." He pronounces it like *yoo-sac.* "Until something changes, that's all that matters."

"These guys sure have you spooked."

"Did you see what they did to that valley? Or the fifteen Black Hawks they brought down?"

"I did, but-"

"There's no *but*, cowboy. If USAC catches us, we're dead. You, me, and this crazy bitch."

Ashley purses her lips but keeps quiet.

"Would they really kill us?" I ask. "Me and Ashley, I mean."

Tuck gives me a long look over. "You wouldn't be the first."

Ashley nods and holds out the blue stone. "It's about this, isn't it?"

Tuck glares. "Let me see that." She hands it over and he chucks it down the hill.

"Hey!" Ashley yells, but it's already gone. Lost in the undergrowth and leaf litter. "What the hell?"

"Doing you a favor," Tuck says. "Asset Command on our ass is bad enough, but if they catch you with one of those..." He trails off and shakes his head. "We need to keep moving."

We all struggle to our feet, and I pat the remaining stones in my pocket. Should I throw them away too? What exactly am I packing here?

Don't be reckless, Clay.

Reckless how, Pops? Tuck says I'm dead either way.

Makes no difference then.

Easy for you to say.

If some rock is worth killing for, it's probably worth carrying.

I guess we'll find out.

We set off again, Baxter leading the way. He seems to have sniffed out some old game trail that takes us deeper and deeper into the woods. It's hard hiking, but the views are sublime: Ancient trees. Mossy stones. Gnarled roots and deadfall. Everything here is so damn stout. I can feel the millennia.

It occurs to me that we may end up spending the night out after all. We're miles from the nearest town. It might not be so bad if this jerk pilot wasn't around. Ashley and I could set up in a little cave, learn the ways of the forest elves...

"Shhhhh."

Suddenly she pulls up short and raises her gun.

"What is it?"

"I heard something."

Tuck drops to his good knee and Baxter growls at my side. We stare into the undergrowth.

"It sounded big," Ashley says. "Maybe a bear."

I creep into her shadow. She's got the pistol after all.

"It's not USAC," says Tuck. "We'd already be dead."

"If it's a bear I'll need a few shots to bring it down."

"You start shooting, USAC will be on us."

"Well, what choice do we have?"

"Depends how you want to die."

"Enough!" Ashley growls.

This is not going well.

Sure hope it's not a bear.

More shuffling. A broken branch. Something big is coming this way.

"Let's fall back." Ashley points to a boulder about ten yards behind. "Higher ground."

No one disagrees, and we creep up the hill to an old hunk of limestone, big as a van. Probably been here a million years.

"You see anything?" Tuck asks.

I don't, and even Baxter seems unsure. We wait a tense moment, then hear rustling again. It sounds like it's just ahead, but all I see is green.

"Anybody there?"

Tuck looks at me like I'm mad, but then a new voice rings out.

"*Clayton Fucking Moore...*" My eyes go wide. "*What in God's good name have you brought down?*"

"I know that voice," Ashley says. She hesitates a beat and lowers her gun.

"*Now Ash, I know you ain't much of a shot, but I'm an easy target...*"

"Arden? Is that you?"

And with that, a hulking figure materializes out of the brush. It's not a bear, but it might as well be. It's probably the largest man I know.

"What the hell?" Tuck shakes his head, confused. Arden wears black cargo pants and weighs at least three hundred pounds. He saunters up and extends a hand.

"Arden Horne, resident bear."

Tuck stares in disbelief while Ashley jumps into his arms. "Wow it's good to see you..."

Arden gives her a squeeze and puts her down. He takes a step back to look everyone over. "Y'all look like you been through it."

"You have no idea, Ard." I offer my hand and he swallows it up.

"Clayton Fucking Moore. I'm just glad to see you alive."

"Been touch and go since this morning."

"Wait, wait, wait," Tuck interjects again. "Where did you even come from? How long has this guy been following us?"

Arden sighs and squares to the pilot. His girth is imposing. Tuck takes a step back.

"Well, I've been tailing y'all for the better part of an hour." He pulls out a rag and wipes his brow. "Had to figure out who was leading who." He glances at Tuck's wounded hand and my busted arm.

"I don't like this," Tuck takes another step back. "I don't like this guy, getting the jump on us. How do we know you're not U.S. Asset Command?"

Arden shrugs. "Well, I ain't even got the jump on you yet. I'm mostly running decoy for ol' Kali here." He nods and we turn to see a giant silver wolf sitting six feet behind us on a log.

Now Tuck really shits himself. "What the – fuck! Jesus!" He scrambles and stumbles and ends up on his ass. The big wolf doesn't flinch.

"Don't think y'all ever met Kali." Arden clicks his tongue and the wolf saunters to his side. Ashley looks at me with a shrug.

"We've got a situation, Ard."

"Seems that way," he nods. "Somebody nuked your valley. I thought the world had come undone." He shakes his head and pulls a silver flask off his belt. Offers it to me. "Now I had to come check what was what. Been hiking half the morning before Kali found your trail."

I take a sip from the flask. It goes down smooth but burns fiery in my gut. Haven't had a bite to eat all day.

"I don't get it," Tuck says, still staring at the wolf. "You live around here? In the woods?"

"Who's asking?"

"He calls himself Tuck," Ashley offers. "Some kind of pilot. He landed in our valley just before the bombs came down."

"Is that so?" Arden takes back the flask.

"It's a long story," Ashley says. "But for now, we need a place to lie low."

"Mmm hmmm." Arden clips the flask back to his belt. It disappears beneath his giant belly. "Just where were y'all headed, anyway?"

"Nowhere," I say with a shrug. "Just hiding out. Getting lost." The wolf watches me as I talk, blue eyes piercing. "Bunch of choppers came down and we booked. Tuck here says they're bad news."

"U. S. Asset Command," Tuck chimes in. "The *worst* news. We need to keep moving if we want to live. How far to your place?"

The wolf studies Tuck and bares her teeth.

"Easy, Kal..." Arden pats her giant head. "What happened to your hand, son?"

Tuck scowls at Ashley and rubs his bandaged limb. Arden chuckles.

"Looks like you got a habit of messing with the wrong folks." He looks around the forest and scratches his chin. "Well, Ashley and Clay always got a place with me. But I need a few assurances before I take in your kind."

"Whatever, fat man." Tuck heaves to his feet with a huff. "I don't have time for your bullshit." He starts tromping down the hill, limping on his bad knee. Arden shakes his head and clicks his tongue. Suddenly the wolf is in Tuck's path.

"What the hell, man?" He staggers back a step. "Call off your dog."

"She ain't my dog," Arden strolls over beside the silver beast. "And these ain't your hills." Tuck takes another fearful step back. Arden leans down and looks him in the eye. "Now I see you're running from something. I've got a place you can lie low, but you need to show your savior some respect." He pulls out his flask again and offers it to Tuck. "Share a drink and shake my hand. Give me your word you won't bring trouble to my home."

Tuck frowns and stares at the proffered flask. I see a swirl of rage behind his eyes, but then they go soft. "All right, man." He takes the flask and puts it to his lips. Gulps once. Twice. Three times. He pulls it away and tips it over. Empty. "You have my word."

They shake hands and some of the tension melts. Kali sits back and Baxter wanders over to sniff her tail.

"Well, all right, then!" Arden says with a flourish. He waves to me and whistles for his wolf. "We got a bit of a hike, but we'll beat nightfall. Kali knows the way."

They both start off and Tuck warily watches them go. Ashley shrugs at me again and sticks the pistol in her pants. "I guess we're going with Arden."

"I guess so."

I look back once and wonder how far USAC lurks behind. This day just keeps getting weirder. I put my head down and follow the wolf.

Part III

Into the Jungle

Chapter 14

I married Ashley five years after Pops died.

We had a modest cowboy wedding. Two-horse affair. Mom came out from Florida and Ash invited a few friends from the service. They were a trip.

"A Texas cowboy! How much shit did he shovel to buy that ring?"

"He runs the ranch, Carl. Pays grunts like me to shovel shit."

"So, you're Texas aristocracy now. Can you buy me a Senate seat?"

On and on and on. They were all jokes and jibes, but you could tell they shared something. After dinner, the group got together for a little toast. Cracked a bottle of Scotch one of the jarheads brought along.

"Three shots," said the gap-toothed fella with a Boston drawl. "One for the fallen. One for the families. And one for the rest of us poor fucks."

"Never forgotten," they all chimed in.

Ashley threw three back without a flinch. Only time I've ever seen her drink.

Now the wedding was sweet, but our engagement was the real story. Ashley and I had been dating two years by then, and she'd long since moved into my bed. Some of the hands already took to calling her, "Mrs. Moore."

I loved Ashley because she was everything I'd never had: Strong, independent, and loyal. I'd spent so many years chasing fickle women. Ashley's honest eyes told a story I could trust.

We were also different in all the right ways. Black and white. Vet and civilian. City girl and country boy. I once asked Ashley what she liked about me and got the best compliment of my life.

"Clay you've got big balls and a bigger heart," she said. "I met a lot of toughs in the army, but you're a man where it counts."

Over time, I came to learn Ashley wasn't all guns and grit. She had a tender side and feminine wants. After two years, the only thing left was to put a ring on it. It was our ranch hand Javier that finally popped the question.

"Hey *Jefe*, when are you going to rope that Mrs. Moore?"

Jav and I were out branding calves, something we still did the old-fashioned way: hot iron on wet hide. We ran a dozen cattle through a squeeze chute and hit them with the same "*MO*" mark Pops had burned for years.

"What do you mean, Jav?"

"*El Toro Negro*. She's the one, no?"

I popped the chute to let a freshly marked calf spring out. "You think she'd make a good wife? She'd be your boss, you know."

"Not my boss, *señor*. Your *padre* put me in charge before he died. I just let you pretend."

I thought on what he said while we finished marking stock. I was prepared to marry Ash, but not sure how to propose. My brain rolled through a dozen dumb ideas while Javier went on about his *loco hermano* down in Mexico.

"Crazy *chocho* hunts cougars now, *sí?* Stalks them through the mountains like he's Bear Grylls."

I didn't know who the Bear fella was, but I was never much into killing for sport.

"*Hombre* says they sell for fifty thousand pesos. I think he's *cagado*."

I knew that to mean, "full of shit," and I suspected he was. Javier was always telling batshit stories about his Mexican fam. But then he dropped something that caught my ear.

"He's trying to get me home for the eclipse next month. Says it's *una tradición*."

"Eclipse? What's that about?"

"*El eclipse de sol, Jefe*. When the moon fucks the sun in the middle of the day."

Of course I knew what an eclipse was, and his description was a bit off. Still, it gave me an idea.

"There's an eclipse next month? Down in Mexico?"

"*Sí señor. Un total*. The path goes right over our village in *Jalisco*."

Wouldn't that be a way to do it? Bring Ashley down to Mexico for a moondance? I could play dumb until the lights went out, then hit her with a ring.

"You ever seen a solar eclipse, Javier?"

"Once, *Jefe*. When I was a boy. *Es la magia*."

Magic.

That's all I needed to hear.

I did some research to narrow down the time and place. Javier was right, his little village would be perfect. But how to get us down there without tipping Ashley off?

Like most things in my life, the answer turned out to be cows. *Corriente* cattle. Mexican beef stock. I told Ashley we were going to browse some Spanish steers and booked a flight into *Guadalajara*. I think she was happy just to get away. In two years we'd hardly spent a night together off-ranch. Javier talked up the romance of his homeland and came along as our guide.

We landed in Mexico the day before the eclipse. Stayed in a big plantation house and felt like rancher royalty. Jav took us out for drinks that night and authentic Mexican *pozole*. He waxed nostalgic while he slurped stew and toasted everyone in the room.

Around two a.m., Ashley and I stumbled back to our suite at the *hacienda*. Well, I stumbled, Ash was stone sober. She helped me over the threshold and into the four-post bed. We made love with the windows open and fell asleep to the sound of bullfrogs.

The next morning, I woke with a headache but didn't care. The day had come. I greeted the sunrise and thanked *el Dios* for clear skies.

Ashley was still asleep, so I geared up. Put on my favorite boots and belt buckle. Checked the ring for the thousandth time. With everything set, I had some coffee sent up and nudged my girl awake.

"*Buenos días, amor.*" Her eyes fluttered open and followed with a smile.

"Morning, Boo."

She drank the coffee in her underwear then put on a sundress. I could have popped the question then and there.

The plan for the day was to meet Javier for breakfast and walk the town. The eclipse was set to peak around noon, and I hoped to meet the moment someplace poignant. Jav promised to make it happen, but when we showed up for breakfast he was nowhere to be found.

"*Pendejo* probably overslept." I was sweating in the morning heat and annoyed to change my plans. Ashley kept it light though.

"We can manage," she said. "Gives me an excuse to practice some *español.*"

73

And so, we spent the morning hand-in-hand strolling cobblestone streets. Ashley turned every head and some twice. I knew with each passing smile I was a lucky man.

Around eleven thirty, people started crowding out and Ashley sniffed something was up. "What's everybody looking at?" People were glancing at the sky and passing around paper glasses. She stopped a nearby *abuela* to ask what was going on.

"*El sol y la luna*," the old woman said, pointing to the sun. Ashley squinted skyward, but it was still too bright to stare. I shrugged and smiled and took her by the hand, looking for a way out of the crowd.

We cut down a narrow alley and into the courtyard of an old church. It was a towering gothic cathedral. A prayer of piled stone. We sat on the lip of a fountain and watched pigeons flit between the spires.

"This is nice, Clay."

"Just you wait."

With five minutes to go, the daylight started to get strange. Colors shifted. Shadows turned funny. More folks gathered in the courtyard as the sun tapered down to a bow. In the final moments before totality, a priest came out of the church and took a spot right next to me. He smiled at Ashley and looked up to the heavens.

Then God gave us a show.

I don't even know how to describe it. In rancher terms, it was like watching a calf born at dawn on Christmas Day. The sun winked away and the stars came out. I got goosebumps as the temp dropped ten degrees.

In the courtyard around us, people gasped and cheered and wept. The church bells rang a chorus while the old priest went down in prayer.

"It's beautiful, Boo."

I took a deep breath and centered myself. I thanked the Lord for the moment and plumbed my pocket for the ring.

"Ashley..."

I went down to a knee and she broke. Just broke. I could hardly move my lips, so I just held out that ring. A simple gold halo like the one in the sky.

"Will you...?"

Ashley shrieked. A wild, primal scream. She heaved and cried and collapsed into my arms. We stayed like that until the sun came back.

74

Finally, she whispered, breathless, "Yes, Clay. Of course."

I smiled and pulled her to her feet. She smoothed out her dress and punched me playfully on the arm. "You know you could have just asked me over dinner."

"I wanted all the heavens here at once." I wiped a tear off her cheek. "That's what I got when I found you."

She laughed and we hugged again. The courtyard around us was raucous and jubilant. A young man slapped me on the back.

"*¡Matrimonio!*" He yelled.

I turned and smiled. "*Sí, matrimonio.*" Marriage.

A woman took Ashley's hand and admired the ring.

"*¡Matrimonio! ¡Matrimonio!*"

More people started cheering and before long we were surrounded. "What's going on?" Ashley said with a laugh.

I just stood there, beaming like a lighthouse. This was our moment. The magic I'd been hoping for. I raised her hand to the sky and the courtyard exploded. People threw flowers and beads. A street band started playing out of nowhere.

"This is incredible, Clay!" My fiancée swayed to the rhythm while tears streamed down her face. "I don't know how you did it."

I don't really know either. Maybe I just got lucky. Maybe some banked up karma paid off. I've always said things work out the way they ought to, and I think that was just our day. The heavenly bodies aligned.

That hour in the church courtyard was the most memorable of my life. I never felt so much love from so many strangers. At some point, Javier showed up a with a bottle of tequila and a drunken grin.

"*¡Felicidades, Jefe!*" He clapped me on the back and forced three shots down my throat. "*¡Viva los Moores!*"

"*¡Viva! ¡Viva!*"

Eventually the party spilled out of the courtyard and into the streets. The whole village seemed drunk off the eclipse, and our *gringo* engagement was just an excuse for more revelry. Ashley and I spent the rest of the day shuffling between bars, everybody and his *hermano* trying to buy me a drink.

When we finally collapsed, buzzing and breathless, in our bedroom back at the *hacienda*, I slipped out of my sweat-stained finery while Ashley admired her ring. We laughed. We kissed. We sang love songs in broken Spanish. I fell asleep feeling like a million *pesos* and woke up to a new day's sun.

Chapter 15

After the wedding, Ashley and I opted for a long honeymoon. Javier tried to talk us back down to Mexico, but Ashley wanted something more private.

"Find me a spot at the end of the world," she said. "Somewhere we can make love on a mountaintop."

I ended up renting a cabin in the wilds of Idaho. Remote. Rustic. Romantic as hell. We rode up on a four-wheeler with two weeks' worth of food. It was paradise.

Those two weeks changed Ashley and me. The land was so beautiful; so healthy and serene. We sang with the birds. Danced with the trees. We hiked up the mountain and made love under the stars.

On the final day, we played chess on the front porch watching mule deer graze the meadow below. Ashley turned to me and said: "I want this."

"This?" I asked. "This cabin?"

"This life," she said. "I want to live like this." She took a long sip of coffee and smiled at the sky.

"What about the ranch?"

"The ranch is our ticket, Clay." She looked at me with something new in her eyes. Some hope I'd never seen there before. "It's good land and you've seen to it. Your father would be proud."

I sure hoped as much.

"But running a ranch is hard work. Not to say that isn't for us, but..." She paused to watch a nuthatch dance across the deck. "I sure would like to settle down for a while."

I thought about her words and gazed off across the hills. The place really was special, but we were young yet to settle down. I turned my focus to the chess board and Ashley's aggressive queen. We swapped a few pawns before she spoke again.

"You own the ranch," Ashley said. "Two thousand acres. Five hundred head." She made another threatening play and I considered how to react.

"You could sell the whole thing for, what? Five million?"

That caught me off guard. I lapsed and blundered and she snatched a hanging rook.

"Sell the ranch?" I muttered. "Pops' ranch?"

"It's your ranch now. Pops gave it to you."

I checked Ashley with my bishop, but it was a lazy move. She blocked and had me running again.

"Five million dollars," she repeated. "We could make that go a long way."

I retreated to a safe square and said nothing. All I could picture was that old timber sign: *Moore's Ranch*. What would Daddy say?

"I know how you feel about your father," Ashley went on. "And I won't push if it's not in your heart." She moved a knight to attack, and I could see the snare closing in.

"But this..." she said, sweeping her arms at the grand expanse. "This speaks to me." She put her hand on my knee and looked into my eyes. "This feels right."

I thought back over all those years of weary ranch work. It was hard living, that was true. But it was good living. And Daddy raised me on it.

"Where would you want to go?" I moved a knight into her path and forced another exchange. Stall tactic.

"Someplace special," Ashely said. "Some perfect piece of land that's just out there waiting for us."

I wasn't used to this starry-eyed version of my girl. Maybe something got to her down in Mexico. Maybe it was the power of this place. She took another sip of coffee while I ruminated on the math.

"Five million dollars?"

"At least."

"And what would we do all day? Once we found this special spot?"

"*This*, Clay. What we've been doing for two weeks." She moved her queen again and put me in a dangerous check. "I know it sounds naïve, but we could live the American dream. Build a little house on the prairie somewhere..."

She started unbuttoning her shirt.

"Live off the land without working so damn hard..."

She slipped it off her shoulders and worked the closure on her bra.

"We'd enjoy our lives, Clay. Every day... and every night." She flashed bedroom eyes and I looked down at the board. I had one move, and it wouldn't matter. Ashley had won.

"You make it sound like a dream, all right."

She stood up from the table and stepped out of her pants. Now naked on the porch and eyeing me like a pigeon hawk.

"Let's think it over," I said. But it was already done. Ashley took me in her arms.

Checkmate.

Chapter 16

And so, we sold the ranch.

It didn't happen right away, of course. I spent the better part of a year hashing things out with lawyers, businessmen, and bankers. A two-thousand-acre land deal is no small thing.

I talked it through with Momma and she was on board from the start.

"I walked away from that life, Clayton. You have every right to do the same."

Mom was quite fond of Ashley, and she told me to defer to my wife's gut from then on. It didn't hurt that I offered her a million out of the final cut.

"Just don't squander the opportunity," Mom said. "That's a lot of money, and you're both still so young."

We ended up selling to a meat mogul out of Iowa. He owned half-a-dozen larger steads and wanted *Moore's* as a startup for his son. Even promised to keep the name.

"Folks around here know *Moore's Ranch*," he said. "Branding is half the battle."

He seemed to know more about business than beef, but when all was said and done we cleared five million, just like Ashley said.

The hardest part was breaking the news to Javier and the staff. We had some hands that had been on twenty years or more. Seen me up from just a boy.

"So, this is how you do me, *pendejo?* Whatever happened to 'bulls before broads'?"

"You just made that up, Javier. Besides, you talked me into tying the knot."

"I kid, *Jefe.* Ashley's a one-in-a-million broad. You don't deserve her."

"I didn't deserve you, either."

We smoked one last together then went our separate ways. Last I heard, he moved back to Mexico to take care of his mom.

At the same time I was working the ranch deal, Ashley scouted land out in eastern Wyoming. We decided on the Cowboy State because it was the least populated and one of the most beautiful. If we couldn't find peace out there, we weren't meant to. Ashley barnstormed every 'For Sale' sign for two hundred miles, but nothing fit her homestead ideal.

"I think we're gonna have to build, Boo." She called me one night from a motel outside Rawlins. "Tomorrow I meet a land agent who's got vacant plots up and down the state. When I find it, I'll know."

"I don't doubt it." If she found a spot half as charming as that hillside in Idaho, I'd sleep happy. We could buy the land and build a house to suit. I just had one request. "Remember to get some water on the property," I said. "A lake or a river. Something clean running through."

"I'll be sure to tell the agent. His name is Dob."

Sure enough, she found our nook and the rest was history. Of course, building a house in the boonies took some doing. Had to lay five miles of access road before any work could even start. I give Ashley a lot of credit: She had a dream and she chased it down. Designed that house from the ground up and hired a dozen contractors to see it through.

On the day we broke ground, Ash and I stood watch as a redhead Canadian boy cranked a backhoe into fresh earth. Ashley kissed me on the cheek and just said, "Thank you."

I looked around and realized I should be the one thanking her. The land was perfect. From the mountains to the valley to our soon-to-be-front door. This was God's country, and we were moving in.

A few days later, we had a crew out setting footings for the foundation. Ashley paced the perimeter while I sat by and smoked.

At one point I heard a rumbling and turned to see a fat man on a four-wheeler coming up the gravel road. He pulled all the way up next to my lawn chair and killed his ride.

"Well, ain't she a beaut?" At first, I thought he was talking about Ashley, and I turned to give him some stink. Then I saw he was just taking in the land. He sat back on the quad with fingers laced across his gut. Wore a smile that said he loved every minute of life.

"Don't think I'll soon get tired of this view," I said.

"I should hope not." The man leaned over and offered an enormous hand. "Arden Horne. Looks like you and I are about to be neighbors."

"Clayton Moore." I shook his hand and offered a cigarette. "That peach over there is my girl, Ash."

He declined the cig and settled back on his ride. "Can't come home smelling like smoke or I'll hear about it," he joked. We watched the work in silence as Ashley yelled to some unseen worker in the pit.

"So, you live nearby?" I asked. "We were under the impression this plot didn't really come with neighbors."

"Oh, I'm around," the big man replied, waving vaguely toward the hills. "Neighbor's a relative term in these parts. I just thought I'd stop by and meet the lucky S.O.B. pitching a 'stead in the valley."

I nodded and smiled. I sure felt lucky.

A few minutes later, Ashley walked over to meet the newcomer. Arden floated to his feet with a crisp salute. He moved easy for a big man.

"Arden Horne," he offered. "Cowboy over here was just telling me you're the queen of this plot."

"That may well be." Ashley shot me a questioning look. "How'd you know I was military?"

Arden eased himself back onto the four-wheeler. "Why them boots and how you walk in 'em," he said. "Same way I made 'ol cowboy here."

I studied my own boots and gave Ashley a shrug. "Arden says we're neighbors. In a relative sense."

The big man laughed. "Well, don't get your hopes up kid," he winked at Ash. "I could fire a .30-06 out my front door and you'd never even hear it."

That meant nothing to me, but it got my wife's attention.
"You shoot?"
"When the better half lets me."
"You serve?"
"Never quite slimmed down to Army standards." He patted his ample belly. "But I come from a long line of grunts."

Arden and Ash went on to talk about guns while I zoned out. She seemed to take a liking to the massive man, and by the end of the conversation they were giggling like a pair of grannies.

"So, what brings a couple of kids out to piss-off Wyoming?" Arden was no old timer but had a decade on Ashley and I, at least.

"Fresh start," Ashley replied. "Recently wed." She flashed a big smile and fingered her ring.

"Well, congrats to you both. You picked a hell of a place to settle down."

We all took a minute to admire the valley. Watched a hawk swoop down and pluck some rodent from the grass.

"Goddamn, it's special out here," Arden said. "Welcome to the neighborhood." I lit up another cigarette while Ashley just beamed.

After that, Arden came around to shoot the shit or shoot something with Ash. They'd go off hunting turkeys on that quad of his. I was glad to see her make a friend.

Once we finished the house and moved in proper, Arden helped us adjust to some of the nuances of frontier life. He looked out for us in a way, but with a light touch.

"Get a dog," he offered one day. "Some big happy hound to roam this plot. You won't regret it."

Arden was always fat and friendly, but cagey about his own affairs. He never let on about where he lived, and we never did meet his girl. We chalked it up to Cowboy State culture. Friendly, but private.

That was just fine by us.

Chapter 17

"Almost there," Arden says. "You can smell the fresh sphagnum."

Whatever that means. Arden's a peculiar cat.

"Hope you've got a hot shower in this hideout, Ard."

For the last three hours we've been whacking straight through Mother Nature's bush. Narrow trails. Steep ravines. I think we crawled through three goddamn caves. The whole time Kali plods along at the head of the pack. She stares me down every time I stop to smoke.

We're losing USAC but it hasn't been easy. The trek's been uphill most of the way and we were already beat down going in. Tuck is basically on one leg at this point. I popped my shoulder again and even Ashley is wearing down.

Somehow Arden takes it all in stride. The big man glides over roots and rocks like he was born in these hills. Maybe he was? At least I understand why he never had us over. I can't wait to meet his wife.

With the sun going down, I'm eager to be indoors again. I feel a sudden longing for my own house: fireplace and easy chair and cozy nights with Ash. This would be about the time I'd pour a glass of whiskey, put on some Morricone, and play chess in my boxers.

Fucking hell.

I hike in silence and wonder what Pops would think of all this.

Look alive, son!

Easy for you to say.

Very funny.

Sorry, that came out wrong.

Go check on your wife.

I sidle up next to Ashley and offer a smile. She looks exhausted.

"Assuming we end up... wherever we're going," she says between breaths, "I expect a full-body massage before bed."

"One-armed massage," I offer, patting my bum shoulder.

"You'll make it work."

We trudge on together as the woods grow darker and more menacing. I hear coyotes in the distance and bats flitting through the trees.

"You know, we used to put in fourteen-hour days at the ranch. Maybe retirement has made us soft."

Ashley scoffs but doesn't look up from her feet. "I also used to hunt terrorists," she says. "Left both of those lives behind."

Can't argue that.

"So, what do you expect of 'ol Arden's place?" I ask. "I always pictured a big log cabin, but now I'm thinking steel-belted treehouse."

That gets a chuckle. "I just hope his wife is my size." Ashley's silks are a tattered mess. She's missing a sleeve and has brambles in her hair. Still looks like a million bucks.

Suddenly, the wolf starts howling and we both stop dead. Takes me a moment to realize that's not the wolf at all. It's Arden.

"Ahhhhooooo," he croons. Hollow and pure. He does a hell of a wolf.

I strain my eyes in the dusky wood and the forest ahead starts glowing. A string of murky lights between two trees. Is this the place?

"Ahhhhoooooooo," Arden howls again as Kali joins in. Their calls are like a warning in the night. I get goosebumps and grab for Ashley's hand.

"Welcome home kids." Arden gestures in the gloom. For a moment I can't see anything, then an earthen structure takes shape.

"Holy sh-" Ashley starts and stops. We both gape at a sloping mound between two giant trees. It's a wide berm with a stone façade. Wooden door. Deep-set portholes. "It's a freaking Hobbit hole."

"Horne hole," Arden chuckles.

"Are you kidding me?" Tuck. Incredulous. "This is where you live?"

"Me, Kali, and Del," Arden says. And with that, the front door opens and out steps the most beautiful man I've ever seen.

Ashley gasps. I'd feel a bit jealous, but I don't have the right.

The man in the doorway is shirtless and shredded. A chiseled Native American, right off the cover of some paperback. He's got olive skin, a sloping nose, and dark hair longer than my wife's. She turns to me with eyes wide.

"I never knew..." She starts, then just smiles. I shrug my good shoulder.

"Greetings, friends." Del spreads his arms in welcome as Kali trots over to his feet. He smiles broadly at Arden.

"These are my folks from the valley," Arden says. "We crossed paths in the woods."

"A fortunate meeting." This Del has a queer calmness about him. *Is that the word they use now?*

Shit, I didn't mean it like that.

"Come inside," Del goes on. "You must be weary from your journey."

Ash and I stand dumbstruck while Tuck hobbles to the doorstep. His mouth hangs slack. He probes at Del with a shaky hand. "Are you... an angel?"

"I am not." Del shakes his head. "Are you?"

Tuck just collapses into his arms.

Chapter 18

"He's lost a lot of blood."

Del washes his hands after treating Tuck and his various wounds. "And that knee is badly sprained."

The pilot snores quietly in the corner of the room.

"He's a tough one, I'll give him that." Arden sits back in a vast recliner. "Pushed harder than any of us to get here."

Del nods thoughtfully. "The mind can drive the body to great things." He turns to me. "May I look at your shoulder?"

"Ashley first. She needs fresh clothes." Ashley bites her lip but doesn't object.

"Of course." Del opens a wooden wardrobe and rummages around. Arden nurses a glass of whiskey and swollen ankles. Ashley and I sit side-by-side on a homespun couch.

"So, how'd you build this place?" The room is cool and cozy. Lit by half-a-dozen oil lamps. "Are we underground, or what?"

"Yes and no," Arden replies. "More like an earthen shell." He points to Del. "It was mostly his doing."

The handsome Indian returns and hands Ashley a neatly folded garment. I notice he's put on a shirt of his own.

"Idaho hemp," Del says. "Not as soft as those silks, but much stronger."

Ashley smiles graciously and stands.

"Washroom's through that door," Arden offers. "Take all the time you need."

Ash kisses me on the cheek and strides away to clean up. Del sits next to me in her place.

"Your shoulder."

I nod and unwrap the sling. My whole arm's swollen and stiff.

"Del knows some native medicine," Arden says. "He's our backcountry doc."

Del produces a bottle of oil and starts massaging my shoulder. "The body heals itself," he says. "I just use some old ways to help it along."

His hands are strong, and the oil smells like ginger. I close my eyes and submit to the old ways.

After a few minutes, I feel a difference. The pain ebbs from a sharp bite to a dull ache. Ashley returns looking cheerful in fresh clothes. "That felt amazing." She reclaims her place on the couch. "Feel free to burn those pajamas."

Del just smiles. Arden swirls his whiskey glass. "I was really scared for you two." His voice is soft and serious now. "We heard those blasts, and thought..." He takes a long sip. "Well, I don't know what we thought." He looks at Del.

"It was quite jarring," Del adds. "Like the Earth itself was coming apart." He bows his head

"Our house shook," Arden goes on. His eyes are glassy. "This house. Dug into the mountain. Fucking *shook*." He takes another drink and stands to refill his glass.

I sit in silence. Transported back to the violence of the morning.

"Mark 82s," Ashley says. "General purpose air-dropped munition." She shrugs. "My best guess, at least. Anything bigger would have been excessive. The target was a plane."

"A plane..." Arden wobbles back over. He's tipsy drunk and less graceful than the man who led us through the woods. "You say this guy just landed in your valley?" He points to Tuck snoozing across the room. "Then a bunch of bombs came down?"

Ashley looks to me to tell the story.

"Well... Bax and I were out walking, you know? Just idling. Doing his business." The bloodhound lays at my feet and I give him a hearty pat. "It's like that most nights. We roam a while. He likes the smells; I like the stars." I think back to where this whole mess started.

"Then we heard this humming noise. Baxter noticed it first and he spooked out. I was just trying to keep up." I remember tailing Baxter when the plane buzzed us over top.

"He overflew us once. Loud and low, but dark. Could barely see him. I figured that was that, and we were heading in when the plane came humming back around."

I stare over at Tuck, still sleeping on his cot. What was he doing, flying like that? Was he even in control? We found him unconscious...

"Was it recon?" Arden asks.

"Hell if I know." I turn and shrug. "He circled back and landed on that flat steppe just south of Dob's. If I'd been asleep, we might never have known."

"What kind of plane?"

"It looked a bit like a Lancer," Ashley says. "But smaller. Definitely a high-altitude rig." She shakes her head. "At first I thought it was some kind of drone. Then we found Tuck."

The room is quiet for a minute. I study Arden's glass and now I want whiskey of my own.

"Did he present himself as hostile?" Del asks.

"He didn't present himself as anything," Ashley says. "No flag. No insignia. He said nothing and then he ran." She laughs. "Probably saved our lives."

"By running?"

"It took us all away from the plane. Far enough, at least. A few minutes later..." She stops and chokes up. "A few minutes later..." Shakes her head. I jump in.

"A few minutes later we had Tuck corralled and I was looking for something to tie him up. I heard this whistling sound, and next thing I knew I was in the air. Ass over teakettle. Landed in the dirt and thought I was dead."

"That whistle was bombs?" Arden asks. "Like they fell from the sky?"

Nobody says anything and Arden gets his answer.

"You got any more of that hooch?"

"Help yourself."

I head over to the little bar top where Arden keeps about a dozen bottles. All whiskey. Kali sits nearby and watches me pour a generous glass. As I make my way back, Del drops a bomb of his own.

"How did the pilot lose his finger?"

A heavy silence fills the room. Finally, Ashley speaks up.

"I shot him."

No elaboration. Del nods but says nothing.

"Look, we still don't know what's what." I take a sip of the whiskey. It's smooth and smoky on my tongue. "The plane, the pilot, the bombs... None of it means anything right now."

Show them your balls.

Very funny, Dad.

You know that's what this is about.

I sigh and fish the stones out of my pocket. "When I searched the plane, I found these." I hand one each to Arden and Del. "There were hundreds of them. Tuck seemed to think they were important."

Arden squints at the blue-green sphere. "Pretty," he muses. "Might make a hell of a whiskey stone." He plops the rock in his drink and giggles. Del looks more serious.

"Stones can carry great power," he says. "Old energies." He looks steady at me. "May I hold this a while?"

"Be my guest. Nothing but trouble since I found it."

Del studies the stone with interest, rolling it around in his muscular hands. A few hits of whiskey have loosened my tongue, and I pop the question that's been on my mind since we arrived.

"So how did you come to meet Arden?"

Del smiles warmly at the thought. "The Old Man brought us together. Just like everything else."

I glance toward Ashley, but she just shrugs. We both turn to Arden, and he's got the same dreamy smile as he studies his whiskey glass.

"So, what..." Ashley starts, but she's interrupted when Tuck vomits onto the floor.

"Aw hell!" Arden cries.

Del stands to attend the sick pilot. "His body is purging toxins."

"Yeah, on my fucking floor!"

"Our floor," Del corrects. "Why don't you boys go drink outside?" He smiles to Ash. "Ashley and I will help this man."

My wife gives me a puzzled look but stands to assist the Indian healer. Arden leads me out the front door, grabbing a bottle of whiskey on his way.

Chapter 19

"Well shit, Clay." Arden tops up his tumbler and sips right off the green stone.

"That's about right." I light up a smoke. The woods are dark and surprisingly loud. Frogs and crickets and God knows what else. "Ashley and I sure appreciate you taking us in."

Arden steps off the porch and strolls into the woods. I move quickly to stay close. Can't see past the tip of my cig.

"Thank Del for that," Arden says. "I wanted to bunker down, but he sent me out."

"You and the wolf."

"Yeah," he chuckles. "Me and the wolf."

I follow the big man through the brush. "Well, I'm glad we finally got to see your home. Meet your... wolf."

Arden huffs as he plows through dark foliage. "I know what you're thinking, Clay."

"Ain't thinking nothing, Ard. Just happy to find friends in the hills."

Arden stops and hands me the whiskey bottle. I take a long drink and pass it back. My head is starting to swim.

"Del's good people," Arden says. "A fucking rock."

"I can see that." I nod in the dark, cigarette bobbing. "Sioux?"

"Blackfoot." Arden hands me the whiskey again. "His full name is Delsin. We've been together twenty years."

"I'll drink to that." I raise the bottle and he clinks it with his glass. "To good people."

"To good people."

We walk on a while in silence. I don't know where he's leading us, but I'm approaching too drunk to care.

"It was Del's idea to set up in these hills. He likes the energy here."

"God's country."

"We lived in a tent for six months while he built that house." Arden laughs. "I thought he was crazy digging out this berm, but now I wouldn't trade it."

91

I pinch out my cigarette and stash the butt in my jeans. Feels wrong to litter out here.

"Real crazy thing," Arden says, "Y'all are the first visitors we've ever had."

"Can't imagine you get much foot traffic." I stumble and crash right into Arden. He stops walking.

"It's more than that," he says, shrugging off my blunder. Maybe he's too drunk to notice. "Del has this way of just... making things happen." He hands me the bottle again and I down one more. That's about my limit.

That's definitely your limit.

Now Pops, I think I've earned a few.

Just keep your guard up.

My guard is... hmmm. I can't feel my guard. I mean my hands. Shit, is Arden still talking?

"...never fully figured it out, but seen him do it enough to respect..." He trails off. "Hey Clay, you all right?" A big hand on my shoulder.

"I'm good, man." I give a thumbs up and blink my eyes a couple of times. We're both quiet and I hear howling on the wind.

"Coyotes," I say. "Kai-oh-tees." They sound far off, but it's a big pack. "Those fuckers roam my valley."

"Yeah, they don't come around here," Arden starts walking again. "Kali sees to that."

I suddenly wish we had the wolf with us. Or Baxter. Something with teeth.

Arden doesn't say anything for a while as we tread deeper into the woods. I'm just following the big man, sheltering in his wake. Suddenly we emerge into a small clearing.

"Oh look, stars."

There's a nice round hole in the treetops and the sky's lit up like Christmas.

"God's country." Arden repeats my mantra and takes a sip of his whiskey. He offers me the bottle but I wave it off.

"Maybe when my head stops spinning." I light up another cigarette like that's going to help.

Arden studies the sky through the canopy. "There's something you need to understand about Del."

"Look, Arden you know I don't judge a man by-"

92

"It ain't that," he cuts me off. "Del's tapped into something. Something powerful."

"Is that so?" I look up at the stars, but my eyes don't seem to focus. Everything feels wobbly and there's a sloshing in my gut.

"Something ancient," Arden goes on. "It's hard to explain."

"He's an interesting cat." I tilt my head, trying not to get the spins. What's Arden on about?

"What if I told you he can make things happen? Things with his mind?"

"I'd ask him to bring back my house."

"I'm serious, Clay."

"Sorry, Ard." I wince and swallow a hiccup. "You mind if I sit down?"

"Have at it."

I plop into the dirt and breathe deep. Arden settles next to me and pours more whiskey. Big man's still going, somehow.

"You probably won't believe me," Arden says, "But I've watched Del make magic for twenty years."

"I'll believe anything right now." I lay on my back and try to focus on the stars. The whole forest spins around me.

Fuck.

Sounds like you had a few too many.

Not helpful, Pops. They got whiskey in heaven?

Who says I'm in heaven?

Oh, shit Pops...

Ha! You're too easy.

Arden continues to talk while I spin. "...like he just sets his mind to it, you know?"

Do I? I just grunt. I think my own mind is shutting down.

"You'll see," Arden says. He takes another swig while I sink into the grass. "Del's probably in there right now, conjuring us a way out of this mess."

What mess?

Oh, right.

Everything.

Chapter 20

"Clay..." A nudge and a whisper. "Clay, wake up."

Fuck that. My head is a blistering knot of-

"Clay! Wake up!"

I crack an eye. It's still dark, but Arden's giant silhouette looms above me.

"Bear, Clay! Bear!"

Now I'm awake.

"You're fucking with me."

"Shhhhh!"

I sit up and try to get my bearings. How long was I asleep?

"In the trees to our left," Arden whispers. "Maybe thirty yards."

I listen close and sure enough I hear something. Rustling. It sounds big.

"I thought you said Kali keeps them away?"

"I said coyotes, not bears."

Adrenaline surges and I suddenly don't feel drunk anymore. Just scared.

"So, what do we do? Did you bring a gun?"

He doesn't answer and I know he didn't.

"Arden?"

"Stay still." The rustling gets closer and more intense. "Stay calm. Don't run."

The clearing is small, no more than thirty feet across. I squint toward the foliage and watch a shape materialize from the dark.

I run.

"Clay!"

I scramble and stumble and plow into the brush.

"Clay, stop!"

I don't know which way I'm going or which way we came from. I'm drunk and blind and running for my life.

"Clay!"

Arden's voice grows distant, but something big follows me through the woods.

Shit. Shit. Shit.

I crash through branches and boughs, stumble over roots.

What are you doing, son?

Shut up. Shut up. Shut up.

You can't outrun a bear!

Shut up! Shut up! Shut up!

Think, son think!

Okay. Keep moving. What are my options?

Climb a tree.

Not with one arm.

Circle back to the house.

I don't know where I am.

Turn and fight.

No way!

Then keep running!

I feel a rush of adrenaline and my focus wipes clear: Just keep moving. Just try to survive.

You can do this!

I bob and weave and dance through the dark forest. I dart around tree trunks and leap over rocks.

That's it, Clay!

I hear grunting and growling and pounding behind me. Is it gaining? Is it fading?

Just keep moving. Don't look back.

I'm amped up. I'm tuned in. I fly through the night like a fucking gazelle.

You will not catch me!

You will not claim me!

I am Clayton motherfucking Moore and I-

I trip.

I go airborne.

The world slows and I study moss on the forest floor. It looks soft but I know it won't be.

I'm fucked.

I brace for impact and wait for life to flash before my eyes. Maybe the bear will trip too. Knock itself out on a rock. Crazier things have happened.

I land with a jolt that blows the air out of my lungs. Roll onto my back and grasp blindly for a weapon. A stick or a rock. God, I wish I had a gun.

The bear lumbers to a stop and stands above me. A hulking shadow with angry eyes and teeth.

Well, fuck you too bear! I never bothered you. I never asked for any of this. I'm just a simple man with a wife and a dog and we had a nice little life until-

A rustling to my left. Something coming through the undergrowth. Probably another goddamn bear.

Ugh.

"Well get on with it, motherf-"

"Woof!"

I know that bark.

"Woof! Woof!"

Balls and business.

"Woof! Woof! Woof!"

Baxter!

The bloodhound steps out of the darkness and onto my chest. He snarls and snaps at the monster looming over us both.

Oh Baxter, you beautiful boy.

The bear growls and the dog howls and I just lay here, two beasts posturing for my life.

That's a hell of a hound you got, son.

That bear must be five times his size, but Baxter holds his ground like a Spartan. I've never been so proud.

A tense standoff ensues. The bear feints and Baxter parries. He's brave, but outmatched. One clean swipe could kill us both. I can't take this. Can't see my dog injured or killed.

"Go on, Baxter," I yell. "Save yourself! Warn the others!"

What am I saying?

The bear's getting frustrated. It bellows and roars and rears back on hind legs. Ten feet tall. Snarling fury.

This must be it.

I love you, Ashley.

Bury me in the valley and never look back.

I close my eyes. I wait for death...

But it never comes.

Pop! Pop! Pop!

Three gunshots. Quick. Efficient. Clean.

I open my eyes.

The bear wavers above me. It moans and teeters and collapses to the earth.

Silent.

Unmoving.

Dead.

Chapter 21

"Don't move."

A woman's voice. Not Ashley's.

I hear a gun click and radio static. I hug my dog.

"God bless you, Baxter," I whisper. "God fucking bless you."

I kiss him and he kisses me back. Slobber and spittle and I'm just happy we're alive.

The giant carcass lays still at me feet. Did that really just happen? I shift for a better look.

"Don't move." That voice again. Cold. Insistent. Who the hell is wandering the woods at this hour?

"I don't know who you are, but thank you for saving my life."

No response. Baxter climbs off me to sniff around the dead bear. My breathing slows. The spinning stops. I don't know who that is or where we are, but for the moment I don't care.

I'm alive.

Holy shit, Pops.

Holy indeed.

Tell me you saw all that.

Every step of the way.

I thought I was fucked.

You were fucked.

I should be dead.

You should be.

But I'm not.

You're not.

I let out a long sigh. These near-death runs will be the death of me. I need to get back to Ashley. I hear radio static again.

"Kirby to Main. Kirby to Main. Target acquired. Over."

Crackle and fuzz.

"Kirby to Main. Kirby to Main. Come in, Main. Over."

Static.

"Goddam it!"

Now I understand my mysterious savior. U.S. Asset Command. I guess they really were hunting us down.

"You got friends out here?" I ask.

No response. She tries her comm again.

"Kirby to Main. Kirby to Main."

Nothing.

"Damn these woods." She turns down her radio. "Where are the others?"

"What others?"

"Don't play dumb. The pilot. The woman. Where are they?"

"Dead, probably." I wince, even at the lie. "I've been on my own since the bombing. Just me and the dog."

"Bullshit." She tries her radio again. Seems frustrated. Maybe out of her element here. "On your feet."

She steps closer and I get a better look. Short. Stocky. Strong. She wears a light helmet and camo fatigues. Gestures with some kind of pistol.

"Let's go."

I hesitate and look for Baxter. He's nose-deep in the dead bear.

"Just please don't shoot my dog."

She doesn't respond, but keeps her gun on me. I climb slowly to my feet. The adrenaline of the chase is gone and everything hurts again.

"Hands on your head."

I raise my right hand while the left hangs limp at my side.

"Shoulder's fucked. Dislocated three times."

She just grunts and moves in to pat me down. Her hands sweep my ankles and up my thighs before landing on a bulge in my right pocket.

"What's this?"

"Dog toy."

"Last chance." She raises the pistol again.

"Jesus, lady. Just take it."

This woman does not fuck around. Reminds me of my wife. She digs into my pocket and fishes out the blue-green stone. Clicks on a small flashlight and looks it over.

"Hmmmmm." She studies me with eyebrows raised. "You boarded the plane." It's not a question.

"I found that on the ground after the bombing. It looked like it might be worth something."

She shakes her head and grabs her radio again. "Kirby to Main. Kirby to Main. Suspect found carrying one unit of V-451. Over." She slips the stone into a pocket and shines the flashlight in my face. "Who do you work for?"

"Nobody." I squint in the harsh light. "I don't even know what's going on."

"What's going on, is you're sneaking around with private property protected under Strategic Interest Initiative 2006.4.18."

"I don't know what any of that means."

"It means you're under arrest by the authority of the United States Asset Command."

She wrenches my arms behind my back and my left shoulder screams.

"Ow! Hey! What are you doing?" I struggle but her grip is iron and I'm out of fight.

"You have the right to remain silent." She slips a zip-tie around my wrists. "Anything you say can and will-"

"Don't move!" Another woman's voice.

"Who's there?" The soldier crouches behind me and shines her light into the dark. "You're both under arrest for illegal possession of a protected asset. Place any weapons on the ground and walk toward me with-"

"I don't think so." Ashley steps out of the shadows holding a pistol of her own. "Release my husband and back the fuck away."

Ashley!

"You're threatening an officer of the United States Asset Command. Further provocation makes you subject to charges of-"

"You better just do what she says." Arden's voice. Somewhere behind us. He pumps a shotgun.

She's outnumbered now but keeps her cool. Back on the radio. "Kirby to Main. Kirby to Main. I've got multiple armed targets at location zero-one-four-"

Arden whistles and a third figure steals out of the brush. The soldier trains her torch and lights up big blue eyes.

"Kali," I whisper. The wolf growls and creeps toward us. All that's left now is for Del to drop out of the sky.

100

"I think you're beat, Ma'am."

I catch a look at the soldier's face. She's young. A scattering of freckles and a scowl of resignation.

For one tense moment there are three guns and a wolf all focused on me. Then my captor relents and lowers her weapon. She pops out the magazine and drops it to the forest floor.

"'Atta girl," Arden says. "What else you got?"

Without speaking, she removes a second pistol and a combat knife from her uniform. Drops both to the ground and puts her hands in the air.

I move to my wife and kiss her cheek. "Boy, do I have a story for you." I then retreat a safe distance and whistle for Baxter. Let the armed folks sort this out.

"What's your business in these hills?" Arden asks.

The soldier stands quiet. Defiant.

"You got a name?"

"She called herself Kirby on the radio," I offer. "Might be a nickname or a call sign."

"Okay, Kirby," Ashley says. "Where's the rest of your unit?"

Her radio crackles with garbled static. Kirby says nothing.

"What do you think, Ard?"

Arden coughs and spits and glances around the wood. "The house is the only place we'll be safe. I say we head back."

"You sure they can't find us there?"

"What did I tell you about Del?"

"I... uh... he..." I don't really remember.

Arden sighs. Somehow in the dark woods I can hear his eyes roll. "Delsin has a way. No one will find us."

Kirby scoffs. "USAC will find you."

Arden ambles around and leans down to inspect the bear. "Three shots, base of the skull." He whistles and turns back to Kirby. "Watch out for this one."

The soldier stands firm but her lips flirt with a smile. Arden retrieves her weapons from the ground and offers me a pistol.

"Make yourself useful."

"Maybe I can just take the knife?"

He shakes his head. "You're lucky you married a real soldier."

Ashley moves in and pats Kirby down. She removes the radio and the blue-green stone. "How'd you get one of these?"

"She took it from my pocket."

Ashley gives Kirby a glare but doesn't say more. She binds the soldier's hands with her own zip-tie.

"Ready to roll out."

Arden takes one more look at the dead bear and shakes his head at me. "Clay, you got some kind of guardian angel."

"More than you know, Arden." I pat my dog and take Ashley by the hand. "More than you know."

Chapter 22

The hike back only takes ten minutes. Turns out my mad dash somehow swung parallel to the house. We arrive to find Del sitting cross-legged in the dirt.

"What's he doing?"

"Meditating."

Arden lets out a quiet howl and Del opens his eyes and smiles. "Welcome back."

"You missed a show, Del." Arden helps him to his feet. "Clay here almost outran a bear."

"Almost?"

"Baxter saved my ass," I add sheepishly. "As did, uh... Kirby here."

Del looks the newcomer up and down. I notice he's shirtless again. "Welcome."

The soldier says nothing.

"How did you guys find me?" I ask.

"It was the damnedest thing," Ashley says. "Del and I were working on Tuck, rewrapping his hand, when Del just stopped and said: *Clay's in trouble.*"

Arden nods and winks at me. Ashley goes on.

"Before I could even ask what he meant, the dogs started going nuts." As if on cue, Baxter wanders to her feet and gets a loving scratch. "So I opened the door, and Baxter here bolted out. Just gone, like a bat out of hell. Kali hung back and stared at me. I didn't know what else to do, so I grabbed some guns and followed her into the woods. At some point I bumped into Arden and we heard gunshots." She turns to me, eyes wide. "I don't know, Boo. It's been a weird fucking day."

"We should get inside," Arden says. "These woods must be crawling with USAC."

"And bears, apparently."

"Everyone is safe here," Del says. For some reason I believe him.

As the group moves indoors, I pull my wife aside. "Hey, go easy on the girl. She saved my life."

"She's USAC. You heard her. She wanted to arrest you."

"Maybe. But she could have shot me and she didn't."

"So what? They bombed our house, Clay. They already *tried* to kill us."

"I know, I know." I pat Ashley on the arm. "We need a good long talk with Kirby and Tuck. A Come-to-Jesus. We'll get to the bottom of all this."

Ashley rolls her eyes.

"Just please take it easy for now. Don't do anything rash."

"Rash? Like what?"

"I don't know, like blow off somebody's finger."

Wrong thing to say, son.

Ashley scowls and turns to stomp inside. "Ashley, wait. Listen-"

She wheels back. "No, *you* listen Clay." She sticks a finger in my face. "I almost died today. *You* almost died today. Multiple times. Our home is destroyed. We're on the run from some army I've never heard of. Fucking *USAC?*" She throws up her hands and looks at me with wild eyes. "We got jumped by a wolf, chased by a bear, almost arrested in the middle of the woods at midnight..." She shakes her head in disbelief. "Sorry if I'm a little *rash* for you, but I am done with this shit."

"I get it. I'm sorry."

She's right.

"You're right."

"We moved out here to find peace, Clay." She shakes her head again. "Our house. Our valley. And now..." Her voice cracks. "And now... what?" She breaks down into my arms.

"We'll be all right," I whisper. "We still have each other. Baxter. Arden and Del." I rub her back with my good hand. "It's been a shit day for everyone, but sometimes that's just how it goes."

Ashley scoffs. "You and your fatalist bullshit."

"It gets me through."

She sighs. "Only my husband, Clayton Fucking Moore, could have his whole life wrecked and shrug it off like, '*Well, you know...*'"

"Isn't that why you married me?"

"That and your junk." She grabs my crotch and we share a long kiss. Finally pull away with a sigh.

Ashley puts her head on my chest. "Stay with me, Boo. No more chasing bears."

"That's not exactly how it went down."

"Just promise."

"I promise."

I squeeze her tight and throw up a prayer. The dark wood hums around us while hungry coyotes call out from afar.

Part IV

Come to Jesus

Chapter 23

I wake to the sound of growling and think: God help me, another bear.

But when I open my eyes, I remember I'm on the floor at Arden and Del's.

I guess it could still be a bear.

I sit up and my shoulder flares. A night on the floor didn't help. I look around the room as morning sun trickles in. Surprisingly bright for a turf lodge in the woods.

Ashley snores on the couch, while Tuck sleeps quietly in the corner. Kali's the one growling as she holds court over our captive marine.

There was a lot of discussion over what to do with Kirby last night. We debated tying her up, locking her down, guarding her in shifts, etc. In the end, Arden convinced us to bind her to the recliner with the dogs on watch.

"We've got a bloodhound and wolf," he said. "Couldn't ask for better sentries." That's how I ended up sleeping on the floor.

She's sitting up now and looks at me with angry eyes. I wonder if she slept. "I gotta pee," Kirby says. She's got short red hair and a strong chin. Can't be much older than twenty-one.

I stand and stretch. Get the blood flowing in my shoulder again. "Arden?" I call. "Del?"

I pop into the washroom to relieve myself. It's not so much a flush toilet as a drainpipe with a seat. Arden explained it runs downhill twenty yards to a creek. The joys of frontier living.

Next to the commode there's a washbasin and a pitcher of well water. I splash a bit on my face, and it feels good. Clean and cool. I study a makeshift shower but can't figure out how it works.

Business done, I step out and return to Kirby. She's in the same position, arms bound to the chair with Kali bristling at her feet. "Really gotta pee, man."

108

"I hear you." I untie her arms and she rubs at swollen wrists. "Through there." I gesture to the door I just came out of. She looks down at the wolf.

I shrug. "Stand down, girl." Kali slinks over and posts up by the front door. Smart pup.

Kirby disappears into the washroom and now Baxter sniffs around my feet. Everyone's gotta pee. I should probably wait for Kirby, but I could also use a smoke. Where's she gonna go?

I turn to Kali. "Keep an eye on things." Giving instructions to a wolf. This is my life now.

Bax and I step out into the cool morning. He runs off to do his business while I take my first look around in daylight.

I can see right away that Del planned his home well. We're sheltered in a dense thicket with just one path in or out. The trees are tall and stout, and the structure fills a mossy berm between two great cottonwood trunks. The whole setup blends right into the forest. If you weren't standing out front, you'd never know it was here.

I smoke my cigarette and listen to the birds. Feel the raw energy. I understand why Del likes it here.

"The Old Man lives in these hills."

I startle and realize he's sitting right next to me.

"Jesus, Del." I shake my head. Step back two feet. "How long have you been there?"

He sits cross legged on the ground. Eyes closed. Same way we found him last night.

"The hour around sunrise is the best for meditation."

"Sorry to interrupt, man."

He smiles but doesn't open his eyes. "There are no interruptions, Clay. Only turns in the river."

I don't know what he's talking about, but it sounds profound.

I give him more space and finish my cigarette. Baxter comes ambling out of the brush and I give him a good once over. Ears, belly, haunch – all his favorite spots. "That's a good boy." The old hound sprawls onto his back.

I love my dog. That should go without saying, but it's worth saying anyway. Outside of Ashley, there is no one more important in my world. Baxter is loyal and loving and he probably saved my life last night. Stood down a goddamn bear.

"A good dog is like the Old Man himself at your side," Del says. Is he reading my mind?

"He's a champ all right." Baxter pops up and walks over to sniff around Del. "Bax, hey. Leave him alone."

"It's no problem," Del says. He still sits lotus-style on the ground. Pets the bloodhound without opening his eyes. "Join me, Clay."

I shrug and look around the little glade. Not sure what I'm looking for. I wonder if Kirby's done in the bathroom. Maybe I should go check on her.

Sit with the man, son.

Yeah, I guess.

He's worth listening to.

I settle to the earth next to my Blackfoot neighbor. My joints ache from a night on the floor, but once I'm down I start to relax.

Nobody speaks for a few minutes. I close my eyes and drift on the sounds of the morning.

"We must stay grounded," Del says after a while.

"Hmm?" My mind swims out of its reverie.

"Do you know the meaning of your name?"

"My name?" That catches me off guard. "Uh... Clay. It's like, earth. I guess."

"Soft earth," he says. "Plastic. Pliable. Clay can be molded into any shape or form."

"Yeah, that makes sense."

"Clay also means mortal," Del adds. "The source of all life."

I ponder this for a while. Never thought much about my own name. Just figured Pops liked the ring of it.

Actually, your mother named you. She thought it sounded country strong.

"My full name is Clayton. I guess my Momma picked it out."

"My full name is Delsin. It means: He is so."

"Interesting."

"My mother wanted a blank slate to be shaped by the Old Man. Like a piece of untouched clay."

This guy sure runs deep.

I like him. A wise old Blackfoot.

He's not that old.

His soul sure is.

110

You know anything about this Old Man he keeps going on about?
You're not ready for that.

"I am so," Delsin repeats. "The most powerful concept there is."
Ask him what he means.

"What do you mean?" I peek at Del next to me and see that he's smiling.

"I exist," he says. "I have agency, awareness, and will." He takes a slow, deep breath. "Master these intentions, and your mind will shape the world."

I'm still not sure what he means, but again, it sounds insightful.
You'll get there, son.

We slide back into silence and I enjoy meditating for a while. I like the smell of the trees. The tickle of breeze on my skin. Del is right, I do feel grounded. After the chaos of yesterday, this is just what I needed.

"Do not be afraid," Del says after a while.

What's that? I open my eyes and take in the forest around me. Everything is as it was. Even Baxter lays peaceful at our feet.

Something is different, though...

I strain and then I hear it. A new sound. Baxter perks up.

"What is that?"

At first, it's just a distant rattle, a vibration on the wind. But it gets louder.

"They will not see us," Del says. He sits in the same position with his eyes closed. I don't know what he's talking about and then I do.

"Helicopters."

The humming grows to a roar as what must be a dozen choppers rumble overhead. Baxter starts barking. Tuck comes scrambling out the door.

"They're on us!" He yells, wide-eyed and frantic. "USAC! We're fucked!"

"Do not be afraid!" Delsin again. He still sits unmoving, but his voice somehow carries over the clamor above. "They will not see us." He repeats. "No one finds us here!"

The words are emphatic. Confident. I want to believe him, but... sheesh. What do you think, Pops?

I think they're getting close.

111

Tuck is panicking. Limping around and waving his arms like a cornered animal.

Del sits like a stone.

I stand and look up but see nothing. The canopy is too thick. That doesn't mean we're invisible, though. Surely, they've got x-ray or infrared or some hotshot imaging tech.

"We gotta get out of here, man!" Tuck screams into my face.

I scan the trees around us. Where would we even go? I look back to Del and he just sits there, silent. Like a crag amidst a storm.

I give Tuck a shrug. He throws up his hands and barrels back into the house.

"Baxter!" I call my dog and he comes. Good boy.

We stand there in the small clearing listening to that roar. The treetops sway in the downdraft, but I never see the sky.

I close my eyes and pray. Open them. Look at Del. Close them again.

I am unseen. I am safe.

I repeat the mantra until the sound recedes. The rumble fades. The trees settle. Everything is calm again.

Delsin opens his eyes and smiles at me. He nods his head like we just shared a joke.

Arden steps through the front door with a shotgun.

"Everybody inside," he says. "We need to talk."

Chapter 24

The house is getting full.

What once seemed a cozy hideaway now hosts a small crowd.

A rundown:

Ashley and I sit on the old couch with Bax curled up between us. My wife tidies her hair and looks refreshed after a night's sleep. She yawns and smiles, and I notice a light seam line still pressed into her face.

Delsin sits on the floor in all his shirtless glory. He looks stoic and thoughtful. Unperturbed by the Blackhawk force that just overflew our nest.

In the corner of the room, USAC Kirby sits on the small cot where Tuck spent the night. She's unrestrained and free to run, but then over by the door we have Kali the white wolf. Anyone in or out will have to go through her, which I find weirdly reassuring. I glance in her direction and those blue eyes meet my gaze.

Arden sits in his huge recliner in the center of everything. He nurses a glass of water and cradles a shotgun. He looks hungover.

Finally, there's Tuck. The short, Asian-American pilot paces the room like a caged racoon. He's got his color back after a night in Del's care, but he's still down a finger and favoring a bad knee. That chopper swarm shook him up pretty bad. Waking to a new housemate didn't help.

"So, let me get this straight..." His eyes are wild and angry. "You got jumped by USAC, so you brought them *here*?"

"She's the only one we saw, Tuck." Arden replies. "Just Kirby."

"Bullshit. What kind of solider patrols by themselves?"

Ashley gives me a look. That's a good question.

"Alone in the woods?" Tuck continues. "At night?"

All eyes turn to Kirby. She puffs out her cheeks but says nothing.

Tuck gets in her face. "What were you doing out there, huh? Some kind of honeypot?"

"Tuck, stand down!" Arden orders. The pilot steps back and crosses his arms. All eyes remain on Kirby.

"Do I have to answer that?"

"Who the hell do you think you-"

"Tuck! Enough!" Arden again. Then softer, to Kirby, "Better start talking, kid."

The young soldier huffs and stares Tuck down. She cracks her knuckles and smooths out a wrinkle in her pants. Making everybody wait.

"Don't make me play the bad cop," Arden says.

"I had to pee."

Tuck scoffs and throws up his hands.

"I was on patrol with three others, and I stepped away to relieve myself. I get bladder shy. I need privacy." Kirby looks around the room. Challenging. Defiant. "I got turned around in the woods and then my radio wouldn't work."

Nobody says anything for a moment. Tuck goes back to pacing.

"SOP would be to stay put and hail my squad leader, but then I heard the bear." Kirby stares me down now. Youthful and fierce. I can't hold her gaze. "So, I pursued," she continues. "And eliminated the threat." She looks around the room. "That's when you all showed up."

"Thank you for that," I add. "For the bear."

Ashley takes my hand and rubs my fingers. She was pretty shaken by the bear encounter and won't let me leave again without a gun.

"Thank your dog," Kirby says, pointing at Baxter. "He bought me time to get the shot."

I give Bax a good rub and he rolls onto his back. Easily the most relaxed in the room.

"So, what's the plan now?" Tuck asks. "We kidnapped a U.S. soldier. We'll have the whole damn army on us before long."

"They won't find us here," Del says, repeating his refrain.

"You keep saying that," Tuck mutters. "But we'll need more than some Blackfoot voodoo to shake USAC." He looks at Kirby. "What were your orders? How many in your patrol?"

Kirby stares and says nothing. Tuck smiles deviously.

"For all they know, you're a deserter now anyway. Don't think Hobbes won't bury you with the rest of us."

114

"Hobbes?" Ashley asks.

"Forget it."

"No, we need answers. Who's Hobbes?"

Tuck sighs. "Hobbes is the man I work for." He gestures to Kirby. "Her too."

"So, he's like your commanding officer?"

"Something like that," Tuck responds. "He heads an organization called *Cygneous*. He also founded USAC."

"He *founded* USAC?"

"Commander-in-chief."

"I thought they were U.S. military?"

"It's a shadow branch that answers directly to Hobbes."

"You're kidding."

"I wish."

"What the fuck?"

Tuck just nods at Ashley. She looks leery and confused.

"So how come I've never heard of this guy? Or *Cygneous*? Or U.S. Asset Command?"

"You're not supposed to. Assuming USAC does its job."

Tuck lets that hang and I get shivers up my spine.

"Sounds sketchy to me," Arden says. "How'd you end up working for Mr. Hobbes?"

"He recruited me," Tuck replies. "I was flying test rigs for Lockheed. Hobbes brought me in and doubled my salary."

"So now you're a test pilot for USAC?"

"For *Cygneous*. That's where the real work is. USAC is more like private security."

"Funded with public dollars," Ashley adds.

Tuck shrugs. "Hobbes has friends *everywhere*."

The room takes all this in. Arden whistles.

I don't like the sound of this.

Me neither, Pops. You think this Hobbes guy wants us dead?

He's got his own army. I'm surprised you're not dead already.

Ashley brings us back to the moment.

"So, you were flying this *Cygneous* plane on behalf of this guy, Hobbes."

"Oliver Hobbes. That's his full name."

"And how'd you end up in our valley?"

115

Tuck hesitates and looks at the floor. Like he'd rather not answer. "I screwed up," he says, finally. "I lost control."

"Care to elaborate?" Arden asks.

"Does it matter?"

"It might."

Tuck sighs. He's giving it up easier now, but I wonder how much is an act. He sits on the floor next to Del and rubs his swollen knee.

"The plane was a prototype. High altitude, long range. I was up there fifteen days."

"Fifteen days?" Ashley gasps.

"I've been told it's a record," Tuck says, pride in his voice. "Longest solo flight in history. Beat some dude in a balloon."

"How did you fly alone for fifteen days? Didn't you sleep?"

"The plane practically flew itself. Just the same big loop through empty airspace. I could roll on autopilot for hours."

"Must get boring."

"It did." Tuck flexes his knee with a wince. "I had a routine where I would sleep for four hours, then wake up and fly for eight. On and off like that."

I remember my search of the plane and that little room with the bedroll. Hell of a place to spend two weeks.

"By day fifteen I had the record. The plane was sound, and I was told to push for twenty. But I was going stir crazy." He looks sheepishly at Ashley. "So I... got a little reckless."

"What does that mean?"

Tuck stares into space and scrunches up his mouth. He looks at Kirby and I see a flash of something. Curiosity? Infatuation?

"I had two Oxys that I smuggled aboard in my personals," Tuck says. "*Cygneous* would have flipped if they found out."

"What are Oxys?" Del asks.

"Oxycodone. Opiate pills." Tuck shrugs. "I needed a little buzz, you know? Fifteen days..."

Del nods, apparently understanding.

"It was stupid. But I was saving them for the day I broke the record. I thought it might take the edge off and boy did it."

"So, you got high," Ashley says. "At forty thousand feet."

"At first, yeah," Tuck sits up tall and takes a breath. "Once I was rolling, I started getting ideas." He glances at Kirby again. "I started climbing."

Tuck stares at the ceiling now. Rubs his chin with a faraway look. "I took it up to 60K. Sixty thousand feet. Almost twice the height of a commercial jet." He smiles dreamily. "At that altitude, it's like being in space. You can see the atmosphere. The curve of the earth." He takes a deep breath. "It's almost spiritual."

"It must be beautiful," Del says.

"It's incredible." Tuck runs a hand through close cropped hair. "So, I was high, and I was... *high*." He smiles at Kirby. "And it was pretty special. But I'm not one-hundred-percent sure what happened next."

"Was your plane even built for that?" Ashley asks.

"She was rated up to sixty-five. And I'd touched that a few times in the sim." Tuck shakes his head. "But I think the Oxys started messing with me."

"Opioids slow everything down," Ashley says. "Your heart rate. Your breathing. Less oxygen to your brain."

"Yeah, I started to get dizzy." Tuck takes a breath to steady himself. "I thought I'd be okay with my mask on, but I guess I passed out."

"Probably hypoxia," Arden adds. "I had a buddy that flew Hornets in Desert Storm. Said he feared blacking out in his own plane more than anything Saddam could throw at him."

"Well, when I woke up, autopilot had kicked in and we were back down to thirty thousand." Tuck frowns at the memory. "I was confused, though. Delusional. Someone kept talking over the radio and they sounded angry. That made me paranoid." He sighs and rubs his eyes. "Then I just wanted to land."

"Why not sleep it off?"

"I wasn't thinking straight. And I was too stoned to use my radio." Tuck stares absently at his hand. Bandage where a finger used to be. "I started thinking they were going to shoot me down."

"Shoot you down?" Del asks. "Who would do that?"

"I don't know. USAC? NORAD? When a plane goes AWOL, they don't fuck around."

Ashley nods. "An unresponsive pilot is serious business. Air Defense would eventually scramble fighters to escort. Downing would be a last resort."

Tuck moans and puts his head in his hands. "I was so stupid." Del pats him on the back and whispers something in his ear. Ashley looks on with pity.

I still don't buy it.

You think he's lying, Pops?

I think he's hiding something. Keep digging.

Eventually, Tuck gathers himself and stands back up. He stretches and resumes pacing.

"So, I was eager to touch down and I didn't care where. I was stupid and scared and not thinking straight. I started looking for highways."

"Highways?" Arden chuckles. "Boy, you were desperate."

"Yeah, I'm not proud of that." Tuck stops pacing to study a wreath of dried flowers on the wall. "Eventually I saw this valley open up. I got really low and gave it a once-over. Looked flat enough."

"You came from the north," I add. "Sailed right over Baxter and I."

"Then I circled back once and decided to land." Tuck laughs to himself. "Drugged up, dizzy, delusional... Still set her down like a newborn baby."

"It looked like a smooth landing."

"In a field with no ground lights." Tuck puffs out his chest. "They don't teach you that one in the sims." He looks to Kirby and she smiles. Something's going on with those two.

"Of course, that was about all I had." Tuck turns to Ashley now. "I passed out in my pilot's chair and that's where you found me."

My wife nods and sits back. "That's quite a story. But you're leaving something out."

Tuck feigns confusion, but quickly drops the act. "You mean the stones?"

Ashley nods again. "You said that's why USAC was coming after us. And Clay saw hundreds of them on the plane."

Now Kirby gives me a glance. I wonder what she knows about all this.

Tuck sighs. "The stones are a *Cygneous* resource." He stares at Kirby. "You could say they're the 'Asset' behind Asset Command."

"And what does that mean?"

"It means they're valuable. Proprietary. Something Hobbes wants to protect."

"So why were you flying around with a plane full of them?"

He rubs his lips and studies the ceiling. "The stones are part of a new stealth technology. They augment the radar signature of an aircraft to make it look like something else."

"A bunch of rocks do that?"

"I don't know all the tech behind it. Something about dynamic magnetic fields. Command had me test it every few hours."

I study Kirby and she's got an odd look. No longer smiling.

"I could make my rig look like a cloud, a commercial jet, a flock of birds..." Tuck spreads his arms wide and smiles. "Or nothing at all."

I notice Del fondling a stone in his hand. The one I gave him last night.

"It's something the nerds at *Cygneous* cooked up. I was only briefed on the broad strokes, but Hobbes was very excited about it."

I watch Del play with the green sphere, rolling it around in his fingers. Kirby watches too and her eyes dart anxiously. Something feels off.

He's lying.

About what, Pops? The stones?

Has to be. You were on that plane.

Yeah, but... I don't really know what I was looking at.

It wasn't stealth tech. We've had that since the eighties.

It does seem odd.

Because it's bullshit. Think it through, son...

I drift back and Tuck is still carrying on "...hope that if we could perfect the system on small aircraft, *Cygneous* could expand applications to-"

"You're lying." I cut him off.

"Excuse me, cowboy?"

"About the stones. That's no radar tech."

Tuck frowns and narrows his eyes. "And what would you know about it?"

I take a deep breath and gather my thoughts.

"Well, I'm no techie," I start. "And I'm no pilot. Hell, I didn't even want to be on that plane." I think back on my nervous stroll through the jet. Tuck folds his arms and says nothing. "But I know stealth technology is nothing new. It's on the Nighthawk. The Raptor. The B-2 Spirit. Anymore, it's baked right into the skin of the plane."

Tuck sighs. "This is leading-edge science, cowboy. You're talking over your head."

"That may be. But you're talking out of your ass."

I let that hang a moment and survey the room. Del studies the stone resting on his palm. Arden rubs his shotgun. Tuck just looks grumpy while Kirby stifles a smile.

Get 'em, son.

I stand.

"And none of that explains the goddamn shelling we took yesterday." I shake my head and step toward Tuck. "Why would USAC bomb the plane like that? The whole damn valley?"

Tuck stands defiant. "You don't know Hobbes. Collateral damage is nothing. He's protecting his asset."

"By blowing it up? What's the man worried about? Some hayseed hacking a stealth jet?"

Tuck shrugs. He glances at Kirby then back to me.

"That plane was in the middle of Nowhere, Wyoming." I look at my wife and she nods encouragement. "Hell, the only folks within twenty miles are standing in this room."

"So?"

"So..." I rub my sore shoulder. "So why would U.S. troops bomb a U.S. plane on U.S. soil?" I sweep my good hand around the room. "Unless they were worried about what *we* might find."

Arden nods. Ashley looks thoughtful.

"It's a good question," Arden says. "We're just a bunch of country folk. What kind of threat are we?"

Tuck shakes his head and says nothing. He looks desperately to Kirby.

You're close, son.

I speak directly to the soldier. "What do you know about all this?"

Kirby considers me a moment. I don't expect her to say anything, but then she starts to laugh.

"I was briefed on you," she says through a chuckle. "Before we went in. They got files on all y'all."

That's the first hint of twang I've heard in her voice. Maybe our vibe is rubbing off.

"I'll admit, yours was pretty light. *Clayton Moore: Rancher. Texan. Smoker.*"

I don't know what all that's about, but now I want a cigarette.

"Your wife is the one we were told to watch out for," Kirby continues. "She's got a dossier ten pages long."

Ashley narrows her eyes but says nothing.

"Mostly boilerplate intel," Kirby goes on. "About your time in service, survival skills, likelihood of being armed."

"USAC knows all that?"

"That and more." Kirby stands from her cot and everyone tenses up. Kali lets out a growl.

"Easy now," Kirby says. "I think your boy here is on to something." She steps over and pats me on my good shoulder. "I never got the full picture either. I'm just a grunt in Hobbes' service." She leans in and winks at me. "But they gave us the same BS about stealth and I never bought it."

I take a small step back. "I heard you on the radio. When you found me in the woods. You took a stone from my pocket and called it in." Kirby nods and removes the rock from her own fatigues. No one ever bothered to take it off her.

"V-451," she says, holding it up for all to see. "That's what my commander called it. How much did you actually get?"

I shrug. "I grabbed a few stones. Tuck threw one in the woods. Arden had one in his drink..."

I look to the big man and he turns up his hands. "Shit, Clay. I dropped everything when that bear came through."

I turn back to Kirby. "I think we have two left."

She nods and holds her stone out to Tuck. "So why don't you tell us what these are really for?"

"I told you," the pilot says, shaking his head. "Prototype stealth technology."

Kirby drills him with a steely gaze.

"What else do you want me to say?"

Kirby smiles but stays silent. Tuck throws up his hands.

"Whose side are you even on? Your *entire mission* is to protect this asset."

121

"It was," Kirby says. "But the situation has changed."

"How so?"

"I'm rethinking my allegiance."

"You're defecting?"

"I'm adapting."

"You're a turncoat."

"I'm pragmatic."

"Oh, blow me."

"Wouldn't you like-"

"Wait!" Ashley jumps in. "I know what it is." She looks at me with wide eyes. "I know what the stones are for."

Tuck groans and Kirby smiles. "I knew you were the smart one here."

Ashley points to the pilot.

"You said you flew for fifteen days."

Tuck shrugs and nods his head. "And then I got high and blew the mission. We covered that."

"What kept you up there so long?"

"I don't know. Willpower?"

Ashley laughs. "I mean your plane." She stares pointedly.

"Um... I guess... I got refueled."

"You guess?"

"USAC kept me topped up." Tuck straightens. "Aerial tanker squad."

"Mmm-hmm," Ashley says. "Were they Extenders or Strats?"

"I think they were... Strats."

"Drop probe or boom?"

Tuck shakes his head. "What is this?" He looks incredulous.

"Something you would remember," Ashley says. "If you actually refueled mid-air."

My wife stands and now most of the room is on their feet. Arden leans forward but doesn't leave his recliner. Del stays rooted to the floor.

"You never used a tanker because you didn't need one," Ashley says. "You flew fifteen days on a single tank of gas. But how?"

Tuck pouts and steps back as Ashley strides toward Kirby. She plucks the stone from her hand.

"Your plane was a prototype all right," Ashley says. "But not for stealth." She raises the stone dramatically. "For *fuel*."

"Yes!" Kirby claps her hands. Ashley bares an awkward smile and soldiers on.

"The stones powered the plane. Like giant batteries."

"How is that possible?" Arden rubs his meaty chin. Ashley commands the room.

"These stones are more than stealth technology," Ashley says. "*Much* more." Her eyes go glassy with realization.

"The stones are *energy*. Free and clean."

"Free energy?" Del speaks up. "If that's true..."

Arden whistles.

Kirby giggles.

Baxter barks for good measure.

Tuck just stands there with his arms crossed. "You think that's it, huh?"

"I do," Ashley says. "Because I've seen these stones before."

Now Tuck steps back in surprise. "Impossible. V-451 is one of the most guarded resources on earth."

"Maybe," Ashley says. "But I know where it came from."

The room goes quiet as all this sinks in. My wife's face shimmers with satisfaction and sweat. But when we lock eyes, I see something darker.

"Sounds like you've got a story, girl." Arden stands and walks over to his husband, still toting the shotgun. He takes the stone from Del and studies it with new interest.

"I do," Ashley replies, more serious now. She sits back on the couch and takes my hand. "A story I've never told anyone. Not even Clay."

I know what she's getting at now.

"Ashley, you don't have to-"

"I do, Boo. It's time."

I take a deep breath and lean into my wife. To support her or me, I'm not sure. "The nightmares..." I whisper. She nods and leans back into me. Stares at the stone for a moment then opens her mouth to speak...

Chapter 25 – Ashley's Story

I was raised by my father.

Corporal James Robert Carter, God rest his soul.

Dad spent twelve years as an MP at Fort Benning and loved every minute of it.

"The Army gave me a life to be proud of," he used to say. "Too many of my friends wound up on drugs or in jail."

Mom hated living on base, so we kept a small flat in East Atlanta. My sister and I saw Dad whenever we could, and we knew enough to be proud of him. Mom made sure of that.

When I was five, Mom got breast cancer and everything changed.

She hid it for a while. Too long, the doctors said. By the time they found the tumors it was too late to slow them down.

I was old enough to see Mom was sick, but too young to appreciate the stakes. My older sister Sage knew better, and she prepared me for the worst.

"Mom is dying," she told me. "It might just be you and me for a while."

Sage was a dynamo. Swagger and brains. Hell, she probably could have raised me if she had to.

Nevertheless, Dad came home. He left the Army and helped Mom through her final days. I could see the weight on him. The pain. He lost his wife and career in one fell swoop. That might break a lesser man, but my father soldiered on.

Over time, we found a new normal. I was young enough to adapt and Sage was too smart to slow down. Dad found a job at the airport and a new flat across town. We all missed Mom. Her laugh. Her fire. Her faith. The tradeoff was more time with our father, and the shared grief brought us closer as a family.

As my sister got older, it became clear she was destined for greatness. Everything just came easy to Sage. She breezed through high school and started getting interest from top universities. Dad got nervous about tuition and began pulling double shifts. We all knew

Sage was worth it, but I hated watching him grind. He stopped making it home for dinner. He was always busy on weekends. I missed the outings we used to share.

Like ballgames. Dad loved him some Atlanta Braves. We'd sit in the bleachers and eat hot dogs and do the tomahawk chop. Dad taught me the rules of baseball and I taught him the chicken dance. It was our time.

One year the team did a "Salute to Service" night. This was just after Desert Storm, so patriotism was running high. Dad wore his old uniform and stood with all the vets for a special ovation. He looked so proud in those Army Greens, probably the first time he'd worn them since Mom passed away. Even the players came out of their dugouts to applaud.

That whole night folks kept coming up to Dad just to shake his hand. White folks. Real respect in their eyes. It was like he was ten feet tall, and I never forgot it. The esteem that uniform could bring.

Flash forward ten years, and Dad's busting ass to put Sage through UNC. I'm coming up on graduation, and worried about how we're going to pay for more school. I was no genius like my sister, but I played a little softball. Could have grabbed a partial scholarship in-state.

Instead, I joined the Army.

Signed my life away on a folding table at the mall.

I remember telling the recruiter I didn't want to burden my family, and I wanted to make my father proud. Instead, Dad was furious.

"Why didn't you talk to me first?" He demanded. "We could have worked something out." He thought it was about the money, but it was more than that. I wanted to wear that uniform. To walk in his boots.

Of course, times were different from when Dad served. He'd never seen live combat, and now the country was fighting two wars. I would likely be deployed and that scared him. Hell, it scared me.

Sage brought us both around. "Ash is gonna fuck some terrorists up! Hooah!" My beautiful, brilliant, bad-mouthed sister. She was behind me all the way. "Dad is proud as shit," she told me. "He just pictured a different life for you."

My first tour was nine months in Iraq. I pushed papers at Al Asad and never left the FOB. I won't say it was the life I expected, but in a way it probably was.

The U.S. military is a fucking marvel. A miracle of manpower and logistics. Sure, it's expensive and antiquated and inefficient, but supporting a quarter million troops in the desert takes some doing. I was proud to play my small role.

Being a black woman was a weird niche though. The black part was actually easy. The Army takes all colors. Sure, you'll find a few racists. You get that everywhere. But in my five years I served alongside every ethnic group under the sun. Africans, Asians, Puerto Ricans, Jews... My bunkmate at basic was a Rwandan refugee. When someone greets you in the Army, the first thing they look for isn't your skin color, it's your rank.

Unless you have breasts.

For all its triumphs on diversity, the Army's gender integration was shit. I get it. War has always been a man's game. You throw two chicks in a platoon of fifty men and things get complicated. Complicated gets people killed.

Still, women want to serve. And some of us want to fight.

After my first tour I volunteered to join a Female Engagement Team. FET's support operations by engaging locals in ways that men can't. You go into these old-world towns in Afghanistan and you need good intelligence. The local women have it, but they don't want to talk to G.I. Joe. Often their culture forbids it. That's where the FETs come in. We'd form relationships with local women, hear their concerns and communicate our goals. We'd swap supplies for critical intel. Share meals and stories of children. It was war with a woman's touch.

After six months of FET work, I felt like I was making a difference. I got called for a special mission and assigned to a squad of Army Rangers north of Kabul. The story was we were looking for a terrorist cell that had gotten their hands on some nuclear material. They were up in the mountains somewhere, cooking up a dirty bomb, and the squad needed my help to root them out.

As soon as I fell in with the Rangers I was in awe. I'd never seen such a disciplined group of soldiers. They were fit and methodical and resolute in their goals. When the squad moved, they moved as one. Everyone knew their roles, and nobody fucked around. I felt like a total imposter, but the squad leader picked me up.

"You're part of this team now," he told me. "You're a Ranger. Just tell us what you need."

Staff Sergeant Hummel was everything I dreamed of in a field commander. Steady and shrewd, Hummel oozed authority. He was a burly black man from Alabama, ten years and two tours my senior. His team was so efficient, he never shouted orders. He'd simply nod his head or wave a hand and ten men would hop to. I just tried to keep up.

Our mission took us way up into the boonies. I'm talking backwaters of the backwater. A narrow strip of Afghan mountains called the Wakhan Corridor. It's remote and rugged and sparsely populated. There are no roads. There was no fighting. We moved mostly on foot and thank God I was in shape.

The alleged terror cell supposedly went by the name, *Bariq*. We humped village to village through the mountains, interrogating every goat herder along the way.

"*Bariq? Bariq?*"

These people looked at me like I was from the moon. I guess to them I could have been. Weeks passed, and we kept pushing father but getting nowhere. I hadn't grabbed a single lead and felt like I was letting the whole team down.

Hummel kept me on point.

"We're getting close," he would say. "Just keep doing what you're doing."

He was supportive when I needed it, but cagey about everything else. I pressed him on what he knew about this terror cell and why we were so far up in the hills.

"Don't worry about the why," he told me. "Just know that your country needs you. Find *Bariq*."

It was an all-or-nothing game, and I had little choice but to soldier on. That's life in the Army sometimes. You're part of a team. You follow orders. Everyone answers to someone, and you know what you need to know.

Finally, after three weeks of hard hiking, I caught a break. We came through a little village near the Tajikistan border. Twelve huts on a mountain pass. I called out a greeting and a young woman came to meet me. She was weathered and beautiful. Juggled two babies while we spoke.

"*Bariq? Bariq?*" I went through the usual song and dance.

"*Bariq!*" Her face lit up with a smile. Not the reaction I was expecting. She handed me one of her babies and fished an object out of her robe. It was a blue-green stone, polished and carved in the shape of a bird. "*Bariq,*" she repeated.

Something about the exchange got Hummel's attention, and he asked to see the stone. He studied it for a few moments then pulled me aside. "Keep her talking while we look around."

I pressed the woman in broken Farsi while the Ranger squad fanned out around me. She started to get nervous, and I offered some gifts to calm her down. Toothpaste. Toilet paper. Simple trinkets from my pack. She took them eagerly then called to another woman who'd been looking on.

"*Bariq,*" she said again, and the woman rolled up her sleeve to reveal a beaded bracelet of the same blue-green stones. She had long hair and amber eyes and spoke a little English.

"Big cave. Not far," the woman said. That got my attention. Maybe this was really it. The cell we'd been searching for. I looked for Hummel and he was prowling through the village with the rest of the squad. They moved carefully with rifles up. I got a weird feeling all of a sudden.

"Staff Sargent!" I called. "This one says there's a cave, not far from here."

Hummel came back over. He had another blue-green stone in his hand. "Show me."

"What's the deal with the stones?" I asked. "Do you think-"

Hummel cut me off. "Show me the cave."

He and I followed the woman with the bracelet down a trail away from the village. Her turquoise veil caught the wind as she stepped over rocks and scree. The rest of the squad stayed behind, and I got that weird feeling again. Were Hummel and I about to take on a terror cell by ourselves?

The woman led us along two tight passes and one precarious ledge. We dipped under some fir trees and suddenly there it was. A gaping hole in the mountain. So big you could drive a truck inside.

"*Bariq,*" the woman said, pointing proudly at the cave. I shouldered my rifle and peered into the darkness.

"Wait here," Hummel said, stepping into the cave by himself. If this was a terrorist stronghold, he was being pretty fucking cavalier. Not the calculating Ranger I knew at all.

I studied the woman and she just smiled at me. I started to think this wasn't the right place at all. Must have been some miscommunication. Maybe *Bariq* meant different things. The vibe was way too casual to be cooking a dirty bomb up here.

After a few minutes, Hummel emerged and gave me a nod. "Good work, private." He pulled out his radio and said something to the team, some code word I wasn't familiar with. Then he gave me a sad kind of look that caught me off guard. Something new in his eyes. Pity? Shame?

He shrugged his shoulders, took a deep breath, and then the gunshots began.

At first, I wasn't sure what was going on. We were far enough from the village that all I heard were muffled pops on the wind. But before long it was unmistakable. Machine gun fire.

The woman's eyes got big and she tried to run. Hummel grabbed her by the arm and threw her to the ground. I started to panic. What was going on? Had the team been ambushed? I looked frantically for a signal from Hummel, but he just stood there, cool as a cucumber. The woman cowered at his feet.

"You did good, kid," he told me. "We couldn't have done it without you."

"Done what?" I asked. "What's going on?"

He sighed and pulled the woman to her feet. She was shaking and crying and moaning with fear.

"Now this can go one of two ways," Hummel said.

"I don't understand," I pleaded. The woman stared at me with frightened eyes. Somewhere back up the mountain, the sound of gunshots tapered off.

"We need you all-in on this," he said. "Otherwise, I have orders."

I shook my head in disbelief. "I still don't..." I was lost for words.

"Don't play dumb, private." Hummel smacked the woman and shoved her back to the ground. "I'll say it once more. This can go *one of two ways.*"

He fixed me with a stony stare and the horror finally sunk in. He wanted me to kill her. The team had wiped out the village and he wanted blood on my hands to buy my silence. Who were these people? What the hell was in that cave?

"I have orders, private." Hummel raised his head. "What's it going to be?" He pulled out his pistol and checked the chamber. Was he going to shoot the woman himself?

No. He could have done that already.

If I didn't do what he wanted, his orders were to kill me.

My stomach dropped. My knees buckled. I bent over and puked into the dirt.

Hummel shook his head. "I'm sorry it has to be this way."

"But why?" I gasped. Still dizzy and sick. "They're civilians..."

"Don't worry about the why," Hummel said. "Just know that your country needs you."

I struggled to meet his eye, but my vision blurred with tears. My heart raced. My hands shook. I wasn't sure I could level a gun if I wanted to. Would Hummel really kill me out here? My own squad commander?

I looked around and realized how easy it would be. We were on the side of a mountain at the end of the world. No one would know. I was the only loose end.

I realized then that I had no choice. For a moment I considered just giving up. Let the bastard kill me. Let me haunt his fucking dreams.

But no, that was futile. The woman was going to die either way. Her village was already gone. I could try and shoot Hummel, but the Rangers would hunt me down. And that's assuming I could get the draw on him.

Hummel's jaw clenched as if he read my thoughts. Another Ranger suddenly appeared next to me. "It's done, sir." I never even heard him approach.

"Time's up," Hummel said. He raised his pistol with a steady hand. "Make your choice."

I drew a deep breath and rose up. Something icy came over me, a numbness spreading out from my heart. I unholstered my sidearm and aimed at the woman weeping in the dirt.

"I'm sorry," I whispered. She screamed and I closed my eyes. "I'll make it right someday."

I fired once. She screamed louder. A primal roar of anguish and pain. My eyes stayed closed and I fired again. A third time. She stopped screaming.

I opened my eyes and it was done.

Chapter 26

"Wow."

Arden leans back and studies the ceiling. "Ash, I had no idea."

My wife shakes her head and wipes tears from her cheeks. "Like I said, I've never told anybody. Not even Clay."

"I'm so sorry." I wrap Ashley in my arms. She feels shaken and frail. Depleted.

Kirby blinks tears from her own eyes. "What happened next?"

"We hiked down the mountain and camped one more night," Ashley says. "The next day, Hummel made a call and we choppered out."

"Did you ever try to talk to him?" Kirby asks. "About the stones or the cave?"

"I didn't talk to anybody." Ashley shakes her head. "I withdrew from FET and spent the rest of my deployment on a cook line. Everyone pretty much left me alone after that, but I could tell they kept eyes on me."

"Hummel and his boys," Arden asks, "You sure they were Rangers?"

Ashley shrugs. "Like I said, he was cagey. 75th Ranger Regiment operates out of Fort Benning where my father served. I tried picking Hummel's brain about it, but he always brushed me off." Ashley gets a far-away look. "Looking back, they were probably something else. Some black squad posing as Rangers. They could have been USAC for all I know."

Everyone ponders that a moment. Del stands up and puts a hand on Ashley's chest. He closes his eyes and recites a prayer.

"You are not the sins of your past," he says. Ashley's lip quivers and she lays her hand over his. "You are love," Del continues. "You are light. You are Ashley Moore." He takes his hand away and smiles.

"Thank you," Ashley mouths, wiping more tears. She shakes her head to clear it. "So... what now?"

"Now?" Arden stands and pumps his shotgun. "Now I want to fuck these assholes up."

"You and me both, Ard," I add. "You think this guy Hobbes is connected?"

"I can maybe speak to that," Tuck says. "Since it's all out there now." He looks somber and serious and turns directly to Ash. "You're right about the stones." She folds her arms and says nothing. "Officially termed V-451, but most of us called it Voltstone."

"Voltstone?"

Tuck extends a hand and Ashley gives him the rock she'd been fondling while telling her story. "It's a naturally occurring mineral, mined somewhere in the Middle East." He gives Ash a knowing look. "The way some of the *Cygneous* guys tell it, there's a whole goddamn mountain out there. It's all been annexed by *Cygneous* and secured by USAC." He walks to the sink and fills a glass of water.

"The stones themselves are inert," Tuck continues. "Pretty colors, but nothing special. It's when you get them wet that something magic happens." He plops the stone in the glass and sets it on a table at the front of the room. Everyone crowds closer for a look.

"Hyper-ionization," Tuck explains. "Voltstones react with water to generate an electric current that you can harness like a battery."

Del studies the glass with interest. "How much current?"

"It depends on the surface area of the stones." He taps Arden on the shoulder and the big man hands him another rock. "This little setup might power a light bulb or two, but when you combine multiple Voltstones you get a catalyzing effect." Tuck drops the second stone into the water glass. "Now you could run a small freezer, or a microwave."

"With two rocks in a glass of water?"

Tuck nods.

"Bullshit."

"Don't believe me? Stick your finger in the glass."

Arden leans in, skeptical look on his face. He licks one of his chubby fingers and dips it into the water.

"Yowch!" He pulls it back out with a start.

Tuck grins. "Anyone else want to try?"

Ashley can't help herself. She slides a finger into the water and quickly jerks it out. "That's amazing." She tries once more with the same result.

"It's a game-changer," Tuck says. "Cheap, clean, affordable power. No combustion. No waste."

"Wait a minute..." I think back to the setup on the aircraft. "I dipped my whole arm in one of those tanks on the plane."

Tuck nods. "There is one catch. Over time, the water runs out of free electrons and the current drops off. You probably stuck your hand in one of the depleted tanks."

I remember the strange sensation I felt. The hum and the warmth and the glow. It all had me hypnotized. "But the rocks themselves never go dead?"

"Never." Tuck shakes his head. "Just cycle the water every few days and you've got permanent juice."

Arden whistles. "It's a miracle."

"It's almost primitive," Ashley says. "Water and stones..."

"A handful of these rocks could power the average home," Tuck says. "Lights, appliances, whatever. A few dozen could supply your whole neighborhood." He lets that sink in, then adds: "It took about two hundred to power the plane."

So, what I thought were fish tanks were actually giant Voltstone batteries. "I guess that explains the buzz we heard. You didn't sound like any normal jet."

"State-of-the-art electric engines," Tuck nods. "Too powerful for any modern battery, but the Voltstones made 'em sing."

"And they got you up to sixty thousand feet? These stones."

"With ease," Tuck says, smiling. "She was a hell of a plane. Could have cruised like that for months."

"But what about the water?" Ashley asks. "You said it runs out of ions over time."

"That's another prototype *Cygneous* was testing. A condenser that pulls moisture from the air to cycle the tanks."

Arden shakes his head. "Sounds like some Skunkworks shit." He frowns. "And this guy Hobbes just blew it all up?"

Tuck shrugs. "The secret is worth more to him than the technology. Hobbes will do anything to keep V-451 under wraps." He glares at Kirby and she slinks away.

"Couldn't he just sell the stuff?" Arden asks. "A whole damn mountain... it must be worth billions."

I think back to some of the oilmen I knew in Texas. All those pumpjacks and pipelines. Live and die by the market price. "He could put a lot of folks out of business too."

Tuck nods. "*Cygneous* gets kickbacks from oil and gas just to keep it all buried. I'm talking Monopoly money. Enough to fund an army." He takes a deep breath and the room goes quiet. We stare at two wet rocks in a glass.

Well, ain't that something?

You believe him now, Pops?

More or less. This guy Hobbes sounds like a piece of work.

It kills me to think what they put Ashley through.

So, what do you plan to do about it?

I just want this to be over.

I don't think you're getting off that easy.

You call this easy? The bombs? The bear? Worst goddamn day of my life.

What about the time that goat kicked you in the-

Oh, come on, Pops.

I'm just sayin', kid. You have the truth now. The world needs to hear it.

Well, that ain't on me.

We'll see...

Baxter whimpers at my feet but I brush him off. A new thought occurs.

"Arden, you guys are off-grid here. Easy juice like this could go a long way."

Arden nods. "We could ditch the old diesel gen for something clean and quiet."

Del nods. "I've lived off-grid most of my life." He runs his fingertip over the glass. "Grew up on a reservation. Everyone was poor." He closes his eyes. "This could change a lot of lives."

Tuck nods and sighs. "Too bad it will never get out. Not as long as Oliver Hobbes has his way."

Ashley stares daggers at the glass. "You know I looked up that word, *Bariq*..." She takes a deep breath and fumbles for my hand. "It's a Quranic name that means 'brilliant' or 'bright'." She starts choking

135

back tears again. "I think those villagers *knew* what was in that mountain." She slumps into my arms. Baxter nudges my foot again.

"Not now, buddy." I comfort my wife.

Nobody speaks for a while. We contemplate the stones and Ashley's sobs.

Then a pistol clicks and the spell is broken.

"Pity party's over."

I turn, dazed. Kirby stands at the back of the room, pointing a handgun.

"Easy now," Arden says.

"Zip it. Drop the shotgun."

"What exactly is-"

"Drop the fucking gun, now!"

Arden obeys. He lays the shotgun at his feet and gives me a nervous look. Ashley pulls out of my shoulder and rubs bleary eyes. "Kirby? What's going on?"

"Where's my radio?" Kirby asks.

"But I thought-"

"Oh, cut the crap. You're all under arrest by the authority of U.S. Asset Command." She meets my eyes with a steely glare. "Radio."

I shrug and Arden speaks up. "Closet. Top shelf."

Kirby glances to the closet but Kali sits bristling in her path. "Call off the wolf."

Nobody moves and the wolf begins to growl. "Call it off or I will shoot-"

"Kali!" Arden whistles and the wolf slowly stalks away.

Kirby shuffles to the closet, keeping her gun trained on the group. She opens the door with one hand and pulls the radio down from the top shelf.

"How did she get a gun?" Ashley whispers.

Arden shakes his head. "We let our guard down. Must have snuck off to the bedroom and found her Glock."

"We could rush her. Five on one, she can't-"

"Don't." I pull my wife close. "Stay with me."

Kirby switches on the radio with one hand and points her pistol with the other.

"Kirby to Main. Kirby to Main. Come in, Main. Over."

The radio hums static and we wait in silence. She tries again.

"Kirby to Main. Kirby to Main. Over."

She waits out the static and waves her pistol at Del. "You there, Blackfoot." Del stands stoic and calm. "Kick that shotgun my way." He steps forward and kicks the weapon a few feet across the room. Returns to Arden's side and takes his hand.

"All the guns on earth won't save your soul."

Kirby hesitates a moment but then the radio snaps to life. "USAC Main. USAC Main. Hailing Private Kirby. Acknowledge transmission. Over."

She smiles and raises the mic. "Private Kirby reporting. Loud and clear, Main."

More static.

"Private Kirby. Repeat squad access code. Over."

Kirby nods. "Bravo. Tango. Charlie. Lunar. Over."

"Standby..."

The radio goes silent and so does the room. Ashley rubs my hand while Baxter roots around my feet. Poor boy was trying to warn me. I'm such an ass.

The radio cracks back to life.

"Private Kirby..." A new voice. Honeyed and sharp. "We were worried about you." Tuck meets my eye and nods.

It's Hobbes.

"Sorry Mr. H." Kirby narrows her eyes. "Couple of rednecks got the jump on me last night. They took my radio and my gun, but I've reestablished control."

"That's good to hear. Status report?"

"We're in some kind of earth house." She scans the room. "I'd estimate about a mile south of my last reported position. Small clearing between two cottonwood trees. Tough to spot until you're right on it." She pauses and looks at her watch. "I heard some choppers about forty-five minutes ago. Flew right over us."

"Excellent, Private. We have teams in the area. What of your captors?"

Kirby smirks. "Real motley crew, sir. There's a fat man and his Indian boy. The cowboy and his wife." Kirby eyes Tuck with a devious look. "Oh, and the pilot's here."

"Is that so?" Pleasant surprise in the man's voice. Tuck buries his face in his hands. "Can you maintain control until a team arrives?"

"Yes sir," Kirby says. "Anyone in here moves and they're dead."

"Tremendous work, Private." Hobbes pauses but holds the channel open. I hear shouts of conversation and an engine firing up. "Remain vigilant. Recovery team: eight minutes out."

"Thank you, sir." Kirby smiles and puffs out her chest.

"Over and out."

Chapter 27

The radio goes silent and Kirby drops it at her feet.

"Eight minutes," she says. "And I meant what I said. Nobody move."

Arden immediately moves, shuffling his bulk in front of Delsin and Ash. Kirby narrows her eyes but doesn't shoot.

"No need to start putting holes in people," Arden says, hands in the air. "I respect your trigger after you triple-tapped that bear." Kirby steadies the gun with both hands. Arden shakes his head and sighs. "So, this is how it's gonna be, huh?"

"This is how it always was."

Arden nods. He pulls out a handkerchief and wipes his brow. "I guess I respect the hustle. Lulled us to sleep and got the drop." He slides the rag back in his pocket and eyes the shotgun on the floor.

"Enough talk," Kirby says. Her eyes are busy, but her face is still.

"All due respect, Private: If I'm about to get wrangled, I'll go out how I please." Arden turns to Del. "You think she'll give us one last roll? I can be quick."

Delsin smiles and his cheeks flush red. He kisses Arden on the forehead while Kirby smirks and checks her watch.

"Seven minutes."

"So, where do you think they'll take us?" Arden asks. "Where's this USAC Main?"

"You'll find out soon enough."

Arden nods and shuffles his feet. Is he inching for the shotgun? Don't do it, Ard.

"I hope we get to meet Hobbes at least." Ashley speaks up. "I'd like to spit in that asshole's face."

Kirby grins. "Try that and it's the last face you'll ever see."

"Oh yeah?" Ashley continues and Arden shuffles again. "Does Oliver Hobbes execute civilians? That's the leader you serve?"

"I do what my country asks of me."

"You're just a lapdog for some psycho."

"Six minutes."

I hear the faint sound now of helicopters on the wind.

"Well," Arden says. "You're not giving me a lot of choice here, Private." He takes another step toward the gun.

"Arden, don't." Ashley reaches out to pull him back, but the big man shrugs her off.

"Don't worry, Ash." He turns and flashes a giant grin.

"Arden, what-" I start but Kirby cuts me off.

"Not one more inch!" She yells, squaring the pistol on Arden. "Step back or I. Will. Shoot."

Arden pauses. Considers. He eyes the shotgun on the floor but it's still five feet away. Kirby's drawn him dead to rights. I pull Ashley close.

Arden cracks his knuckles and coils like he's about to lunge. Then does something else.

"Ahhhoooooooo!"

He throws back his head and howls. Long and low like the first time we showed up at the house.

"Ahhhhhhhooooooooooo!" He's really into it this time. Eyes closed. Lips shaking.

"Stop that!" Kirby yells. "Step back!"

"Don't do it, Ard," Ashley whispers. Arden takes a deep breath and pans around the room...

Then he goes for it.

It's slow and telegraphed and clumsy as hell. In one ungainly lunge, the big man falls forward like a bellyflop. Kirby puts two in his shoulder before he hits the ground.

Then a white blur takes her by the throat.

Kali.

The wolf vaults the recliner and hits Kirby like a truck. She drops the gun and they go down in a maul.

Snarling. Screaming. Struggling.

There's a sickening crunch and the screams turn to gargles. Then moans. Then nothing.

"Holy shit."

Tuck is the first to move. He shuffles past Arden and picks up the shotgun. He shoulders it anxiously, eyes on the wolf. Del mumbles a prayer while Ashley rushes to Arden, sitting him up with a grunt.

140

"She sure can shoot," Arden says. He probes his shoulder and watches Kirby bleed out. "Godspeed, kid."

"Arden you dumb son of a-" Ashley works fast, pulling off his shirt to examine the wound. "I see two entry holes but only one exit. Second shot probably hit bone."

Arden lifts his arm with a wince. "Feels about right."

"Del, I need something to staunch the bleeding. Pillows, towels, whatever you've got."

Del grabs some linens off the couch and kneels next to his husband. "That was very brave," he says. "And very dumb." He leans down and they share a kiss.

"Aw Del..." Arden pulls away with misty eyes. "You know my time ain't up yet."

Delsin just nods.

It occurs to me I'm the only one in the room doing nothing. I reach down and absently pet my dog.

You're in shock, son.

The wolf... The screams...

You've seen death before.

Never like that.

Deal with it later. The clock's ticking...

Shit, he's right. USAC is bearing down in what – five minutes? Less? I shake my head to clear it and try not to look at all the blood.

"What now?" I mutter but nobody hears me. Ashley and Del are fussing over Arden. My voice feels small in my throat.

"What now?" I speak up. Louder this time. Tuck snaps out of his own trance and stares at me. He looks like he's seen a ghost.

"They're coming," he says. "We have to run."

"Where?" I ask. "They'll chase us down." I glance at Kirby's body on the floor. Everything's cloudy and slow.

"I'm in no shape to run," Arden says. "But y'all are welcome to try."

Ashley holds a makeshift compress against his shoulder. Her hands are red with Arden's blood. "Clay's right," she says, not looking up from her work. "We wouldn't get far." There's a sadness in her voice. Like the game is over and she knows it.

"No." Tuck says. "Dammit, no! We can't give up now." He looks frantically around the room. "How many guns do we have?"

Arden grunts. "Not enough."

"We can't win a shootout." Ashley looks up at me with teary eyes. "We'd be slaughtered..." I kneel down and wrap her in my arms.

"It's okay," I whisper, but I don't believe it. "We'll be okay." Ashley keeps her hands to Arden's shoulder as she lays her head on mine.

Tuck paces nervously around the room. He opens the front door and looks out. "Fuck it," he says. The helicopters are getting louder. "I'm going for it."

Nobody offers to join him. Arden just nods his head. "Good luck, son."

Tuck hesitates at the threshold. He takes a deep breath then slips out without a word.

Ashley checks on Arden's wound. "You need a hospital," she says.

"Hope Hobbes has a good surgeon."

I can't believe we're about to become prisoners of some madman's army. I study the stones on the table. The cause of all this chaos. "Fucking Hobbes," I mutter under my breath. Everyone's quiet as we contemplate our fleeting freedom.

"There might be a way," Del says after a moment.

"A way to what?"

"A way out." He looks at me. "There's a cave."

"Aww, shit," Arden says. "You talking about Grover's?"

"What's Grover's?"

"It's a cave all right," Arden says. "More like an underground river."

"Where does it lead?"

Arden shrugs. He looks at Del.

"We've never explored it," Del says. "But there's an entrance a few hundred yards from here."

Everyone's quiet for a moment. I hear a thousand helicopters bearing down.

"Well it ain't for me," Arden says. "But y'all might have a chance if you leave now."

"We're not leaving you," Ashley says.

"Somebody ought to get out," he protests. "They could kill us all on sight."

"Would they do that?"

Nobody says anything. Nobody knows.

Del puts a hand on my shoulder. "Come with me."

"Me?" I look to Ashley for reassurance. Her eyes are glassy and cold.

"Maybe Del's right," she says.

"Maybe what?"

She puts a hand on my arm, slick with Arden's blood. "If we all get caught, it's over. You and Del, take the stones. Get someplace safe." She looks to Del and he nods. "As long as you're out there, Hobbes can't kill us. He can't risk you guys exposing the truth."

My head spins. I can't believe what I'm hearing. "Can't kill you?" The words chafe my throat and make me want to puke. "How do you even-"

Ashley stands and pulls me to my feet. Del leans into Arden and starts muttering sweet goodbyes. What the hell is going on?

"Boo..." Ashley takes a deep breath and takes me in her arms. I squeeze so goddamn tight my shoulder pops out.

"Boo..." she says again, whispering in my ear. "It's the only way."

I close my eyes and shake my head.

No.

No. No. No. No. No!

I can't leave my wife. I won't. I bury my face in her hair. Tears run down my cheeks.

"I'm sorry, Clay."

She tries to wriggle free, but I refuse to let go.

"Clay..." She struggles in my arms. Don't let go...

"Clay!" She pushes free with a shove and my dead arm drops to my side. She grabs it and roughly jerks the joint back into its socket. Pain and adrenaline blast through my head while Ashley gets right in my face.

"Clayton Fucking Moore," she says. "You are going to leave here with Del and *get someplace safe*." Her eyes are fiery now. "Swim, hike, climb, fly – I don't care! You get out. Do you understand?"

"Yes..." My voice feels pathetic and small.

"You take those stones and you get someplace safe then you *come and find me*."

"Yes ma'am."

143

"You and Del put your big, beautiful heads together and you save our asses. You got it? Come for us!"

"Yes ma'am!"

Del pushes two wet stones into my hands. "Hold these." I shove them deep into my pocket.

Ashley picks up Kirby's pistol and checks the magazine. "Ten rounds left." She hands it to me butt first but I have nowhere to put it. I clutch the gun like a dead fish.

"You can do this," Ashley says. "Come and find me." She pulls me in for one more hug. "I love you," she whispers. I don't even have words. She knows how I feel.

Del taps me on the shoulder. "We have to go."

I take a deep breath and pull away from my wife. She smiles and brushes hair from her face. I swallow and blink tears from my eyes.

"See you on the other side, cowboy," Arden says. Del leans down for one more kiss and as he pulls away Arden slaps him on the ass. "Now go!"

Del nods and shoulders a pack. We float toward the door and the sound of approaching helicopters. Del glances out. "All clear."

I take one last look at my wife. She's down on the floor with Arden, holding back his blood. "Come and find me, Clay Moore!" I nod and salute and slip out the door.

"This way." Del leads me around the side of the house. "Stay quiet. Stay low."

The shimmering green is disorienting after the dim interior of the home. I blink away tears and follow Del blindly over the sloping mound of his home. The choppers sound like they're everywhere, but I can't see anything through the trees.

We climb over fallen logs and push through dense brush. I think about my wife and the weight of the Glock in my hand. I pray I don't hear gunshots. I wonder if we'll run into Tuck.

"Down!" Del whispers and we both crouch behind a mossy trunk. He holds a finger to his lips and I suck in my breath. I hear a rustling and peek around the tree to see a team of four commandoes, creeping through the undergrowth. They're all decked out in tactical gear and carrying machine guns. Marching for my wife.

144

I clench the pistol and want to scream, but Del lays a steady hand on my arm. "Stay calm," he mouths. I think. His eyes are tranquil and I ease out my breath.

When the team moves out of earshot, we resume our creep in the other direction. I'm hypersensitive now, tracking every hint of movement or sound. I feel like I'm being followed and turn to see an old bloodhound nosing along my tracks.

"Baxter!" I'm both elated and scared. Happy to have my dog with me, but nervous about him tagging along. Don't we have to swim through a cave?

Del glances back and just nods. Nothing to do about it now. He waves us on and after a few more minutes we reach a round hole in the earth.

"Grover's Cave." I almost don't see it at first. A shadowy gap about three feet across, ringed by creepers and moss. I lean down and hear water rushing below.

"Why do you call it Grover's?"

Del sighs. "We had another dog, years ago..." He looks around with sad eyes, like he's not sure he'll ever see these woods again. "Grover and Arden went walking one night and the dog fell in this hole."

"Jesus, Del..."

"It was a tragic start to our lives here." He picks up a rock and drops it into the void. A second later I hear the splash. "About fifteen feet."

Del takes off his pack and opens the zipper. "This bag is waterproof. Give me the gun and anything you don't want to get wet." I hand Del the pistol, happy to be rid of it; and a crumpled pack of cigarettes with four or five left.

"Better take these too." I fish the stones out of my pocket. "Don't need them zapping my nuts." Del nods and zips everything into the bag. He looks down at Baxter.

"He can swim, right?"

"Shit, I think so. You didn't ask about me, though."

Del smiles and puts a hand on my shoulder. "I'm not worried about you, Clay." He says it with a wink. What's that supposed to mean?

Del gestures to the hole. "You want to go first?" I grit my teeth and nod, bend down and scoop Baxter with my good arm. Get ready, boy.

"Every year since Grover died," Del says, "We've come to this cave to make an offering and a prayer." He bows his head to the cavern. "His spirit will see us through."

I cradle my dog and think about poor Grover, lost and drifting in the dark. "How do you know he died?" I ask. "Maybe the old boy's waiting for us at the other end."

Del smiles and gives Baxter a scratch. "Let's find out."

I take one last look in the direction of the house. My wife. My best friend.

"Stay strong," I whisper. For Ashley or myself, I'm not sure.

I close my eyes and step into the void.

Part V

The Old Man

Chapter 28

Darkness.

Water.

Stone.

I cling to my dog.

Poor Baxter.

We've been drifting for hours.

There's no light. No exits. No options.

Just three bodies, tired and treading.

Del is somewhere ahead, humming a tune. The sound echoes through the cavern and helps me stay close. It's my link to reality. That and the dog.

Baxter paddles beside me and we keep each other afloat. He's waterlogged and weary. We all are.

"Hang in there, buddy." I press my nose against damp fur. "We need to ride this out for Ash."

Ashley.

Sweet lord, my sweet wife. Taken by some monster. I rack back and forth between panic and shame. I shouldn't have left her.

You had no choice.

Bullshit, Pops.

She told you to go.

She was being brave.

It's done.

I sniffle and sob in the darkness. Tears mix with cave water on my cheeks. Limestone and salt.

I think about ol' Grover drifting in the dark. Did he make it? Did he drown? Did he blame Arden for his plight? I squeeze Baxter and he whimpers. Licks the snot off my face.

Thirty-some hours ago we were just out walking. A man and his hound. Then this plane and pilot and stones and bombs and guns and choppers and blood.

I think about Kirby. Screaming and thrashing. Didn't deserve what she got... Or did she?

I think about Arden, saving all our asses. Took two bullets so his wolf could get the drop. He'll take care of Ashley. Or vice versa.

I think about my wife. Where is she? How is she? *"Come and find me Clay Moore!"*

I'll try baby. But how?

Where do we start? What do we do? Del will have a plan. He's strong and fearless and wise. Could probably charm his way shirtless into USAC Main.

I listen for his hum and realize I don't hear it. It's been a constant chorus for hours, and now it's stopped.

"Del?" My voice sounds tiny in the hollow cave.

"Del?" I hear a rush of water, like rapids picking up steam.

"Delsin, you there?"

Nothing.

Shit.

"Del!"

Baxter thrashes and barks. I grapple and cling and fight hard to hang on. Can't lose him too. "Stay with me boy."

The roar gets louder and we pick up speed. Coming up on something bad.

"Delsin!"

So helpless. Cold and wet and tired and blind. I try to paddle against the current, but I've got one good arm and it's clinging to a bloodhound.

Oh Baxter, I'm so sorry. Poor dog never asked for this. Just followed me out like a Good Boy. He whimpers and moans and I try to catch his frightened eyes and then it hits me: I can see.

I can see!

I squint in the dark and make out light up ahead. The cave opens up, but into what I can't tell. Looks like the sky. Sounds like a waterfall.

We pick up speed and I kick, but my feet are numb. Whole body's numb. My left arm feels dead, like it's not part of me anymore.

I pull Baxter close and we fight the flow together. He's stronger than me, but less graceful. Not a swimmer. A paw hits my cheek and takes skin. I taste blood.

"Ow! Dammit..."

Not your fault, boy, not your fault. None of this is your...

"Clay!"

What's that? "Delsin?!"

"Over here!"

I blink water from my eyes and spot Del. He's standing on some rocks at the mouth of the cave. Coming up fast.

"Waterfall!" He cries. I think? It's so loud. He waves his arms and I try to work his way. I grit and kick and flail, but everything feels stiff and clunky and broke.

"I can't!" I spit a mouthful of water. Can't fight the current. Can barely hang on to my dog.

Del hollers again, but it's lost in the roar. He's holding something. A branch over the water. It's thick and stout and maybe I can grab on. I nod my head and bear down.

Thirty feet now. Coming up fast. The river ahead disappears into space. Del stands ready. Is he shirtless again? I twist against the current. We'll get one shot at this.

Do it for Ashley.

Don't act like I'm not!

I squeeze Baxter with my good arm and focus on the branch. "Whatever happens, I won't let you go."

I strain my left hand out of the water. Shoulder screams. I scream. Del braces on the rocks.

Fifteen feet. Ten. Five. The roar builds to a crescendo. The cavern drops away. I reach and stretch and my fingers catch wood.

"Hold!" Del screams as he fights to pull me in. "Hold!"

My shoulder flares in agony. Sinew stretches and tears. Del inches us to shore, but it's slow. Too slow. Baxter squirms and I squeeze, but we can't hang on much longer. My shoulder's pulling out. Fingers losing grip. The current is too strong and the dog is too heavy and the waterfall roars and oh God Ashley I'm so sorry-

Bonk.

My head hits a rock. I see stars. Hands grab me roughly by the collar and pull me up, up, up out of the water. Somehow, I drag Baxter along.

I'm heaved onto a flat slab of stone. It scrapes my skin and I don't care. It's the first solid thing I've felt in hours. I sputter and cough and spit up water. Roll onto my back and blood runs into my eyes.

"We made it."

Del stands over me. Muscles dripping with cave water. What a fucking man.

I lift my head and we're on a pile of rocks. There's a sloping hill behind us, and a thirty-foot plunge to a rocky pool below.

"Holy shit, Del." Baxter finds his footing and shakes water from his fur. He barks once. Twice. Three times. A prayer for ol' Grover that the darkness barks back.

Chapter 29

After catching our breath, Del and I hike down the hill and officially out of the Chaplains.

The transition is abrupt. Slope turns to flatland and the forest thins out. I look back at wooded hills, looming piously above. Can't decide if they were savior or curse.

"You know where we are?"

Del studies the land like a menu and shakes his head. We start walking and I hate it. Wet clothes chafe my skin. Feet blister in my boots. I'm dizzy from hunger and heartache and a head wound.

"You got a plan?" I ask after a few minutes.

Del just nods and walks on. He's quiet since fishing me off that waterfall. Probably thinking about Ard.

We follow the river downstream but otherwise nowhere in particular. Baxter trundles along in the lead and seems like the only one enjoying himself. I'm glad he's along.

After an hour, Del stops and pulls some jerky from his pack. We eat in silence and toss pieces that Baxter chomps out of the air. Then we walk some more.

The trees thin out and the sun gets high and hot. It cooks the water from my clothes, and I wish they were cool and wet again. My stomach growls for more jerky. I know Del can hear it, but he doesn't say so.

"How much food you got in that bag?"

"Day or two."

The man doesn't take a hint. I stop and kneel and drink some water from the river. It's cool and earthy and fills my stomach.

"Help me up?"

Del takes my right hand and pulls me to my feet. My left arm flops painfully and I stifle a curse.

"Hmpf." I grunt and grit and spit. Shoulder's so messed up I'll need surgery just to lift a smoke.

Del looks thoughtful and pulls off his shirt. Here we go...

"Ain't no time for a swim, Del."

Instead, he ties a sling and loops it around my neck. I tuck my left arm away and it feels better. I nod a sheepish thanks and we walk on.

At least the view is good. Puffy clouds and prairie grass and Ponderosa pines. I count six different types of wildflower. Summertime in God's Country.

"When was the last time you came down from the hills?"

"Years."

Del's on a silent schtick, but I'm not giving up.

"Used to see Arden roll around on that quad. You never joined him?"

Del just shakes his head.

"I guess Ashley and I didn't leave the valley much." Bringing it up makes me happy and sad. "Hell of a place to call home."

Del nods. "Good energy."

"God's Country."

He gives me a knowing look like we're on the same page, but I'm not sure we are.

"Maybe when all's said and done, you can help me build one of those earth houses."

Del shrugs and looks distant. Now I think I made *him* sad.

Let the man be, son.

What's he on now, Pops?

Patience.

Seems like even Pops is laying low.

I stew in silence, and we trudge another mile. Hopelessness creeps in and I wonder how the hell we're supposed to save Ashley and Ard? We don't know where they are. We don't know where we are. Could walk this backcountry for days without seeing a soul.

"One more mile," Del says, shocking me out of my trance.

I shake my head to clear it. Did I think out loud? I squint at Del, and he smiles.

"Then we'll find a vehicle."

"We'll find one?"

"One more mile."

"Hmmpf." I'm not impressed. "If you say so."

Back to silence. Footfalls. A warbler sings.

"So, is that what you've been at this whole time?" My tone is nastier than I intend, but I lean into it. "Conjuring up some miracle?"

154

Del smiles again. His easy air is back. "I've been working on our next step. A way forward."

"A way forward..." I look back to the receding hills. "You've been working on it?"

Del nods. "Just one more mile."

I spit in the dirt. This is so stupid.

"Hang in there, Clay."

Was I thinking out loud again? Can he read my thoughts?

Del pats me on the back, careful to avoid my left shoulder. "Have a little faith."

I grumble and spit. "Faith?" I give him a hard look like *don't start with me right now.*

Del nods and says nothing. He turns and walks backwards a few steps, staring at the hills like he might catch sight of Ashley and Ard. I whistle for Bax and the bloodhound's ass-up in a juniper. Wags his way back over and falls in stride.

"Do you remember what I said about my name?" Delsin asks.

"Not really." Feels like lifetimes ago. Was that this morning?

"It means: He is so."

"That so?"

Del chuckles like we're playing a game. He bends down and picks a flower without breaking stride. He's shirtless and smiling and goddamn relaxed. I feel like a pile of nails.

"Are you a religious man, Clay?"

"Not so much."

"But you must believe in something?"

"I guess."

Del lifts an eyebrow. He wants more.

"I always just kind of felt like things worked out."

Del nods and studies his flower. Slim red petals. Indian Paintbrush.

"Not like destiny or fate..." It always sounds stupid when I say it. "Just like – what happens is what happens, you know?"

Del tucks the flower behind his ear. "That makes sense."

"It does?"

We ponder that together in silence. I can't decide if it's brilliant or stupid, but at least I got him talking again.

"What do Blackfeet believe?"

Del smiles skyward. "My people tell tales of a creator." He takes a breath and closes his eyes. "An Old Man who put everything in its place."

"Sounds about right."

"You have thoughts on the creator, Clay?"

"We're not on good terms right now."

Del grins like we're joking again. He pulls the flower from his ear and hands it to me while we walk. "What do you suppose that's made of?"

"The flower?" I roll it between my fingers like a cigarette. "Well, there's a stem, and some petals, and..."

Del shakes his head. "Think deeper, Clay."

I think deeper. Try to remember my old textbook. "I guess it's like, plant cells, right? Like DNA?"

Del nods. "And what about the cells? What are they made of?"

"You mean like, atoms and shit?"

"Atoms and shit, yes."

"Don't play with me, man."

"I'm not playing." He raises a hand in surrender. "What about those atoms, Clay? What are they made of?"

I roll my eyes and shrug.

"Even tinier particles," he offers. "Like electrons and quarks."

"Sounds about right."

"So, what are those made of?"

"Is there a point to all this?"

"A big one."

"Well, just take me there, Del."

"It's better if you get there yourself."

"I'm feeling pretty lost right now."

He scrunches up his face. Wipes some black hair off his brow. "Look at the flower."

"I'm looking."

"Forget all that other stuff."

"Forgetting."

"What's it *made* of?" He emphasizes that word like it means something.

"Atoms and protons and-"

"But what are they, Clay? What are protons? What is anything?"

"Shit, Del. I don't know..." I try to picture a proton.

Del sighs. "The whole world is made of tiny things. Where do you think they came from?"

"You mean like the creator? The Old Man?"

Del nods and waves me to continue.

"Well, I guess he made the protons."

"And...?"

"And the flowers... And the trees... And the mountains, and... pretty much everything else."

Del smiles. "God's Country."

"I'll give the Old Man his due."

"He also made you and me," Del says.

"Sure enough."

"And Ashley and Arden."

"Fine work."

"Kirby and Hobbes..."

I can't hide my frown. Del leans into the challenge. "You think he didn't?"

"I'm not saying that."

We walk a minute in silence. Not ready to go where Del's taking me.

"Look, if you're trying to-"

"What's it all *made of*, Clay?"

"I don't know, dammit!"

"Okay, okay..." Del bows his head and backs off. Baxter smells my anger and tenses up. I take some deep breaths.

Relax, son.

Pops, I ain't in the mood.

He's trying to teach you something.

Well, I ain't trying to learn.

I pull out a cigarette and my Bic. Flick the lighter ten times before it flares. The smoke grabs my lungs and helps me relax.

"Can I get one?"

I hand Del a crumpled Camel that he lights in one shot. Dangles off his lip like an old pro.

"I didn't know you smoked."

"It's been a while."

We walk and smoke in silence. The sun dips behind a cloud and the air cools.

"One more mile?"

"Less, now."

I study the terrain ahead and see we're coming up on a cluster of pines. The river veers east but we don't and five minutes later we're back in the woods. Baxter jogs ahead and I let him.

"Just beyond these trees," Del says.

"You're sure then?"

He smiles and winks at me. "It is so."

His cig has burned down to a nub but he's still kissing it. I pinch mine out and pray to the Old Man he's right.

Chapter 30

Just past the pines we hit a dirt road. It's empty and rutted and riddled with weeds.

"This should be the spot," Del says.

I look left and right. Barely a towpath through the scrub. Wide enough for two horses.

Del sits on a rock and opens his pack. "You want some more jerky?"

I don't know whether to laugh or cry, but I'll take that jerky. I sit beside Del, and we munch salted beef. Bax hops up for a share.

"So, we just wait?"

"Shouldn't be long."

The road winds in from the west and disappears downhill to the east. It connects nothing to nowhere, and I can only guess the last time it's seen a car.

"You said there'd be a vehicle."

Del nods. "Blue Mercedes with the windows down."

"Okay now you're playing with me."

"Wait and see." Del smiles and picks beef bits from his teeth.

I hang my head and groan. "This all feels hopeless."

Del pats me on the back and Baxter nuzzles my chin. He smells like jerky and juniper.

Hang in there, son.

Easy for you to say, Pops.

You don't have faith in the man?

I don't have faith in anything right now.

Maybe that's your problem.

I stand and sigh and pull out my smokes. Two left.

"You want one?" Del waves me off.

I take a deep drag and survey my surroundings. The sun has started wheeling to our west and the pines cast spotty shadows. The land slopes gently south, and it's just humps and hillocks for miles. Who even runs a road out here?

"You don't believe me, do you?"

I turn with a shrug. "Come on, Del." I tap some ash on the road and study the man square. "A blue Mercedes?"

Del nods and stands. He brushes off his backside and stretches muscled arms. Cracks his neck. Cracks his knuckles. Bax and I both take a step back.

"I'm not here to fuck around with you, Clay." That's the first time I've heard the man curse. "I'm lost out here, same as you." He takes a step toward me, pecs puffed out. "My man is missing, same as yours."

Well it's my girl, but point taken.

"I swam through that cave and almost died on those rocks and left my own husband bleeding on the floor." He takes a deep breath and stares me down. Wind whips the hair around his face.

"Shit Del, I'm sorry."

We hold that gaze a moment then something snaps. I bow my head and offer the cig. "Blue Mercedes," I nod. Del grabs the smoke and takes a long draw. He cranes his head back and blows a billow to the sky.

"Clayton Fucking Moore," he barks it out like Arden. "We are going to get your wife back." He hands me the cigarette.

"And your husband," I add.

Del nods. "And to do that, we must remember what we are."

I take another draw and exhale through my nose. The smoke stings and it helps me focus. "What do you mean?"

Del starts pacing a circle around Baxter and I. We rotate to stay with him.

"You remember what I said about the flower?"

Keep an open mind son.

"You kept asking me what it's made of." Del nods and studies his feet while he walks. "We broke it down to tiny things, but that's where I got stuck."

Del ponders for a moment. "Let's try it from the other direction. What do you know of the Old Man?"

"You mean God? Nothing, really. Not for certain, at least."

"And why is that?"

"The Old Man's a cagey bastard." I pinch the ember off my cigarette and snuff it out with my boot. "He keeps his cards close to the vest."

160

"But you have theories? Beliefs?"

"Everyone does," I shrug. "Mama used to say there's a thousand names for God, but they're all spelled the same."

Del smiles. "I like that."

"I never really understood it."

"There are countless stories," Del continues. "But no one truly *knows.*"

"Ain't met the man yet."

Del stops pacing and looks me in the eye. "So, the world runs on faith."

I shrug.

"None of us know the truth."

"Kirby might."

"Ahhh," Del raises a finger. "But are you willing to die to find out?"

"Not until Ashley's safe."

Baxter barks an agreement and Del stares off down the road. If the Old Man really wanted my attention, now would be a good time to send a sign.

"I used to be like you," Del says, still eyeing the horizon. He spreads his arms then sits down in the road. I wait a beat then walk around to check him out. He's meditating again.

"So that's it?"

Del grins but says nothing. I watch his chest rise and fall. Guess that's it.

I let out a long sigh. "Maybe we should walk some more." Ants prowl the earth at my feet. Only traffic we're likely to get out here. "We could follow the road."

I study the dirt lane as it sweeps east and disappears. Must lead somewhere.

Fuck it.

I start walking. "Catch up when you're ready." Baxter hops to my side like the Good Boy he is.

We mosey a hundred yards and I start to feel better. This road will get me to a town, and I'll go from there. Maybe the police will help if they buy my story. Then again, USAC probably has eyes on every burg. I'll have to play close to the vest, like the Old Man.

The image makes me chuckle. Old greybeard palming a flush draw. I wish I shared Del's faith.

You're pressing on alone?

Once I catch a ride, I'll double back for Del. Find me a blue Mercedes.

You think he's full of it.

You know something I don't?

Pops goes quiet but I know he's still with me. I fall into a strut and crack a smile. For the first time all day it feels like I'm in control. Clayton Fucking Moore, coming for you, baby.

Baxter woofs his support and I reach down to pat his head. Looking back up the road I can just spot the old Blackfoot, half-lotus in the dirt. I also see the dark shape of our pack. Shit. I could really use some jerky. And that gun.

I hesitate on some backcountry brink. Should I go back? Push on? What would Ashley do?

She wouldn't leave the gun, that's for sure.

Sigh...

I turn and start trudging back toward Del. A hint of dark clouds on the horizon threaten rain. We should probably stick together. Baxter follows on without complaint, sniffing out whatever he missed on the first pass.

Those Voltstones are in the pack, too.

Yeah, yeah, I'm walking back.

All of a sudden, Bax rears on alert.

"What is it, boy?" Probably just some prairie rat, but could be bigger game. I need to get that gun.

"Let's go." I pick up my pace toward Del, but Bax is barking back the other way. I have flashbacks to that night in the valley. The buzz. The plane. Bloodhound always sniffs it out first.

I break into a run and holler Del out of his trance. "Something's coming!" Could be coyotes, or a bear. USAC convoy on patrol. I race to the pack and fumble for the 9mm. It's cold and heavy and smells like cave water.

"Baxter!"

He rumbles back my way, sounding off to the west. I see dust rising off the road and check the safety on the gun like Ashley taught me. I try to aim down the sight but it's hard to steady with one hand.

Del stands and we wait. Vehicle drawing closer. Baxter wants to go after it and keeps looking at me for the okay.

"Hang back, boy."

"Put the gun down, Clay." I turn and see Del with his palms up. "These are friends."

"How do you know?"

"Listen..."

I cock an ear and try to tune out the dog. Is that music? Sounds like a rock song.

I dip the gun back into the pack but keep a ready hand on it. From fifty yards out it looks like just a lone car. A blue fucking Mercedes. Del steps into the road and waves the approaching vehicle to a stop.

"Greetings, friend!" Del hails the driver with a kindly salute. "We've found ourselves a bit lost."

A black man with a bushy beard turns down his music and gawks. He looks around, uncertain, like it might be trap.

"Forgive our ragged looks," Del says. "Hard country out here."

The man's eyes go back and forth between Del's abs and my arm. I offer a hangdog half-shrug and he relaxes a bit.

"Actually, we're a bit lost too." His voice is husky and soft. "You know the way back to the interstate?"

"We're not lost!" A child's voice rings out from the passenger seat, and a young boy leans forward to give us a look. "GPS says five miles to the turn."

The man rolls his eyes and drums his fingers on the wheel. He glances at our pack, and I realize I've still got my hand on the gun. "We just need a lift to the nearest town," I offer, pulling out a handful of jerky and a smile. "Y'all like beef sticks?"

"We've got soda!" The boy calls, hoisting a two-liter bottle like a trophy. "Is that a bloodhound?"

Baxter woofs and wags an affirmative. The kid grins and his father shrugs. "We're heading east if that works for you."

I shoulder the backpack. "Anywhere but here."

163

Chapter 31

"My name's Patrick," says our driver, easing back up to speed on the bumpy road. "This is my son, Carl."

The boy turns and studies us from the front seat. He wears thick-rimmed glasses and fondles a smartphone. "We're on a road trip."

"Nice to meet you," Del smiles at the boy. "I'm Del and this is Clay."

"Are you an Indian?"

"Carl..."

"What?" He brushes off his dad and studies Del with probing eyes. "He looks like an Indian."

Patrick sighs and finds my eyes in the mirror. "We're not from around here." He prods his son on the knee. "Apologize to the man."

"No need," Del says with a wave. "I am Blackfoot and proud. Good eyes, son."

"We're black and proud," the boy responds. He reaches out a hand and we both shake. Baxter follows up with a lick.

"How old are you, kid?"

"Ten years and two days," Carl responds with a toothy smile.

"Well happy birthday."

"Thanks... Look what I got!" He waggles the smartphone and hands it to Del. "It's an iPhone."

Del grabs the mobile and studies it like an artifact.

"Do Blackfeet use smartphones?"

"Some of us do." Del returns the device. "But I'm a bit off-grid."

"You live around here?" Patrick asks.

"I've got a place up in the hills. Not much cell reception though."

Carl bends down and flicks through icons and apps. "I've got *YouTube* and *Minecraft* and *Pokémon* and *Snake*." He nudges drooping specs back up his nose. "Have you ever played *Zombie Football?*"

I shake my head. "I mostly stick to chess."

Two swipes and a tap later, Carl flashes a small chessboard on the screen. "I've got that, too."

"Pretty cool, kid."

"We've been visiting my mom," Patrick says. "Over in Chugwater."

"We're from Ohio," Carl chimes in.

"Well, that is a long trip."

"One thousand, four hundred and twenty-two miles to go," Carl adds with another smile. "According to Google Maps."

Patrick nods and eases the car over a rocky wash. "Probably take three days," he says. "At least, that was the plan..."

I study the rolling plains out the window. We're still in the middle of nowhere. I've never been to Chugwater, but I can bet it ain't much. "So, how'd y'all end up way out here?"

"Pronghorns!" Carl shouts with glee. "We saw a herd from the highway and followed them off road."

Patrick shrugs and eyes me again in the mirror. "Carl convinced me this trail would take us back to the main drag."

"It will," Carl insists. "Just three-point-eight miles to go." He uncaps his big bottle of soda and offers me a sip. It's sickly sweet and I feign a smile.

"Beautiful creatures," Del says. "Pronghorn antelope. You were lucky to see a herd like that."

"It was awesome," Carl says, eyes back on his phone. "Have you ever seen a pronghorn, Clay?"

Takes me a second to realize he's talking to me. "Uh, yeah..." I think back. "We've had herds graze our valley from time to time. My wife calls them 'Devil Deer'. Because of the horns."

"That's cool. Where's your wife?" I have a moment of panic and look bug-eyed at Del. I hesitate too long, and Carl looks up at me, expectant.

"She's visiting friends." It's a shitty lie, and Patrick sniffs it out immediately. He gives me a leery look in the rearview mirror. "I'm actually trying to get back to town so I can call her."

"You can use this." Carl offers his iPhone and I'm scrambling again.

"Uh, I couldn't," I stammer. "It's long distance."

Carl shrugs it off, but Patrick narrows his eyes further. "Carl, how much farther to the main road?"

165

"Two-point-nine miles," Carl says, oblivious to the rising tension. "Then another four-and-a-half to the interstate."

"Maybe we'll just drop our friends there," Patrick says. "Let Mr. Clay phone his wife."

"That's fine by me. Y'all done more than enough."

Bax whimpers on the seat next to me and I lay a hand to calm him down. Carl studies me and the dog. "What happened to your arm?"

Jesus, this kid.

"I fell." The words come quicker this time but no less suspicious. "Dislocated my shoulder." I rub the joint and wince.

"How'd you fall?" Patrick asks, mean mugging the rearview again. Keep your eyes on the road, buddy.

Del comes to my aid this time. "We were caving," he says. "Clay slipped on some slickrock and took a tumble. I had to fish him out of the creek." I nod sheepishly but I don't think Patrick buys it.

"Wow, you went spelunking?" Carl gets excited again. "What's the name of the cave? How deep did you go?"

"Grover's Cave," I reply, happy to have an honest answer. "And we went all the way through."

"That's so cool," Carl fiddles with his phone. "Dad, can we check out Grover's Cave?"

"Maybe next time." The road straightens out and Patrick picks up speed. "How far to the turn?"

"Less than two miles." We ride quiet for a spell and I enjoy the break.

"That's weird," Carl says after a few minutes. "No search results for Grover's Cave. You sure you got the name right?"

I shrug and Patrick gives me more stinkeye in the mirror. I'm about out of rope with this guy.

"It's a little-known tract," Del offers. "Way up in the hills. Clay and I are probably the only two that have ever been through it."

"Wow," Carl says, smitten. "You guys are like Indiana Jones."

"Don't give us too much credit."

"How far to the turn, son?"

"Point four miles then make a left."

No signs of life yet, but the terrain has opened up. We're into rocky shrubland now with knots of juniper and skunkbush. Not as pretty as my valley. God's Country lite.

166

"This should be it," Carl says as we approach an empty two-lane road. Lonely rural route but at least it's paved. Patrick makes the turn and punches up to speed.

"First town we hit I'll drop you two and be on our way," Patrick says. "Long haul back to Ohio."

"We appreciate you taking us this far."

"Next town looks like Willow," Carl chimes in. "Fourteen-point-eight miles." Patrick frowns and hits the gas a little harder. Welcome to Wyoming, bud.

We cruise in silence for a few minutes and I think about next steps. We'll need a car, but I doubt we find anything in Willow. Probably hitch a ride on to Cheyenne and regroup. I could use a doctor for my arm, but hate to be set back more than a day. Ashley is waiting.

Then what?

Do we reach out to *Cygneous*? Try to parlay with Hobbes? I'd like to make sure Ashley and Arden are okay, but we can't just give ourselves away without a plan. We probably need some help. A scientist or engineer. Someone who would understand the stones and what to-

"Shit!" Patrick curses and hammers the brakes. He stares wide-eyed in the mirror but for once he's not looking at me. "Cops."

I swivel back and see flashing red-and-blues. Where'd he come from? A moment later, the siren kicks up.

"What's the limit here?" Patrick asks.

"Probably fifty-five on the rural route."

"Shit. Shit. Shit." Patrick smacks the steering wheel. "He got me."

"Daddy!" Carl cries.

"It's okay, son." He eases to a stop on the soft shoulder. "Remember what we talked about: No backtalk. Hands in your lap."

"Are we in trouble, Dad?"

"Just a ticket son." Patrick looks around and straightens his beard. "Stay cool. Be quiet. Follow my lead."

The officer pulls over behind us but stays in his car.

"How fast were you going?" I ask.

"Seventy, seventy-five..." He glares at me like it's my fault. "As soon as this is over, you two are out of my car and we're gone."

I raise my palm in submission. I understand why he's nervous, but Del and I have our own problems with USAC. Do the cops know

167

about us? APB on a cowboy and Indian? I hate to see Carl and Patrick caught up in our shit.

"Nothing to worry about," Del says. Unruffled as always.

"What would you know?" Patrick snaps. "I'm an out-of-state black man lost in Wyoming." He shakes his head. "Even-odds this pig's already cooked up some phantom rap."

"Easy now," I plead. "We're not all racists out here."

"Yeah? How many black folks you know in this state?"

I want to start in about Ashley, but Del waves me off. I offer Carl a smile and feel it go crooked. Poor kid straightens up in his seat.

"Everybody just be cool," Patrick says through deep breaths. "This isn't my first rodeo."

We all sit and face forward. I hear the door slam as the officer exits his car. Baxter looks at me cockeyed and I stroke his fur to calm us both down.

"Jesus..." Patrick mutters, and I turn to see what's up. A lone officer crab-walks toward us with a hand on his gun. He's tall and broad and scowls behind mirrored shades. Patrick rolls his window down and we wait.

"License and registration."

Patrick hands the cards he had ready in his lap. I'm behind Carl on the passenger's side and have to crane down to see the towering cop's face.

"You know why I stopped you today?" The officer leans down and muscles bulge beneath his shirt.

"Yes sir." Patrick responds. "Speeding, sir."

"Eighty-one in a fifty," the cop eyes the ID without lifting his shades. "What's the hurry there, Pat?"

"Eighty-one...?" Patrick sounds peeved but gathers himself. "Just lost track, sir. I apologize."

"Mmmmhmmm..." He taps Patrick's license on the car door. "Long way from Ohio."

"Visiting family, sir." Patrick looks straight ahead while he talks. "My mom over in Chugwater."

"Chugwater." Officer says it almost like an accusation. "How'd you end up on my rural route?"

"Scenic detour, sir."

"We were tracking pronghorns." Carl chimes in.

The officer leans down and lifts his shades. Eyeballs Carl in the passenger seat. "Didn't ask you, kid." Carl pales and straightens up.

"Tell me Pat..." He drops his shades back over his eyes. "You been drinking today?"

"No sir." Patrick hesitates a moment then turns to the cop. "I go by Patrick."

The officer scrunches up his face and sniffs. "You sure that's not beer I smell? Maybe malt liquor?"

Patrick's voice goes cold and hard. "Not on me sir."

"Any drugs in the car? Illegal substances I need to know about?"

"No sir."

"Have you ever used illegal drugs, Pat?"

"Ever used...?"

"It's a simple question."

"No sir."

"You got any warrants? Felony convictions? DUIs?"

"No sir."

"Hmmmmmm..." The officer leans back and looks the vehicle up and down. Drums his hands on the rooftop. "This your car, Pat?"

"Yes sir."

"You got proof of ownership?"

"Right there on my registration."

"Any weapons in the vehicle?"

"No sir."

"Any guns, knives, or explosives?"

"No sir."

"Any gold, jewelry or gemstones?"

"Excuse me?"

This is getting weird. What does he mean by gemstones? Is this guy USAC? I clutch the pack on my lap and realize with horror there's a stolen pistol inside.

"We're just on the lookout for some contraband," the officer says. "Had some burglaries in the area."

"I wouldn't know anything about that, sir."

The officer stares down with a smirk. He puckers and spits and then Del speaks up from the back seat. "Is there a problem here, officer?"

169

The cop turns, annoyed. Del rolls down his window and smiles, still shirtless.

"Put some clothes on, prairie nigger."

Carl gasps and Patrick winces, but Del plays it cool. "What an unpleasant thing to say."

The officer snickers and snorts. "I get enough of you 'skins running moonshine down the twenty-five." He hocks at his feet and spit dribbles down his chin. "You're lucky I'm not allowed on Indian land..."

This is getting out of hand.

This guy is nuts, Pops.

Do something.

Like what?

You don't have time for his bullshit. Step in and talk him down.

"Um... sir?" I speak up before I even know what to say. "I've got an appointment over in Willow. You think we could move this along?"

The officer pulls his shades and squints like he just noticed me. "You got an appointment? In Willow?"

"Yes sir." I pray he doesn't press for details.

Go on the offensive, kid.

How do I do that?

He's just an old dumb racist. Put it on him.

"Uh, I'm sorry officer..." I scan for the name on his badge. "Lavigne. I just moved up from Texas and was looking to meet a fella about some chicken wire." I kick some extra twang into my voice, but Officer Lavigne just looks confused. "We had some car trouble 'round the way, and these boys here were kind enough to offer me a lift."

Lavigne rolls his tongue around his mouth. "To Willow?"

Why does he keep saying it like that?

"Yes sir. You seem like a capable ranger, sir. But if it's all the same to you I'd like to make this meeting, or I'll have the missus on my ass."

Lavigne gives me a quizzical look, Del and Patrick momentarily forgotten. At least I've got him off his game.

Go for the kill, son.

I'm pulling this straight out of my ass.

Well, finish him.

"Uhh... Lavigne... that's a French name, right? I knew a Lavigne ran a ranch outside Lubbock? Y'all related?"

170

The officer narrows his eyes. "Don't think so."

"You sure? He was a tall, forthright fella like yourself. Real salt-of-the-earth folk, you know?" I flash my best good-ol-boy grin. "Sumbitch used to go on about *Pyrenees pork*. 'So juicy you could drink it,' he'd say. Sounded like bullshit to me, but the man knew his meat. What part of France you from?"

Ol' Lavigne seizes up like I hit him. "France...?" He mutters. "I'm American."

"Ah, well..." I smile and shrug. "I guess we're all Americans here, then."

Lavigne says nothing but I can hear his teeth grind. He eyes me hard, face set in a scowl. I feel the gun in my lap and the sweat on my brow. Finally, the officer huffs and turns back to Patrick. "You're getting a ticket." He stomps back to his car. Everyone lets out a breath.

"Smooth talking, Clay." Del smiles at me.

"I'm sorry what he said to you, Del. That ain't right."

Del shrugs and waves it off. "Nothing I haven't heard before."

Patrick nods his head in the front seat. "You okay, son?" He puts a calming hand on Carl's knee. The kid looks spooked, iPhone forgotten in his lap. "We'll be moving on soon."

We all sit and wait. Five minutes turns into ten turns into twenty.

"What's taking so long?"

"He's digging," Patrick says, eyes hard in the rearview. "Running my name through every database he's got. Probably phoning friends in Ohio."

"Are you in trouble, Daddy?"

Patrick shakes his head. "Don't worry, son. My record's clean."

My stomach rumbles and I pull a bite of beef stick out of the pack. Pray we find a decent meal in Willow.

A few more minutes and Lavigne finally gets out of his car. He shuffles back over and hands Patrick some paperwork. "Eighty-one in a fifty," he says. "Four-hundred dollars and two points on your license." Patrick frowns but says nothing.

"If you'd like to contest, you have a court date in Willow six weeks from tomorrow." He flashes a big, shit-eating grin. "'Course I understand if y'all can't make it out from Ohio."

"Yes sir."

"Drive safe, now," the officer calls. "Don't want to be seeing me again."

He turns and starts back toward his car. As he passes Del's open window, he eyes Baxter between us on the back seat. "Pretty dog. I used to breed bloodhounds for K-9." He reaches down looking for a pet. "Come here, boy."

Baxter clambers to his feet, and as he does his paw catches one of the bag straps and pulls it off my lap. Before I know what's happened, the gun lies bare-ass on the mat.

Oh God son, you left the bag open.

I pray Lavigne won't see it, but he does. I watch his eyes get big and his jaw get tight and the next thing I know he's got his pistol in my face.

"Don't move!"

"Officer, I-"

"Cram it, cowboy! Hands in the air!"

Shit. Shit. Shit.

"Anybody moves gets shot. The kid. The dog. Try me, motherfuckers!"

Fuck. Fuck. Fuck.

"Officer, please. It's my gun."

"Too late for that." Lavigne reaches down and opens the rear door. "I asked about weapons in the vehicle. You are legally obligated to declare a concealed firearm." He hits me with an ugly sneer. "Now you're all going to jail."

I'd drop my head in my hands but I'm afraid to move. Instead, I catch Patrick's angry eyes in the mirror.

"Here's what's going to happen," Lavigne says, eyeing me down a .22. "One by one, you'll each get out of the car and onto your knees. Keep your hands in the air and don't move without my order." He takes a step back and nods to Del. "You first, Squanto."

Del eases out of the car and onto the pavement. Baxter hops out behind him and squats on the side of the road.

"You're next, cowboy. Don't even think about reaching for that piece." I keep my right hand high and my eyes on Lavigne and awkwardly shuffle out the door. He pats me down rough, giving my bad shoulder a squeeze. "That hurt?"

I grit my teeth and say nothing. Patrick gets out next then finally Carl. Poor kid shudders with fear. Lavigne zip-ties the other three with

172

their hands behind their back, then stands over me and pulls out a pair of silver cuffs.

"No easy way to do this," he grins, then proceeds to handcuff my right wrist to my left ankle. "That oughta hold ya." I'm hunched over and miserable. Afraid to meet anyone's eyes.

Party restrained, Lavigne holsters the gun and calls for backup on his radio. He pulls the backpack out of the car but leaves the pistol untouched on the floor.

"Appointment in Willow, huh?" He chuckles and leans against the Mercedes as he roots through the contents of our bag. "Might have to reschedule."

I hang my head and listen to Carl quietly cry. The pavement burns and my shoulder aches and I'm folded like a five-dollar bill.

Lavigne helps himself to a beef stick and my last cigarette.

Then he pets my goddamn dog.

Chapter 32

One hour later, we're in a rusty cell in downtown Willow. Downtown ain't much, basically two gas pumps and a traffic light. Lavigne's one-room jailhouse shares a parking lot with the Sunoco.

"Y'all sit tight for a minute," he says as he locks Del, Patrick, Carl and I in the spartan cell. "I'll see if I can find you a couple of lawyers." Then he laughs and disappears out the door.

No one says anything for a few minutes as the weight of our troubles sink in. Patrick sits with Carl on the lumpy cot, comforting the boy as he sniffles and sobs. Carl keeps eyeing me with a teary look of disbelief, while Patrick ignores me altogether.

Boy I really fucked things this time, Pops.

Doesn't look good, kid.

Not even half a day out, and I bumble into Johnny Law.

At least he hasn't outed you.

Won't take long. He'll run that pistol and find it's stolen off a dead soldier. Few phone calls later we'll be property of USAC. At least I'll get to see Ashley again.

So you think.

I drop an audible grunt and pace across the cell. Del meditates in one corner while Baxter naps on the floor outside the cell. I give the iron a smack, but no one seems to flinch.

"I'm sorry guys," I announce to the quiet room. "It was my gun. I'll sign something so there's nothing on y'all. Lavigne will have to cut you loose before long."

My grumbling gut is the only response I get. I'm hungry and tired and could really use a smoke. There's a bag of chips and a pack of Camels on the desk across the room. A gun cabinet in one corner and a couple of pinups on the wall. That's about it for ambiance. Lavigne brought us in with a short, potbellied officer named Mooch. Far as I can tell they're the only law for miles.

"Where do you think they went?" Nobody responds and I go back to pacing the cell. There's a little window set high in the wall, about a foot square. Enough to see a patch of sky and dark clouds on the move. "Looks like we're in for a stormy night."

Patrick glances at the window, then turns to meet my gaze. "Carl and I should be in Nebraska by now." He shakes his head at the hostile confines. "Holiday Inn in North Platte."

"I'm so sorry..." I run a hand through my hair and toe the brick wall with my boot. "You bailed us out of a bad spot. You deserve better."

Patrick scratches his chin through the thick beard. "What were you guys really doing out there? Caving? With no gear?"

I shrug and turn away. What do I even tell the man?

"You should have said something about the gun," he goes on. "You put us all at risk."

"It's not that simple."

"It's not?" Patrick raises his voice and Carl's eyes get wide. "Forget it..." He shakes his head and turns back to his son. "Just like the bangers back home," he shrugs. "Everyone's a gangster until they get caught."

I wince and whisper. "It ain't like that."

"I bet it ain't."

"I hate guns."

"Yeah, I can tell."

I look to Del but he's no help. Turn back to Patrick: "I don't know what to say."

He hits me with a hard stare. "I'll be sure to pass that on to my son."

We sit in silence for twenty minutes before the officers return. Lavigne sits at the desk and starts making phone calls, while Mooch munches fast food out of a paper bag. My stomach growls just watching him.

"You think we could get some fries or something?"

The portly officer smirks and tosses a few on the floor. Baxter gobbles them up with delight.

"Maybe something for the kid?" I plead. "I'm the guilty man here. You can let these folks go." Mooch shakes his head and chews open-mouthed on some cheeseburger. Carl stays quiet but licks his lips.

The wind picks up outside and raindrops start to splatter the small window. Mooch grins and follows my gaze. "Gon' be a big one," he says between bites of burger. "Tornado watch." Lavigne hangs up his phone and marches over to the cell.

"Moore!" He calls out. "Where in God's name did you get that gun?"

I shrug and say nothing. Right to remain silent.

"That Glock is fucking military!" Lavigne barges on. "Something called Asset Command? What ain't you telling me, cowboy?"

Mooch chokes on a bite of food and Lavigne smacks him on the back. He spits a soggy lump onto the floor and I wince as Baxter slurps it up.

"Chew your food, goddammit." Lavigne turns back and smiles at me through the bars. "I gotta make a few more calls."

He stalks back over to the desk and starts rifling through our bag. Pulls out one of the Voltstones and fumbles it onto the floor. "What the..." The green marble rolls across the room and under the bars into our cell. Everyone just watches as I pick it up and pocket the rock.

"What you got there, Moore?" Lavigne calls from the desk. I shrug and he smiles. "You can hold that for now. Something to keep your nuts warm."

Lavigne chuckles at his own joke and goes back to making calls. The wind and rain intensify outside, and a crack of thunder makes us all jump. Mooch steps out to eyeball the storm.

"Hang in there, boy." I squat down to pet Baxter through the bars. Poor hound never did like thunder. Carl cozies up to his father and wrings his hands nervously in his lap.

I get an idea.

"Here you go, son." I pull the Voltstone out of my pocket and offer it to Carl. "That there's a special stone." Patrick looks incredulous but Carl is intrigued.

"What is it?" The boy asks, rolling the rock around in his hand.

"They call it Voltstone. Came all the way from the Middle East."

"Voltstone?" Carl studies the rock and rubs a finger over colorful swirls. "It's pretty."

"Powerful too." I glance over at Del and see he's cracked an eye in my direction. "You could probably charge your iPhone with that thing."

176

Patrick gives me a suspicious look. "What do you mean?"

I shrug and sit next to him on the cot. "Something about ionized current. You gotta put it in water."

Patrick's not buying it. "Why don't you give it back to the man, Carl."

"No, no, please." I shake my head and turn up my palm. "A gift for the boy's troubles." I glance across the room and lower my voice. "Just don't show that to Lavigne."

Carl nods and pockets the stone. I don't know what I'm angling for here, but I figure at least one of the Voltstones oughta make it out. I stand and stretch and walk back to the other side of the cell. Raindrops pound the window above my head.

Patrick gives me a long look over. "You better not be setting us up."

I roll my eyes to the ceiling. "Come on man. Give me a little credit."

"Everything that comes out of your mouth sounds like bullshit."

He's right. I get it. I wouldn't believe my story either.

I think about the plane and the bombs and our dark swim through the cave. "I just want my wife back," I sigh. To my surprise, Patrick softens and stands.

"I'm sorry," he says. "My wife left me too." He puts a hand on Carl's shoulder. "Walked out on me and the boy three years ago. Shacked up with some deejay."

"Ashley didn't leave!" I get angry, then catch myself. "She's out there waiting for me." I swallow hard and my eyes tear up.

"I know the feeling." Patrick takes a step toward me. "I thought it was a phase and I could win her back. Certainly, for the boy-"

"You don't understand," I interrupt. "My wife didn't leave. She was... taken."

"Taken?" Patrick furrows his brow. "Like kidnapped?"

"My husband too," Del says without opening his eyes. "After he was shot with that pistol."

Patrick swivels between the Blackfoot on the floor and the gun on Lavigne's desk. "You guys messing with me?"

"I wish."

"So, your spouses were kidnapped?"

I nod.

"And *shot?*"

Del nods.

"By whom?" He's flustered now. Might as well go all-in.

"You ever heard of Oliver Hobbes?"

"I know him!" Carl chimes in. "He owns *AMPersand.*"

"*AMPersand?*" I narrow my eyes at the boy.

"One of the top eSports teams." Carl jumps off the cot now, clearly excited. "*Counter Strike, Overwatch, Fortnite...*" We all stare like he's speaking Spanish. "You've never heard of eSports?"

Del smiles. "I don't get out much, son."

"Well, it's like competitive video games. They play big arenas and live streams with thousands of viewers."

"Oliver Hobbes is a gamer?"

"I don't think he plays," Carl says. "But he owns a team." He pats his pockets in frustration. "I wish I had my phone I could tell you more."

"eSports, huh?" I raise an eyebrow at Del and he shrugs.

"*AMPersand* is legit," Carl says. "I've watched their streams. Hobbes brings in top talent."

"You know anything else about the guy?"

"Not really. Just that he's like... a billionaire."

"So I've heard." Rain lashes the window and wind whistles outside.

"Wait a minute," Patrick cuts in. "So, this eSports guy kidnapped your wife?"

"You should tell the police!" Carl adds.

I glance across the room at Officer Lavigne. He's got a phone to his ear and speaks in hushed tones.

"These guys won't help us." I shake my head. "He's probably on the phone with Hobbes' people right now."

"Or..." Del suddenly stands and stretches his legs. "Maybe Lavigne will let us go." He winks and pats me on the arm.

"What are you on now, Del?" I roll my eyes.

"Just had a chat with the Old Man."

"Who's the Old Man?" Carl asks.

Del just smiles and looks toward the window as a siren starts to scream outside.

Chapter 33

Mooch tumbles through the door and shakes water off his hat. "Stovepipe spotted off the forty-five," he calls out.

"Shit!" Lavine drops the phone and leaps from his desk. He pushes Mooch aside and peers out through driving rain. "I got work to do here. Think you can go spot?"

"On it, boss." Mooch throws a clumsy salute and slips back out into the rain. Lavigne frowns and stalks over to our cell.

"Seems like we've got a situation," he says. "Tornado about five miles south. Happens this time of year."

I've seen my share of Wyoming storms, including some nasty spin-ups in the flatland. "Anything out there, boss?"

Lavigne narrows his eyes and swallows. "Couple of homes. A grocery." He's holding something back.

"Are we safe here, Dad?" Carl hugs his pops while Patrick stares the officer down.

"We're all right," Lavigne says, eyeing the boy. "Storm shelter 'round back if things get hairy." He spits on the cement floor and rubs it out with his shoe. Then he turns to me. "You want to start talking about that gun? I'm getting the runaround from USAC."

"You called USAC?"

"They called me." Lavigne huffs and spits again. "After I ran a trace on that Glock. Asking a lot of funny questions."

"That sounds about right."

Lavigne looks us up and down. "Just what are you boys into?"

I side-eye Patrick and shrug. "You wouldn't believe us if we told you, sir."

"Try me."

A loud thunderclap makes the lights blink and everyone jumps. Radio cackles on the desk and Lavigne hustles over.

"Big one, sir..." Sounds like Mooch through rain and fuzz. "Quarter mile East of the cemetery, about to jump the river..."

Lavigne's jaw tightens and he drums a finger on the desk. "Can you tell which way it's moving?" He peeks out the door as rain whips in through the void.

The radio hangs quiet for ten seconds. Fifteen. Twenty...

"Mooch, you copy? How far to the eastern 'steads?"

Lavigne waits, face set in a frown. I know that look now.

"You got people out there."

He eyes me hard and tries the radio again. "Mooch! What's the status? Mooch!"

After ten more seconds of silence, he stomps back and tries the phone. Toggles the switch a few times then buries it back in the cradle.

"Line dead?"

Lavigne eyes me again but says nothing. Stands like a statue in the middle of the room.

"Maybe we should get to the shelter." Wind whistles outside and bulbs flicker overhead and Lavigne rocks with indecision. Finally grabs his hat and charges for the door.

"Wait!" Patrick yells. "You can't leave us here!" Carl starts crying and Baxter rears up. Lavigne hesitates at the threshold and eyes me hard once more.

"Do it for the boy," I say, just as the lights go out.

Chapter 34

"Everyone on me!"

Lavigne manages to pop our cell in the dark and get everyone huddled by the front door. Only light to see by is what flashes across the sky.

"Stay tight to the man in front! Keep one hand on the wall!"

I crouch behind Del and brace for the chaos outside. Wind rocks the building as raindrops hammer the door.

"We go east around the building to the lee side! Stay low and keep up!"

Lavigne shouts orders and I work my free hand into Baxter's collar. "Hang in there, boy."

Lavigne stands in front followed by Patrick, Carl, Delsin, Baxter and me. Conga line to the shelter out back. The wind howls and the old jailhouse groans and Lavigne yells something but it's lost in the roar. Suddenly the door is open and the storm hits me in the face.

"Move! Move! Move!" The group staggers off, but I can barely keep my feet. Rain hits me side-on like a firehose. It floods up my nose and into my boots. I close my eyes and keep my good hand tight to the dog.

"Turn! Turn!"

I think that's Lavigne. We get around the corner and the wind slacks a bit. I squint through the deluge and stumble into Del. "This is crazy!"

Del says nothing but grabs my shirt to keep me close. Thirty more feet and we round another corner back into the maelstrom.

"Keep your heads down!" I hang tight to Baxter as we blunder blind through ankle-deep slosh.

"Almost there!" Lavigne calls as a web of lightning reveals the low, flat doors of a shelter. Thunder cracks and Baxter jumps and Carl goes down with a splash. Del drags the boy to his feet and Patrick wraps him in a bear hug against the wind.

"Get it open!" He yells as Lavigne fumbles with a set of keys. "Hurry!" The tall cop shakes and stutters and drops the keyring in the wash at his feet.

"Aw, hell!" He goes down to a knee. Roots through black water as rain curtains in from all sides.

Baxter is barking. Carl is crying. Patrick is screaming. Lavigne is swearing. Somehow through it all Del meets my eyes and smiles.

What the hell?

Do not be afraid.

Is that you, Pops? No... Something different.

Come and find me Clay Moore...

I close my eyes and let go.

I see Ashley on a morning walk in the valley. Kicking up dewdrops, smiling behind a coffee cup.

Now we're in a courtyard. Mexico. Midday. Church bells and cobblestones and a halo in the sky.

Back on the ranch. Herding stock. Ashley sits high on a black Morgan and doffs her cap.

I open my eyes.

Patrick carries Carl down through open cellar doors. Lavigne waves Del behind and reaches for my hand. "Come on, Moore!" I float to the doorway and follow Baxter down rickety steps. Lavigne heaves the doors shut behind us with a bang.

"Whew."

It's pitch dark and I stumble into Del. Soaked to the bone. Shoulder throbs. Eyeballs sting from water and grit.

I've seen my share of weather but that's the wrath of God out there.

Someone takes my hand. "We're safe now," Del says.

"Are you sure?" Carl asks. The storm doors rattle and drip. I give Del's hand a squeeze.

Lavigne sighs in the dark. "This is as safe as it gets out here." There's worry in his voice.

"Your folks got a shelter?"

"Nope."

The word hangs like cobwebs in a crypt. Baxter finds my feet and I join him on the damp floor. Slowly stroke his fur and it calms us both down.

"They'll be all right," Del says.

"The fuck are you to talk?" Lavigne snaps.

Del says nothing more. He sits beside me and takes my hand again. I lean in close and listen to him hum.

Five minutes pass. Ten. Lavigne tries his radio and gets static. Pops a door briefly and gets wet.

"See anything?"

"No."

He climbs back down and paces like a caged bull. Back and forth in a restless circuit. Wet boots on cold concrete.

Five more minutes. The radio cackles again but nothing distinct.

"Mooch? Mooch, is that you?"

Fuzz. Lavigne stomps and swears.

"They'll be all right," Del says again. This time Lavigne lets it go. Maybe he wants to believe.

More minutes pass. Finally, there's a break in the rain.

"I think it's stopping," Carl cautiously rallies the group. Baxter hops up and shakes the murk from his fur. Lavigne nudges the door ajar.

"It's quiet," Patrick says. "Is it over?"

Lavigne grunts and heaves out into the night. He doesn't wait but the rest of us do.

"Should we follow?" Patrick asks.

"I'm in no rush."

"We're needed," Del says. He stands and pulls me up by my good hand. Wet clothes cling to my skin for the second time today. Del tromps up out of the cellar and Baxter is quick to follow. Then Patrick and his boy.

Best get on, son.

What, back in the cell? Wait for USAC?

The Old Man's got other plans for you now.

I hope you're right, Pops.

Climb the steps and see.

I creep my way into the muggy night. Rain falls gently like the credits of a movie. Lightning crawls away to the east.

"Clay, over here!"

I see the group huddled around something across the lot. Jog over and realize it's a downed pole.

"Snapped like a twig."

"Watch the wire." Patrick ushers Carl back.

183

I scan the surroundings for more damage but there ain't much here. The Sunoco roof looks crooked but it might have already been that way. Suddenly the radio jumps to life.

"Lavigne! Lavigne! Code red! Come in!"

The officer fumbles with his handset and almost drops it to the pavement.

"Mooch, what's the status? Are the houses okay?"

A long pause. Nobody breathes.

"It's bad, boss," Mooch comes back. "Direct hit on multiple 'steads. Get down here ASAP!"

Lavigne goes pale. "What about Molly? And the baby? Were we hit?"

He turns to me with a quivering lip. I try to project some calm.

"It's bad, boss..." Mooch drops into static and Lavigne closes his eyes. Thunder pops and we wait. "...going in, now," Mooch continues. "Get down here, boss. Bring all hands! Over!"

The radio goes dead and thunder pops again. Lavigne sags in his boots.

"You heard the man," Del speaks up. "All hands." He claps three times and Lavigne comes to life.

"Everybody to the cruiser," he calls, setting off toward his car. We scramble through puddles in the parking lot as Lavigne pauses at the driver's door. "You're up front with me, Moore." He takes a deep breath and crosses himself. "I hope that bloodhound's ready to work."

Chapter 35

The cruiser whips along wet pavement, too fast for the two-lane country road.

"Easy, man!" Patrick calls from the caged back seat. Lavigne just punches it faster.

"How far?" I ask.

Lavigne says nothing. The car bounces over branches in the roadway. I sit shotgun and hug Baxter with one arm.

Suddenly we crest a ridge and there's a car in our path. Mooch's cruiser. Lavigne slams the brakes and we fishtail hard into the grass. He's out the door and running before we make a full stop.

"Jesus!" Patrick calls. "He could have got us killed."

"Where's he going?" Carl asks.

I watch Lavigne recede at a sprint across a dark field. He slips and falls and clambers back to his feet.

"Clay, we need your help." I turn and see Del push uselessly on the cruiser door. They won't open from the inside. I hop out and free the group and we slog off into the lumpy prairie.

"Anyone see anything?"

Baxter jogs ahead and I let him go. "Lavigne!" My voice blows away on the wind. The cop's disappeared from view but I can read his trail in the muddy turf. "He went this way."

Del picks up the pace and I stagger into a jog. My shin cracks something hard and I go facedown into the mud.

"Dammit!"

Patrick leans down to help but my free hand is slick with filth. I roll over and reach back for whatever tripped me up. "What the...?"

It's a vacuum. One of those vintage metal uprights that must weigh twenty pounds. The heavy base is half stuck in the earth and the damn thing tripped me like a curb.

"What's that doing here?"

"Come on." I fight to my feet and blunder on. Baxter barks and shadows roam the dark fifty yards ahead. I leap over a footstool and a garbage can.

"Watch your feet!"

The debris picks up and we're forced to slow down. I stagger over a chunk of slate roof and smell gas.

"Hold up." I wave Patrick and Carl to a stop. "We're close."

"Over here!" Del's call rings out from the darkness and beside me Patrick gasps.

"Good lord..."

"What is it?" Carl asks. Then he sees. "Oh, wow..."

In the middle of the field, beneath the flickering bolts of receding clouds, sits a heaping mound that was once a home.

"Molly!" Lavigne's voice now. Urgent and scared. "Molly!"

"Come on!" Del calls, and we hustle through debris to the outskirts of the house proper. I hobble up next to the shirtless Blackfoot and lean on his shoulder to catch my breath.

"Molly!" Another voice. Mooch. The paunchy policeman steps around a battered chimney and calls to us. "Start digging!" He yells. "Lavigne's wife and kid!"

This gets Patrick's attention. "There's a kid?"

"Little girl," Mooch replies, rooting through the rubble. "Eight months."

Holy shit.

Lavigne said they had no basement. No shelter.

Shit. Shit. Shit.

"Fan out," Del says.

I stagger forward onto unsteady heaps of lumber and brick. "Molly!" Something shifts and I wobble on my feet. "Molly!" The whole house is obliterated. Unrecognizable. Broken glass and busted drywall. Tangles of plywood and pipe. "Molly!"

I try to pull a two-by-four but it won't budge. Twist a piece of clapboard and get splinters in my palm.

"Molly!"

This is bad.

"Molly!"

It's like a bomb went off.

"Molly!"

Could someone even survive this mess?

Bear down, son. Find them.

I'm trying, Pops.

Find them.

I balance on a butt joint and study the wreckage around me. "Molly!"

I can do this. I grew up in tornado alley. We never took a direct hit, but hunkered down more times than I can count.

Remember the drills, son.

Whenever the sirens went off, first choice was always underground. Failing that, interior bathroom or a closet.

"Molly!"

The debris pile peaks toward the center. If Molly had time that's where she should be.

Call your hound.

"Baxter!" He barks a response but I can't place it. "Baxter!" Where is that dog?

Suddenly Bax bounds over a bedframe and he's at my feet. Rowdy as hell. "Easy, boy." We're on a pile of shifting shrapnel with bodies underneath. "Be careful. Move slow."

The bloodhound follows his nose and I follow him. We pick our way through rubble. "Molly!" I pray we're not too late. "Molly!"

Lavigne comes up behind and grabs my arm. His eyes are frantic. Hands bloody and scratched. "They have to be here!" He points to the raised mound amongst the wreckage. "Hall closet. Safest place."

"Well, start digging then." I pull a few bricks off the pile, but I'm near useless with one hand. Lavigne bends over and tears through chunks of his broken home.

"Molly!" He's screaming himself hoarse. "Molly!" Del comes over and takes command.

"Dig carefully," he says. "We don't want to collapse the pile." He hefts a light fixture and tosses it aside. "Lift and remove."

The rest of the group descends on the heap and I back off. I call Baxter to my feet and he looks up with wild eyes. "You smell anything, boy?" He knows the stakes are high and wants to deliver. I wave him back into the fray. "Find the kid!" Baxter goes nose-down and ass-up and huffs it all in. He squirms around Carl and through Del's legs and then stops.

"Woof!"

Nose down. Ass up. Double check.

"Woof! Woof!"

He's sure.

"Baxter's got something!" He's sniffs around a slab of plaster and scrabbles with his paws. "Under there!"

I call him back as Lavigne races to the spot. "Molly!" The panicked cop wills his wife to respond.

"Easy," Del says, stepping in to help. "Lift and remove. We'll get them out."

Lavigne doesn't seem to hear and digs his way down like a badger. "Molly!" He sweats and shovels and strains. "Mollllllllyyy!" He struggles with a length of lumber and puts his whole heart into heaving it off the pile.

"I see something!" Carl calls as Lavigne opens up a cavity full of clothes. I see it too. Movement beneath the mass.

"Molly!" Lavigne wrenches out a pile of pants and there she is. Bloody and busted with a baby to her breast. She opens crusted eyes and Lavigne bursts into tears.

"Oh, Molly..."

"We got you, ma'am," Del says. He pulls away a web of rebar perched precariously over the hole. "Don't try to move yet."

Molly lies contorted beneath the debris, linens packed tight around her body. "Looks like she covered herself in clothes," Patrick says. "Must have raced into the closet and pulled them down on top of her."

"Her and the baby," I nod. Molly mutters something but it's too weak to hear. She squirms and lifts the child, wrapped in its own swaddle of sheets. Lavigne gingerly takes the bundle and rocks it in is arms.

"Isabelle..." he coos, tears dripping off his nose. "I was so scared..." Molly tries to speak again but it comes out a staggered groan.

"Stay calm, Mrs. Lavigne." Del methodically clears the cocoon of shrapnel. "We're here for you." Baxter hops down next to the wounded woman and licks her face. She weakly pushes him away and tries to speak again.

"What's wrong?" Lavigne speaks up, nervous tenor back in his voice. "Hey, Moore. What's wrong with her?"

"She's in shock," I say, watching Mooch and Del dig out. "Probably has a concussion."

"No," Lavigne says, more urgent this time. "Isabelle. She's not crying."

This gets everyone's attention, and the work stops briefly as all eyes turn to the tiny babe in Lavigne's giant hands. "She's blue," he adds, pleading with helpless eyes. "Isabelle..."

Now Patrick snaps into action. "Give her here. Quickly." He takes the bundle and carries her away from the fray. He lays the baby on a slab of old countertop and puts an ear to her chest.

"You some kind of doctor?"

"Quiet." Patrick works quickly, unwrapping the child and checking the body for injuries. Isabelle's skin is pallid and her limbs droop like rags. "No signs of trauma, but her pulse is faint." He leans down and starts breathing into her mouth.

Lavigne looks on helpless, eyes darting between his daughter and wife. "Go help dig!" I tell him, but he just stares at me like a puppy while Patrick pumps the baby's chest.

"Come on, Isabelle," he murmurs while he works. "Come back to us, dear."

I pull Carl close and whisper in his ear. "Where'd your dad learn CPR?"

"I don't know," Carl shrugs. "Dad's an electrician."

That might explain it. Risk of shock or falling on the job could stop a man's heart. I once saw a high school coach bring his quarterback around after a knock. Never seen mouth-to-mouth on a baby, though.

"Come on, Patrick." I squeeze Carl's hand and pray we're not about to watch the girl die. "Maybe we should help dig," I offer, but the boy pulls from my grip and runs over to his father.

"What can I do, Dad?"

"Hold her head."

Carl cradles the baby's skull while his dad delivers more breaths.

"Tickle her feet."

He flicks a tiny foot and Isabelle's leg starts to twitch.

"She's moving!"

Patrick never breaks rhythm. Pump, pump, breathe. Pump, pump, breathe.

Lavigne hunches nearby, frozen with fear.

Pump, pump, breathe. Pump, pump, breathe.

Carl pinches a toe and the baby kicks again. Stronger this time.

"It's working!"

Pump, pump, breathe.

"Come on, girl..."

Pump, pump, breathe.

Carl's glasses slide off and he lets them fall. Patrick's beard gleams with saliva and sweat.

Pump, pump, breathe.

Pump, pump, breathe.

Anything you can do, Pops?

This is out of my hands.

Pump, pump, breathe.

Pump, pump, breathe.

I turn to see Mooch and Del helping Molly to her feet. She wobbles and sways and climbs gingerly out of the hole. "My baby..." She calls through clenched teeth. Lavigne moves to meet her when suddenly Isabelle cries out.

"Waaaaaaaaaaahhhhhh!"

The sound is tortured and shrill. Pure anguish from the poor child. But she's back.

"Isabelle!" Lavgine rushes to his daughter and scoops her off the slab. Patrick steps back to catch his breath as Molly collapses against her husband. The family breaks down into a huddle of weeping and wails.

"Ambulance en route," Mooch declares, holstering his radio. He claps Delsin on the back and shakes his hand. "Thank God you folks were here."

I realize I've been holding my breath and let out a good long sigh. Patrick turns to me and smiles. "Where'd you learn that?" I ask.

"Known CPR for years," Patrick shrugs. "First time I've ever had to use it." He leans down and wraps Carl in a hug. "Great work, kid."

"You saved her, Dad!"

"We all did."

I whistle for Baxter and give him the love he deserves. If not for his nose, or Patrick's breath, or Del's strong hand, little Isabelle might not have come out alive. It's a sobering thought, and I let it wash over me until my eyes blur and my knees go weak.

"Easy there." Del scoops me up before I drop. I lean on him and let go. Just let the tears come out in a rush. "It's all right," Del says. But it's not.

It's all wrong.

My wife. My shoulder. The river. The jail. The storm. I'm not built for this.

Of course you are, son.

Aw hell, Pops.

You're built for exactly this.

I just want my wife back.

Then go get her.

I think about Ashley and the tears come harder. Del gives me a shoulder and everyone else gives space. The world around us is a soggy, shattered mess, and I match my pitch to poor Isabelle as we weep helplessly in the dark.

Chapter 36

"Walk with me, Moore."

Lavigne claps me on the back and leads me away from the crowd. EMTs have arrived for Molly and Isabelle, while stunned neighbors chat up Patrick and Del. I've got my shit back together after a good cry, but wading through the wreckage brings back demons of its own.

"I'm sorry about your house," I mutter as we step through the remains of what used to be Lavigne's kitchen.

"Yeah..." His eyes go glassy, like he can't see the destruction for what it is yet. "Thank God for insurance."

"You got a place to stay?"

He eyeballs me like he hasn't thought that far. Maybe he's just surprised that I care. "Hey, I was shit to you guys back there on the road," he says. "I want to apologize to you, and your black friend. And the Indian."

"You can tell 'em yourself."

Lavigne looks back toward Patrick then meets my eyes again. "I want you to be straight with me, Moore." He pulls out a damp cigarette and passes it to me, butt first. "What's USAC?"

I take the proffered lighter and somehow spark it on the first try. The smoke fills my lungs like an old friend. I exhale to the sky and decide to tell the truth.

"United States Asset Command," I say, as Lavigne lights up a smoke of his own. "Private military run by a billionaire. They bombed my house and took my wife."

Lavigne nods like I just relayed a football score. Maybe he's still in shock. "How'd you get the gun?"

"USAC soldier tried to take us in." I glance over at the shirtless Blackfoot who meets my eyes. "Del and I got away."

"Mmm hmm." Lavigne smokes slowly and taps the butt after every puff. He nudges a piece of broken tile with his toe. "And the soldier?"

I take a long drag and think about Kirby and the wolf. Not going there. "Del and I got away."

Lavigne nods. "But they took your wife?"

"And Del's husband."

He eyes Del from a distance and smiles. "USAC is thirsty for you boys," he says after a long drag. "Guy on the phone claimed you've been racking up bodies."

"Bodies?" I balk at that and hope my shock reads legit. "What do you think?"

He contemplates, saying nothing. Eyes float over the wreckage and finally back to me. "I don't see it." He shakes his head.

I take a last puff off the dwindling cig and give the man an earnest look. "I'm no killer."

Lavigne nods. "Why'd they take your wife?"

I pinch the cherry off my smoke and spit where it hits the ground. "We're caught up in something we didn't ask for."

He bends down and retrieves a child's toothbrush. Sighs and tosses it like a spent match. "I know the feeling." He offers a hand and I take it. "Thanks for saving my kid."

"The men you should be thanking are over there." I point to Patrick and Del.

Lavigne shrugs. "I'll have Mooch give y'all a ride to your car." He turns and starts back toward the small crowd around his wife and child. "If you're smart, you'll be gone before USAC rolls in."

I'm struck still for a moment then hurry back to his side. "These are dangerous people," I say. "You're just going to cut us loose?"

"I'm keeping the gun," he says. "Tell 'em y'all escaped in the storm." He turns to me with tired eyes. "Go find your wife, Clay Moore."

Relief washes over me like a cloudburst. He's giving us a chance. I don't know what to say so I say nothing. Jog over to Patrick and Del.

"Lavigne's letting us go."

Patrick's eyes go big with surprise, but Del just nods like he expected it. I watch Lavigne pass instructions to Mooch, and the portly cop nods our way. Everyone looks ready to bolt but there's one more thing I need before this all sits right.

"Lavigne!" I call, just as he's about to check on Molly and Isabelle. "Hey!" I frantically wave him over. His eyes go cross, but he obliges and shuffles to where we stand.

"What is it, Moore?" His voice is gruff and annoyed. "I told you to get gone."

I step back and nudge Del forward next to Patrick and Carl. "The men who saved your daughter's life."

Lavigne stares for a moment, trying to be hard. Then something gives and his shoulders relax. He offers a hand and Del swallows it up. "Thank you." The words are quiet but the eyes sincere. He turns to Carl next, and finally Patrick.

"Sorry for the trouble," Lavigne says. "I'll owe you forever."

Patrick nods and shakes his hand. "Right place at the right time."

Lavigne chokes back a tear and turns away. "Mooch," he calls. "Give these men a ride to their car."

Chapter 37

Ten minutes later, we're back where Lavigne pulled us over. Patrick's Mercedes sits unmoved on the side of the highway.

"Good luck," Mooch says before speeding off. Baxter growls at the vehicle and I half-expect USAC commandos to start jumping out of the brush.

"We should get moving," I urge, and everyone piles into the car without another word.

"Where to?" Patrick turns to me. Am I in charge now? Carl excitedly powers up his phone and flicks through missed alerts.

"Bring up your map, kid." He nods and swipes and passes the device to me.

"We can't risk going through Willow, but there's a dirt road through a ranch about three miles back." I pinch and poke at the silky screen. "That will get us south, then I say we blast east like a spooked steer."

"Sounds like a plan." Patrick starts the car and wastes no time whipping us around. Feels good to be on the move again, but I won't sleep sound until we're far from here.

We hit the dirt road and bounce along the outskirts of a quiet ranch. My mind drifts to simpler times: baling hay, herding cows, morning rides with Pops.

"What's that?" Carl taps twice against his window and snaps me out of my trance. I squint through the dark and see lights coming in fast from the west.

"Kill the engine," I say. "And the lamps."

Patrick gives me wide eye in the mirror but complies without a word. We soon sit quietly in the dark.

"USAC," I whisper. Rotors thump and engines drone as helicopters sweep our way across the prairie.

"Jesus." Patrick gasps. "This is for you?"

I just nod and watch the lights in the sky. I don't think they'll see us down here, but if they do it's over. I count six black choppers coming in hot.

No one says a word. They're pushing all-out for Willow and rush over us at full speed.

"Let's move," I say as the lights recede to the east. Patrick lets out a breath and starts the car. Baxter whines with all the tension and I try to calm him down.

"Another mile south and we'll hit the highway. Head east and don't look back." I hand the iPhone back to Carl. "Take us as far as you can, kid." He nods and gulps and dives facedown into his screen.

I feel a hand on my shoulder. Del. His eyes say relax, so I lean back and try. I need a meal and a bed and a smoke and my wife. I close my eyes and drift to thoughts of Ashley. Baxter curls up at my side as we bounce along the dirt road.

The next thing I know we're on a highway someplace else.

"Welcome back." Del smiles and rubs my shoulder again.

"Was I asleep?"

"About two hours."

I shake my head and rub dry eyes. "Anyone got water?" My back is stiff and my throat is parched. Carl hands me his giant bottle of soda and I slurp the sweet drink down.

"Where are we?" The land outside is dark and flat with nothing to see. The clock on the dash says 12:45.

"Nebraska," says Patrick. His droopy eyes meet mine in mirror. "Just outside North Platte."

"You need a break? Let me drive for a bit." I'm groggy but Patrick looks worse. He nods and a few minutes later we pull into a gas station to change places.

Del runs inside – shirtless – and comes back with hot coffee and a pack of cigarettes. I could kiss him and I almost do. I pound a Camel on the curb and then we're back on the road.

Patrick and Carl doze in the back seat while Del joins me up front. We share the coffee and listen to a radio show about aliens. Del takes the wheel around four, and by sunrise we're somewhere in the middle of Iowa.

196

"Breakfast," Del declares as he pulls into the lot of some greasy spoon. We're all famished and queue up a small feast of breakfast breads and meats. I start to feel human again.

"God, I needed this."

"Mmmrmph," Carl mumbles through a mouthful of home fries. Del smiles and works through a three-cheese omelet. He wears a too-tight tee-shirt borrowed from Patrick, and our young waitress can't stop fussing over him.

"More hot water for your tea, sweetheart?" Del nods and extends his mug. She leans way over and fills it up. "Where you folks headed?"

Patrick eyes me across the table and I return a slight shrug. That's still up in the air.

"Pittsburgh," Carl jumps in. "For the gaming convention."

Nice deception, kid.

I think.

"Gaming...?" The poor girl is confused and not the only one.

"Video games," Carl says. "Dad promised to take me for my birthday. And I got this new phone, look!" He waves the iPhone precariously over a plate of pancakes. Our waitress smiles and starts to back off.

"Well happy birthday to you, son." She scans the room and straightens her hair. "If any of y'all need help while you're in town, my name's Therese." She winks at Del and wanders off to other tables.

I grin behind my coffee mug. "Barking up the wrong tree there, Therese."

"She's sweet," Del says with a smile.

"I bet you get a lot of that," Patrick says.

"I really don't get out much."

"So, what's your deal?" Carl asks between bites of buttered toast. "You live in some Indian town?"

"Carl..." Patrick rolls his eyes apologetically. "Let the man eat."

"It's okay," Del says. "I actually own a house in the hills with my husband."

Carl shovels more sausage into his mouth, still clutching his phone in one hand. "Are Indians allowed to be gay?"

"Carl!"

"What? Some religions aren't."

"Blackfoot isn't a religion, son. It's a tribe." He eyes Del warily, already out of his depth. "Maybe both?"

"I'm just a man," Del says, taking a slow sip of tea. "I can be whatever I want."

"Hear, hear." I raise my mug to Del and we clink.

Carl shrugs and tosses a slice of bacon under the table. The hostess was kind enough to let us bring Baxter inside. "So how did you know?" he asks.

"Know what, son?"

"About the officer..." Carl stops eating a moment to focus on his thought. "You said he would let us go, and he did."

Now that is a good question. Del's been right about a lot of things he had no business knowing. The blue Mercedes. Lavigne letting us go. Hell, he said Molly and Isabelle would be all right, and they were. I think back to something Arden said in the woods the other night when we got drunk watching the stars.

"Del's tapped into something. Something powerful..."

I can't pretend I haven't seen it. He'll meditate a while and make some declaration and there it is. He tried preaching me that Old Man schtick, but I never quite caught on.

"The ol' Blackfoot voodoo, eh Del?" It was supposed to be a joke but feels awkward and rude.

Del smiles and swirls the dregs of tea in his mug. "Nothing so complicated as that," he says. "Just a way of seeing things as they are."

"Something you learned from the Blackfeet?" Carl asks.

"Actually, something I learned in prison."

We all seize up at that. Patrick drops his fork and I choke some coffee down the wrong pipe.

"Prison?" I grunt and reach for a glass of water. "You were in-" The rest is lost in a fit of sputters and coughs.

Del just smiles, amused.

"Woah!" Carl says. "What did you do?"

The stoic Blackfoot smooths his long hair and lifts an empty mug. Therese shows up in a blink to fill his tea while the rest of us look on. "Thanks, dear," Del says, and the waitress all but floats away. Del takes a sip and licks his lips and sweeps his eyes around the table. "You boys want to hear a story?"

"Hell, yes!" Carl says.

"Carl..." his father scolds again but I can tell he's curious.

"I can't believe you went to prison, Del." I shake my head in surprise. "Is that where you learned you were..." I stop myself but not in time. Second stupid thing I've said in five minutes.

"Oh, I knew that long before." Del grins as I try to shrink down into my shirt. "But it's where I learned to be free."

Chapter 38 – Del's Story

I was born angry.

Came out and cried for three straight days.

"Yours were screams of fury," my mother told me. "Red-faced rage at the world you came into."

That world was the Ki'sómma Sovereign Territory, a North Dakota reservation near the Canadian border, and I was right to hate it.

It was brutal country. Windswept hardscrabble and scrub. There were few trees. Fewer animals. We didn't even have fresh water on our land.

I lived with Mom and Dad in a rusty trailer at the end of a dirt road. Things were bad and I knew it. My youthful innocence scoured away. I mouthed off. Got into fights. Made friends just to steal from their homes.

Winters were the worst. Six months of hoarfrost and chill. The snow would drift up to our doorknob. I got used to not feeling my toes.

When I was ten, Dad lost his job at the oil field he'd worked for years. He hurt his back hauling chain, and they denied him disability by claiming he was drunk. He wasn't. My father never drank. But he was no match for the lawyers who knew half the Rez was sauced.

With Dad out of work, we sold our trailer and moved in with my aunt. Nine of us in a three-room house. I stopped coming home after school and fell in with a group of older boys who'd been similarly displaced. I was young and dumb and didn't understand what I was into. We'd roll around in an overstuffed pickup, chasing girls and teasing dogs.

It broke my mother's heart to see me so listless, but there was little she could do. Mom was a simple woman. Kind-hearted but feeble. Years later I would learn she suffered early-onset dementia, and the more I grew up the less she seemed to notice me at all.

There were other good folks in the community, and a few tried to reach me along the way. A coach named Red Crow introduced me to the weight room, and I found an outlet there for some of my rage.

Weights were a springboard for me. A chance to take charge and better myself. I filled out fast. Got big. Felt strong. I'd spend hours flexing in the mirror and began to fall in love with my own physique.

This was a revelation I was ready for. I never cared much for my female peers. While other boys bragged about their sexual exploits, I was more interested in exploring myself. Once I saw what I could be – abs, pecs, biceps, quads – I knew what I was after.

It first showed up in the form of a classmate named Mouse. Mouse and I shared a schedule freshman year, and as I started filling out my tees, he started giving me the eye. Our first time was in a broom closet behind the gym. It was messy but exhilarating. Angry sex. The only way I knew how.

Mouse and I stayed close throughout high school, and he chilled me out a bit. I had my weights and my man. I still hated the world, but at least I was getting laid.

Then it all went to hell.

Mouse was a beautiful boy. High cheekbones, feathered lips. He was tender and dreamy and everything I was not.

He wanted to be an actor, and we dreamed of running off to Hollywood as soon as we finished school. It was mostly fantasy, but a part of me thinks we might have pulled it off. He had the face. I had the body. There's always work for good looking men.

Our problem was we had no money. Didn't even know what it was like to have money. Most of the reservation jobs were unskilled with low pay. There was contract oil work off the Rez, but it was hard labor. Just ask my father. I figured I'd end up in those fields, but Mouse was no roughneck. He sought a different way.

It was the shoes I noticed first. Mouse showed up to class one day in brand new Chuck Taylors. I heard the soles squeak and my jaw dropped. Everyone's did. Those were hundred-dollar kicks. Mouse shrugged off his classmates' ribbing and called the shoes a gift from his mom.

A few days later he had a new hat. Then designer jeans. He was cagey about it, but I knew something was up. When he bought me dinner one night with a hundred-dollar bill, I sat him down for a talk.

"Where'd you get this money, man?"

"I found a job... off the Rez."

"Off the Rez? Doing what?"

His grin was sheepish, and I didn't need much more to piece it out. Mouse was turning tricks.

Turned out there was a whole flock of white folks who would pay good money to lay a good-looking Blackfoot. Mouse wasn't the only one whoring off the reservation, but as far as I knew he was the only male. That meant he brought a good price, and he claimed to have half-a-dozen regulars lined up to get a mouse in their bed.

"This is our ticket out," he told me. "A few months of this and we're in Hollywood. Hell, one of these guys might take us there."

Mouse was his same starry-eyed self, but I was mad. I didn't mind that he was sleeping around, it was just the unfairness of it all. This poor boy pleasing old men for pocket cash. One more injustice in my unjust world.

"It's good money," Mouse promised me. "Most of these guys are really nice."

"Most of them?"

He never got specific, but I understood the stakes. Mouse was vulnerable. He was pretty and naïve. Off the Rez, our people were always second class. All it took was one bad apple, and I knew before long Mouse would find him.

One day he didn't show up to school. That was rare for Mouse. He was an average student, but reliable. Social. I tracked down his sister who said he hadn't come home the night before. She thought he was with me.

The next day Mouse was still AWOL, and I ducked out of school to scout his usual haunts. I ran into his mother at the laundromat, where she all but broke down crying into my chest.

"Please find my baby boy!"

"Maybe he finally ran off to Hollywood," I offered, but we both knew better. Mother and I spun our wheels the rest of the day and the ensuing sleepless night. When Mouse didn't surface by day three, we started checking hospitals. That's when we found him in an ICU.

"He came in as a John Doe," the doctor told us. "Found unconscious in a motel room with a pile of cocaine. He's been in a coma for thirty-six hours."

Mouse's mother wept by the bedside while I peppered the staff for clues.

"Who found him? Why was he there? Mouse didn't do drugs..."

Nobody had answers but a picture was coming clear: Mouse met up with one of his Johns and overdosed on coke. The guy probably bailed and left him for dead.

It made my blood boil. Old rage came flooding back. I sat in a chair and watched my friend lie comatose while his mother wept. We kept vigil through another sleepless night, and the next day the Old Man sent a miracle.

Mouse woke up.

Just like that.

He opened his eyes and his mother screamed and nurses poured into the room. I stood back while half the hospital fussed over his bed. At one point he caught my eyes and smiled. Silent tears on both our cheeks.

When things settled down, doctors explained Mouse would be laid up for a while. The cocaine had shredded his system, taxing kidneys, heart, and lungs. He couldn't remember how much he did. He didn't know how long he'd slept. He was shaky and shattered and sickly and slow. But he was alive.

I stayed by Mouse's bedside for a day and a half. Doctors and nurses and family came and went. When we finally got a moment in private, I dove in.

"What was his name?"

Mouse winced and shook his head.

"His name," I said. "The man who did this to you."

"I don't remember," Mouse said meekly. His eyes drooped and his tongue lolled out. "Most of them never gave a real name."

"What do you remember?" I waited patiently while Mouse meditated on my words. My hands worked in and out of fists. My biceps coiled and unwound.

"His car," Mouse finally spoke up. "He picked me up in a blue wagon."

"Anything else?"

"He works in the oil fields."

"You're sure?"

Mouse closed his eyes and choked something back. "Don't do anything stupid, Del." He opened them and gave me a helpless stare. "Please."

"I'll do what I have to."

Mouse dropped his head and drifted off and I quietly slipped out of the room.

My first stop was a friend of my father's. Big Russ. I barged into his house to find him shirtless, sipping a beer.

"Need to borrow your revolver."

Russ eyed me with a curious glare. "Borrow?"

"Scare off some possums."

He frowned and took a pull off his beer. Maybe I should have knocked. I scanned the room for a place to sit, but there was none. "Ma says they're into her beet patch."

"I bet they are," Russ said. "You sure this isn't about something else?"

He already sniffed out my bull, but I was too stubborn to pivot. I thought about Mouse on a ventilator and IVs. "Can I borrow it or not?"

Big Russ sighed and downed the last of his beer. He crushed the can and stood to face me, equal height but opposite build. His thick belly brushed my shirt.

After a few seconds of staredown, Russ turned and went to a high cupboard on the wall. He pulled out a lockbox and sat back down in his chair. "What kind of possums?" He asked as he worked an old pitted key into the lock.

I ignored the question and watched hungrily as he pulled out a shiny Colt Peacemaker. The long-barreled six-shooter was straight out of a cowboy flick. It made me both eager and ill.

Russ sighed and looked the gun over. He took out a rag and wiped down the barrel and grip. I first thought he was cleaning it for me, then I realized he was rubbing out his prints.

"She's not registered," Russ said with a glance. "So it won't come back to me." He popped the cylinder and gave it a spin. "Course you can go down just for holding it."

I nodded and licked my lips. Righteous adrenaline flooded my veins. Russ finished his work and set the gun on the table, daring me to pick it up. "Think it through now, son."

I waited a beat then dove on the weapon. It was warm and weighty in my hands.

"It's beautiful," I said, losing myself in the polished steel.

"It's deadly," Russ said with a frown. "Maybe this is a bad idea..."

I clutched the gun to my chest like a treasure. "I'll have it back in a day or two."

"That's not the point."

"I need to get these possums."

"You trying to kill 'em?"

"Just give them a scare."

Big Russ nodded slowly and pursed his lips. "I heard what happened to Mouse."

I squeezed the Colt tighter at the sound of his name. Closed my eyes and let the rage run through me.

"Good kid," Russ went on. "I'm sure he wouldn't want you getting yourself in trouble."

Eyes still closed, I shook my head. The gun under my nose smelled like oil and ash.

The next morning, I hitched a ride to the oil fields with one of the men who still worked there. I told him I had a job interview, and he was nice enough not to ask me about missing school.

We pulled into a sprawling dirt lot with a few hundred cars. Bleary-eyed roughnecks downed cigarettes and coffee as they marched toward a cluster of trailers.

Which of these men left Mouse to die?

The revolver hung heavy in the back of my pants.

I slipped away from my ride and lost myself in the crowd. Listened to men grunt and fart and joke about their wives. Kept my eye out for a blue wagon.

"Hey kid, you lost?" Big, bearded fella hollering at me behind crooked teeth.

"Another redskin wandered off the Rez." A few men laughed and I cut a sharp left down a row of parked cars.

Blue wagon. Blue wagon. Blue wagon...

I prowled to the end of the line then back down the next row.

Blue wagon. Blue wagon. Blue wagon...

I took three passes before stumbling on it. A baby blue station wagon with rusted rims. The car sat crooked on a spare tire.

Really, Mouse?

I glanced around for watchers, but I was out at the edge of the lot. Hesitated a moment then tried the door.

Click.

Of course this idiot wouldn't lock his car. I slipped into the driver's seat and set the gun on my lap. The car smelled like cigarettes and mud.

What now?

My plan had been to camp out in the guy's car and surprise him. Pop up and flash steel until he shit his pants. Now I considered my options:

Steal the car? Burn it? Slash his tires? Cut his brakes?

Any one of these might have kept me out of trouble, but none would sate my rage. Mouse had nearly died. Used up and tossed like a piece of trash. Somewhere amidst all these drills and derricks was the culprit. I would make him pay.

So, I sat.

All day.

Nine hours.

I baked and brooded and fondled the gun. I rifled his glove box and peed on the floor. By the end I was dehydrated and delirious. Slipped into the back seat and crouched in my own piss.

At some point, a man climbed in front and started the car. He didn't notice me. Didn't notice the smell. He lit up a cigarette and hummed along to the radio. I let him get a few miles then I pounced.

"Don't move, faggot." I pressed the barrel of the revolver to the base of his skull. His eyes went wide in the mirror and he dropped the cigarette in his lap.

"Ow... shit. Ow!" He scrambled as the cig burned a hole in his pants. He lurched with the wheel and almost ran us off the road. Finally, he grabbed the butt and tossed it out the window.

"Easy, man," he said. "Just take my wallet. Take whatever."

He tried to get a look at me in the mirror, but I stayed low. Only let him see my eyes.

"Pull over in the next drive," I said. We were rolling through empty country, and I didn't know where he lived. If I was going to shoot the guy, I needed him to park the car.

"Who are you? What do you want?"

I jabbed the gun hard into the back of his neck. "I said: pull over." He cursed and coughed and turned into the mouth of a dirt drive. Car parked. Engine off. My moment of truth had arrived.

"You know why I'm here." Voice cold and detached. I fed off the rage and it felt right.

"I don't, really. I swear."

Another jab with the Peacemaker. "Take a guess, faggot."

"Are you..." he stammered. "Is this about... the kid?"

Waves of satisfaction rolled through me. I had the right man.

"I never meant for him to get hurt," he went on. "I told him to take it easy, but..."

"You left him for dead."

"I'm sorry..." Tears coming now. Sweat oozing from his scalp. "I panicked. I didn't know what to do."

"You could have helped him."

"I didn't know what to say..." He trembled and sobbed and I made sure he felt the gun against his skin. One quick pull could end it. "Please..." he carried on. "I was scared. I have a family."

"So did Mouse."

The man broke down and I felt no pity. He was the worst kind of scumbag. Fake-ass family man, cheating on his wife. Lying to his children. Lying to himself. He chased a secret fantasy that blew up in his face. Thought he could walk away.

"I'm sorry..." He whispered. "Is... is he dead?"

I felt a surge of revulsion. He didn't even know. I shook my head and blinked my eyes and let the rage take over. I screamed. I swung. I cracked the revolver against his skull. Again. And again. And again.

The man slumped over. Unconscious. Maybe dead. Blood flecked the windshield and bits of skin stuck to the gun. I stared at the weapon in my shaking hand and dropped it to the floor. I leaned back and let out a long breath. No going back.

I climbed out of the car and stretched my legs. It felt good to stand. Get the blood flowing. I looked around at the desolate country. My home, but not for long. I never even thought about running.

I flagged down a passing car.

The man didn't die. He suffered a fractured skull and brain bleed. His lawyer claimed he lost sight in one eye.

I pled guilty to aggravated assault and was sentenced to ten years. My mother wept at the courthouse. Sadness, confusion, and shame. I could barely meet her eyes, but she still threw me support.

"Be strong, Delsin," she called as the bailiff perp-walked me out. "Never forget who you are."

Who was I, though? Just a broken kid from a broken world. I tried to right things and made them worse.

The victim's family also came for the sentencing. Pretty wife and polished kids. They sat and stared daggers and I felt their hate.

I wasn't proud of what I did. It didn't help Mouse and it didn't help me. I'd hurt someone. Badly. Worst of all I was still angry, and I had ten years to ride that rage.

As I entered the system, my life was no longer my own. I was told when to eat, when to sleep, when to piss. A ward of the state. Shackles and cellblocks and long, dark nights.

I bounced around between cliques. The natives. The gays. I hit the weights and acted hard, but inside I was breaking down. I grew lonely and destitute. Prowled my cage and counted hours in the day.

I might have tried to end it. The thought crossed my mind. But at some point, my second year in, a hand reached out and plucked me from the darkness.

Her name was Dixie. A 250-pound prison guard from Tennessee. Dixie transferred to my block and immediately made her presence known.

"I'm not here to take shit from any of y'all." She strutted down the aisle, eyeballing every cell. "You won't be my first rodeo, but I can be your last." Dixie moved like a silverback. I'd never seen such swagger. She stopped in front of my cell and puffed out her ample chest. "I could kill a man with these," she said with a smirk. "Ain't as much fun as it sounds."

Dixie was that rare breed of hardass that genuinely cared. She was tough because she had to be, but she counseled cons and did favors and treated us with respect.

A few days on the job she popped my cell door and stepped inside. Sat down on my bed with a creak, the small cot straining under her mass. I didn't know what to say so I just stared at her a while. No one had taken personal interest in me for months.

"So, what's your story?" She finally blurted out.

"Uhh... my name's Del." I offered my hand. Dixie grabbed and shook and looked me in the eye.

"Where you from, Del?"

"Ki'sómma Sovereign Territory," I said. "Blackfeet Rez up north."

"Hmmm," she nodded. "You might be my first Blackfoot."

"There's a few of us in here."

"Well, I'm from Knoxville," Dixie said. "Smoky mountains." She looked around my sparse cell and rubbed her chin. "Dakotas seem nice, but it's shit cold."

I chuckled at that. "Wait until winter."

"You mean this ain't winter?" Her eyes bugged out and I chuckled again. It was October. We sat in silence for a moment and I ruminated on winters past. That brought back thoughts of family. Thoughts of Mouse.

"You want to know what I did?"

Dixie scoffed. "I don't care what you did." She leaned in close and dropped her voice. "When I was fifteen I broke my boyfriend's jaw with an ash tray." She grinned at the memory. "If he wasn't such a pussy, I'd be in here with y'all."

With that, she slapped me on the knee and stood. "Nice to meet you, Del." She stepped out of the cell and turned back. "Don't fuck around and we'll be all right." She locked up and walked off and I was alone again.

Dixie fast became a favorite on the block, and every few days she stopped by my cell for a chat. I still felt angry and hopeless, but her humanity slowly chipped away my shell.

One time she walked by to find me fuming. I'd just met with my lawyer who said our last appeal had been denied. It was official now. Ten years in, no way out. He urged me to stay straight for parole, but I couldn't see it. I was angry and desperate and looking to lash out.

"Del!" Dixie called as she watched me pace my cell. "What's got into you?"

I stomped and spit and smacked my hand against the bars. "Fucking lawyers!" I was out of options. Trapped.

"Heard that before," Dixie said. "What they get you on now?"

I kicked my cot and punched the wall. I was hurting myself more than the cell. "Out of appeals," I fumed. "Nine fucking years." That was the sentence I had left. "Nine fucking years!" I toppled a trash can and sat down in a huff.

"That's a long time," Dixie said. "Do you deserve it?"

That caught me off guard. I gave her a righteous glare like I'd been wounded, but she just looked back with honest eyes. We had a brief staring contest, then I dropped my head. "I don't know," I mumbled. "Probably."

Dixie nodded and leaned against the bars. She let the silence hang a while, left me alone with my thoughts. Finally, she said: "You know the difference between you and me, Del?"

"Is that a trick question?"

"Humor me."

I frowned and studied the plump female guard outside my cell. We were different in almost every way: Race, gender, birthplace, build. She was a world apart, but only one thing really mattered.

"The bars," I said. "You're on one side, I'm on the other."

Dixie nodded again. She drummed her fingers on the steel slats of my cage. "These bars bother you, don't they?"

"What do you think?"

"What if I told you it didn't have to be this way?"

"You gonna bust me out?"

"Not me, Del." She smiled and let that hang. What was she getting at? I stood and paced the cell again, lost in thoughts of escape.

"What would it feel like?" Dixie asked.

"Huh?"

"Freedom," she said. "How would that feel? To you?"

I closed my eyes and imagined myself just walking out. No more bars. No more cuffs. Just the sky overhead and the earth at my feet. I visualized getting into a car and driving off. Picking up Mouse and cruising to California. Starring in movies. Buying a home.

I lived in this scene for a while. Lost track of time. My breathing slowed and my body relaxed and I smiled without even meaning to. I finally opened my eyes to tell Dixie what I'd felt, but she was gone.

"Dixie?" I went to the bars and craned my neck but couldn't see her in either direction. How long had I been daydreaming? I sat back on the bed and slipped into the fantasy again. I felt the sun on my face. The wind in my hair. Mouse's hand in mine.

But then I opened my eyes and I was back in the cell. Cold concrete floor. Toilet by the bed. I could smell my own piss. I sighed and lay back and felt hopeless again. Nice trick Dixie pulled, but I was still doing nine years. I zoned out a while until I heard tapping outside. Dixie must be back. I sat up to confront the big guard but there was no one there.

"Dixie?"

The whole block was quiet, but this tiny sound: tap, tap, tap.

"Dixie?"

Tap, tap, tap.

What was that? I stood up from the bed and walked to the bars. Nothing. No one. Still, that sound: tap, tap, tap.

"Hello?"

Finally, I glanced down and there it was. A mouse. Small and brown and scratching the cell door at my feet.

"What the...?"

I'd never seen a mouse on the block before. I stared in wonder and it looked up at me, tiny paws tapping steel.

"Where did you come from?"

The little rodent squeaked and skittered back and forth. I grinned at his antics and looked around for something to offer. A few crumbs. A piece of food. I rifled through the trash on the floor and found a crust of three-day-old bread. I squatted down and the mouse munched for a few minutes while I lost myself again.

Thoughts of freedom. A life renewed.

The mouse polished off the last of the bread and chirped twice. It looked at me - fucking *looked* at me - then turned tail and darted off.

I watched it go and thought: Someday that will be me.

The next time Dixie came around I told her what had happened. My daydream. The mouse. She grinned and asked, "How did it feel?"

211

"It felt free," I said. "Liberating." Then reality crashed back and I frowned. "But I'm still in here." I kicked glumly at the bars.

"For now, yes. But not forever."

"Nine years might as well be."

"That's a long time," she nodded. "In nine years, that mouse will be dead."

"Is that supposed to make me feel better?"

"Does it?"

She stared me down with those earnest eyes. For a tough-talking prison guard, Dixie sure could make you think.

"Listen Del," she opened the door and sat down next to me on the bed. "There are things we can change, and things we can't. Your crime. That mouse. These bars." She paused to consider her words. "But you have more power than you think... Up here." She looked me in the eye and tapped me on the forehead. I wasn't sure what she was getting at, but I desperately wanted to believe.

"When I told you to feel free," she said, "You were free."

"I guess..."

"You felt it, right?"

I nodded.

"You experienced it?"

I shrugged.

"So, what's the difference?"

"I'm not free."

"But you felt it."

"But I'm not."

Dixie sighed and stood to face me. "I know it's hard..." She clicked her tongue and set hands on meaty hips. "But it's all in your mind, Del."

I opened my mouth to object again, but she cut me off. "No more excuses." The words came out steady and strong. "You want to be free? Master your mind."

"Master my mind..."

"Visualize your freedom. Meditate on it. Walk this block like a free man." She surveyed my unkempt compartment. "It's the one thing they can't take from you."

I nodded and listened as an inmate screamed obscenities somewhere down the block. Dixie rolled her eyes and set them back on me. "Most of the cons in here can't do it," she said. "Too stupid or stubborn." Something crashed down the hall and Dixie turned with a sigh. She exited the cell and stared me down once more. "But I believe in you."

I shrugged. "Master my mind?"

"Walk like a free man."

"And this cell won't bother me anymore?"

Dixie chuckled and slid the heavy door into place. "Delsin," she said, "If you really set your mind to it, you'll walk right through the fucking walls."

Chapter 39

Del sits back and sips his tea. He's attracted a small crowd of diner folk to hear his story. An elderly dame in a church hat pats his arm.

"Did you ever get back to Mouse?" she asks, dabbing a kerchief to one eye.

Del shakes his head. "I never set foot back on the Rez. Paroled after five years and I went straight into a halfway house."

"You never went back?" Patrick asks. "But you put yourself in prison for that kid."

Del shrugs. "I did what I did." He takes another sip of tea and studies the faces around him. "It was never really about Mouse. It was the hate that I carried. Dixie helped me see that."

Everyone's quiet a beat to soak that in. Carl chews a piece of toast and nudges his glasses up his nose. "Did you really walk through the walls?"

"In a sense," Del flashes a smile. "I did the work. I mastered my mind." He winks at the boy. "I read. I studied. I meditated. I prayed. I believed I was free, and one day I walked out."

"But it took four years."

"Real change takes time."

"How'd you get out early?" I ask.

Del turns grave and sets his face in a frown. "My mother died." He puts his teacup down and folds his hands. "I got that news and decided I was done. Six weeks later I made parole."

"Just like that?"

"Just like that."

I shake my head and look down at my lap. Del has everyone at a loss for words.

"I call bullshit."

Well, not everyone. A twentysomething kid with deep eyes and acne scars looks on from an adjacent table. "Story sounds fake to me." The assembled diners mutter disapproval, but the young man holds his chin out firm.

214

"Which part, son?" Del remains unflapped.

"All of it." The boy smirks and his tone turns sarcastic. "*Master your mind. Walk through the walls. I'm a queer Blackfoot.*"

Patrick rises to confront the young man, but Del stops him with an outstretched hand. He closes his eyes and the crowd looks on. After a moment, he smiles. "That's my story, son. Good luck writing your own."

The kid snorts and munches sausage with an open mouth. "Whatever, faggot."

More murmurs through the crowd. Patrick again tries to move on the boy and this time I stand to join him.

"Please," Del says, stopping us both in our tracks. "Let him be."

The old lady in the church hat stares daggers. "You need to learn respect, young man."

The boy chuckles and wipes crumbs off his chin. "You're all a bunch of faggots."

Gasps and glares and now the crowd is riled up. The kid stands like he's ready to fight them all.

"Is there a problem here?" Diner boss steps into the fray. He's got syrup stains on his blue tie.

"No problem, sir." Del rises to his feet. The boy takes it as a challenge and widens his stance.

"You wanna go?"

"Please gentlemen-"

"It's okay," Del spreads his arms and everyone hangs in the balance. Therese chews on a coffee stir. Church hat clutches her pearls.

"Del..." I whisper but he just closes his eyes. "We don't have time for this."

The young man whistles and taunts. "I'll lay you out, bitch." He cracks his knuckles and bobs on his feet. Del just stands like a statue.

One beat. Two.

Finally, he opens his eyes.

"I knew a lot of kids like you in prison," Del says. He takes a long sip of chamomile and looks down in his cup. "Most of them are still in there."

The boy blinks and frowns. He looks ready to retort, but then the fight fades out of him. He sits down and attacks a plate of pancakes instead.

The crowd melts away.

Patrick nods his head in admiration. He hands Therese cash for the meal, but she never takes her eyes off Del.

"That's one way to handle a bully," I say. Ol' Blackfoot never ceases to amaze. He turns to me with surprising intensity in his eyes.

"You were right," he says. "We don't have time for this." He puts a heavy hand on my good shoulder. "Let's go find Arden and Ash."

Ten minutes later, we pull into a nearby motel.

"I need a proper bed," Patrick says. "We all do."

No objections. We drove all night and slept shifts in the car.

"Let's get a couple of rooms," Patrick suggests. "Drive more this evening."

I study the small-town accommodations and consider our options. "You guys are heading to Ohio?"

Patrick nods. "We can take you as far as Dayton." He squints in the morning sunshine. "Assuming... that's where you want to go?"

I shrug and pull out a cigarette. A good smoke and pace will help me think. "Honestly," I light up with a laugh. "I have no fucking idea what we're doing." Patrick frowns but Carl grins at the swear. "Sorry kid."

I march a few strides across the lot then back toward the group. Smoke and pace.

"My wife is still missing." I smoke and I pace. "USAC hunting us down." Bax walks at my side for a lap then gives up. "We have no plan, no resources..." Smoke and pace. Smoke and pace. "We're up against an army and we have... what? One Voltstone left?"

Carl pulls the marbled rock out of his pocket and I'm relieved to see he still has it.

"We'll think of something," Del says. I keep pacing and keep smoking.

"What – in Ohio?" I gesture vaguely to the east. "Best guess: Ashley and Arden are in Montana somewhere."

"Why do you think that?" Patrick asks.

216

"Something the pilot said..." I think back on what Tuck told us about USAC Main. Running ops out of Billings, was it? What even happened to Tuck? I'm so fucking lost.

I finish my smoke but keep pacing. Light up another mid-stride. "We need to reach them somehow." I smoke and I pace and I spit and I think. "Ashley and Arden... Hobbes... Hell, if we could just make contact..."

I sit down on a parking block and nurse my cigarette. Baxter nuzzles my leg and I'm grateful for it.

"Why don't you call them?" Carl offers. I study the boy like he's simple, but his eyes are sincere.

"We're on the run, kid." I shake my head and tap my cig. "We shook USAC once. Can't give ourselves away without a plan."

Carl nods. "What if you don't have to?" He pulls out his smartphone and putters around on the screen. "Make a VOIP call." He offers the device, but I just stare dumbly.

"A what?"

"Voice over IP," Carl says. "It's like a phone call using the internet."

I frown and consider. "Can't they still track that?"

"Not with a VPN." Carl swipes some more and pulls up another app that I find similarly inscrutable. "Virtual Private Network. You route your traffic through a proxy server to make it look like you're logged in someplace else."

I glance at Del and he shrugs. Patrick looks on with a hint of pride. "How do you know this stuff, kid?"

Carl grins ear to ear. "I watch a lot of gaming streams. Korea. Singapore. Japan. VPN helps me get around the geo-blocks."

I stub out my cigarette and consider lighting a third. Climb to my feet and resume pacing. "So, you're saying..." I piece things together as I walk... "We could use your phone to make an untraceable internet call?"

"Exactly!" Carl stands tall and fixes his specs. Maybe he's on to something.

"But who would we call?" Del asks. "I doubt USAC is in the phone book."

"No, but *Cygneous* is. Hobbes' umbrella company."

We all stare at each other while Carl bobs on his toes. He rummages through the touchscreen and offers it to me a third time. "*Cygneous Client Services*. Got a number right here."

I take a long, deep breath. Sure would be nice to hear Ashely's voice. Or at least parlay with Hobbes. "I guess it's worth a shot."

"Fuck yeah!"

"Carl!"

"Sorry, Dad."

That's probably my fault.

"Let's get some rooms," I say. "Everybody shower and clean up. We meet in an hour and make the call."

Patrick goes in to book the rooms because he's the only one with cash. Carl fiddles with the phone while Del unloads the car.

I light up another cigarette.

Smoke and pace.

Chapter 40

"You sure about this?"

I sit across form Carl on a thick motel mattress, staring at his blinking phone.

"I'm using a VPN app to route our connection through Kansas City," Carl says. "Even if *Cygneous* tracks inbound calls, our location and IP address will be encrypted."

"Why Kansas City?"

Carl shrugs. "Make them think we headed south? It's close enough to be believable but far enough not to give us away."

I turn to Patrick with eyebrows raised. "This kid is ten?"

"I don't know where he gets it. You can thank my mom for the phone."

Happy birthday, kid.

Del sits on a pillow by the mini fridge, Baxter curled at his side. "So, what's the plan?" he asks. "We call the main line, ask for Ashley and Arden?"

"Good question. Maybe we can get through to Hobbes somehow. Make him deal with us directly."

"The billionaire CEO?"

"You got a better idea?"

Patrick sits across from us and scribbles on a motel notepad. "What's our leverage?" He asks. "We'll probably have to work up the chain."

I gesture to Carl. "Still got that stone, kid?" He pulls the blue-green marble from his pocket and sets it by the phone. It practically glows against the dingy motel bedsheet. "This is our leverage."

"One Voltstone?"

"Hobbes doesn't know how many we have. Tell him we've got ten."

"The stones don't really matter," Del says. "We have the truth." He pets the dog and stares into space. I sense new resolve in my Blackfoot friend. Maybe dredging up Mouse's memory lit a fire.

"We have the truth, and he has our spouses."

Patrick nods, focused. Carl looks on for my signal. I take a deep breath.

Any advice here, Pops?

Don't let them push you around.

I just want Ashley back.

Then stay on that phone until you've heard her voice.

I'll try.

You remember how we break a wild bull, son?

Sate him with food.

Good. What else?

Talk to him. Calm and confident.

Then what?

Let him lead himself into the pen.

Go get 'em, cowboy.

"Hit it, Carl."

The boy nods and taps the screen. He puts the phone on speaker and we listen to it ring.

"*Cygneous* Client Services. How may I direct your call?" Young male voice. Midwestern drawl.

"I'd like to speak with Oliver Hobbes."

"Mr. Hobbes doesn't take unsolicited calls. Can I connect you with another department?"

"I need Hobbes," I say. Glance around the room for reassurance. "Or someone high up at USAC."

Slight hesitation. Tapping on a keyboard.

"We have no department by that name, sir. Perhaps you've reached the wrong organization."

I exhale and lean over the phone. Don't give in to the runaround. "Hobbes and I need to parley. He knows what it's about."

The young receptionist sighs. "Sir, this is an engineering firm, unless you have-"

"Listen, kid." I cut him off. "I'm not here to waste your time, so don't waste mine." Carl glares down at the phone. Baxter perks up at my tone. "I've got business with Oliver Hobbes. If you can't help me, put on someone who can."

A quiet grumble and more tapping. Patrick nods encouragement and scribbles on his pad. The voice on the phone comes back curt and cold. "One moment, please." Cut to muzak. I let out a breath.

"You're doing good," Del says. He strokes Baxter who lays his head on Del's knee. Thirty seconds later the muzak drops and a new voice picks up.

"*Cygneous* Client Services, Communications Department. How can I help you?" Female this time. Warm and friendly. Play nice.

"Yes, I'd like to speak with Mr. Oliver Hobbes. Can you connect me through?"

"Mmmm hmmm. And what is this regarding?"

I turn to Carl and he shrugs. Patrick scribbles something on his pad and holds it up. One word: *Investment.*

"Yeah, I'm... looking to make an investment in one of *Cygneous'* technologies."

"I see..." Hint of condescension. I don't think she buys it. "Why don't I connect you with the finance department?"

Patrick shakes his head.

"No thank you, ma'am. I need to deal with Hobbes directly."

"Mr. Hobbes is very busy." I hear idle tapping on a keyboard. "Let me put you through to the sales team."

"No, wait..." This isn't getting anywhere. Quit beating around the bush. "Put me through to Oliver Hobbes. Tell him Clay Moore has his Voltstone."

This brings a pause. The tapping stops. I almost think the line went dead until the woman's voice comes back. "Is this some kind of prank?" Her tone has changed. Conspiratorial and low.

"No prank, ma'am. I got business. Get me Hobbes."

Muttering and shuffling. "Please hold." More muzak. I sit back and exhale again.

"Climb the ladder," Patrick says with a thumbs up.

"That Voltstone comment got her attention," says Del.

"Cat's out of the bag now."

We sit in silence for a few minutes as the muzak drones on. I start to wonder if we may actually get to Hobbes this time.

Calm and confident. Let the bull lead himself in.

Finally, a voice comes back on the line. Professional. Dispassionate.

"Mr. Moore."

"Hobbes?"

"Mr. Hobbes is very busy. I speak on his behalf. Call me Charles."

"You know what this is about, Charles?"

"I do, Mr. Moore. You've stolen some of our property."

That's rich.

"Your goons kidnapped my wife."

"Your wife is being detained for violation of the Strategic Interest Initiative 2006.4.18."

"Bullshit."

"She's also under investigation in the death of Private Stephanie Kirby, United States Asset Command."

"Kirby was killed by a wolf."

"That investigation is ongoing."

Patrick holds up the notepad: *He's trying to scare you. Stay focused.* I nod my head and let out a breath.

"I want to speak with Ashley."

"I'm afraid that's not possible."

"Where is she?"

"Your wife is in a secure facility commensurate with the charges against her."

"What about Arden?"

"Mr. Horne is in the same facility, facing the same charges."

"Arden was shot..." I glance at Del. Face blank but eyes intense. "What's his condition?"

"Mr. Horne is stable. He's been treated for his injuries and monitored by medical staff." A chuckle through the phone. Almost taunting. "We're not barbarians, Mr. Moore. The prisoners are being cared for, but they remain our prisoners."

Prisoners. My wife. I fumble for a cigarette and light up with shaky hands.

"I want to talk to Ashley."

"I'm afraid that's not possible."

"Put her on the phone."

"I can't do that."

"Then put Hobbes on the phone."

"I can't do that either."

I grunt and spit smoke. Fuck this guy. Patrick holds up the pad with a new scribble: *Voltstone.*

"You're not leaving me many options here, Charles."

"You don't have any options, Mr. Moore."

"I've got one..." I lift the stone off the bed and study its blue-green swirls. "I'll go public." Heads bob around the room. "Tell the world what you're up to."

"The law is on our side here, Mr. Moore." Charles' voice stays emotionless and flat. "Theft. Conspiracy. Homicide. You'll all have your day in court."

"I'll go public with the stones," I barrel on. "Live demo on the six o-clock news. Tune in and watch your empire crumble."

A pause.

"That would be unwise, Mr. Moore."

Now I pause. Let him hang a bit. Patrick scribbles on his pad then flashes a new suggestion: *We have a buyer.* I nod and say nothing. Charles presses again.

"Mr. Moore?"

"Sorry, Charles. Got a buyer on the other line. Is fifty grand a fair price for ten Voltstones? What do you guys usually charge?"

Carl snickers and covers his mouth. I tap my cig into an empty cup.

"You're going to sell the stones?" Charles asks.

"Only if the demo goes well. My buyer needs to see they're legit. I guess we'll find out tonight, huh?"

More silence. I'm bluffing my ass off.

"You're playing a dangerous game, Mr. Moore."

"Put my wife on the phone."

Muffled silence. Conferring behind the scenes. Carl nods. Patrick scribbles. Del runs his hand through Baxter's fur.

"If I let you speak with your wife, you won't pull this stunt on the news."

"Put her on and let's find out."

"We need assurances, Mr. Moore."

"I assure you that if I don't hear Ashley's voice soon, this shit goes viral by the end of the day."

A sigh. A click. Did he hang up? I look around the room. Patrick shrugs. Del raises a hand. The line hangs empty. No dial tone. No muzak. A minute passes. Two. And then...

"Clayton?" Shaky and soft. My wife.

"Ashley!" Emotions flood and my eyes go to glass. Tears. Shakes. Shock. Relief. "Are you okay?"

"Oh, Boo..." It's Ashley all right. Her voice sounds tinny and small. Something rumbles in the background. Indistinct shouts. "Are you safe?" she asks.

"We're good," I say. "Del and I got out. We're with friends."

"Thank God..." She sounds distracted. Unsure. My shoulder starts to throb. "Stay away, Boo..." she whispers, almost breathless. "Don't let them catch you."

"Ashley, what's wrong? Have they hurt you?" Anger flares and I want to punch the phone.

"It's not that..." Barely a whisper. "They'll kill you, Clay." She means it. She's scared.

"They already tried. In the valley. In the woods."

"They won't stop."

"I'll come for you."

"Oh, Boo..." She breaks down into tears.

"Ashley..." I want to hug her so bad. "Ashley, it's okay. I'm fine. We'll get through this."

"You don't understand..." She shudders and sobs. Sniffle. Snort. "Hobbes wants you *dead*." A harsh whisper. Heavy breaths. "You have to *run*, Clay."

"We've been running." I glance around the room. Del looks solemn. Carl looks scared. "We're coming for you, Ashley. I promise."

"Please, Clay..." She sounds broken and frail. Like I've never heard before. "Just disappear for a while. Don't worry about me."

"*Don't worry about you?*" I almost laugh. I almost puke. Then something new takes hold. A flush in my veins. Maybe it's hate. Maybe it's love. I lift the phone off the bed and speak straight into the mic.

"Listen to me, Ash." Silence. She's listening.

"For thirteen years you've been my rock. Fuckin' granite, baby. Foundation of my world."

I close my eyes and picture Ashley at my side. I can feel her. Like she's here.

"I am what I am because of you. I was a slapdick ranch boy, and now I'm a man. You're stronger than me. Smarter than me. You're my soldier and my lover and my saint."

Faint sobs over the line, but I push on. Don't know when I'll get this chance again.

"Nothing scares me anymore, Ash. Not Hobbes and his army. Not *Cygneous* and their stones. I've been blown up and beat down and chased by a goddamn bear. I swam through a cave. Walked through a twister. I watched a man bring a baby back to life."

I glance at Patrick and he stares back. Notepad in his lap. Fire in his eyes.

"And through it all - through every last goddamn thing... I thought of you. Your smile. Your smell. Your voice in my ear. We're one, you and me. Twin flames on the same candle. Two sides of the same coin."

I don't know where I'm getting these words, but when I see Del smiling I know they're all right.

"I'm coming for you, now. I've got Del and Baxter and we're coming. Patrick and Carl and this Old ass Man. Let Arden know. Let everybody know. We're coming."

Patrick nods. Baxter barks. I feel electric. Alive.

"Nothing can stop this, Ashley. I'll walk through fucking fire if I have to." I blink away tears. "You know that."

I pause. She whispers. "I know, Clay..."

"I love you."

"Thank you, Boo."

"Keep your head up."

"I'm trying."

A gulp and a huff. Ashley gathers herself. When she speaks again her voice is stronger.

"Come and find me, Clay Moore."

"If it's the last thing I do."

She chuckles. I smile.

"I miss you," she says. Then her voice drops again. "They're afraid of you, Clay. Afraid of what you know."

"I just want you back."

"Just be careful..." A pause and a breath. Muffled noises on the line. Then a whisper. "Get wise, Clay."

"Get what?"

"Get wise."

"Wise is more of your thing, Ash."

"You need the help. Trust me."

"I'm not sure I understand."

"Just go get *wise*... You'll figure it out." Another pause. Heavy breaths. "I can't say more."

"Okay."

A long sigh. "It's good to hear your voice."

"You too, babe."

"I tried to be strong, but..." Her words come fast and clipped. "You and Del went out that door... I didn't know... Arden and Kirby... So much blood... USAC came in with guns drawn... I thought they would kill us."

I shudder and pinch out my cig. My girl's been through it. Someone's going to pay.

"How'd you get this number, Clay?"

"Persistence." I smile at Carl. "And some help from new friends."

"Please be careful."

"I've tamed bigger bulls."

Another chuckle. At least I got her smiling.

"Thanks for calling, Clay."

"Tell Arden to be strong."

Ashley snorts. "Arden's a fucking horse."

I smile at Del. "Ain't that the truth."

"Time's up." A new voice on the line.

"Get wise, Clay..." Last thing I hear then Ashley's gone. I zone out for a moment then realize someone is still talking.

"Mr. Moore?"

"Charles?"

"This is Oliver Hobbes."

Woah.

"Inspiring speech, Mr. Moore." There's an edge to Hobbes' voice. It brings nervous looks around the room.

"You heard all that, huh?"

"I heard enough."

"Well, I meant everything I said."

"I'm sure you did."

Silence. Something's off. Maybe he's trying to stall me? Trace the call?

"I want my wife back, Hobbes."

"We all want things, Mr. Moore."

"This isn't that complicated."

"Oh, it's *very* complicated."

More silence. Like he's playing with me. I look to Patrick and he shrugs. Carl shrinks back like Hobbes might reach through the phone.

"Let's make a deal, then."

"You have nothing to offer."

"I have your stones. I know your secrets."

"That's precisely why we can't negotiate."

"I don't understand."

"Of course, you don't."

What is he getting at? My high melts away. He's pushed me off my game.

That's his style, son. Tame the bull.

"What do you want, sir?"

"Truthfully? I want you all dead."

"Excuse me?"

"You, Clay Moore. Your wife. Your friends. I want you dead and buried. It's the only way."

Del frowns. Carl gasps. I blubber my words. "Th- that seems extreme..."

Another sigh. Like he's bored with me. "That's the game you're playing."

I take a deep breath. I don't know what to say.

"Tell me, Mr. Moore, had you heard of Voltstone before?"

"What do you mean?"

"I mean before all this. Before you boarded my plane and stole my property. Did you know of these electric stones?"

"I did not."

"And why do you think that is?"

Feed him, son.

"Because you keep them secret."

"Not just me," Hobbes replies. "Me and *Cygneous*. Me and my army." He chuckles, like the thought delights him. "A lot of people are willing to do a lot of things to protect what we've built."

I ponder the stakes. "That's why you bombed my valley."

"That's why we do *everything*, Mr. Moore." His voice turns hostile. Threatening. "We've waged wars to stop people like you. Burned cities to the ground."

"For some stones?"

"Not just stones..." His voice slows down. "The world order is at stake."

I take a deep breath. This is over my head.

Let him lead himself in.

"So, where do we go from here?"

Hobbes doesn't respond. I hear voices and shuffling, like he's getting pulled away.

"I have to go, Mr. Moore."

"Wait, what? Let's make a deal."

"You have nothing to offer."

"But what about Arshley... I mean Arden... I mean...?" My mind is a blur. This isn't working.

"Bring me the pilot." Hobbes' words are cold and abrupt.

"The pilot?" Does he mean Tuck? Last I saw he disappeared out Del's door with a shotgun. Does Hobbes think he's with us?

"I'll be in Pittsburgh in three days. Meet me at the Allegheny Convention Center. Bring the pilot and the stones."

"But I don't-"

"Three days, Mr. Moore."

My thoughts spin in circles. "But what about Ashley?"

"I'll bring the prisoners to Pittsburgh. Meet my terms or everyone dies."

"Sir, you can't..."

"I can and I will. This is not a negotiation. It's a promise."

My gut goes weak. Head feels faint. I want to scream and curse and run.

"I'll be there, but-"

"No *buts*, Mr. Moore. Be there or your wife is dead."

"Sir, please-"

"Dead."

Hobbes ends the call.

Part VI

Get Wise

Chapter 41

"Ugggh..."

I hang my head and stare at dingy motel carpet. Del rubs my back while Baxter licks my hand. I'm shook. We're all shook. Carl is wobbly and pale. Patrick looks like he could puke.

"I'm sorry, guys..."

They didn't sign up for this. Hobbes just threatened everyone's life. He promised to kill Ashley and demanded I bring him Tuck. Fucking Tuck?

"Who is this pilot?" Patrick finally asks.

"The guy that started all this." I sigh and lift my head. Somber eyes around the room. "He landed his plane in my valley three nights ago. Followed us to Del's place in the woods but split with USAC bearing down."

"Do you think he got off the mountain?" Del asks.

"Who knows..." I shake my head. "Hobbes must think he's with us, but Tuck could be anywhere." I look to Patrick and shrug. "Wyoming... Canada... Might as well be on the moon."

Patrick nods. He understands the stakes. "I'm sorry, Clay."

"Fucking hell..." I feel lost again. No way we'll find Tuck. So how to get Ashley back?

Get wise, Clay.

What did she mean by that? She wants me to be wiser, but I can't think my way out of this. Hell, Ashley's twice as smart as I am. And she's still only half as smart as...

"That's it!" I pop up and startle the room. "Sage!"

"What now?" Carl asks.

"Ashley's sister, Sage. That's what she must have meant by, *Get wise.*" It's something at least. A place to start. "Sage has a PhD in astrophysics. She's the smartest cat I've ever met."

Patrick nods slowly. "So, where's Sage?"

"Columbus, Ohio." I marvel at the thought. "We're already heading that way. Then Hobbes wants to meet in Pittsburgh..."

I look to Del and he smiles. "The Old Man guides our path."

"You're telling me."

I'm still scared for Ashley, but I push it from my mind. What choice do I have? If we can get to Sage, maybe she can help. Help us find Tuck, or rescue Ash, or fucking murder Hobbes.

I turn to Patrick. "Can you take us to Columbus? Get us to Ashley's sister then you can wash your hands of this whole thing."

Patrick gulps. He doesn't look convinced. "What are the odds Hobbes leaves Carl and I alone?"

I don't know what to say so I just look at the floor. The room is quiet and still. I feel like shit for getting Patrick and his son involved. Hell, Delsin too. None of these folks deserve the trouble. They'd all be safe at home if not for me.

It ain't on you, kid.

I don't even know anymore, Pops.

Just keep trying to do the right thing.

And what's the right thing here? Assuming I could even find Tuck, how would I turn him over to Hobbes?

Suddenly, Baxter starts barking. Full-throated fury.

"What is it boy?" I grab his collar but that just riles him up more. He jumps and pulls and woofs and wails. Finally, I let him go. "Baxter!" He bounds to the door. Yapping his ass off. Is somebody outside?

I wave to Carl and he moves behind his father. Del steps to my side and we face the door.

"Anyone out there?" No answer, but Bax keeps barking like he's on fire. Is it the cops? USAC? Maybe Hobbes bluffed long enough to trace the call.

Shit. Shit. Shit. Can't we catch a break?

I clench my teeth and scan the room for a weapon. Lavigne took our pistol. Even the TV's bolted down. Not like it matters if we're facing live soldiers out there.

I turn to Del and shrug. He leans to the peephole and gasps. "What is it?"

Del waves me back. I try to pull Baxter but he's still going nuts, claws scrabbling against the floor.

I step aside and let come what may.

Del throws open the door.

The first thing I see is a shotgun.
The second is Tuck.

Chapter 42

Tuck charges through the door and slams it shut behind him. Before anyone can react, Baxter pounces and all hell breaks loose.

"Get him off me!" The pilot yells. He swings his shotgun like a club, and I lurch back and forth to avoid the barrel.

Carl screams. Patrick throws him to the floor and dives onto his son. I try to control Baxter as Del grabs for Tuck.

"Tuck! What are you-"

"Call off your dog!"

"Baxter!"

Ol' hound won't listen. He's out for blood. These two have history.

"Baxter!"

I need to get him under control before someone gets shot. Tuck kicks wildly and flails with his shotgun. Is it loaded? I don't want to know.

"Baxter!"

I grapple in the scrum and feel my shoulder wrench. Not again...

"Baxter! Heel!" I put something different into my voice. My own balls and business. Bax hesitates and gives me a look. "Sit! Now!"

He growls at Tuck but backs off. Tuck scrambles to his feet and trains the shotgun on my dog.

"No." I step in front of the barrel.

"Your dog is fucking crazy!"

I stand my ground. Done letting assholes hurt the ones I love.

We stare each other down as Baxter barks away behind me. Tuck looks haggard and spent. He wears the same tattered flight suit and has scratches all over his face. His hand is still wrapped from where Ashley took a chunk.

"Enough." Del steps in and puts a hand on the gun. Tuck turns like he's seeing him for the first time. He finally shakes his head and drops the weapon to the floor. He lets out a long breath and all but deflates onto the bed.

"It's okay," I motion to Patrick and Carl. They stagger to unsteady feet as Patrick maintains a shield in front of his son.

"What the hell, Clay?"

"Patrick, Carl..." I shrug toward the bed. "This is Tuck."

"The pilot?"

"One and the same."

Patrick stares in disbelief. "But how...?"

"That's a great question." I turn to the panting pilot. "How'd you find us here, Tuck?"

He holds up a hand, still catching his breath. "I followed you," he says between heaves.

"Followed us? From Wyoming?" Del and I exchange skeptical looks.

"I know it sounds crazy..." Tuck tries to stand but sits back down with a wince. He curses quietly and rubs his knee. Patrick shuffles over and picks up the shotgun.

"What the hell, Tuck?" I can't believe I'm looking at this guy. We left him on a hilltop eight hundred miles away. Then he shows up at our door? Five minutes after Hobbes' ultimatum?

Shit.

It's a trap.

I walk to the window and peek out through the blinds. The motel lot is quiet, but something feels off. I pop the door and look around. There's a windowless van across the street. USAC? I shut the door and throw the bolt.

"Relax, Clay."

I march over to Patrick and take the shotgun. Check the chamber and count two fresh shells.

"I'm here alone, I swear."

"Bullshit." I walk back to Tuck and stick the barrel in his face. "How did you find us?"

He shrugs. "It was an accident."

"Bullshit." The gun feels cold and wicked in my hand. Would I kill this man? I need him to get to Ashley. But he could already be working with Hobbes...

"Start talking."

"You won't shoot me."

"Start talking!"

235

Tuck grins. I remember that snarky smile. "You're not a violent person, Clay. Now your wife on the other hand..."

I swing the barrel and connect with his head. Steel meets skull.

Tuck groans and goes down in a heap. Carl screams. Del steps up and puts a hand on my shoulder. "Please don't."

The heavy gun trembles in my hand. What did I just do?

Tuck moans and rolls around on the bed. He's conscious, but barely. Bleeding from his ear. Carl is crying. Patrick looks like he's ready to bolt.

Del reaches for the gun and I let him have it. I feel clammy all over. Need a cigarette.

Without a word I step outside and slam the door. Let them sort it out.

I smoke and I pace and await the USAC ambush. An old lady gets into the van across the street and drives away. Am I being too paranoid here?

The pressure's getting to you, son.

This is crazy, Pops.

You need to keep your cool.

Hobbes wants to kill Ashley. To kill all of us! Then Tuck just shows up out of nowhere...

I take a deep drag and let it out slow. Pops is right. I have to stay cool. Focus on getting to Ash.

I finish the smoke and take a breath of clean air. My shoulder feels loose but intact. That's a win, I guess. Also, nobody jumped me yet. Maybe Tuck is telling the truth. I hope I didn't hurt him too badly...

I shake my head and feel kinship with my wife. When Ashley met Tuck, she did the same thing. Clocked him out cold that first night in the valley, then blew off his finger the next day. Something about this guy just pushes our buttons.

I step back into the room and Baxter greets me like it's been years. "Easy boy..."

Del sits on the bed and holds a bloody towel to Tuck's head.

"He gonna be all right?"

"We need some ice," Del says.

Tuck glares at me but says nothing. I turn to Carl who looks like he could curl up into a ball.

"Why don't you fetch some ice, son?"

Carl looks to his father who nods and takes his hand. Patrick grabs the bucket and they slip together out the door.

"I'm sorry I hit you."

No one says anything. Tuck won't even look at me.

"Keep my wife's name out of your mouth."

Tuck sighs and slowly nods. "Where is she?"

"Detained by USAC. Arden too. We're working to get them back."

"You got a plan?"

"Not really. We just talked to Hobbes and he said-"

"You talked to Hobbes?" Tuck bolts upright and looks around. "Where? How?"

"On the phone," I say. "Carl made an encrypted call."

Tuck goes pale like he's seen a ghost. Could also be blood loss. Del coaxes him back down onto a pillow and presses a clean towel against his head.

"You can't negotiate with Hobbes," Tuck says, studying the ceiling. "He'll kill us all before making a deal."

"He suggested as much."

"He means it." Tuck sits up again and stares me down. "I've seen it." He narrows his eyes. "Your wife has seen it."

I nod and look down at my boots. The room is quiet and we all startle when Carl comes back with the ice. Del wraps a new compress and Carl huddles with his dad.

"Hobbes said to meet him in Pittsburgh. First I want to stop in Columbus and see a friend."

"What's in Pittsburgh?"

"Not sure. Hobbes said he would be there in three days, and that we should bring..." I trail off.

"Bring what?"

Nobody says anything. Tuck seems to figure it out.

"Bring me," he says. Voice flat and unsurprised.

Again, no one responds. Tuck sighs. He looks like hell. Bandaged hand. Crooked knee. Dented skull.

"I never thought we'd see you again, Tuck."

He grins. "Not so easy to get rid of me."

"How'd you get away from USAC?"

He grins even wider. "I stole a bird."

"You what?"

Tuck sits up and waves Delsin off. His head has stopped bleeding, but he's still wobbly and pale. I offer some water and he chugs it. Offer a cigarette and takes that too.

"When Kirby went down, I panicked." Tuck stares off and smokes slow. "I thought we'd all die on that hill."

I think back to the chaos in Del's home. Kirby shot Arden then Kali went at her. Ripped the poor girl's throat out. USAC would have stormed in to see one of their own dead on the floor. No wonder Tuck ran.

"I figured my best chance was to go it alone. But I ran uphill instead of down. Thought that might throw off any tail."

Del and I had worked our way downslope to the cave. I remember we passed a few commandoes along the way.

"USAC was everywhere though," Tuck says. "I heard choppers and shouts and thought for sure I was toast." He stares off through the smoky haze. "I freaked and dove into this little hollow. Buried myself in brush and didn't move for hours."

I picture Tuck curled up in some thorny nook, covered in spiders.

"Twice I heard them get close. I'm talking feet away. I had the shotgun ready and it's a miracle nobody died."

Tuck takes a drag and breaks his thousand-yard stare. Looks right at me.

"I moved when it got dark," he says. "Hadn't heard anyone for an hour and I was soaking in my own piss. I kept pushing uphill but everything hurt. Especially my knee. I was stumbling blind and afraid for my life. Finally, I reached this clearing on the peak. Top of the fucking mountain, there's a goddamn helicopter."

"I've been up there," Del says. "Arden calls it Bald Crown."

"Well, whatever you guys call it, USAC landed a chopper in the gap. Left one man guarding it and I put a slug in his leg."

"Jesus, Tuck."

He waves me off. "I did what I had to, Clay. You need to be prepared to do the same."

I frown and think on this. Could I really shoot a man? If my life depended on it?

"Your wife would do it," Tuck says. "Hell, she *has* done it. And before you go jumping on me let me finish my story."

It stings but he's right. I suppose I'd pull a trigger for Ashley. That's the only way.

"So I climb in behind the stick, but I've never flown a helicopter before. I've got five-thousand hours in fixed-wing aircraft." He sighs and runs a hand over short hair. "I did some runs in a sim way back, but no nighttime takeoffs." He flashes a cocky smile. "Almost clipped a skid but I got her up."

"You must be some pilot, Tuck."

"I've been around..." He pauses, considering. "It was dicey though. Choppers climb fast but everything's in flux. Roll, pitch, yaw... I was lurching like a drunk." He shakes his head and stubs out the cig. "I can fly planes in my sleep. Just point and shoot. That helo made me fight for every inch."

"You got out though."

"I did. Climbed to three thousand feet and turned north. Figured I'd push for Canada."

"In a USAC aircraft? Seems like they'd be all over you."

"No doubt," Tuck says. "But when I turned on the radio, they were talking about you boys instead. Whole USAC band was buzzing about this jailhouse in Willow."

I nod. "We got pulled over. Local cop hauled me in on a gun charge."

"Awww, Clay. You're better than that." Tuck squints at me. "But when I heard you were out there, something just... came over me." He sits back, face turning serious. "I couldn't believe anyone else got off the mountain. Y'all had USAC tripping over themselves. Made me want to come help."

"Why risk yourself for us?"

Tuck shrugs. "Hobbes will hunt me forever. I can't go back to *Cygneous*." He looks down at his bandaged hand. "In a weird way, you folks are all I got."

He sounds sincere, but I've still got questions.

"But we never saw you in Willow. How the hell'd you find us in Iowa?"

He chuckles. "You won't believe this shit." Quick glance around the room. "I started flying down to Willow when I ran into weather. Crazy storm. Supercell as big as the county."

"Yeah, we had a tornado on the ground."

"I believe it," Tuck says. "I was already over my head, and it started raining sideways. Had to put her down in a field. Thank God it was so flat."

I think back to our trek around the jailhouse. We could barely keep our feet in those winds, I can't imagine flying through them.

"It was a rough landing," Tuck says, reading my thoughts. "Put the bird out of commission so I walked to the nearest road. Waited in the rain with my thumb out but no one came by. Fucking Wyoming."

"You hitched a ride?"

"Tried to. But it was the middle of nowhere. Decided to walk east, staggering through this downpour. Eventually I came across a car on the shoulder. Blue Mercedes. Ohio plates. Seemed out of place, but the doors were unlocked and I wanted out of the hail."

"You sheltered in our car?" Patrick looks aghast. Like he's been violated.

"Any port in a storm," Tuck shrugs. "When the rain finally let up, I saw police lights coming down the road." He snorts a laugh. "I kind of panicked and jumped in the trunk."

"You didn't."

Tuck just smiles and nods. Patrick looks confused.

"All the way from Willow?"

"At least I got some sleep."

"No fucking way," Patrick says. A rare curse from him.

Tuck stretches out on the bed. "I'm a short guy, so it could have been worse." He smiles at Patrick. "Thanks for packing light."

I shake my head. "Jesus, Tuck."

"You don't believe me, do you?"

"I don't know what to believe." We drove all night. Eight hundred miles.

"I believe him," Carl chimes in. Tuck turns to the boy as if registering him for the first time. "I heard something," Carl says, "Last night while Del was driving and everyone else was asleep." He looks at his father, a little uncertain. "It was like a shuffling in the trunk. But I never said anything because I wasn't sure."

Tuck smiles. "Good ears, kid."

I never heard shit, but I remember Baxter growling when we got back to the car. Probably smelled Tuck the whole time. Can't fool a bloodhound.

"Well hell, Tuck..." I let out a long sigh. "I don't even know what to say."

"Don't say anything, Clay Moore." He smiles and sinks into the pillow. "I'm here now, and I'm going to help you take down Oliver Hobbes."

"I just want Ashley back."

"We'll do that too." He closes his eyes and I study faces around the room. Del offers a smile and a shrug. Carl seems contemplative. Patrick just looks drained.

"Maybe we all need some shut-eye," I offer. Patrick nods wearily and ushers his son out the door. Del stretches out on the floor and motions me to take the bed.

Tuck is already snoring. He smells like blood, sweat, and piss. I curl up next to him and sleep like I'm dead.

Chapter 43

I wake to a dark room. Alone. How long did I sleep?

I ease up in bed and rub my eyes. My shoulder feels better. Everything feels better. I check the bathroom door and find it locked.

Knock, knock. "Hello?"

Shower running. Muffled singing. Rumpled flight suit on the floor.

I step outside where it's humid and warm. Twilit sky. Summer stars. I light up a smoke and take a few minutes' peace.

My mind feels light. Music floats out an open door. Children crowd an ice cream shop across the street.

This is nice.

Small town America.

I've spent so much time in our lonely valley, I forget how soothing society can be.

A bark breaks my daydream and here comes my dog. I smile as Baxter runs over and Del follows behind. "We took a walk," he says. He looks clean and refreshed and holds a bag full of clothes. "Found a thrift store down the street." He primps the collar on a beige Oxford. "Grabbed some things for you and Tuck."

As if on cue, our room door opens and Tuck steps out. He's naked but for a white motel towel around his waist.

"Best shower I've ever had."

"How about some new clothes?"

"Fuckin' A!"

Tuck gestures for a cigarette and I light him up. He stands a head shorter than Del but sports a muscular physique. Not big, but fit. A trim pilot's build. His knee is visibly swollen and his hand needs redressed. Still smokes with a smile.

"So, what's the plan, boys?"

I shrug. "For now? Drive east. I want to see Sage in Columbus. Hobbes said to meet him in Pittsburgh in three days."

Tuck nods and crosses his arms. "Hobbes is full of shit."

"I don't trust him either, but-"

242

"He'll lead us right into an ambush. Whatever's in Pittsburgh, it won't be good."

"He said he would bring Ashley and Arden."

"I bet he did."

I frown. "So, what do you propose?"

Tuck dribbles smoke out of his mouth and sucks it back in through his nose. "We need to expose him. Blow the lid off the whole thing."

"You mean Voltstone?"

"Voltstone. *Cygneous.* USAC. All of it."

"And what about Ashley and Ard?"

"All of it," Tuck repeats. He flicks his still burning cigarette under a car and I cringe. "Who's this chick in Columbus?"

"Ashley's sister, Sage. Brilliant woman. I think she can help."

Tuck shrugs and stares off into space. "She hot?"

I roll my eyes at Del. "She's a PhD."

"That's not what I asked."

"She's out of your league, Tuck."

He smiles and stretches and flexes in his towel. I point to the bloody bandage on his hand.

"Maybe we should visit a clinic first."

Tuck frowns but doesn't disagree. "How's your shoulder?"

"Feels better, but I could use some pain pills and proper sling."

Tuck nods. "Maybe I can get some Oxys." He fakes a punch at my shoulder, and we all step inside. I take a long, hot shower and put on the fresh clothes Del brought back. He bought me blue jeans and a brick hat. Almost feel like a cowboy again. Tuck sports a pink pullover and track pants while Del strips down to a muscle tee.

We head to the local ER where nurses throw a fit over Tuck's hand. He ends up with twelve stitches and a steroid shot. We're there for four hours.

In the meantime, a kindly black doctor performs an MRI which shows "significant tissue damage" in my shoulder. He recommends surgery and fits me for a proper sling. We finally walk out around midnight, high on Percocet, and pile into Patrick's Mercedes for another all-night drive.

"No trunk!" Tuck declares as he hops in the front seat without asking. Patrick takes the wheel while everyone else squeezes into the back. It's a long, lonely haul, and as we speed down dark highways the boy fills us in on what he's learned about Hobbes.

"There's an e-sports event in Pittsburgh this weekend," Carl explains. "Hobbes will be there to promote *AMPersand*. He's also part of a panel on competitive gaming."

"Where's the event?" I ask.

"Allegheny Convention Center."

"Odd place for a hostage exchange."

"Don't let the public setting fool you," Tuck chimes in from the front seat. "Hobbes never goes anywhere without security detail. He's protected like a head of state."

"And you think he's up to something?"

"I'm sure he is," Tuck replies. "He'll have the whole place crawling with USAC goons. One misstep and they whisk you into an unmarked van."

Carl cringes in the light of his phone. He brings up an image and hands it to me. "That's Hobbes."

"That's Hobbes?"

The man doesn't look anything like I expected. On the phone he sounded authoritative and sharp. I pictured a clean-cut bigwig in a ten-thousand-dollar suit. But in the photo, he just looks... drab. He's balding and chubby with mushy red cheeks. He looks dehydrated. Or drunk.

Tuck laughs. "Not the Bond villain you imagined?"

"Not at all."

"Looks can be deceiving," Tuck says. "That man has the net worth of a small country, and an army to defend it. He also has powerful friends."

I nod and stare at the image of Oliver Hobbes. He reminds me of a grimy barkeep I knew in Texas. The guy once pinched Ashley's butt and she laid him out. God, I miss her.

The screen goes dark and I hand it back to Carl. I shake my head to clear it and settle back into the seat. Dark fields roll by outside the window. We're somewhere in eastern Illinois.

You'll get her back, son.

God, I hope so.

Go see Sage. She can help.

We need friends right now.

I'm still not sure about this pilot.

Me neither, Pops.

I sigh and pet the dog at my feet. He's been so good through all this. Loyal hound at the ready. If we were home this would be about time for a late-night walk. A starry stroll through the valley. I get an idea.

"Hey Patrick..." He's been cruising on autopilot for hours. Increasingly dreamy and quiet. "Can you pull over for a few?"

Patrick zones back in and rubs bleary eyes. "Pull over? Here?"

We're running I-74 through the middle of nowhere. Endless acres of cornfields and soy.

"Wherever's safe," I say. "Baxter and I need to stretch our legs." Patrick nods and pulls off on a grassy berm. He throws the car in park and leans back to rest his eyes.

"We'll just be a few minutes." I pop the door and Baxter hops out. He sniffs along the shoulder like a gourmet buffet. "This way, boy." I lead him down a small slope into a budding field of corn. The stalks come up to my armpits as I wade between two rows.

"God's country..."

So much peace amidst a world of chaos.

Crickets. Dewdrops. Sweet corn on the breeze.

Maybe we'll be all right.

Chapter 44

Tuck takes the wheel and drives like a madman. We reach Ohio before dawn.

The sunrise is beautiful. Pink fingers tickle the sky. We blow through Dayton without a word, but I catch the angst on Patrick's face.

Pronghorns. That's what brought us together. A detour and a chance encounter and a ride out of the hills. Since then, it's just been one mess after another.

I think Hobbes' threats shook Patrick up. Then when Tuck barged in with that shotgun he was done. I can't blame the man. He's got a son to worry about. Watching Carl these few days got me wondering about being a dad myself. Ash and I never took a serious run at kids. Maybe we're missing out.

We roll into Columbus with the morning rush. Carl navigates to the Ohio State campus, and even looks up Sage's building on the web. We swing past a giant football stadium and cruise a tree-lined street. Students scoot across the road without a glance.

"Nice campus," Del says. "I don't think I've ever been this far east."

We pull up next to a stately brick building called Fadziah Hall. "Department of Astrophysics," Carl says. "Sage Carter's office should be on the third floor."

We start piling out of the car when Patrick calls a halt. "Listen guys..." I have a hunch what he's about to say. "I think this is where Carl and I leave you."

"What? Noooo!" Carl tries to protest, but his dad silences him with a hand. "This is getting too thick for us," he says. "I hope you get your people back. I sincerely do. But I'm not up for tangling with this Oliver Hobbes."

"But I want to see the game convention!" Carl was buzzing half the night about catching the event in Pittsburgh.

"I'm sorry, son." Patrick strokes his thick beard. "Mr. Tuck here thinks it's a trap. Mercenaries and unmarked vans..." Tuck shrugs and folds his arms. Patrick eyes his bandaged hand and my slinged-up shoulder. "I can't risk Carl getting hurt."

I nod down at my feet. I'd feel like hell if something happened to the kid on account of me. This is probably for the best.

"I appreciate you getting us all this way." I meet Patrick's eyes and hold them. "I know we didn't start out on the best terms, but if not for you and Carl..." I trail off. Not sure what else to say.

"Happy to play our part," Patrick says. "But I think that part is over."

"Where will you go?" Del asks. "Back to Dayton?"

Patrick shakes his head. "Somewhere south. I have a friend..." Carl looks confused, but I see what his father's getting at. Disappear for a while. He's thought this through.

"Well, best of luck to you." I offer a hand and Patrick shakes it firm.

"Go get your wife back." He turns to Del. "And your husband."

Del smiles and slaps him on the shoulder. "It's already done, friend."

Baxter lets out a whoop and slobbers Carl's hand one last time. With that we're out of the car and watch the blue Mercedes drive away.

"Godspeed," Del says. I study the sidewalk and gather my thoughts. I'll miss Patrick's calm demeanor and Carl's millennial savvy. "Remember why we're here, Clay." Del rouses me from my contemplation. I nod and look up at the towering academic building. Dark windows line the façade and burly arches frame the door. I lead our group to the entrance but hesitate at the threshold. What do we do with Baxter?

Before I can make any kind of decision, an Asian girl with a giant purse steps out and squeals at the sight of the bloodhound.

"What a precious doggo!" She squats down to pet Baxter and he woofs in appreciation. I notice Tuck push out his chest, but the girl seems wholly absorbed in giving love to the dog. "What's his name?"

"Uh... this is Baxter."

"OMG, Baxter!" She speaks some kind of internet shorthand, but seems to know her way around a hound. I get an idea.

"Hey, listen..." The girl looks up at me with pretty eyes and dimpled cheeks. Black hair spills from a messy bun. "My friends and I

247

have a meeting here in Fadziah Hall, but I don't think we can bring the dog inside. Would you mind watching Baxter for a bit?"

"Yaaaaaas! I will totes chill with your dog!" Her slang is puzzling, but I admire the young woman's vigor. She pulls out a big pink smartphone and starts snapping selfies with Bax at her feet.

"Are you sure? You don't have class or something? I don't know how long we'll be."

"No problem, cowboy." She checks her phone. "I just met with my advisor. No class until three."

I glance at Del and he shrugs. Tuck ogles the girl a bit more than seems appropriate and I begin to pull him inside. "Let's go, guys... Thank you so much, ma'am."

We enter into a large foyer with shiny floors. A group of students pause mid-convo and stare at our secondhand clothes.

"Which way to the stairs?"

A scruffy kid in a ballcap points down the hall to our left. "Cool hat!" he calls as we shuffle away.

I hit the oak steps and take them two at a time. On the way up we pass three young ladies who flash three big smiles at Del.

"Man, you could be swimming in sorority chicks," Tuck declares as we reach the third floor. He gawks at a curvy blonde in tiny shorts bouncing down the stairs.

"I'm married," Del says with a shrug.

"And he's gay," I add.

"You're missing out," Tuck says.

Del winks and claps him on the back. "Maybe *you* are."

Tuck frowns and averts his eyes. "Let's find Sage."

We prowl the narrow hallway, peeking into open doors. Our search takes us two-thirds of the way around the building before I recognize a familiar nameplate: Sage Carter, PhD. I knock twice and the door drifts ajar. "Doctor Carter?"

Sage looks up from a fancy tablet and spits out a mouthful of tea.

"Clayton Fucking Moore!?" I guess I get that a lot. "Holy shit!" She jumps to her feet and practically vaults the cluttered desk. "Great to see you, cowboy!" We embrace as old friends and my thoughts turn to Ashley. Sage's pixie frame is nothing like her sister's, but they both smell the same.

Finally, she steps back and waves us into the room. "Welcome, welcome..." She clears books off a couple of chairs and settles back behind the desk. It's been about six months since I've seen Sage and she's grown an imposing afro. A small woman with big presence. I've never met anyone so self-assured.

"So, what's the old joke?" She asks, eyeing Tuck and Del at my sides. "A cowboy, an Indian, and a..." she points probingly at Tuck.

"Uh... Vietnamese-American," he stammers.

"Well," Sage raises her arms with a flourish, "We're two Turks short of a proper orgy, but I can make this work." Del laughs and sits in one of the chairs.

"Easy, Sage," I say, dropping into the other. "I'm married to your sister."

"Mmm hmm..." She turns to Del. "And this tall drink of rainwater?"

"Spoken for," he answers with a polite nod. Sage finally turns to Tuck, still standing awkwardly by the door.

"Um... s-sure?" He fumbles his words behind a sheepish grin. It's cute to see the cocky pilot so cowed.

Sage bellows a laugh. "Put that on ice. What brings you boys to my office on a Wednesday morning? Where's Ashley?"

"Actually, Sage..." Here comes the hard part. "That's what we're here to talk to you about."

Her mouth droops and her eyes narrow. Sunny to serious in a heartbeat. "What's wrong." It's more a declaration than a question, and as I walk her through our last few days, Sage grows increasingly focused and grim. She only interrupts once: when I describe the bombing of our house in the valley.

"Oh, Clay..." She shakes her head and drums white gloss nails on the desk. "That's a crime against God."

I nod in agreement. Sage loved our land out west. She'd spend a week in Wyoming every year and was always despondent to leave.

"So..." she says heavily after coming up to speed. "How do we get my sister back?"

Tuck steps forward and stands tall. "We hit Hobbes where it hurts. The one thing that means more to him than money or stones."

Del and I exchange a shrug, but Sage picks up the ball. "His reputation."

Tuck grins. "Clay said you were smart."

"You don't get where I am without knowing your way around an alpha male."

He nods. "*Cygneous* has a lot of stakeholders. If we can undermine confidence in Hobbes' management over Voltstone, we can gain leverage in our bid to free Ashley and Arden."

"But what's to stop Hobbes from just killing them?" My own question makes me queasy. "He already threatened as much. Now you want to backdoor the man?"

"It sounds heartless," Sage reaches across the desk and takes my hand, "But Ashley isn't a threat to Hobbes right now. Not while he has her locked up."

"She's right," Tuck adds. "The biggest threats to *Cygneous* are the people in this room. As long as we walk free, Hobbes' won't hurt Arden or Ash."

Del nods slowly like he gets it. I can't say I feel the same. "But you said this guy was crazy," I protest. "A psychopath." My eyes jump from Sage to Tuck. "You said he'd kill us all before making a deal."

"I did," Tuck nods. "And he will. But only once he holds all the cards."

Sage squeezes my hand and I see Ashley in her face. Same sloping nose. Same expressive eyes. "Ash is a strong girl," she says. "We'll get her back in one piece."

I huff and stand and step to the window. This talk turned heavy, and I need a moment to cleanse.

Sage and Tuck carry on while I watch students roam the courtyard below. They all look so breezy and pure. Young folks with big dreams.

I gaze across the grassy quad when something familiar catches my eye. Baxter. He's lazing next to a wrought bench with his temporary handler. The bubbly girl seems to have attracted an admirer in a sportcoat. He sits stoically while she talks with her hands.

I watch the pair for a moment and the man almost seems to look at me. It's hard to tell from this distance, but his head tilts up and drops down again. Then a second time. A third. Suddenly he stands and marches away, leaving the girl flailing alone on the bench. She seems confused. Angry. She yells something after him and even Bax pops up to bark.

I watch the man retreat when he turns to look at me again. This time he makes eye contact and mutters into his lapel.

Shit.

"Uh, guys..."

Sage and Tuck are carrying on about psycho Hobbes.

"Guys, I think we've been made."

Tuck strides to the window.

"Sportcoat. Twelve o'clock." I point him out.

Tuck nods. "USAC spotter. Probably just called in the cavalry."

"Jesus. What do we do?"

"We need to split."

Sage squeezes in and leans against the glass. "Is that Baxter?"

"Yeah, I left him with a student on the way in."

"Oh my God, Claire..."

"The Asian girl? You know her?"

"She's my top grad student." Sage fumbles for her phone and cues up a call. Down on the bench, Claire digs through her giant purse.

"Doctor Carter?"

"Claire, honey, I need you to take the dog and meet me around the side door of Fadziah Hall."

"OMG Doctor, I just got ghosted by this Chad in a-"

"Claire, listen: Don't follow that man. Don't ask questions. Take the dog. Side door. Two minutes."

"O-okay Doctor..." The girl looks around anxiously and Sage hangs up her phone.

"That's your grad student?"

"Claire's solid." Sage kicks off a pair of pumps and pulls tennis shoes from under her desk.

In the quad below I watch poor Claire stalk nervously toward the building. She gets ten feet then turns back for her purse. On the second attempt she loses a shoe.

"You got someplace we can lay low?"

Sage nods. "Let's get to my car." She turns to Tuck. "What am I up against here?"

Tuck scratches his chin. "In public like this, Hobbes should hold back the big guns." He peers out the window at the quiet campus. "But USAC has urban assault squads. On par with the Rangers."

"How soon you think they'll be here?"

Tuck shrugs. "If they were watching you, they've got a team on standby. Ten minutes by helo. Maybe less."

"Helicopters?" Tuck nods and Sage rolls wide eyes. "What. The. Fuck. Clay?"

Del steps to my defense. "We didn't ask for any of this, Doctor."

"I understand." She unlocks a desk drawer and pulls out a giant revolver.

"Jesus! You keep that in your office?"

"Do you watch the news, Clay?" She calmly checks the barrel and shoves extra ammo into her purse. "Let's move."

We follow her out of the office and down the narrow hall. A gawky student in short pants tries to intercept, but Sage blows right by. "Not now, Trevor!"

She leads us past the main staircase and through a small door between two bathrooms. "Plumbing access," Sage declares. We duck beneath exposed piping and ducts. "Down the hatch." She lifts a metal grate with a piercing creak to reveal rungs descending into darkness.

Del starts down without a word but Tuck and I hang back. "Couldn't we take the stairs?" I ask, contemplating how to climb with one arm.

"This ladder runs right down to a side door. It's direct and discreet. Could be other spotters in the building."

I nod and mount the metal ladder. The first few moves are clumsy until I find a rhythm for one-armed descent. Step down, lean in, grab the next rung. Step down, lean in, grab the next rung. It's awkward and slow but it's progress. Just over my head, Tuck climbs down in a similar fashion.

"Don't look up my dress!" I hear Sage call from above. I ignore the dust in my eyes and the drop below my feet. Finally, my boots meet cement. We're in some sort of dark, mechanical crawl space. A pump purrs noisily nearby.

"How do you know about this place?"

Sage looks me dead in the eye. "A few years ago, I hooked up with one of the janitors in here. She liked the cold floor."

I frown. Del grins. Tuck grins even larger.

Sage steps around dripping PVC and cracks a metal door. "Claire!" She hisses. Sunlight spills through the void followed by Claire's panicked face.

"Doctor Carter?" She looks sweaty and flushed. Baxter noses around her feet. "What's going on?"

"Is anyone around?" Sage asks. "Anyone follow you here?"

"N-no..." Claire stammers, glancing over her shoulder. "I don't think so."

Sage slips out the door and motions us to follow. We emerge from the dark, dank sump room into a sunlit garden. Del admires a blooming bougainvillea.

"I'm parked in a faculty garage a few blocks from here," Sage says. "Everyone stay on me. If you see something suspicious, call it out." She sets off through a cluster of hostas while the rest of us stand gawking in her wake.

"She's amazing," Tuck says.

"Sage doesn't fuck around."

"WTF is going on right now?" Poor Claire looks despondent. Del offers a hand and words of comfort as he leads her through the drooping foliage.

I wish someone would do the same for me.

Chapter 45

We're almost to the garage when the first shots ring out.

"Shooter!" Tuck calls. "Get down!"

Bullets whizz past my head and wing through a metal crosswalk sign.

"Are you kidding me?!" Sage sounds more angry than scared. "There are kids around!"

I peek back and there's sportcoat, sighting down a pistol from a block away. It's a desperate, dangerous shot. Scary reminder of how bad Hobbes wants us dead.

Sage yells something else but all I hear is pounding in my ears. It occurs to me this is the first time I've ever been shot at. I feel frantic and vulnerable and scan desperately for cover. That's when I realize I've lost the rest of my group.

All around me, students swerve and scramble and scream. I crash head-on into a lanky kid on a longboard and we both go tumbling to the pavement.

"What the hell, man?" His nose is bloody and he looks ready to fight. When a bullet strikes the sidewalk he takes off without a word.

Instinct takes over and I roll blindly to my right. The concrete is not kind to my swollen shoulder, but I'd stumble down a stairwell if it meant not getting shot. My progress ends at a stiff hedgerow, and I clamber around behind it for some semblance of cover.

"Sage!" I call hopelessly. "Del! Tuck!" Even Baxter disappeared on me. Where did everyone go? I'm huddled amidst the landscaping in front of another academic hall. I don't hear any more gunshots, but something else catches my ear.

"Clay!"

I whip around but can't place it.

"Clayton Fucking Moore!"

It's Sage and she's behind me. A hand waves from an open ground-floor window.

"Run!"

I do as I'm told. Pop into a crouch and charge for the window. Bullets rip through foliage as the shooter draws a bead. I move without thinking. Adrenal-fueled flight. I reach the window at full speed and launch like a linebacker into the void.

"Gotcha!" Del steps up to catch me and we fall heavily to the floor. Moments later the windowpane explodes.

"Stay down!" Sage growls, as if I needed to be told. We're in a wide office surrounded by thick books and broken glass. Del, Tuck, Sage, Claire, and Bax hold down various sections of the floor. A bald professor cowers underneath his desk.

"Sage led us in a side door," Del whispers. "You must have missed the cue."

"Thanks for the heads up."

Baxter plods over and leans against my legs. He's panting and shaking and scared. Poor boy.

"What's going on?" The trembling professor looks like he could shit himself.

"Campus shooter," Sage declares. "Shelter in place."

Without another word she pops up and takes a stance beside the window. Big hair. Big gun. Small dress. Sage cuts quite a figure.

"What are you doing?" Tuck asks.

"Ending this."

She hefts the gun and peeks around the splintered frame.

"Do you see him?"

She shakes her head. I move against every urge to self-preserve and join Sage on the opposite side of the window.

The scene outside is surprisingly calm. Most bystanders have fled the area with the sportcoat nowhere to be seen. I watch a trio of campus cops sweep the street with guns drawn. More law enforcement should arrive soon. Will that keep USAC at bay?

"Let's move," Sage says.

I'd rather not, but she's clearly in charge. Sage pulls Claire to her feet and waves Tuck to follow. We slip out the office door and I hear the old professor sigh with relief. Sage leads us down the hall and into a stairwell.

"Where are we going?"

"To my car."

"Up the stairs?"

"You'll see."

No more questions as we race up four flights and onto the roof.

"Sage?"

"This is Holt Hall," she says, striding along a tarry ridge. "My car is in South Garage. The two buildings are practically adjacent."

"Practically?"

We wade to the roof's edge and a knee-high wall that overlooks the parking garage next door.

"There's a six-foot gap." Sage declares.

"That's six feet?"

"Give or take."

It looks like a chasm. The Grand fucking Canyon. I peer over the edge and see nothing but death.

"You can do it," Sage says. "We're a bit higher than the garage, so gravity should work in our favor."

"Are you kidding?"

Is she kidding?

"Get a running start and take off right here." Sage smacks her hand against the low wall. "You'll clear the gap."

I gawk incredulously at the rest of the group. "But what about Baxter?" I plead.

"I got him," Del scoops the hound in his muscled arms.

"Tuck has a bad knee."

"I'll do anything for you, Sage."

"Claire can't make that jump."

"Hey, I'm an all-state hurdler, asshole!"

I exhaust a heavy sigh. Everyone looks at me like I'm the crazy one.

"Clay, you can head back down and meet us at the car," Sage says. "Watch out for the man with the gun."

I stand at the ledge and glance over once more. Fuck. Fuck. Fuck.

You can do it, son.

Are you kidding, Pops? If I fall, I'm crippled. Or dead.

Then don't fall.

I take a deep breath and study faces in turn. Del, Tuck, Sage, Claire. All windblown and waiting on me. Even Bax drools with resolve.

Aww, hell.

I nod to Sage. She nods to Tuck. Without a word he steps up and eyeballs the gap. Prods a testing boot atop the low wall then paces off a running start.

"If I fall, I got a brother in Fresno," Tuck says. "Make sure he gets my bike."

"But we don't even know your-"

Before I can finish, Tuck charges the ledge, plants a foot, and vaults with a primal scream. The plucky pilot flails through space and crashes to the parking deck with feet to spare.

"Woooooooop!" Tuck roars in the face of death. "Who's next?"

I shy back as Del steps forward, Baxter cradled in his arms like a potato sack. He kisses the dog and closes his eyes and hums something to himself. I'd kill for a cup of that Zen.

My Blackfoot friend squares to the ledge, takes two powerful strides, and leaps the gap like a panther. He lands on his feet and releases the hound. Baxter barks like they just stepped out to piss.

"You're up, Clay." Sage directs me with insistent eyes. I could protest, but what's the point? I stop myself from looking down and look up instead. Blue sky, puffy clouds. Perfect summer morning.

I glance across at Del and he smiles at me. Little head nod of encouragement. Time to cowboy up.

I retreat from the ledge as far as I can. Ten feet. Twenty. Long running start. Sage gives me a withering stare but says nothing. From back here I can't see my landing zone. Just a low wall and empty space. A leap of faith. I rub my eyes and picture my wife. Got another story for you, Ash.

"Do I have time for a cigarette?"

Before Sage can scold me again, I'm off. Legs move on their own. One arm pumps, one tight at my side. I block everything out but the squat launch wall. It's covered in bird shit. Here we go.

Plant. Push. Soar.

OHMYFUCKINGGODTHISIS-

I crash into Del. Big strapping lad slows my momentum and my feet feel pavement again.

"Attaboy, Clay." He claps me on the back. I let out a breath I'd been holding and look back over the edge. Can't help myself. A girl in a blue sun dress gapes up at me, mouth ajar. I flash a sheepish grin just as the sportcoat steps into the narrow alley. He cranes his neck, lifts his arm, and cracks off two quick rounds.

"Down!" I yell. Mostly to myself. I scramble away from the ledge and wave to Sage on the other side. "It's him!" She nods and takes Claire by the hand. The poor girl looks ashen, but Sage says something that takes the knock out of her knees. They stand and face us across the void.

"Be safe, girls..." I whisper. Claire kicks off clompy shoes and slings her purse across her chest. Sage dangles the revolver like some cartoon hero. She meets my eyes and gives a curt nod, then they're off.

Side-by-side. Leaning into the sprint. Sage runs trim and agile while Claire takes long, loping strides. They reach the wall in unison and launch like a couple of track stars.

Airborne.

Gunshots.

Pop! Pop! Pop!

I hit the deck out of instinct and pray the wild rounds miss their mark. Sage lands light on her feet and just keeps running. Claire stumbles into Tuck and looks ready to puke.

"Come on!" Sage disappears down a concrete ramp to the level below. I stand dumb trying to process what we just did when I hear a rumbling on the breeze.

"What is that?" Claire asks between heavy breaths.

I know that sound.

"Trouble," Tuck says. He drapes an arm around Claire and leads her toward the ramp. Baxter sounds off while Del points to the horizon. Two choppers chew up blue sky.

"It never ends, does it, Del?"

"Everything ends, Clay."

He smiles and jogs off like life's a big game to him. Maybe it is. I wait a beat and light a smoke because Fuck You I earned it. Stand atop the deck and watch death approach at speed.

Chapter 46

Sage's car sits alone on the third floor of the garage. It's a jet-black Tesla that has Tuck beside himself.

"You drive a Model S!" He seizes the front seat and runs a hand over every surface he can reach.

"Performance edition," Sage replies as she straps in. "Buckle up."

Del and I sandwich Claire in the back seat as she pulls Baxter onto her lap. She's barefoot and sweaty and all her hair escaped its bun.

"Thanks for watching my dog." I sheepishly doff the hat that's somehow still on my head. Claire breaks into a nervous smile and hugs the bloodhound tight.

"He's a good doggo." She rubs Bax under his chin and he practically purrs.

"Sorry about all this, Claire," Sage says as she pushes a button to start the car. I brace for a grumbling roar, but barely hear the electric engine at all. Across the dash, a vibrant console blinks to life.

"Everybody strapped in?"

Sage backs out of the parking spot and surveys the quiet garage. Tuck fiddles with the Tesla's touchscreen like an excited child. "This is so coo-"

Sage hits the accelerator and we surge forward like a speedboat. She whips down the ramp and around three turns before I realize I'm holding my breath. "Eyes peeled," she declares, studying parked cars for a lurking sportcoat. We race down each level until we reach the ground floor. A reversing Honda blares its horn as Sage swerves to avoid a crash.

"Jesus!" Tuck calls, bouncing in his seat.

"I said buckle up!"

Sage lines up a clear run to the exit, picking up speed as we approach the lowered gate. A panicked parking attendant leans out of the gatehouse just as a sportcoat appears behind an SUV.

"Duck!"

Before I get the chance, he points his pistol and punches two clean holes in the windshield. Claire and I scream while Sage shimmies the wheel and lays on the gas. Sportcoat steps back and lines up another shot when he's suddenly hit from behind.

"Oh my God!" Claire yells.

The valiant parking attendant clocks our USAC goon and tackles him hard to the ground. Ol' sport never saw it coming. His head hits concrete and the gun skids beneath a parked car.

"That was awesome!" Tuck declares.

"The hero we need," says Del.

Sage crashes through the gate and out of the garage. She skids around a curb onto a wide campus boulevard. "Is anybody hurt?" We take a quick self-scan, but no one appears to be shot. Tuck bumped his head and Claire took a shard of glass to the ear. Del removes his shirt to press against the bleeding wound. Claire seems to forget her trauma as soon as she sees his abs.

"We need to get away from the university," Sage says, swerving around light campus traffic. "What happened to those choppers?"

We all crane to get a look at the sky but see nothing. Sage opens the sunroof and warm air comes gushing in.

"You plan to take this beast to top speed?" Tuck asks.

"I told you to buckle up."

Rather than obey, Tuck turns around and ogles Claire in the backseat. "Try not to bleed on this swanky leather- OW!"

Sage cuffs him hard on the back of the head. He spins around and shuts up but still neglects to fasten his belt.

"Who was that guy?" Claire asks.

"The man in the sportcoat is part of an organization called USAC," I say. "They've got us on the run right now."

"They kidnapped my sister," Sage adds from the front.

"Shit, Doc. For realz?"

"For realz."

Sage rounds onto a main road that runs parallel to campus. She weaves methodically through traffic as we snake toward downtown.

I lean back and revel in the rush of another close call. I should have known they'd be watching Sage. I feel bad leading USAC here, but who knew they would shoot up a campus like that? Maybe Tuck's right. We can't trust Hobbes for shit. If he hurts one hair on Ashley's-

"Look out!" Tuck screams as a black SUV lurches abruptly into our lane. Sage slams the brakes and stops on a dime alongside a small cross street. Two big men in big sportcoats climb out with big guns.

"Shit. Shit. Shit." Sage hits the gas again and the car leaps forward like a missile. She pulls hard on the wheel and smacks our back end against the driver's side of the SUV. The impact staggers our assailants and sends one man stumbling into oncoming traffic. The other fires off a burst but we're already gone. Whipping down a narrow side street lined tight with parked cars.

"They're everywhere!" Tuck cries as a different SUV appears snug on our ass. Sage pushes the speedometer up to fifty, and we clip a side mirror with a crack that makes everyone jump.

"This car's not made for these streets," Tuck complains. "Anywhere we can open her up?"

"I'm trying." Sage steadies the wheel as her eyes dart between the rearview and the road. She drifts slightly over center and adds even more speed. "Hang on." We all grab handholds or each other. Claire hooks an arm through mine and puts a bracing hand on Baxter.

"Ready..." Sage lines up a maneuver and I'm glad she's the one at the wheel. We whip past parked cars way too fast as the SUV stays tight on our tail.

"Now!"

She slams the brakes and fishtails into an adjacent alley. Tires screech and we sway like cornstalks but Sage threads the needle. Our tail turns late and the SUV skids broadside into a parked sedan.

"Let's fuckin' go!" Tuck pumps his fist as we put distance on the USAC wreck. Sage makes a quick turn off the alley and pops out onto a two-lane road.

"Did we lose them?" Del asks.

"Probably not." Sage turns again onto a bigger avenue with signs for an approaching interstate. "Two miles to the freeway," she says. "What happened to those helicopters?"

I study the sky but see no choppers. Just clean blue like a gas flame. Traffic is light and we zip along until Sage hits the brakes with a curse.

"Dammit." She stops short of a flashing railroad gate as a freight train rumbles by.

"A train? Seriously?" Claire looks around frantically as we get boxed in by idling traffic. "Who even rides trains anymore?"

Sage lets out a sigh and rolls her eyes in the mirror. "It's a cargo train, dear. No getting by."

Tuck fidgets anxiously and tries to look in every direction. "We're sitting ducks here," he complains. "Can't you go around?"

"Go around the train?" Sage rolls her eyes again.

"I don't like this."

"I told you to buckle up."

We sit in anxious silence as the train chugs and tension grows. Bax pops up and sniffs at Claire's bloody ear.

"Baxter, no..."

"It's okay," she says. "Who's a good doggo?" Claire pulls a phone from her giant purse and starts narrating some kind of video.

"Hey peeps! Claire Bear here in the back of a Tesla with my new best friend..." She makes a kissing face and drags Baxter's drooling mug into the frame. "We're on the run from some baddies, but I've got the world's sweetest baby here to protect me!"

"What are you doing?" Tuck asks.

"Livestreaming, durr. It helps with my nerves."

"Turn that off!" He grabs for the phone, but Claire jerks it away. "You'll expose our position!"

"You think the bad guys follow me on Facebook?"

"I don't know, but it's terrible OPSEC."

"Chill, Karen." Claire settles back behind the camera. "I already made like three TikToks today..."

"Tik-whats?"

"Enough!" Sage cuts in, hands tight on the wheel. "Claire, no livestreams. Tuck, fasten your damn seatbelt." They apologize in unison but neither heeds her demands. I listen to the rumble of boxcars while Claire mimes some viral dance beside me.

We sit like ducks another minute before Del breaks the silence. "Hmmmmm..."

"What's up, Del?"

"Anyone hear that?"

The screechy clanks of the train are too loud to make out much, but soon Sage picks it up.

"Helicopters," she says.

Tuck sticks his head out the sunroof then drops back down. "We gotta move," he says. "What's the plan, Sage?"

"I don't know."

"How long is this train?"

"I don't know!"

We sit. We wait. The endless train rolls on. Car after car after car after car.

Claire whispers into her phone beside me. "So now we're being hunted by some kind of mercs. *Literal* black helicopters. It's like an episode of *Homeland*."

Tuck pokes his head out again. "I don't see anything," he says, but the rotor drone grows louder. They're close. "Where are they coming from?"

"I don't know." Sage again.

"Can they see us?"

"I DON'T FUCKING KNOW!"

Everyone shuts up and even Baxter cowers down. Claire turns her livestream to the sunroof and lets the soundtrack speak for itself.

Ca-chunk. Ca-chunk. Ca-chunk. Ca-chunk.

Thup-a-ta-thup-a-ta-thup-a-ta-thup-a-ta.

Tuck groans and balls fists into his eyes. Sage chokes the wheel with an iron grip. Even Del looks nervous. I lean into Claire and we both stroke Baxter for support. The thumping and the chunking build to a crescendo, and finally two black choppers emerge over trees to our left.

"Here we go..."

"Shit. Shit. Shit. Shit."

One helo swoops circles around our position, while the other holds a hover about a hundred feet off the ground. All around us, bystanders gawk at the aerial display.

"Is this for real?" Claire shouts but I can barely hear her. Sage lays on the horn but it's all futile. We're stuck. Fifty cars stacked up behind us with a freight train blocking our front. Guard rails shut down any path left or right. We have literally nowhere to go.

Tuck almost bails. I can see it in his eyes. He's got one hand on the door when ropes start dropping from the sky.

"No!" Claire gasps and grabs my hand. She's still filming on her cell and points the camera out the window to my left. The floating chopper holds position as black-clad commandoes abseil from the open door.

"This is it," Tuck cries. "It's over."

Sage revs the engine and creeps to within inches of the lowered gate. USAC soldiers glide down thick cables into a parking lot across the road. The first man hits the deck and takes off running toward our position. He wears full tactical gear and wields an assault rifle. Suddenly I miss ol' sportcoat.

"We're fucked. We're fucked. We're fucked. We're fucked!"

Tuck is despondent. Claire shocked speechless. Del hangs his head in quiet prayer.

"The train!" Sage calls. "I see the end!"

I peek to our right down the tracks and sure enough there's a slow-rolling caboose. I swing my head left as more soldiers hit the ground and fan out. They swoop in all directions, setting a perimeter, but no one's opened fire yet. The street is packed with bystanders but that didn't stop them before.

"Hang on..." Sage chomps at the bit, Tesla coiled to strike. "We can make it!" My life's in her hands but there's worse places to be.

Whatcha think, Pops?

These boys look mean. Y'all better get.

I watch a jack-booted commando sprint balls-out toward our car. He vaults the guard rail with a grin on his face. Where do they find these guys?

"Time's up."

"Hold on!"

The final train car screeches past and Sage puts the pedal to the floor. We take off like a rocket as I'm thrown back hard against the seat.

"GAAAAAAAAAA!" Sage screams. Claire screams. Baxter screams. Everybody screams. The crossing ramps up to an incline and we blast through the wooden gate like a toothpick. The Tesla goes airborne – absolute fucking liftoff – and we never even touch the tracks.

We land rough on the other side but Sage somehow keeps it on the road. I hear gunshots and throw my body over Claire. Del does the same and we knock heads. I see stars. For a moment I think I might be shot.

"Go! Go! Go! Go!"

Somebody screams. Probably Tuck. I keep my head down and study the floorboards. At some point Claire dropped her phone and I stare dumbly at my own face livestreaming to the world. A splatter of messages scroll by:

Be safe, Claire Bear.
THIS IS SO INTENSE!
More DOGGO please...
What a time to be alive.

Chapter 47

We hit the freeway and Sage pours it on. Eighty. Ninety. One hundred miles per.

The ride is smooth and quiet as Sage uses all three lanes to snake through southbound traffic.

"Doc, you drive like a boss." Claire keeps filming as we fly past cars like they're standing still.

"I need to focus," Sage says. "Keep your eyes peeled and call out threats."

We zip by a school bus as kids smear the windows. Wide eyes. Open mouths. Little fingers smudge the glass. It takes me a moment to realize they aren't gawking at our blazing Tesla, but the whirlybird chasing us down.

"Helicopter. Five o'clock." I declare the obvious. We somehow slipped the commandos at the train, but that second USAC chopper has us dead to rights.

Sage doesn't even blink. "Tuck, what's the chance we can outrun it?"

"Uhhh, zero percent." He twists around to get eyes on the bird. "That's a Sikorsky Black Hawk. It can cruise almost two hundred miles an hour." He turns back to the dash as we overtake a sporty Mazda. "I love this car, Sage, but you can't outrun a helicopter."

"Okay, plan B..." She weaves hard around a rusty pickup, briefly drifting onto the shoulder.

"What's plan B?"

"You're the pilot, Tuck. Give me a plan B!"

Tuck seems flustered, but Sage is all business. She waits a beat behind a three-truck convoy, then swoops past like a stock car pro.

"Um, well..." Tuck gathers himself as Claire leans forward to stick her camera in his face. "The chopper's biggest advantage is freedom of movement. As long as they can see us, they can follow us anywhere."

"So we need to hide."

"Possibly..." Tuck takes another look behind and I see sweat slick on his brow. "A garage or tunnel would give us cover, but we could also end up trapped."

"Plan C then."

"Head toward an airport? Restricted airspace? Although USAC might get clearance..."

"Plan D?"

"Shit Sage, I don't know."

"Plan D, Tuck!"

"Right, well... We could try something unexpected. Like a diversion. Throw the spotters off, then-"

"Plan D! Hold on!"

In one quick clip, Sage slams the brakes and whips the car into a vicious skid. The sharp deceleration grabs the belt and grinds my shoulder into dust. No fun, but Tuck gets it worse. He's tossed turvy like a bull rider. Shoulda buckled up.

"What are you doing?" Claire screams as Sage flips a full one-eighty. We skid through the grassy median then start back the other way.

"Something unexpected."

I scan for the chopper as panicked drivers honk and swerve. We're clear of the road but against the grain. It's got everyone spooked, including myself.

"Did we lose them?" Del sounds hopeful.

"Not yet." Sage punches the pedal and her Tesla shows its stuff. Zero to sixty on a turf track. Not bad. We come up on a gap in the divider and Sage swerves right through it. Whips into northbound traffic to a chorus of horns.

"Sorry!"

"Jesus, Doctor..." Claire is flushed, but still filming. She leans down to Baxter for another play-by-play. "We just pulled a U-turn on the freeway!" She hugs the hound close and he looks like he could barf. Ain't the only one.

A minute of cruise then I hear the chopper again. Took a big loop around but it's still on us. "Bird's back," I declare.

Tuck turns for a view and nods his assent. "Looks like they backed off a bit. Your crazy U-turn bought us some space."

"It's a start." Sage shoots past a flatbed and checks all her mirrors.

"This helicopter is still chasing our car," Claire whispers into her phone. "I don't know what they want, but these guys keep shooting at us." She pats a probing hand to her ear. "Look I'm bleeding! From the glass. This is so crazy, guys. I'm glad I can, like, document what's going on because if we-"

Sage suddenly careens across three lanes and Claire's commentary slips into a squeal. We narrowly avoid sideswiping a station wagon as we whip through the merge lane and down a narrow ramp.

"Plan E," Sage says. "Off the freeway."

"You could have warned us!" Claire cuddles up to Del and resumes blubbering into her phone. "I think I've got whiplash." She frowns to the camera and fixes her hair. Del puts a strong hand on her neck and Claire's eyes go gooey. Ol' Blackfoot's a heartbreaker.

"Bear with me," Sage says, cruising down the ramp and onto a four-lane road. Traffic is slower but thinner. We zoom past stoplights, strip malls, and suburban sprawl. Makes me miss Wyoming.

"You're heading away from the city," Tuck says.

"There's a big park, about five miles from here. Lots of trees. Lots of cover."

"Worth a shot." Tuck turns back to study the chopper as Sage barrels through a yellow light.

"You need to buckle up," she says. We fly past a kid on a motorcycle and he glares like we just smacked him. Leans into a racing crouch and opens up his hog. "Oh, for fuck's sake..." He pulls even with the Tesla and now we're in a race. "Back off, kid!" Sage is not amused, but the kid matches our speed. He pulls tight to Tuck's window and bares a shit-eating grin.

"What is he doing?" Del asks.

"He wants to race," Claire says, holding her phone to the window for a better view.

"Not the fucking time." Sage snarls and pushes past seventy. We're well over the limit on streets not made for speed. A Honda honks angrily as he's run off the road.

"We need to lose him," Sage says. "Tuck, grab my purse." He lifts the handbag from between his feet and stares dumbly at Sage. "Do it," she says without taking eyes off the road.

"You want me to-"

"Just scare him. Get him off my ass!"

Tuck nods and pulls out the revolver. He rolls down his window and we're hit with waves of roar: The wind, the bike, the chopper. Mr. Moto just grins like it's some kind of game.

"Back off!" Tuck yells but it's lost in the din. He raises the revolver and the kid's face goes white. He brakes hard and just like that, he's gone.

"Nice work," Sage eases off the speed and falls in behind a minivan.

"OMG did you see his face?" Claire giggles and mugs for the livestream. "Don't mess with my crew, bitches!"

"Easy, Claire..." We make a soft right and USAC follows with a lazy bank. "We've still got problems."

We graze the outskirts of suburbia and start pushing into parkland. Less traffic and more trees. I see a sign for Buckeye State Forest just as the chopper starts reeling us back in.

"They're trying something." Tuck is floppy and antsy and still beltless in the front seat. The helicopter drops elevation and adds speed, sweeping around to parallel our driver's side. It's a menacing move and I get chills in my nuts.

"What are they doing?" Claire leans across my lap to film the chopper, then recoils with a scream when a gun barrel pokes out.

"Get down!" Sage screams and veers hard onto the shoulder. I can't hear the shots over everything else, but I see the muzzle flash and chunks of asphalt kick up against the windows.

"Warning shots," Tuck calls out. "They're trying to scare us."

"Well, it worked!" Claire cowers over Baxter for another livestream aside. "This is so messed up right now..." She snorts a big snot wad up her nose. "I'm just gonna hug this doggo and read all your comments. Someone tell my mom I love her."

Del pats her on the back as Sage make two quick turns and has us closing on Buckeye Forest. We've escaped the crush of suburbia into a nice rural green. Cedars and maples and... buckeyes, I guess.

"What's the plan, Sage?"

"Into the woods."

"Is that gonna lose 'em?"

"It's our only chance."

The copter swings around and opens fire again. This time they put holes in the hood and we almost end up in a ditch.

"This isn't working!" Tuck yells. "They're going to waste us!"

"Shoot back!" Sage replies.

Tuck grits his teeth and hefts the revolver. He rolls down his window and takes aim at the multimillion-dollar war machine outside.

Pop! Pop! Pop! Pop! Pop! Pop!

This time I hear the shots as Tuck empties his cylinder. Not sure if he hit anything but the bird backs off.

"Nice shooting," Sage offers.

"That's just gonna piss them off."

"They were already pissed." Sage peels down a narrow drive into our first semblance of cover. Big beech trees line the road and obscure the view, but USAC shoots again anyway.

Brat-at-at-at-at-at-at!

Now it sounds like ten guns at once and might as well be. Branches and leaf bits rain down as bullets shred the canopy. Something *thunks* beneath the car as one of the tires goes flat. We lurch and waver but Sage somehow stays on the road.

"Yeah, they're pissed."

"Keep going!" Claire calls. "They can't see us through the trees."

With the firepower they've got I'm not sure it matters. But Sage pours it on, and I love her for it.

"Hang on!" She puts the pedal down and we wind deeper into the woods. Left and right and up and down. We hug the hills. We paint the curves. It's like poetry. A symphony. A ballet of momentum and speed.

The road is our bitch and I want to believe and then out steps this deer.

"Look out!" Claire screams but it's too late.

For us.

For the deer.

For this beautiful car.

We crash headlong through a twelve-point buck. The hood crumples and the windshield explodes. Blood and glass fill the car and Sage finally loses control.

We spin. We screech. We flail.

I grasp blindly for Baxter and wait for the impact.

BOOM!

There it is.

I buck hard against the belt and then there's no more movement.

Just darkness and pain.

Chapter 48

"We dead, Del?"

"Not yet, Clay."

"What'd we hit?"

"Couple of trees."

"Everybody okay?"

"Hold still."

Strong hands work my seatbelt and release me with a *click*. I slouch forward and seek my bearings.

"Baxter?"

Head hazy and sore. Shoulder feels hollow. I wipe blood out of my eyes.

"Come to me, Clay."

Del again. He's outside the car trying to coax me through the door. I shift my weight and everything hurts. Feels like a bomb went off. I would know.

"That's it..." Del holds my hand as I slide off the seat onto a mossy grade. My legs wobble and creak but they bear my weight. Nothing broken. Del presses a bloody shirt to my forehead.

"Nasty cut above your eye," he says. "Otherwise, you look intact. Thank the Old Man you wore your seatbelt."

I nod and wince and study Del up and down. He's shirtless and sweaty, but not much worse for wear. Couple of nicks. A bruise on his chest. Crazy for everything we've been through.

"What happened to the chopper?"

He points a finger skyward and twirls it around. I hear the hum of the helicopter but can't see through the thick canopy. We're deep in the woods now. I feel an odd sense of safety, but I know that won't last.

"Too dense here to land," Del says. "But they're staying close. Probably sending backup."

"Where is everybody?"

Del bites his lip and puts a hand on my arm. "Why don't you take a minute, Clay. Catch your breath."

Something's up. Someone must be hurt. Baxter? "Where's Baxter?"

I shake my head to clear it but still feel thick and slow. After the chaos of the chase and the violence of the crash, my world won't settle. My balance wavers. Del props me up. "Easy, cowboy," he says. "Take it slow."

I fight to focus on a blur in the road. Baxter. Hobbling my way with a limp. Aw, hell.

"Baxter's okay," Del reassures. "Just favoring his leg."

Poor dog settles heavy at my feet. He looks whooped but wears a bloodhound smile. He's damp and shaky. I fight back a tear. "I'm so sorry, boy..."

Del rubs my back and we all take a moment. That was a mother of a wreck. Too fast around tight turns. The deer. The trees. Poor Bax didn't have a seatbelt. Come to think of it, neither did...

"Tuck? Where's Tuck? And Sage and Claire?"

Del says nothing but turns his gaze to the woods. I follow with my head and it swims. Stings. Must be concussed. I look past the mangled car and see figures in the trees.

"Sage!" I call out and a head turns my way. An arm waves. Someone calls back but I've got ringing in my ears. "What happened?" I ask Del.

"It's Tuck," he says. Solemn and straight and I know it's bad.
"Shit."

Del nods and motions toward the trees. "When you're ready."
Shit.

I lurch and lumber and limp into the woods. Baxter follows at my feet and Del at my back. Don't think I'd get far without 'em.

"Tuck?"

I trip over a rock and Del catches me.
"Claire?"

I lean against a fat trunk and feel like falling asleep.

"Over here, Clay." It's Sage. I think. I stumble through some thorny brush and into someone's arms.

"Woah, there..." It is Sage. All five-foot-three of her props me up. "Here, sit." She guides me to a flat rock and eases my sore self down. God, she's strong. Just like her sister.

"That Clay?"

Tuck's voice. I squint and stare as my brain tries to catch up. A scene resolves:

Claire. Barefoot. Kneeling in the dirt. Black hair spills around her head like oil.

She's holding something. A hand. Bloody. There's a lump and some branches and a boot and - Oh God.

"Tuck?"

A cough and a wheeze. "It's me, cowboy."

"Tuck, what...?"

I don't know what to say. It's not even clear what I'm looking at. I see legs and arms... but no person. Everything is wrong. The angles are off. Bones protrude. Blood seeps. Is that a lung?

Tuck gags as he fights for a voice. "You got a smoke, Clay?"

I pull out a roughed cigarette and pass it to Tuck with shaky hands. Claire lights the end off his bloody lips.

"Jesus, Tuck."

He takes a drag and smiles. One eye swollen shut. "Probably shoulda buckled up."

Sage folds her arms and shakes her head. Claire snorts back a tear.

"We need to get you to a hospital."

Tuck just keeps smoking and grinning. Nothing moves besides his face.

He's got one foot out the door, son.

Tuck's a fighter, Pops. Maybe we can save him.

A man knows when his time has come. You'll understand someday.

I watch Tuck smoke, his gaze faraway. There's a peace there, I guess.

"Does it hurt?"

"I'm past pain, Clay."

"You said you had a brother?"

"Miles Nguyen. Fresno. He's all I got."

"I'll see that he gets word."

274

Tuck eases out a sigh as blood drips from his nose. "You're a good man, Clay." He pauses. A chickadee chirps nearby. "I knew you and Ashley were the right folks for the job."

I glance sidelong at Del. "We just fell into this, Tuck." I picture Ashley and Ard. Better halves. "But we'll keep fighting 'til our people are safe."

Tuck smiles and fixes me with his tired eye. "You don't understand, Clay..." He takes a slow drag. "This was no accident. None of it." He coughs around the stubby butt of the cig. "I knew what I was doing when I landed that plane."

"What are you talking about, Tuck?" He must be delusional now. Death throes. It happens to folks.

"I mean that night in the valley..." His face gets all dreamy like he's back there. "I did it on purpose, Clay. I picked your backyard. I wanted you and Ashley to find those stones."

"Don't bullshit me, man."

"You know I'm not." Strength floods into his voice. Strength and pain. "Not with my dying words."

He looks to Claire and she lifts the fading cigarette from his lips. Takes her own puff off the bloody butt then stubs it out.

"Tuck, I..." I'm at a loss for words. My brain feels full of slugs. Del puts a hand on my shoulder and I try to piece together what's going on.

"But you said you were flying for *Cygneous*. Fifteen days." I light up my own smoke to steady my nerves. "You took some pills and blacked out. Had to ditch on our land."

"Most of that's true." Tuck says as Claire rubs his arm. I wonder if he even feels it. "But I went up there with a plan to go AWOL. And I landed right where you and Ash would find me."

"Me and Ash?" I shake my head, but it doesn't clear. "But we're just random folk. How could you even know who we were?"

Tuck's mouth goes slack and I wonder if he's gone. Then he sucks in a breath and speaks.

"I was *there*, Clay..." He pauses and you could hear a bug fart. "Afghanistan. '05. Embedded with your wife in the hills around Bariq."

"No way."

"Way." That shit-eating grin. Missing a few teeth now.

"You were a Ranger?"

"We weren't really Rangers. That was a cover. We were a merc squad Hobbes put together to find the Voltstone cave."

"Ashley would have remembered you."

"I wore a beard back then and we barely spoke." Tuck frowns. "She probably buried it after all the trauma. I know I tried..." His gaze gets distant then he snaps back again. "Hell, she might have known. That morning when she shot me. Something in her eyes..."

I look at his bandaged hand with its dirty, bloodstained wrap. A thousand thoughts tangle in my brain but only two words get to my mouth. "Jesus, Tuck."

He closes his eye for a while and I hear the faint sound of a vehicle on the road.

"I'm sorry, Clay." I'm dizzy and he's dying so I just let Tuck talk.

"I lost a piece of myself that day. Sold my soul to Oliver Hobbes. I was young and trying to prove something and boy did I. Proved I was a monster. Over the years flying for *Cygneous*, I came to loathe what I'd become. Hobbes paid me well. He pays everybody well. He put me through flight school. But the price was too much. The screams. The blood. Sins I could never atone for..."

He pauses for a raspy breath then carries on.

"It was a dumbass plan. I knew it would probably kill me and I made peace with that. I needed help, but nobody inside *Cygneous* wanted any part. Crossing Hobbes is a death wish and a ticket off the gravy train. No one outside would believe me... and then I remembered your wife. Ashley Carter. The reluctant killer. I remembered that pain in her eyes. The shame. The hate. That stayed with me like everything else.

It took some work to find her. She'd changed her name and fell off the map. Finally tracked her to a land deed in Wyoming. Way the fuck out. I couldn't just knock on the door, and I felt bad putting it on her at all. But a part of me thought maybe she'd seize the chance for redemption. Or revenge. Or whatever she wanted it to be.

So that night on the plane, after three hundred hours of flying, I treated myself to a couple of pills and set the trap. I planted a seed and put it in your hands to see what you and Ashley might grow with it. I didn't think they'd bomb your land, Clay. I knew they'd come after us, but that caught me off guard. I'm sorry for what I brought down on you. On everyone. My penance has come, and I deserve it."

Tuck pauses, breath gone faint. Behind me in the road, a car door slams. Maybe it's USAC. Maybe it's the Old Man come for Tuck's soul.

"I think that's all he's got," Del says.

I nod. It feels like an ending. Claire weeps softly. Wind rustles the leaves. Somewhere above, the chopper drones on. I sit in that moment as footsteps stomp through the brush.

"Claire?"

Nobody moves. Like the voice doesn't sync with our reality.

"Claire, are you-" A young man steps into the clearing. Blonde hair. Gumboots. He takes a look at Tuck and chokes something back. "Woah..."

Claire glances up and slowly registers the new face. "Sean?"

"I was fishing nearby," the young man says. "I got a bunch of texts and turned on your livestream." He shakes his head. "What's going on, Claire?"

She stands without a word and leans into his arms. The tears flow harder, and Sean runs a hand through her tangled hair.

"This is our friend, Tuck," Del offers. "We're gonna let him rest now."

Sean nods and his mouth goes tight. The gravity seems to hit him. To hit all of us.

Suddenly Tuck snaps open his eye. "You all need to go." His voice is weak, but the words are firm.

"We can sit with you awhile, Tuck."

"You don't have a while." He nods weakly to the sky. "Get the hell out of here. Go finish the job."

Del looks at me and nods. He peers toward the road then back to the new arrival. "What are you driving, Sean?"

The kid gulps and gathers himself. Claire stands barefoot on the toes of his rubber boots. "I've got a four-by-four pickup," he says, then nods to the unseen helicopter above. "I know a shortcut through an old horse trail. Should get us out of here unseen."

Sage takes a long, deep breath and looks me in the eye. "What choice do we have?"

"None that I can figure."

She leans down close to Tuck. "You take care, friend."

He smiles but his eyes stay closed. Claire kisses him on the forehead then walks away without a word. Del puts a hand on Tuck's shoulder and bows his head in prayer. They all start back to the road, but my feet won't seem to move.

Time to be going, son.

Feels wrong leaving a man to die, Pops.

It's all you can do for him now.

I stand there watching Tuck's chest rise and fall. I don't know how I feel about what he told me. I don't know how I feel about what comes next. All I know is I'm on the verge of something, and here lies the man that started it all.

"Say Hi to my Pops, Tuck."

"I'll do that, Clay." The words catch me off guard and Tuck smiles. "But you gotta do something for me."

"What's that?"

He cracks an eyelid. Squinty. Slow. "When you finally take down Hobbes..." He pauses for breath. "Kick him in the nuts for me."

Tuck grins. I grin. Somewhere in the brush, a cardinal sings.

"Well all right, then."

I doff my hat and that's that. Turn and walk and leave Tuck to it.

Part VII

Front Toward Enemy

"A new viral video taking the internet by storm appears to show a high-speed chase between a civilian vehicle and a pair of military helicopters. Claire Dahlia Boheme, a postgraduate student at The Ohio State University, began broadcasting on Facebook Live around ten a.m. this morning, narrating from the back seat of a car as it sped through Columbus, Ohio streets. The livestream gained attention as the vehicle made a number of dramatic evasive maneuvers in the face of aggression from the helicopters and their crew.

Miss Boheme expressed shock and fear as black-clad soldiers strafed the vehicle and performed an airdrop alongside a congested urban roadway. The livestream peaked at around 10,000 viewers as the car sped down the winding roads of Buckeye Forest, then abruptly ended with what appeared to be a high-speed collision sending the vehicle off the road.

Emergency responders arrived to find a heavily damaged Tesla Model S registered to Dr. Sage Carter, a professor of astrophysics at The Ohio State University. Police recovered one unidentified body from the accident scene, but the whereabouts of the vehicle's other occupants, including Miss Boheme, are currently unknown.

Military enthusiasts across the country have speculated about the identity and objective of the mysterious units seen in Columbus. As conspiracy theories abound, the unmarked helicopters have been labeled everything from private military contractors to an unregulated militia. Some have described the incident as an elaborate training exercise, while others are writing it off as a Hollywood stunt.

One theory gaining traction on social media is that the soldiers seen on video belong to a little-known branch of the Defense Department called United States Asset Command. This public-private security force is rumored to take directives from unknown American business leaders, and harbors unusual authority to conduct operations on U.S. soil.

While our sources at the Pentagon confirmed the existence of a minor branch called Asset Command, they would not provide any details on USAC's jurisdiction, chain of command, or potential involvement in this morning's incident.

In other news..."

Chapter 49

Well, the cat's out of the bag.

Bull's out of the barn.

The pig's out of the pantry if that's more your thing.

Turns out our little jaunt through Columbus made national news, and now "#USAC" is trending online. I'm not sure if that's good or bad.

Claire says all the publicity gives us leverage. She's got a platform now. Internet famous. We could threaten Hobbes to go public unless he gives up Ashley and Ard. Of course, we already tried that, and he vowed to kill everyone. So I don't know.

We're safe for the moment. Claire's boy Sean got us out of the woods and all the way to Pittsburgh. We're holed up in a hotel, but no cheapie this time. Sage reserved a suite at the fucking Ritz. Swankiest spot in the city. We've got a hot tub and silk sheets and a twenty-four-hour butler. Even brought up a cushy bed for the dog.

Sage paid in Bitcoin and booked the room under a fake name. *Esperanza Bellatrix.* She said we could use the pampering, and I'm in no shape to disagree. I hurt. That wreck took all my aches and turned them up to 11. My shoulder is mush. My brain is concussed. I spent the first day in the hot tub and the second day in bed. Now it's day three and I can finally walk a bit.

Tomorrow we meet Hobbes at the big gaming convention. I try not to get my hopes too high about seeing Ashley, but it's all I care about now. I can tell Del is antsy too. We'll get 'em back or burn this motherfucker down.

One way or another, it's about to end.

Chapter 50

"Arden would love this."

Del sits cross-legged on a massive ottoman, eating ice cream. We just had breakfast and he ordered a chocolate cone for dessert.

"It's been years since I've had ice cream," he says. "We never had this kind of stuff at the house."

I think back to his cozy hole in the hills. Simpler life. Simpler times. I hope he gets back there. My own home is just a bombed-out crater now. No going back to that.

I guess I have Tuck to blame. Cocky S.O.B. brought it all down on us. I've been wrestling with his deathbed confession and still don't know where I stand. He claimed he knew Ashley. Wanted her help with Hobbes. Well, now he's dead and she's a hostage all because of these goddamn stones.

Del would say to trust in the Old Man. Ashley would say to look out for ourselves. I'll keep doing both and see what comes.

"This food is amazing." Sage polishes off the last of a bacon breakfast sandwich. "Well worth the thirty-dollar upcharge."

"You're my hero, Doctor C." Claire lies prone on a king-sized bed, Baxter curled up at her side. "This room was made for Instagram."

"No social," Sage says emphatically. "Not until we know the situation with Hobbes."

I light up a smoke and sip my morning coffee. I'm buried in an easy chair as big as my truck. Del is right, Arden would love this place. So would Ashley for that matter. She'd rock a satin robe and live off room service. When this is all over, I'm taking her someplace nice.

"So, what's the plan, anyway?" Claire sits up in bed and takes a long pull off a bottle of bubble tea.

I look to Del. Del looks to Sage. Sage looks back to me.

"Well..." I take a puff off the cigarette to buy some time. "Right now, we don't really have one."

Sage wipes her mouth on a napkin and crumples it onto her plate. "What did Hobbes say when you talked to him?"

"He just said to meet him at the convention center. We didn't even know it was a gaming thing."

"And he said he'd bring Ashley?"

"He said he'd kill her if we don't show up."

Sage stands to pace the room. "So what's his angle? Inviting you to a public event?"

"It was more of an ultimatum than an invite," Del says. He pops the last bit of waffle cone into his mouth. "Hobbes talks like he wants nothing to do with us, but I think we've got more leverage than he lets on."

"Because of the stones?"

Del nods.

"And how many do we have?"

Del frowns.

"Just one," I say, "But Hobbes doesn't know that."

"And you think he'll trade the hostages for one wayward Voltstone?"

"Unlikely."

"So, what else will it take?"

I shrug. "He also wanted Tuck."

Sage furrows her brow. Claire taps on her phone. Nobody talks for a minute.

"So, this guy is like some big gaming hotshot?" Claire finally asks.

I nod. "He owns an e-sports team."

"But he's also a secret supervillain?"

"With a merc army."

She puckers her lips and makes a soft smooching sound. Baxter perks up and kisses her on the mouth.

"I don't know much about villains," she says. "But I know gamers. They're quirky, but principled. If the community found out Hobbes was a war criminal, they'd eat him alive."

"Hell, a lot of folks would." I stub out my cigarette in frustration. "That's why he kills people to cover it up."

A silence grabs the room and only Sage has the balls to break it. "So, you want to bargain with him?"

"Whatever gets Ashley back."

"And what about exposing *Cygneous* and Voltstone?"

"Fuck all that."

"But Tuck said-"

286

"I don't care what Tuck said." I stand and walk to the glass that makes up the north wall of our suite. It's a hell of a view from the thirty-fifth floor. "I just want Ashley safe."

Sage follows me to the window and puts a soft hand on my back. "We all want the same thing, Clay." She leans against my shoulder and we look down on Pittsburgh together. Sharp, angular buildings. Smooth, sweeping bridges. Two fat rivers sculpt the city to a point.

"Del, you said we have some leverage over Hobbes?" Sage steps away and I miss her closeness.

"I think he's afraid of us," Del says. "He's taking risks."

"He's definitely thrown his weight around."

"Those choppers were *crazy*," Claire says. "Just dropping soldiers in the middle of Columbus. And that shooter on campus?" Her eyes go wide. "Hobbes must have known that would make the news."

Sage steps behind an oak bar top rimmed with stately brass. "I think Del's right," she says, drumming her fingers on the hardwood. "Hobbes came after us because he sees us as a threat. That's why he had a gunman watching my office. That's why he sent helicopters to hunt us down."

"That's why he bombed my land and kidnapped my wife."

"And that's *exactly* why he'll never strike a deal." Sage punctuates her point with a fist to the wood.

"We have to try, Sage."

She shakes her head. "You don't get it, Clay. Even if we had a thousand Voltstones, we could never give Hobbes what he really wants."

"And what is that?"

"Our silence."

She lets the word hang like a slaughtered pig.

"Maybe we could sign something," I offer. "Like a contract. A non-disclosure form."

Sage scoffs. "Never happen. Hobbes sits on secret tech and a pile of bodies. You can't bury that with an NDA."

"We could offer."

"Would you trust him? Would Ashley?" She scowls out the window and shakes her head. "You'd spend the rest of your life looking over your shoulder, waiting for that other shoe to drop."

I let out a long sigh and lean hard against the glass. "Well give me something, Sage. You're the smartest person I know."

"I'm working on a plan, but you're not going to like it."

"Does it get Ashley and Arden back safe?"

"I think it's our best chance."

"Then I love it."

"Claire, can you look up the convention schedule? When is Hobbes supposed to speak?"

Claire fiddles with her phone while Baxter licks her bare feet. "He's on a panel at noon. *Revenue Streams in Competitive Gaming.* Other guests include... some PlayStation exec and a venture capitalist. Blech."

"Will they be taking audience questions?"

Claire nods. "Twenty-minute Q&A."

"Perfect." Sage pulls a can of strawberry seltzer from behind the bar. "Maybe we can make him sweat a bit."

"You want to confront Hobbes during the panel?"

"Tactfully." She chugs the fizzy drink and rips an enormous belch.

"I don't know, Sage." I shake my head. "We'll be lucky if USAC doesn't just nab us at the door."

"I may have a solution for that." Claire leaps from the bed into some sort of pop star pose. Coy smile. Kinky hips. Hands curled in the shape of a heart.

"I don't get it."

"Ever heard of cosplay?"

Sage snorts. "Oh, fuck yes."

"What's cosplay?"

"It's when people dress up as their favorite characters," Sage explains. "From movies, games, comics. Pretty standard at conventions like this."

Claire giggles and frolics to a small video screen set in the wall. She taps a command and moments later a face appears.

"Yes, madam?" That's Pickerington, our on-call butler. He brings food, runs errands, whatever we need. Nice perk with the twelve-hundred-dollar suite.

"Pickerington, what's the nearest shopping mall?"

"That would be... Nine Acres. An upscale megamall four miles south."

Pick's a good dude. I was skeptical at first, but the old Englishman has been solid. He brought me painkillers and smokes. Picked up shoes for Claire. He even gave Baxter a walk.

"Sounds perfect," Claire chirps. "Can you give a girl a ride?"

"I can arrange transport at the lady's pleasure."

"You're the man, Pick. We'll be down in ten."

She ends the call and turns around with a grin. "Who's ready to get freaky?"

I give Sage a desperate look. "Are we really doing this?"

"It's good cover, Clay." She touches up her makeup as Claire readies her giant purse. "You'll have to trust the girls on this one."

Del stands with a chuckle and pulls on a shirt. I guess this is happening. My first cosplay.

"It's a freaking Con, Clay." Claire reads the doubt in my face and blows it away with a wink. "The best way to blend in is to stand out."

Chapter 51

Three hours and three hundred dollars later, we're back at the hotel with full costume attire.

Claire dragged us through a dozen stores but got everything we needed: clothes, makeup, accessories, props... that girl knows her way around a shopping mall.

When I show up at the convention tomorrow, I'll do so in the image of a digital cowboy named Arthur Morgan. Claire called him the "gruff protagonist" of open-world western *Red Dead Redemption 2.*

I've never played the game. Never played any of these games. But I feel more comfortable about the getup than I thought I would. It's mostly standard ranch wear: canvas, cotton, and leather - roughed up for that 1890s feel. I got a grizzly hat and a gun belt, but feel a bit dopey with my arm in a sling. Claire says that just adds to the mystique. Tell folks I got shot robbing a train.

Del is dressing up as a God. Burly Greek fella from a game called *God of War.* The costume includes a big fake beard, lots of war paint, leather gauntlets and a battle axe. It's a fierce look.

Sage did well too. She's a stealthy killer from *Assassins Creed.* Her character free-climbs buildings in light boots and a hooded cloak. Death from above.

All in all, our looks are legit. For a first-time cosplayer, I'm even having a bit of fun.

And then there's Claire.

Ho-ly Claire.

Claire's attending the convention as something she calls, "Sexy Link". It's her take on the young elfish hero from *The Legend of Zelda.* She's got fake pointy ears and a floppy green cap. A long plastic sword, colorful shield, and... not much else. The purpose of the costume seems to be exposing maximum skin. Her only cover is a brown leather bikini and a microskirt. It's a showstopper.

The plan, as far as I can tell, is to ambush Hobbes' during his panel appearance. Claire will serve as honeypot, buttering him up before hitting him with hard questions about *Cygneous*, USAC, and Voltstone.

Hobbes is an old pro who should dodge them all, but he's also an arrogant S.O.B., and Sage thinks we can rile him up in front of the crowd. She'll film the exchange and broadcast live on Claire's Facebook feed. It's a ready platform to start building a public case that Hobbes is doing evil. That's phase one.

Phase two is intercept. As soon as the panel is over, Del and I will corner Hobbes and demand to see Arden and Ash. We'll offer him a Voltstone (our only Voltstone) as a gesture of good faith. Assuming he's hot from the panel he should be ready to hear us out.

The goal is to locate our spouses. That's the only goal. Whatever goes down needs to put me in a room with my wife. I'll rip Hobbes' ears off if I have to. He can have mine if that's what it takes. We'll make our stand, right there, in front of a bunch of costumed gamers.

It's a shit plan. Sage said I wouldn't like it and I don't. But we don't hold a lot of cards here. We have to act strong, steer Hobbes, and sell out for Arden and Ash. If Hobbes won't give them up, then it's on to phase three: Dead Man's Switch.

Sage had me record a video. An impassioned plea for the release of my wife. It's a short clip, just three minutes long, but it hits every one of Hobbes' pain points and paints him for the psychopath he is. I don't know if it will rate. I don't know if it will matter. Sage wants me to be "the public face of resistance" whatever that's supposed to mean. I'm only doing it to save Ash.

The video is queued up on a twenty-four-hour delay. If the timer runs out, my mug goes live across five social media sites and creates a big viral headache for Oliver Hobbes. The only way to stop it is with a single password on a single device - both in the safe possession of our man Pickerington at the hotel. He was a champ about the whole thing. Wary of our motives, but a willing accomplice. The five hundred bucks Sage slipped him couldn't have hurt.

If Hobbes won't meet us at the convention, the video goes live. If he tries to capture, kill, or hurt someone, the video goes live. If he plays games or backs out or can't deliver, the video goes live. If he hurts Ashley or Arden, the video goes live. It's a threat he can't murder away, and it's about all we've got.

Now we wait. The convention starts in nine hours, and I can't sleep. Neither can Del. Go figure. The girls zonk on their king bed while Blackfoot and I share a smoke on the balcony. Stars twinkle above and Pittsburgh twinkles below. Not exactly God's Country, but maybe in its own way.

"You think we can pull this off?"

"I think we can do anything, Clay."

"There you go again."

Del smiles and takes a puff of his cig. This is the second time I've seen him smoke, so I guess he lets loose more than he lets on. Apparently Arden keeps a pot patch up in the hills. Could sure go for some of that right now.

"I miss Arden a lot," Del says. He takes another drag and the ember glows orange in the dark. "For twenty years I never knew a day without him. Now I'm on my own out here. I feel naked sometimes."

"You could throw a shirt on once in a while."

A knowing grin. "It's been a weird week." He pauses to admire the city below. "In a way, it's been nice. A chance to reconnect with something. But I'm ready to get back home."

"You don't worry about your man?"

"Of course I do. I'm human. Arden's human. We left him bloody and hurt..." He trails off. "But I know we'll be together again." Del's tone is resolute. "I live in that feeling, Clay. Nothing can push me off."

I study his face in the moonlight. Calm. Confident. "I wish I had what you have, Del."

"You might be closer than you think."

I sigh. Big cloud of smoke in the night. I won't know peace until Ashley is safe. Her smell. Her smile. Her skin...

"You remember our talk by the river, Clay?" Del pulls me out of my thoughts but I'm not ready. I can almost taste her. Rosehip and coffee and sugar and sweat.

"What's that?"

"After the cave. Before we met Patrick and Carl. I was trying to show you something." Del takes a slow draw and taps ash into a glass tray. "Maybe you're ready now."

"Maybe I am."

A smile. A nod. Del digs into his pocket and pulls out a crumpled flower. Indian paintbrush. It curls like a spider in his palm.

"That damn flower."

"What's it made of, Clay?"

I give him a long, hard look. Del's eyes are honest. His smile is pure. We're in the same cell and he's offering me a key. I just wish I could grab it.

"Go back to the beginning." He stubs out his cigarette and leans forward in his chair.

"The beginning of what?"

"There is only one beginning."

"That's deep, Del."

"I'm a deep motherfucker, Clay."

I get caught on the draw and snort smoke into my nose. My breath burns and my eyes tear up, but it feels good to laugh. Ol' Blackfoot gets me sometimes.

"Alright, man..." I pinch out my cig with snotty fingers. "In the beginning..." I tip my head back to that Pittsburgh sky. "In the beginning there was nothing."

Del nods and waves me on.

"Nothing but the Old Man. Whatever you want to call him."

"So, what happened?"

I shrug. "Old Man made the world." I pull out another cigarette because it's that kind of conversation.

"He made it all?"

"Far as I know."

"So, what's it all made of?"

That question again.

"What's the substance of it, Clay?" Del's eyes twinkle like the dawn of time. "You. Me. That flower. This table." He smacks the surface with a force that makes me jump. "There's something real here." He leans back and steeples his hands. "So, what is it?"

I take a deep breath and a long drag. Step back to see myself in full:

This rancher's son.

Far from home.

Chasing down the devil and talking God with a Blackfoot.

Well...

Maybe I finally see what he's getting at. All those old truths rolled into one.

"It's him."

293

He raises a brow. I crack a door in my mind and it blows right off its hinge. "It's the Old Man. All of it." I knock slowly on the table as Del nods along. "God didn't just make this world... He became it."

He became it.

I kill the cig and stand on shaky legs. Del grins a toothy smile and guides me across the balcony. We look down on Pittsburgh together.

"He became it," Del repeats once more. "It's a simple truth, but it changes the way you see everything."

I study the world below with fresh eyes. The Old Man winks back from a thousand points of light.

"Holy shit, Del..."

"It's scary at first."

"It's a lot to process."

"It's supposed to be." Del's long hair swims against the stars. I stare into the night and stroke stubble on my chin.

"So does that mean we're all like... pieces of the Old Man?"

"You could call it that."

"And everyone's connected. But it's deeper than that."

"Everyone's *accountable*. We're our own creators." Del sweeps a hand across the world below. "It's a story we wrote for ourselves."

"Damn, Del..." I try to wrap my mind around his words. "Then why is everything so fucked up?"

"I can't answer that." He looks down with a frown. "Maybe it's part of the experience. Maybe we lost our way." He turns and puts a finger in my chest. "What I can tell you is that *you* made this world, Clay Moore. This is your story. So, if something is broken you can always fix it."

"But-"

"No buts." He grabs my shoulders and stills my breath. "You're God's fucking cowboy..." Del leans in and plants a kiss on my mouth. "Start acting like it."

He walks off without another word.

Wow.

I stand silent for a minute while my head spins. If only Pops could see me now.

I see you, son.

I don't even know what to say.

Your friend's a wise man.

How come you never told me all this?

It wasn't my place.

Did you meet the Old Man when you died?

It ain't like that.

So where do I go from here?

Wherever you want. It's your story.

I want Ashley back.

So go get her.

And what about Hobbes?

It's your story.

Damn, Pops.

You'll get there, son...

I sit back down and light one last cig. I feel like a weight's come off my shoulders and a new one's settled down. There's no hiding anymore. No excuses.

He became it.

We became us.

I smile and sigh and raise my hand in salute.

I guess I know what I'm made of now.

Chapter 52

"Rise and shine, cowboy!"

I creep into consciousness and crack one eye. Claire leans down with a shiny smile. Her hair is pinned back and - Oh God she's naked!

I snap awake and shake my head and see she's not naked at all. She's in full costume. Green skirt. Leather bra. I count fifteen freckles and a mole on her hip. Will they really let her in the door like that?

"Today's the day, Clay!" She shrieks and giggles and bounces off across the room.

Today's the day.

I sit up in the recliner. Must have passed out here after my nightcap with Del. I catch his eye by the bartop and he smiles through a big fake beard. Red paint streaks his torso like a tribal tattoo.

"Up and at 'em, Clay." Sage pulls a droopy hood over her eyes and studies the look in a mirror. Everyone's already costumed up.

"Why didn't anyone wake me?"

"You looked so cute and peaceful." Claire calibrates an elfish cap so her hair spills out just so. "I've never seen anyone smile in their sleep like that."

I groan as Baxter hops onto the chair with me. "What time is it?"

Sage struts over and drops a pile of coswear on my lap. "Time to get dressed. Pickerington calls our car in twenty minutes."

The name of the old English butler gets my wheels spinning again. I remember what we're up against today. What we're trying to pull off.

I shudder and sigh and stretch what I can without pain. My shoulder's tight and could use a soak in the tub. No time. I climb into my getup as Baxter sniffs around my feet. "We're getting momma back today, boy." He woofs his appreciation and I woof back. Let's do this thing.

I cap the costume with my new grizzly hat. Black oilskin with a rawhide hatband. Beautiful piece. I flick the brim and Claire fakes a swoon.

"Catch me at the saloon, partner!"

"Sorry ma'am. This cowboy's spoken for."

Giggles all around.

Del and I help Sage strap into her boots when the video screen chimes a call from Pick. "Your vehicle awaits at the main entrance."

"Thanks Pick!" Claire gives everyone a once over as I struggle not to do the same to her. "Looking good, crew." She pops off a few selfies. "I so wish I could share these."

Sage shakes her head and slips a dagger into her cloak. "Today's about business." She nods to Del and I in turn. "Let's fucking roll."

Five minutes later we're crossing the lobby like a catwalk. Claire takes the lead and most of the attention, but Del the shirtless warrior gets his share of gawk.

Pickerington waits at the entrance and greets us with a practiced nod. Old pro doesn't even flinch as Claire kisses him on the cheek. "You look smashing, dear. I pity your foes."

She playfully twirls her plastic sword then climbs in the back of an idling Town Car. Sage, Del and Baxter follow suit, and I'm about to sit shotgun when something catches my eye across the lot.

Three black SUV's. Shiny and sharp. Parked nose-to-tail across a dozen spaces. A trio of sportcoats stand by at parade rest.

"Who's that?" The men look bored, but their jackets bulge with muscles and menace.

"The hotel hosts numerous VIPs," Pickerington says. "We keep our guests' privacy in confidence."

I guess it could be anyone, but those sportcoats look familiar...

"What's up, Clay?" Sage leans out the door and peeks up from under her hood.

"What do you make of this crew?"

She swivels for a glance as one of the sportcoats looks our way.

"They could be anyone, Clay."

"Could be."

"You think Hobbes followed us here?"

I shrug. Sage frowns. We both stare. One of the sportcoats fiddles with his shades.

Sage pulls out her phone and waves Pickerington in close. "You have my number, Pick." She points to an image on the screen and I'm shocked to see Ashley's smiling face. "If you see this woman, call me ASAP. It's my sister."

The butler just nods and files it away, along with a fifty-dollar bill Sage secretes from her cloak. "Otherwise, you know the plan," she says.

Pickerington nods again and without a word ushers me into the front seat of the car. The driver taps his horn and we roll out.

"Next stop: *Greater Allegheny Gaming Convention*!"

Claire's having fun, but those sportcoats put me sour. Are those *Cygneous* vehicles? USAC? Could Ashley be tied up in one of those tinted SUVs? The thought gives me goosebumps and I choke on a bit of phlegm.

You made this world, Clay. If something's broken, you can always fix it.

Del's words rattle like guitar strings in my brain.

Chapter 53

I don't know what to expect walking into the *Greater Allegheny Gaming Convention*. This is my first trip to any kind of 'Con'.

I went to a state fair once. Lots of cattle auctions. I guess I pictured something like a big horse show with less mud.

Instead, I'm hit with rap music and lasers.

"Welcome to *GAG Con*!" A black girl with two-tone hair hands me an event map. "Don't forget to visit *Bubble Bobble Dome*."

I assume she's joking.

Walking into the convention hall is sensory overload. Sights and sounds fight for my attention like a night on the Vegas strip.

"Let's hit some merch booths!"

Claire turns every head strutting the floor in her skimpy attire. It's weird at first, but I soon see crazy costumes are the norm around here. Everyone's spiffed up like actors or aliens or anime girls. One guy looks like he's made of Tetris blocks.

We spend our first hour wandering as Claire pauses for mock sword fights and selfies. These are her people. Del and I mostly hang back, but he attracts a group of lovestruck schoolgirls who titter ten feet behind wherever we go.

No one seems to care about my cowboy kit, but folks sure like taking pictures with my dog. Claire fixed Baxter up like some kind of *Pokémon*, and the kids love him.

Amidst all this, Sage floats in and out like a ghost. She's here, she's there, slinking through the crowd looking for signs of USAC. Nothing yet. It's early and Hobbes' panel doesn't start until noon.

In the meantime, we roam the floor and it's a fucking trip.

The whole thing has a made-for-internet vibe. Everyone wants you to blast their hashtag or download their app.

"Follow our speedruns on Twitch!" Somebody yells. I don't know what any of that means.

Half the crowd walks with their cell phone out, while some folks straight-up strap cameras to their gear. Walking past a booth for some game-themed soda, I'm jumped by a pair of touts who stick a blue can in my face.

"Can you handle the PIXEL punch?"

I'm so spooked I jump back and knock some poor princess on her ass.

"Let's try a game, Clay."

Claire pulls me into a queue to play something called *BoneBreakers.* After twenty minutes I'm led to a console and a controller and a kid who can't stop laughing. It doesn't end well.

After that embarrassment, we line up to try some virtual reality. This time I'm fit with hi-tech headgear and dropped in a virtual jungle. It's immersive as hell, and I'm having fun until some psycho comes at me with a machete.

That's enough gaming.

Del and I find a food court for some hot dogs and a breather.

"This place is a trip."

Del nods and munches a mustard coney. "I've never seen anything like it."

We watch a pair of kids dressed as *Spider-Man* chase each other around a nearby table.

"I wonder what Ashley and Arden would think."

"You'll find out soon enough." Del smiles through a mouthful of bun.

I lean down and feed Baxter some French fries at my feet. One of the Spidey kids comes over with a pizza slice.

"Can I feed your dog?"

I shrug. "Baxter loves pizza."

The boy giggles while Bax slurps the whole slice right off his hand. Then he looks up at me.

"Are you Arthur Morgan?"

Am I? Shit. I forgot my character's name. Del bails me out.

"The one and only outlaw..." He leans down and lowers his voice. "Don't tell the sheriff."

"I won't."

The kid looks around like the sheriff might be listening.

"Thank you kindly, *Batman.*"

"No, it's *Spider-Man*!" He shoots me with imaginary webs while I hit him back with finger guns. We all have a chuckle and he runs off. Cute kid.

I space out for a bit before Del brings me back around.

"You ever thought about having kids, Clay?"

"Thought about it."

"Never pulled the trigger?"

I shrug. "We got comfortable after we sold the ranch. We've been happy. Never felt like we were missing much."

"Children aren't about filling a void."

"True enough."

After Ashley and I got married, I sort of assumed a kid would come next. That's what people did. But then we settled down and got Baxter and stopped talking about it. Maybe we have been missing out.

"What about you and Arden?"

"We could adopt," Del says with a nod. "But we'd have to move. Never get approved living up in those hills."

"Well, that's a damn shame." Arden and Del have a beautiful home. A kid would be lucky to come up there. "I think you'd make a hell of a dad, Del."

He smiles in a way I haven't seen yet. Like I caught him off guard for once. "Likewise, Clayton." We tap cups in a toast and watch kids amongst the crowd. Some look like little angels while others raise hell. I wonder how Ashley and I would do.

Just then, a rustle in the masses grabs my eye. Heads turn and bodies shift and out of the rabble pops Oliver fucking Hobbes. He's stooped over a cellphone and surrounded by sportcoats. I can smell him from here.

"You seeing this?"

The group moves quickly to a side door marked: *No Entry.* I scan like Ashley might be part of the entourage, but of course she's not. Does that mean she's here, though? In a back room somewhere? A car outside? Or still stuffed in a cell back at USAC Main? The thought makes my blood boil.

As Hobbes and crew slip through the private door, a hooded figure peels off the throng and makes for our table. Sage.

"He's here."

"We saw."

Everyone nods.

"Where do you think that door leads?" Del asks.

"Want me to follow them?" Sage is all business today, but I don't want her walking into a bad time.

"Let's stick together for now. Where's Claire?"

On cue, the half-naked elf appears at my side. "What a bunch of wankers," she says. "Walking through here like they own the place."

"The panel starts in thirty minutes. You still up for this?"

Claire narrows her eyes and pulls out her plastic sword. She parries a few fake blows then swipes down hard on the table. "Let's gut these motherfuckers."

All eyes go wide as Claire juts her chin in contempt. "Yeah," she says. "I'm ready."

Nods around the table as Del and I stand. Baxter's up quick and alert. He can sense the change in the air. Oliver Hobbes is here.

I pat my pocket for our lonely Voltstone. It's bone dry, but I swear I feel a pulse. Maybe it's my own. Maybe it's my wife's.

Maybe it's all the same now.

Chapter 54

Hobbes' panel takes place in an auditorium off the main drag. The room seats about three hundred, and looks to be half full.

Revenue Streams in Competitive Gaming.

The crowd here is noticeably buttoned-up compared to the riffraff outside. More suits and less cosplay. A handful of sportcoats prowl the perimeter.

Del and I enter together and take seats at the back. I keep waiting for USAC to pounce on us, but it doesn't happen. Maybe it's the costumes. Maybe they're laying low for now. We sit in tense silence as Baxter lounges at our feet.

Sage slips in behind and stalks all the way to the front. She sits as close to the stage as possible and checks the angle on her phone. She'll be filming the action for Claire's live stream.

Hobbes and the other panelists chat amongst themselves while the crowd settles. There's a lot of gladhanding, but the smiles are fake as hell.

Hobbes himself looks bored. He scans the room often but never meets my eyes.

Where's my wife, you fucker?

I seethe in silence until Del calms me with a smile.

"Relax," he says. "This is your story."

I nod.

This is my story.

Just before the panel starts, Claire comes waltzing in. I can tell she's arrived by the craning necks and murmurs. She takes her own seat near the front and blows a kiss to Oliver Hobbes.

"Welcome to the latest installment in our *GAGCon Discussion Series!*" The event moderator is a tall, busty woman in a blue power suit. She introduces each panelist to modest applause, then starts into a rather dry discussion of E-sports economics.

"Mr. Hobbes, you employ more than two hundred elite gamers with *AMPersand*. How do you navigate the balance between versatility and marketability?"

"Well Wanda..." Hobbes drones on about some back-slapping bullshit. He sounds less menacing than he did on the phone, but I take that as an act for the suits. I hope Claire can rile him up.

The panel drags on and I grow anxious. Hobbes takes questions. The other guests take questions. The only thing I take away is that these guys are loaded. Apparently *AMPersand* is a hundred-million-dollar franchise, but it's just a side gig for Oliver Hobbes.

Finally, the moderator opens the floor to the audience. Our time has arrived. Hobbes fields a few softballs from *AMP* fanboys before Claire gets her turn. She stands tall, sweeps hair off her face, adjusts her skirt with a shimmy, and starts in for the kill.

"Mr. Hobbes, what would you say are the biggest obstacles to penetrating your product into emerging markets?"

"Well, that's a good question. We're still far below market saturation in countries like Brazil, Turkey, and Malaysia, but these communities are some of the most enthusiastic toward the *AMPersand* product. The accessibility gap remains the high price of gaming hardware. Consoles and computers and high-end peripherals represent a prohibitive entry point, even for many middle-class families. Hence, we focus most of our efforts on branding and engaging these customers across mobile platforms."

"Interesting. And what about rural communities?"

"Well, if you're talking about undeveloped regions of developing nations, then it's typically an infrastructure issue. We can't promote online gaming in an Afghan village without reliable broadband. That's on local governments to fix. But we're always monitoring the global landscape and *AMPersand* is primed to step into untapped markets as conditions evolve."

"Fascinating, Mr. Hobbes." Claire bobs her head to some imaginary beat. "So, what if people in these communities had reliable access to affordable energy? Could that sort of technological democratization spark a paradigm shift in competitive gaming?"

Hobbes frowns. "I'm not quite sure what you're getting at."

"Access, Mr. Hobbes." Claire pulls out her plastic sword and twirls it casually in her hand. "A power source so rudimentary, even an

Afghan farmer can use it. You could cut out the middleman in some of these bureaucratic states, and get ahead of lagging infrastructure and reliance on unreliable governments."

I'm shocked by Claire's performance, but I probably shouldn't be. She's a doctoral student under Sage's wing. Of course she's smart as hell. The ditz schtick just flipped off like a switch.

Now the moderator steps in. "I'm sorry Miss, are you talking about some kind of plug-and-play renewable technology? Because that's not really the subject of this discussion."

"I'm talking about Voltstone."

Even from back here I can see Hobbes clench his jaw. A few sportcoats perk up like they heard a magic word.

"I'm not familiar with that term," the moderator says.

"Then I shall enlighten you!" Claire wades past a group of slack-jaws and bounds into the aisle. She twirls on her toes and pulls out a blue stone. "Behold! The next generation in affordable consumer energy."

Claire milks the moment as Hobbes starts to squirm. Everyone else looks curious but confused.

"Cheap. Clean. Efficient and abundant. These unassuming stones represent a revolution in localized energy solutions." Claire must have practiced this speech. "With just a handful of these colorful rocks, you could power your home, start your car, accelerate entire *communities* out of poverty. There's just one catch..." She holds the room with a dramatic pause... "Oliver Hobbes will kill you if you try."

A moment of stunned silence, then all hell breaks loose.

"Ma'am that is quite enough!" The moderator pleads.

"Let her speak!" Someone calls from the crowd. "Sexy Link!"

Claire stands tall and defiant. She ignores the heckles and keeps her gaze on Hobbes. To his credit, he stays composed. The commotion dies down as the room awaits his response.

"That's a serious accusation you've made, young lady."

"Well, you're a seriously fucked up dude."

The crowd erupts again as sportcoats start moving in on Claire. I don't know if any of this helps our cause, but I hope Sage is getting it on film.

"What do we do?" I turn to Del but he's not even there. I spot him swimming through bodies up ahead, trying to get to Claire. It's a valiant effort, but the sportcoats are almost on her.

That's when she comes alive.

She drops the first guy with a spinning kick to the face. It's a beautiful blur of a pirouette that draws gasps and cheers from the crowd.

"Holy shit!"

"What a move!"

The second guy can barely react before Claire swoops low and drives her prop sword into his gut.

"Sexy Link!"

"She can fight!"

The crowd seems to think it's some kind of show, but sportcoat number three gets wise and takes a defensive stance. He parries a groin shot while his comrade sneaks up and grabs Claire from behind.

"Let go of me!"

She struggles and squirms, but the bear hug holds. The pair wrestle to the front of the room and disappear through a door behind the stage.

"Hey, bring her back!"

Now I'm the one standing and screaming.

"You can't do this, Hobbes. Let the girl go!"

His gaze finally finds me, and his face finds a snarl.

"That's right, asshole. Your business is with me. Let her go!"

Hobbes shakes his head. "She slandered my name and assaulted my men." He waves to the sportcoats writhing on the floor. "She must face charges."

"Coward!" I'm fired up now. "You prey on innocents. You hide behind thugs. Come down and face me like a man!"

Hobbes sighs and stands. For a moment I think he might actually come at me, but more sportcoats start bearing down instead.

"It didn't have to be this way, Mr. Moore."

"Bullshit!" I brace for a fight but I'm no Claire Boheme. "You bombed my house! You kidnapped my wife." I backpedal into an aisle as the crowd around me scatters. "Where's Ashley, you prick? Where's Arden Horne?"

I stand ready as Hobbes' men close in from either side. I won't last long against these brutes, but I won't shut up either.

"This psycho slaughtered a village!"

I scream and froth as folks cower around the room.

"Oliver Hobbes is a killer! Everything she said is true!"

"Arrest him."

Hobbes gives the signal, and the first man makes his move. I swing wildly with my good hand and the thug swings back. One of our punches lands.

"Oooowwww..."

My ears ring. My eyes blur. My jaw feels loose. I brace blindly for a second shot, but it never comes. Instead, I hear a scream.

"Arrrggggh... Get him off!"

I squint through tears to see a sportcoat brawling with a bloodhound.

My fucking hero.

"Get this thing off me!"

Baxter growls and I can tell he means business. Literally got the guy by the balls.

"Shoot the dog."

"No!"

"Shoot it!"

"Baxter!"

I lunge to pull him off, but strong hands hold me from behind.

"Don't shoot him, please!"

The sportcoat screams and Baxter snarls and the two stay locked in a vicious struggle. A nearby agent pulls a pistol.

"Nooooo!"

He points it at my dog.

"Baxter, let go!"

I surge and strain but can't break free.

"Baxter!"

Something finally gets through, and the hound backs off. The wounded sportcoat crawls away, but his friend leans in with the gun.

"Run, Bax. Please..."

Baxter meets my eyes and something new flows between us. Some ancient fire. Bits of the Old Man.

Thanks for the help, friend. I owe you another one.

He woofs like he gets it.

Our story ain't done yet. Go on and we'll catch up.

307

Old hound nods at me. Fucking *nods* at me. Then darts off and disappears out the back. The sportcoat holsters his gun and I sigh with relief.

"Okay, Hobbes. I called off my dog. Now call off yours."

Claire and Baxter took out three sportcoats, but six more stand ready to pounce. Hobbes looks at me with murder in his eyes. He nods and a forearm slips around my neck.

"Hey, wai-"

The sportcoat clamps down and my breath cuts off. Sleeper hold. Squeezing like a vice. My vision tunnels and my legs go weak. I have fleeting thoughts of Ashley then it all fades to black.

Chapter 55

I come to on a floor. Dark. Dizzy. Bound by hands and feet.

It's quiet. Soft carpet. Where the hell am I?

"Hello?"

Someone grunts. Not alone. Could be a guard, or one of those sportcoats we roughed up. Neither bodes well for me. At least Baxter got away.

I wonder who else made it out. Delsin? Sage? I didn't see much after that sportcoat put me in a sleeper. All I know is Claire got dragged out the stage door.

"Is that you, Claire?"

Another grunt. Big and masculine. Probably not Claire.

"Guess again, cowboy."

That voice. It couldn't be...

"Arden?"

"Clayton Fucking Moore."

"Arden!"

I roll across the floor and lean into his bulk. He finds my hand with a squeeze. Big, sweaty bear paw. I hear him cry but don't say anything. After a time, we roll apart.

"You're here to save me."

"Something like that."

"Bout time y'all showed up."

"We've been trying, Ard."

"I don't doubt it."

He's quiet for a spell and I listen to him breathe. Doesn't sound well.

"How's your shoulder?"

"Fucked up. How's yours?"

"Same."

"They shot Kali."

"Oh, Ard..."

"First man through the door. Put a bullet between her eyes."

309

"I'm so sorry."

He's quiet again. Slow, labored breaths. I think about his white wolf and those icy eyes.

"What about Baxter?"

"He's all right."

"Glad to hear it."

"Where are we, Arden?"

"Some swank hotel."

"You're kidding."

"Penthouse suite. Locked in a closet."

Those sportcoats this morning. I knew something was off...

"Believe it or not, I think I have a room downstairs."

"Well, I hope you got whiskey."

"I hope you got smokes."

Chuckles. A cough.

"You don't sound so good, Ard."

"I've been better."

"That was a brave thing you did."

"I got shot."

"You bought us time."

"Well, what'd you do with it?"

I sigh. What do I tell him? How to give the man hope?

"We met Ashley's sister."

"I bet she's legit."

"She is. USAC's been hot, but Sage kept us clear."

"Is that so?"

"Well..." I scramble for words. "We outran some choppers and crashed in the woods. Hightailed to Pittsburgh. Tuck was with us, but... he didn't make it."

"I'm sorry to hear that."

"Sage booked a suite in this fancy hotel. We went to a gamer con, all dressed up. You should see Del."

"I'd like to."

Another pregnant pause. Arden's heavy breath.

"That the end of the story?"

I sigh. "It didn't go down how we planned. I got nabbed. So did our girl, Claire. She took a few with her, though."

"Sounds like y'all been busy."

310

"This isn't over, Ard. Sage is still out there. So is Del. I think..."

A pained grunt.

"The cavalry's coming. You just gotta have faith."

"Now you sound like my husband."

"Del's rubbed off on me a bit."

"I'll try not to take that the wrong way."

I sigh again. Poor Arden. I can't imagine what he's been through. Shot through and locked up and missing his man. There's something else I need to ask, but I've been holding back. Arden takes it up for me.

"She's not here, Clay."

My heart sinks. I don't have words to respond.

"She might be around, but I haven't seen her. They separated us a few days back."

"Why'd they separate you?"

"We were talking. Plotting. You know how she is."

"I do."

If Ashley's not with Arden, where could she be?

"How long have you been in here?"

"Hard to say. At least a day, but I've lost track of time. Every so often some thug brings me to the bathroom."

"Have you seen anyone else in the suite?"

"Couple of heavies prowling around. Hobbes comes and goes. Last time I went to piss they were bringing in a call girl."

"A call girl?"

"Chinese chick wearing next to nothing. She was fightin' everybody though."

"That sounds like Claire. Grad student under Ashley's sister. She's no call girl."

"Well, I pity the man that tries to make her one."

"Did you see where they took her? How big is the suite?"

"Shit, I've seen three different bathrooms just to piss. Hobbes could house an army up here."

Maybe Ashley is around after all. Some bathroom or closet. The thought gives me goosebumps.

"I need to look around the place."

"Good luck with that."

311

I shimmy over and try the door, but it holds firm. The damn carpet's so thick I can't peek underneath.

"I need to get out and look for Ash."

"Like I said, I've been out to piss and that's it."

"Well, I gotta piss."

BANG! BANG! BANG!

I sit up and pound the door. My left arm is still slung high, and now my wrists are tied together across my chest. It's at least more comfortable than the pretzel job Lavigne put me in.

"Open up! I need to piss!"

BANG! BANG! BANG!

I listen at the door but it's quiet.

"You sure somebody's out there?"

"Somebody is."

BANG! BANG! BANG!

"Toilet! I need a toilet!"

Now I hear muffled grumbling as footsteps approach the door.

"Good luck, cowboy."

"We got this, Arden."

A lock turns and the door pulls open. Bright light blinds my darkroom eyes.

"What do you want?"

"I need to pee. Gonna burst over here."

A hulking figure looms over me in a black sportcoat. He wears a handgun on his hip and a rifle on his shoulder. Probably another pistol or two up his ass.

"Bathroom break's not for 30 minutes."

"I can't hold it that long!"

"Not my problem."

He moves to close the door and I shove my legs through the gap.

"Please, buddy! I ain't pissed myself since preschool. Give a man some dignity."

He stares down with menace as I do my best to look pathetic. We lock eyes for a moment, and I go for it. That Old Man flow.

We're the same stuff, brother. Let this cowboy work.

He frowns like he farted, then looks around the room. A snort. A shrug. He reaches down to lift me roughly by my left shoulder.

"Owww! Easy man, that's dislocated!"

He smirks and shoves me out of the closet. My feet are still tied together, and I immediately fall flat on my face.

"Dammit! What's your problem?"

He leans over with a snarl. "Your dog mauled my partner. He's in the hospital right now getting his balls stitched."

Attaboy, Baxter.

"I'm sorry about your friend's balls." I keep my eyes down this time. "Old hound was just protecting his people. Same as y'all."

The big man sighs. "Get up."

"My feet are tied." I squirm around for effect. He sighs again and bends down to clip the zip tie at my ankles. I stand and flex my useless hands.

"You gonna hold my dick for me too?"

The guard glares with absolute menace. He sticks his semi-auto in my face as he cuts my wrists free.

"One false move and I'll fuck you up."

"I can see that." I shake the blood back into my limbs. "Which way to the can?"

He jabs me with the gun barrel, and I set off stumbling across the room. The space is large and luxurious. Plush furniture. Posh decor. Hardwood stairs lead up to a loft while big glass doors reveal a private balcony outside.

Arden wasn't kidding. Hobbes could house an army up here.

"Right." Another jab with the gun and I veer around a massive leather couch. A sportcoat snores loudly while two more munch sandwiches on either side.

In all, I count half-a-dozen USAC guards in various postures around the room. A fat black man sits at attention next to a closed door. He holds a rifle across his lap and watches my every move.

Is Ashley behind that door?

I want to scream at him: *Is Ashley behind that door!?*

"Over here." The sportcoat leading me points to his bathroom of choice. "Leave it open."

I walk into a majestic marbled washroom with floor-to-ceiling mirrors. I catch a glimpse of myself and stop short. I look ridiculous. Still mocked up like an outlaw with his arm in a sling.

I take a long leak and splash water on my face. The sink is shiny chrome. The toilet jingles while I pee. Everything in here is fancy as hell. I need to find Ashley and Claire.

"Time's up!"

My friend with the rifle knocks on the doorframe and orders me out. In a moment of random agency, I pocket a lump of soap. It feels like a win, somehow. Secret soap.

"Back to the closet."

He waves his gun around like a pecker, and I wonder if this guy's in the closet himself. I walk as slow as I can get away with. The big black guard keeps eyeing me like I stole something. Does he know about the soap?

IS ASHLEY BEHIND THAT DOOR?!

I ponder a charge. Just bum rush like a raging bull. But there's no point. I'd end a bloody smear on the carpet, and Ashley deserves better.

"Move along."

The sportcoat prods me, but I hesitate. I need to reach her somehow. To connect. To let her know.

"Ashley!"

The fat guard shifts on his stool.

"Ashley, are you in there?"

Sportcoat shoves me from behind and I fall to the floor.

"Ashley, I'm here for you!"

"That's enough!"

My escort yanks me to my feet while the door guard hefts his rifle. I take two steps and trip over a low table. Hit the floor to buy more time.

"Ashley! Claire! It's going to be okay!"

I hope they can hear me. This place has dense doors, but something must get through.

"Ashley!"

I roll under the table and blank my mind.

I'm here, Ash.

I reach for her. Like flowers feeling for the sun.

I've learned some things. I see it now.

"That's enough!" The sportcoats close in and I brace for pain, but then something catches my eye beneath the door:

Fingers.

Brown and beautiful. Poking out with a ring I'd recognize from Mars.

Hey, Boo.

They wiggle and wave. No one notices but me.

I found you.

I'm swept up in a scrum and manhandled across the room. Sportcoats toss me in the closet where I hit the wall hard and collapse to the floor.

"No more piss breaks for you!"

The door slams. The lock clicks. Voices fade, then it's quiet again. Just Arden's labored breathing mixed with mine.

"How'd you do, cowboy?"

My head swims with excitement and pain.

"She's here, Arden."

I see stars in the darkness.

She's here.

Chapter 56

Hours pass. I lose track of time and space.

Arden's not much for talking, but I share stories of our journey. The cave. The storm. The helicopters. The chase.

At one point I hear sounds of commotion through the heavy door. Yelling. Banging. Maybe Ashley is killing them all.

Arden and I lie quietly in the darkness, until someone drags us out into the light.

"Put him over there."

Hobbes' voice. I'm dropped on a couch in front of a giant TV. Arden is eased down next to me. They're gentler with him, but he's twice my size.

I look around for Ashley and Claire but see neither. There's an ugly new guard in front of the same closed door.

"Turn it on."

Hobbes stands by the bar with a bottle in his hand. He drains a beer and opens another. Someone cues up a news report on the big TV.

"... *shocking footage from the Greater Allegheny Gaming Convention, where violence broke out this afternoon during a panel discussion featuring industry icon Oliver Hobbes. The video, streamed via Facebook by recent viral sensation Claire Boheme, reveals a heated verbal confrontation over Hobbes' alleged suppression of energy technology. The billionaire mogul, known for his leadership over technology firm Cygneous and gaming franchise AMPersand, directed private security to detain Miss Boheme, resulting in an altercation as she was removed from the room. An unidentified man dressed as a cowboy was also forcibly detained.*"

Unidentified cowboy. Pops would be proud.

"*Oliver Hobbes has so far offered no public comments on the incident, but a spokesperson for Cygneous called it: "A desperate stunt in pursuit of viral fame." The internet has responded with more speculation about Miss Boheme, and the relationship between today's incident and a recent high-speed chase she broadcast from central Ohio. Some are questioning Hobbes' aggressive use of private security, while others allege he holds broad command authority over a range of military assets. The event has inspired several popular hashtags trending across social media, including #GAGbrawl, #voltstone, and #FreeClaire. The whereabouts of Miss Boheme and any potential accomplices are currently unknown..."*

"Turn it off."

The TV goes black, and a fat silence takes the room. A bunch of gun barrels bob in my direction. Hobbes wouldn't kill me here, would he?

Would he?

BOOM!

Something crashes and everybody jumps. I brace for bullets, but it sounds like Hobbes smashed a bottle in the sink. I keep my eyes forward. He pops a fresh beer with a soft hiss.

"That was some stunt you pulled."

Hobbes slowly walks around and sits across from Arden and I. His tie is loose at the collar. Sweat beads on his brow. He sips beer from the bottle and glares at me.

"You're playing with fire, Clay Moore."

"A fire you started."

He smirks and sets his beer on the table.

"I've played this game before. I know how it ends."

"You've bombed houses and kidnapped families?"

"Yes."

Another tense silence. Arden breathes heavily next to me. Now that I'm finally seated across from Oliver Hobbes, I see a bit of the man behind the monster. Hungry eyes. Wrinkled lips. I bet he's got a tiny dick.

"Is something funny?"

I shake my head, but can't wipe the grin. What is Hobbes but a lost soul like the rest of us? Some wayward shard of the Old Man.

Still a piece of shit, though.

"You know what I want, Hobbes."

A fiendish smirk. "You want what all simple men want: a cold beer and a warm cunt." He burps in my face.

"Ashley's a lot more than that."

"Of course she is." Hobbes snaps his fingers and more bottles appear. He hands one to me, but I give it to Arden instead.

"That's your problem, Moore..." Hobbes shakes his head. "Everything is there for the taking, but you just pass it along."

"You don't know shit about me."

"I know your father left you a ranch."

"You don't know shit about my dad."

Hobbes smiles and sighs. "I'm sure he was a fine man." He offers me another beer, but again I refuse. "The world needs men like him. Just as it needs men like me."

"Con men and killers?"

"Leaders."

I can't help but scoff. "What kind of leader kills women and kids? What kind of leader hides resources from the world?"

"Leadership is sacrifice." Hobbes stands and prowls slowly while he talks. "Everyone wants to be in charge, but few are willing to do what it takes."

"Maybe the rest of us have a conscience."

"Maybe so." Hobbes shrugs. He pulls out a smartphone and fiddles while everyone waits.

"So where do we go from here?" I ask.

"I haven't decided yet."

"You want to throttle a few kittens first?"

Hobbes doesn't react, but one of his hired guns snorts.

"This may surprise you, Mr. Moore, but my motives transcend simple violence and greed."

"Are you kidding?" I make a dramatic show of looking around. "We're in a penthouse suite surrounded by guns. All I see is violence and greed."

"That's because you're missing the big picture."

"Man, you're so full of shit." I turn to Arden and shake my head. "Nothing this guy says means a damn thing."

Arden nods. "All hat and no cattle."

Hobbes' mouth goes tight and his head tips slowly to one side. "No cattle, you say?" He gets a weird look in his eye and gulps the rest of his beer. "Bring them out."

Two sportcoats march toward the closed door and it takes me a moment to appreciate what's going on. *Bring them out.* That can only mean one thing. An oafish lackey fumbles with a set of keys while Hobbes stands by grinning like Mr. Burns.

Bring them out.

I slide to the edge of the couch. Arden puts a heavy hand on my knee. The clumsy sportcoat drops the keys twice before finally getting them into the lock.

Click.

The door swings wide.

The room is dark, and I stand to get a better look. I wait an agonizing beat. Then two. I'm about to make a move, when out comes Claire Boheme.

She looks drowsy and disheveled, still dressed down as Sexy Link. The sportcoat leads her at gunpoint while Hobbes ogles her up and down. It's gross and I want to punch him. Then my wife steps through the door.

My first feeling is love. Just heart-swelling love to see Ashley's face after almost a week. I move instinctively toward her, and a dozen guns turn toward me. I don't stop until one of the sportcoats puts a barrel to my chest.

"That's close enough, Mr. Moore."

"Ashley..."

She's led over next to Claire and her eyes meet mine. The whole world stops. Hobbes. Arden. Sportcoats. Guns. Nothing moves. Nothing breathes. Nothing exists but Ashley Moore and me. We speak through our eyes.

Are you okay?

Be careful, Boo.

I'm here for you now.

It's not over yet...

I reach out with my mind and take Ashley in my arms. I stroke her hair and kiss her mouth and feel her chest and hear her heart and then Oliver Hobbes slaps her hard across the face.

Time starts back up again.

"Gaauuggh!"

I unleash some kind of guttural roar, like a cow under a hot brand. Ashley, for her part, barely reacts. She doesn't whimper or cower or cry out in shock. Almost like she's been hit before.

"Do you see it now, Mr. Moore?"

319

"You goddamn cocksucking son of a-"

He hits her again. An open-handed slap that sends blood dripping off her nose.

"You fuck! What the fuck?" I'm white-hot rage and it takes three sportcoats to hold me back. "I'll kill you, Hobbes. I burn you alive if you so much as-"

This time he winds up and punches Claire in the gut. Her eyes bug out, and she collapses to the floor. She was not ready for that.

"Aaauuugghh! Why? You sick fuck!"

"Do you see it now, Mr. Moore?"

"They can't even defend themselves!"

"They'll be fine." Hobbes flexes his hand and nods to one of his lackeys. The sportcoat drags Claire to her feet and leads them both to a squat settee against the wall. They slump there together. Claire, teary and wheezing. Ashley, stoic and hard.

"Leadership is sacrifice." Hobbes repeats his mantra. "I don't want to hurt your friends, but I have to show you I'm willing to do what it takes." I say nothing. I'm done baiting this fuck. "I've earned my power, Mr. Moore, and you can see what separates us now."

"I can see it, all right."

Hobbes smiles and opens another beer. "You might find it cruel, but the whole world is cruel. I'd rather be in my shoes than yours."

I sit back down and stew. I turn to Arden, but he won't meet my eyes. I turn to Ashley and her face is cement. What I wouldn't give to see her smile again.

"What do you want, Hobbes?"

He leans down and offers me a bottle of beer. Third time. I finally accept and take a long swig. Maybe he's breaking me down.

"I want to protect what's mine," Hobbes says. "What I've worked so hard to build."

"Your Voltstone empire."

"And the power it holds."

"Well, I'm not standing in your way."

"I'll be the judge of that."

I take another swig of beer. Some hoppy highbrow import. It tastes like piss.

"Your pilot is dead."

"Yes. Unfortunate. I was hoping to make an example out of him."

"Tuck really shook you up, didn't he?"

"Just a few loose ends. Nothing I can't clean up."

"Is that what we are to you? Loose ends?"

Hobbes smiles. Mischievous. Unhinged.

"Would you like to hear a story, Mr. Moore?"

"Do I have a choice?"

"It might give you some perspective."

"Then I'm gonna need another beer."

I chug the remains of my bottle and wait for round two. I try to calculate my odds of smashing the glass and killing Hobbes with a jagged edge. I bet Ashley could pull it off.

"And how about one for my wife? And Claire? And a freshie for Arden, here?"

My wife doesn't even drink, but I'm playing the hand I've got. Hobbes considers a moment, then nods and fresh bottles appear. A sportcoat offers one to Ashley and she just glares at him. Little she can do with both hands behind her back.

"Cut them free," Hobbes says, and the sportcoat clips the ties around Claire and Ashley's wrists. I mug for Ashley like I won something, but there are still too many guns in the room to tip the scales. She takes the drink and sips slowly without a word.

Hobbes knocks back his own and reaches for another. This guy can drink. He sits in silence for a heavy minute, collecting whatever batshit thoughts hold court inside his brain. I'm about to break the silence when Oliver Hobbes begins his tale...

Chapter 57 – Hobbes' Story

I was fifteen when I realized I could rule the world.

It hit me like a drug. Like a needle in the arm.

Before that I was lazy. Cocksure son of a car salesman. We had money, but no power. Means without mystique. Life was comfortable, and that was enough. Until I saw another way.

It was my first summer job. Caddie at the local boys' club, hauling bags for all the swinging dicks. I'd get up with the sun and walk fairways for tips.

"Beautiful drive, sir."

"Seven should carry the water."

"Back pin is your sweet spot."

These men were a different breed from my father. Bankers, brokers, and lawyers. They'd drink and smoke and talk business and sex. I'd lurk in the wings and wipe mud off their balls.

I was only fifteen, but I wanted what they had. Nice clothes. Nice clubs. Pretty cars. Pretty wives. I saved some money and bought a big flashy watch. It was a brick of a piece, but it put swagger in my stride.

Maybe I could be a big swinging dick someday? Work hard. Play hard. Climb the ladder. Step on toes.

I came to idolize those men as masters of the universe.

But those men were nothing.

I learned that the day she showed up.

It started with a phone call. Rainy August morning, lazing about the caddyshack. The boss' phone rang and he went silent for a full minute.

"Is this for real?"

Apparently it was. Without another word, he hung up and let out a low whistle.

"VIP coming through," he announced. "I need everyone's dicks in a row the next few days."

He wouldn't say more, but rumors got the clubhouse buzzing. Who was the VIP? We had some pro athletes tee up now and then. They'd get lots of gladhanding, but kept it low key.

This was different.

The whole club went into overdrive dolling up the place. They had me washing windows in the pro shop when one of the regulars came blasting in.

"What's this about my tee time getting pushed tomorrow?"

He was wet and angry and looking for someone to ream. He turned to me like I had something to do with it.

"I've been going off at nine for five goddamn years. Who the hell thinks they're taking my slot?"

I shrugged and mumbled and double-timed my streaky windows. The clubhouse manager bailed me out.

"Andy! Get in here!" He called the guy into his office and closed the door. Five minutes later, Andy barreled out again cussing to himself.

Who was pulling rank on all the swinging dicks?

I went home that night and got my gear in order. Cleaned my shoes. Pressed my shirt. Cut my hair. Dreamed about carrying bags for POTUS and his men.

I made sure to be the first caddie on site the next morning. Boss gave me a queer look and a cup of coffee.

"You really want this one, huh?" He looked me up and down and must have liked what he saw. "Tell you what: tip out your mates anything over two-hundred. Hang tight in the clubhouse and I'll call you when she's ready."

She?

The VIP?

This alpha swinging dick was a She?

Now my head was spinning as I waited for the call. I'd spent the whole summer building up the club regulars, and here came some broad making everyone bend the knee.

Whatever her deal, I was excited to land the loop and a fat tip along with it. I sprinted to the caddyshack when my name was called, and met with a sober looking group that proved to be her entourage.

"This is Oliver Hobbes," my boss addressed the crowd. "He's young but he's good. Knows the course. Won't get in anyone's way." He looked at me with this last part and I filed away the subtext.

One of the lackeys eyed me over and whispered something to a colleague. I counted three men and one woman. They all wore golf shirts and sunglasses and pistols. One carried a briefcase. Not the foursome I expected.

"She plays fast," the woman said to me. She had sharp black hair and small gold earrings. Quite beautiful despite a scar across her forehead. "You need to hustle to beat her to every ball."

"Understood."

"Keep the club heads clean and the talk to a minimum. If she asks you a question, don't bullshit. She'll know."

"Yes ma'am."

"Take this bag to the first tee and we'll meet you when she's ready."

I hoisted a beautiful leather golf bag and jogged to the opening tee box. The grounds were quiet. Everyone waiting on a whale.

I used the interim to take stock of her gear. Chromed irons. Titanium driver. Shit I'd never seen before. (This was 1988.) She had three sleeves of balls with custom paint: little red ladybugs and a single boldface word: *MARIQUITA.*

Just exactly who's bag was I about to carry? Some mystery bitch with ladybug balls usurped the whole fucking club?

I stood tall and waited. The sun burned off morning clouds. Her entourage came over and took positions around the tee. Sunglasses. Pistols. Briefcase. Same crew I'd seen before.

Still no VIP.

Ten more minutes passed, everyone just standing around. I suddenly had to pee and that's when she showed up.

"Incoming," said one of the lackeys, and we all straightened our stance. Next came the hum of a golf cart and up pulled the club president himself.

"...anything else during your stay I will personally see it done."

He hopped off and hustled - fucking *hustled* - around to the passenger side to escort his charge.

"*Muchas gracias,*" she said. "That will be all."

"Enjoy your round." He climbed back in the cart, then almost as an afterthought shot me a glare.

Don't fuck this up, Hobbes.

The cart sped away and there she stood. Short. Wiry. Wavy dark hair. She wore a bright red skirt and metal spikes that clacked the cart path as she approached the first tee.

"*Buenas días*, Mariquita," said the man with the briefcase. She walked straight toward me and I was ready with the driver.

"Fairway slopes to the right." I handed her the club, and she took a few practice swings. Smooth. Compact. Powerful. "Aim for the big spruce to cut the dogleg down."

She nodded, teed up one of her fancy balls, and striped a drive exactly where I'd pointed. Ninety percent of the club regs couldn't do that.

I admired the flight for a moment before I realized the whole group was already marching in its wake. I scrambled to catch up, barely winning the race to the next shot. They were right when they said Mariquita played fast. She stalked down that fairway like she owned it, surveying her domain behind mirrored aviator shades.

It took a few holes to get her cadence down, but I soon started earning my keep. I helped read a green and she buried the putt. Offered an iron and set up a bird. It was easy when she hit everything so clean, so straight, so true. I started thinking she must be an old tour pro. A barnstorming vet.

Then she had a man killed on the fourteenth green.

I think that's what happened. I'll never know for sure. She'd just drilled a three-wood to the back fringe, and I was busting ass to get an early look at an eagle putt. I set down the bag and squatted behind the ball. A minute passed but no one else showed up. I stood to see the whole entourage huddled around a greenside bunker, and I jogged over to investigate.

"Looks like a slippery left-to-right that should speed up as-"

Mariquita stopped me with a finger. A single firm gesture that froze my mouth and my feet. She spoke in hushed tones to the man with the briefcase, and I caught random clips of Spanish words.

"*Pagar dinero... consecuencias... la última vez...*"

The discussion grew heated and there appeared to be some disagreement within the group. One of the lackeys raised his voice but quickly backed off. Whatever they were discussing, Mariquita got her way. The debate ended when she made an emphatic swipe with her hand, and the man opened his briefcase to reveal a fancy satellite phone. It looked like something out of a movie. He dialed a number and spoke two quick words then hung up. I never caught what he said, but Mariquita nodded and lit up some kind of cigarillo while they continued to wait.

It was at this point she seemed to notice I was still standing nearby. I tried to back off, but she waved me over and offered me a smoke. I really didn't want it, and I had a weird feeling about whatever was going on, but by then I was at the mercy of Mariquita and the group. I sparked up and sputtered and they all had a good laugh. Maybe I helped break the tension.

A few minutes later the phone rang, and Mr. Briefcase held it to his ear. He didn't say anything, but nodded to Mariquita and she let out a long sigh. The woman with the scar recited a prayer, then they all crossed themselves and looked up to the sky.

It was an eerie intermission, but Mariquita broke the spell by stomping out her smoke and clapping me on the back.

"¡Vámonos!"

She marched to the ball with a spring in her step, two-putted for birdie and went on to card a superlative 73. As we parted ways after the round, her female companion slipped a wad of hundred-dollar bills into my hand and invited me to join them again.

"That's the best I've seen her play in a while. Same time tomorrow morning?"

I nodded absently but couldn't stop staring at the pistol on her hip. She caught me looking and hitched up her belt.

"You did well today. Just remember that Mariquita values her privacy."

She palmed me another Benjamin and sent me on my way. I went home and laid out my haul: five hundred dollars. More than I'd spent on that fancy watch. I was high on fresh cash, but questions kept me up half the night. Who was Mariquita? Why the guns and the briefcase and the drama on the fourteenth green?

I showed up dutifully the next morning. Groggy, but ready to work. The round went more or less the same, though she didn't play as well and the phone never came out. She got testy after slicing a few on the back nine and sent one of her lackeys into the water to fetch a ball.

326

They seemed happy enough with my work, and I netted another four hundred bucks after tipping out some clubhouse staff. The other caddies were jealous and probing. "Who is she? What's with the entourage? How does she play?"

Nobody knew shit, but the rumors were flying. Most people assumed she was a drug dealer. One guy swore he'd seen her on *America's Most Wanted*. My favorite was the bartender who said she was the deposed queen of Cuba, and we were giving her asylum in exchange for Soviet nuclear codes.

Whatever the case, she brought Nine Pines Golf and Country Club to its knees. As her caddy for a few days, I enjoyed some notoriety myself. It was heady stuff.

I spent the second night pondering what to do with my newfound wealth. I was suddenly less interested in flashy material ends. Shiny watches. Speedy cars. These were just toys in the face of Mariquita's power. I watched her leave the golf course in a helicopter. She had a mystique that put the local swinging dicks to shame.

The next morning, I was up and at it again. She brought a playing partner this time, an older Asian man with tattoos on his neck. My buddy Goose got picked for the bag and couldn't stop smiling. I tried to coach him up as we waited on the first tee.

"This is big time, Goose. It's good money if you're on point."

"I want to see if this woman eats babies like they say."

"It's not like that. But her whole entourage is armed."

"What are they packing? Uzis? Kalashnikovs?"

"I don't know. Pistols. They've also got a satellite phone in a briefcase."

"Pistols? I thought she was some guerrilla narco."

"She's legit, Goose. Don't drop a club or cross her line."

"We'll see. You know anything about the chink I'm toting for?"

I winced at the slur. Goose's father was a club member, and he often rode a high horse through the caddyshack. I assumed Goose got the loop on privilege, but he was in over his head with this group.

"I don't know anything, and you're best not to ask questions."

Goose shrugged and rooted through the guy's bag. He pulled out a driver; this big, ornate cudgel with a clubhead painted like a duck.

"Look at this shit." He took a few practice swings while I busied myself with a fresh sleeve of Mariquita's ladybug balls. A moment later we heard a furious scream, and Goose and I both turned to see the Asian man storming our way.

"Oh, crap..."

He wagged a finger and bugged his eyes and spit a stream of inscrutable rage. I don't know if it was Chinese or Korean or what, but his message was clear: *Put down my fucking club.*

Goose cowed and raised his hands while the guy marched right up into his face. Balled fists. Bulging veins. I've never seen someone so upset. Goose looked like he was going to faint, and I felt a sliver of pity for my friend. He wasn't a bad kid. Just cocky and stupid and hadn't learned better. Well, he was about to.

Just as I considered stepping in, the Asian guy reached back and wrenched a 9-iron from his bag. He twirled it once then swung full bore into the side of Goose's head.

The sound was horrific. I'll never forget it. This wet, heavy *thunk* as Goose's skull cracked and the club broke off at the shaft. Goose made a queer groan and dropped like a sack. His eyes stayed open, and I was sure he was dead.

Then the guy turned to me. Flecks of blood on his face and a crazy glint in his eye. He ground his teeth and heaved his breath and held the broken club handle like a baton.

I froze.

I thought about running. I thought about screaming. I thought about grabbing one of Mariquita's clubs in self-defense. Instead, I just stood there and watched my life flash before my eyes. It was short and meaningless. The next thing I knew, one of Mariquita's henchmen had a pistol to the guy's head.

"Stand down."

Still, nobody moved. A tense standoff had just become more so with the addition of a gun. I glanced at Goose and saw blood dribbling out of his mouth. A second henchman reached down and checked his pulse.

"*¿Qué sucedió?*"

Mariquita strolled onto the tee box. She wore a wide-brim fedora and held a cup of lemonade. The Asian guy finally relaxed. He gave her a slight bow, and the henchman's gun returned to his hip. They went back and forth in Spanish while Mariquita nodded and sipped her drink. I just stood there trying not to puke.

At one point she leaned over Goose's body and made a "*tsk tsk*" sound. Her female companion started giving instructions and one of the others tended Goose's wounds. The satellite phone came out, and after a few minutes I heard the drone of an approaching helicopter.

"Would you like to ride with him?"

It took me a moment to realize Mariquita was now talking to me. My tongue knotted in my mouth.

"Whuh..."

"We'll take him to a hospital. A good one."

"Is he... dead?"

"Not yet. Your friend is young. If his will is strong, he'll pull through."

I stuttered and groaned. Mariquita offered me a sip of lemonade and the cool drink loosened my lips.

"Why would he do that?"

We both turned to the tattooed Asian man, now sitting calmly in the grass.

"He claims that club holds the spirit of his father. Your friend was wrong to play with it."

"But Goose was just messing around. He didn't even fight back."

Mariquita shrugged. "Messing around with something sacred to a powerful man. A hard lesson learned."

"But that isn't fair."

"And what would have been fair?"

She studied me pointedly and I withered beneath her gaze. She finished the lemonade and passed the cup off to a waiting hand.

"People decide what's fair. Today it was that man with that club. Are you prepared to do something about it?"

"I don't..." I studied my shoes, defeated. "He should go to jail."

"Maybe he will." Mariquita waved her briefcase over.

"Goose's dad is a lawyer."

"I know plenty of lawyers."

"He's a member at this club."

"This club?" She looked around theatrically. Her entourage loomed and the chopper grew louder. Point made.

Her lackey opened the briefcase and she pulled out a banded stack of cash. She rifled hundred-dollar bills with her thumb then offered the wad to me.

"You've been a good help. We appreciate your continued discretion."

I gawked at what must have been ten grand held in front of my face.

"You're buying me off?"

"Ensuring your cooperation."

She tipped her head toward Goose. A subtle threat. Still, I balked.

"But Goose is my friend."

He wasn't, really. A schoolmate. A coworker. We were hardly close. It still felt like a betrayal.

"And Mr. Park is mine." She pulled another wad from the briefcase and slapped both stacks into my hand. They were crisp and heavy. Practically stung my palm.

"H... how much is that?"

"Twenty thousand dollars."

My breath caught and I met Mariquita's eyes. There was something different there. A certainty I'd never seen before. This woman would eat my lunch whether I took her money or not.

I pocketed the cash.

"Wise decision." She leaned back and smiled. "You can spend that money, or you can build something with it. Find the right hustle and you'll rule the fucking world."

She patted me on the shoulder and started barking orders to her team. The chopper grew to a roar as it crested the treeline a hundred yards away. I stood there, still unable to move, still processing the bulge in my pocket and the blood in the grass. The Asian man retrieved his duck head driver and whispered to it like a fussy baby. The whole tee box bustled while I stayed rooted to the spot.

"Go on now, kid."

It was the woman with the scar. She had her pistol in hand as she scanned the surroundings. That was my cue to get lost. I glanced at Goose and he stared back with lifeless eyes. I took off and ran aimlessly down the fairway. I didn't want to set foot in the caddyshack. Never again. I was done with this club and all the limp dicks who ran it. I was about to duck into the woods when I took one last look back toward the tee.

There was Mariquita: standing tall amidst the chaos. Sat phone in her hand. Cigarillo in her mouth. She caught my eye and waved as a helicopter landed at her feet.

Chapter 58

Hobbes pauses and the room takes a breath.

"That's quite a story, Hobbes."

His eyes are vacant and there's sweat on his chin. I'm not sure if it's the memory or the beer.

"What happened to Goose?"

Hobbes shakes himself back into the present. "Goose survived but he never recovered. Too much blood in the brain. He spends his days in a wheelchair, painting still-lifes. They're terrible."

Arden grunts. "And these psychos are your role models? The ones that crippled your friend?"

"They taught me about power." Hobbes narrows his eyes. "Twenty years later I returned the favor."

"You tracked them down?"

"Mariquita's in the wind, but Mr. Park got what was coming to him."

One of the sportcoats snickers and Hobbes quiets him with a glare.

"I took that money and built an empire. Just like Mariquita suggested. I started with a question: What did people really want?"

Hobbes signals and someone brings him yet another beer. He sits heavily across from me and paws at his forehead.

"Then I pushed myself to think bigger: What did *powerful* people want? Corporations. Politicians. Billionaires. What would get me a seat with the brokers who ran the world?"

He raises a brow like he expects me to answer, but before I can open my mouth he barges on.

"Resources, Mr. Moore. Pure, potent, natural resources."

He says that word with a Cheshire grin. I'm pretty sure he's made this speech before.

"All of *life* is a battle for resources. Be it fish in a pond or cities on a hill. We compete for the same food, the same water, the same rocks."

Hobbes takes a long drink. His cheeks and nose are red. I glance over at Ashley, and she looks back at me with tired eyes.

"I aimed high but took my time," Hobbes carries on. "Mariquita gave me that luxury. I put myself through school with a degree in geoscience and an MBA. I founded *Cygneous* as a surveying and consulting firm, working with mining interests to locate new deposits around the world. In 2004 we got a contract to assess mineral reserves in Afghanistan. We stumbled upon something bigger than we ever imagined."

"Your Voltstone mine."

"Not just a mine, but a *mountain*. Ten billion tons of the stuff by our estimates."

"Good God." I choke on my beer. "You could power half the planet."

Hobbes nods and smiles. He's showing off now.

"If the world was ready, perhaps. But all those billionaires and bureaucrats - the power brokers I'd been seeking out – were willing to pay handsomely to keep Voltstone under wraps."

"So, you covered it all up?"

"I seized an opportunity with the world's elite."

I shake my head. Hobbes sets down his beer.

"You might see it as a moral failing, Mr. Moore, but I chose powerful friends over powerful enemies. Now I'm one of the richest men on earth."

He stands and spreads his arms. Basking in the breadth of his empire.

"Sounds like some Machiavellian bullshit."

Heads turn and I'm surprised to see Claire speaking up. She's got some of her color back and she narrows her eyes at Hobbes. "Your friend got ganked, so you became this evil boss. Most people try to find a middle ground."

Hobbes shakes his head. "You're not getting it. Goose *was* the middle ground. He was well off. White privilege. Connected father. None of it mattered. They told Goose's dad he walked into a backswing. You think the old man took that lying down?"

Claire shrugs and Hobbes steps menacingly toward her.

"He went on a crusade to avenge his son. Pulled every legal string he had. Six months later he turned up in a ditch." Claire frowns and Hobbes continues on. "This is the way it's always been. Machiavelli knew that centuries ago. Nothing has changed."

Hobbes folds his arms and Claire sits back. He sure paints a bleak picture. Money. Manipulation. Murder. The currencies of power. There has to be another way.

Of course there is, son.

Hard to see it in this room, Pops.

Who's the most powerful person you know?

You mean besides this guy with the army?

You know what I mean.

I nudge Arden. "You and Del ever talk about the Old Man?"

"Of course."

"What do you think he'd say to all this?"

Arden pauses to consider. "I could never paint it like Del, but there might be something there."

Hobbes hears our chatter and levels a glare. "Do you see it now, Mr. Moore?"

"You've made your point." I stand and look him in the eye. "I'm sorry about your friend."

"Don't be. Goose was a fool. There's a reason we both ended up where we did."

"I guess everyone eventually gets what they deserve."

Hobbes grins. Drunk and toothy. "Sounds like you finally understand your place."

"I'm getting there." I look to my wife. Her hair's a mottled mess and her cheek puffs where Hobbes slapped her. She smiles at me in spite of everything.

Come and find me, Clay Moore...

I take a deep breath and close my eyes. It's time to have a word with the Old Man. I let everything relax and the world drops away. My mind casts out like an ember on the wind.

"Clay?"

Arden's voice but I tune it out.

"Clay, you all right?"

Del said everything connects back to the Old Man. Every atom. Every flower. If that's true, I should be able to find the thread. Maybe give it a little pull...

"What is he doing?"

"What are you doing, Boo?"

Ashley and Claire. Hang in there, girls. I squeeze my eyes tighter and float out a little farther.

What's the plan here, son?

The Old Man, Pops. I'm gonna find him and we're gonna end this.

That's a bold play.

It seems to work for Del.

Del's been at it a long time.

I just need to find the thread.

"We don't have time for this." Hobbes' voice. Grumpy and gruff. "Tie him up and throw him back in the closet."

Shit. I feel rough hands on my arm. I smell sportcoats and sweat.

Time's running out, son.

I bear down and barrel through the void. There's a connection here, I know it.

Better hurry.

Where's the thread, Pops?

What thread?

The Old Man's thread. The one that connects everything back to him.

You are the damn thread.

Oh.

I slam on the brakes. The world grinds to a halt.

What did you think it all meant?

I don't know. I just wanted to find the Old Man.

It's all the Old Man.

Of course.

Every atom. Every flower.

Every cowboy and every stone.

You see it now.

I think I do.

So go get him.

I pull my mind back and turn my gaze in. Voices muffle and bodies jostle and I think I just got hit with a gun.

Godspeed, Clay Moore.

Come with me, Pops.

This is where I leave you.

But I can't do it alone.

No one's ever alone...

335

Aw hell, Pops.

Pops?

Guess that's it.

Come and find me, Clay Moore...

A different voice. Not Pops. Not Ashley either. Could it be? I dive deeper inside.

"God, he's like a dead weight."

"Fat ass cowboy."

I feel myself being dragged across the floor. My shoulder stings and my hip burns but I block it all out. The Old Man is here. Always has been. I catch a glimpse of something and follow it down, down, down....

"Better snap to, Clay."

"Please wake up, Boo!"

Arden. Ashley. It's okay guys, I promise. I can find him. I can feel him. I see a door and I push for it. I reach the knob and then I'm falling...

Falling...

Falling...

I hit earth. Frozen and firm. A jolt through my shoulder and a scrape on my chin. I climb slowly to my feet as grass crunches beneath my boots.

"Hello?"

Where am I? It's cold and dark and empty. I hear coyotes. I smell dog.

"Baxter?"

Something woofs and rubs past my leg. Soft and warm. I reach for his scruff.

"Where are we, Bax?"

He woofs again and my head starts to clear. My eyes find focus. A new scene resolves.

Welcome home, Clay.

We've come back to the valley. Blue hills and buffalo grass and look at those fucking stars.

God's country.

Of course. We were there all along.

You see it now.

Does that mean you're...?

Come and find me.

I walk. We walk. Baxter leads like a good boy. The night is cold and the wind is sharp, not at all like the summer eve we left. Baxter keeps his nose down and I double-time to keep up. We skirt Dob's at a horse's length, moving east toward the Chaplain Hills.

Everything's as it should be, but not. There are no craters. No rubble. No bombed-out remains. The earth is smooth and the air smells of juniper. Maybe none of it really happened. Maybe it was all a dream.

"Woof."

Baxter's on to something. His ears twitch and his tail whips around like a hose.

"What is it boy? You smell coyote?"

Hate to get mixed up with a prairie pack on a cold night like this. Ashley always tells me to bring a gun but I never do.

"Maybe we should turn back."

I look west to the house. Smoke slides from the chimney and warm light tickles the eaves. Is that a face in the window? I wave but can't tell if she waves back.

"Let's go home, Bax."

I wheel around and set course but ol' Baxter has other plans. A woof and a whimper and he's run out thirty feet.

"Baxter!"

He's going the wrong way. Down the valley. Toward the hills. I just want to go home. Curl up with Ashley and be done with all this.

"Woof!"

Off to my right. "What are you on, Bax?"

"Woof!"

"Let's call it, buddy! Hustle back to momma."

"Woof!"

He keeps barking and keeps straying and I keep after him without much choice.

"Where'd you go, boy?"

"Woof! Woof!"

I close to the spot and he's circling something in the grass. Awfully proud of himself. He yields the find as I step up.

"All right, Baxter. What is it?"

"Woof! Woof!"

I lean down and squint but it's too dark to see. No moon tonight. I pat for my lighter but come up empty.

"Well, I can't see shit. Help a cowboy out."

He ducks down and scoops something into his mouth, then drops a warm, wet weight into my palm.

"Oh, gross, Bax. What is...?"

My first thought is a dead rat or a fresh turd. Ol' hound's not above hauling either around in his maw. But then I get a weird feeling across my fingers. Like an electric pulse.

"Jesus, Bax..."

It's some kind of stone. Smooth and solid and slick with bloodhound drool. I raise it high and the surface catches starlight.

"What in the world?"

Baxter woofs and wags. A cold wind cuts but the stone grows hot in my hand.

You know what it is.

It feels familiar.

Everything is familiar.

I rub my thumb across colorful veins. Green and blue and electric and alive. I've seen this before.

You've seen everything before.

I reach back and remember. The buzz of a plane. A shock in the water. A cave at the end of the world.

It's a Voltstone.

Correct.

Oliver Hobbes tried to kill me over this.

And how did he do?

I'm still standing. I think.

But you're in trouble.

We're all in trouble. Ashley, Arden, Claire...

So why are you here, Clay Moore?

I'm looking for the Old Man.

It's all the Old Man.

Of course.

Every atom. Every flower.

Every cowboy and every stone.

You see it now.

I think I do.

338

So go get him.

But I feel like I'm running in circles.

Because you keep asking the same questions.

I study the stone as it pulses in my hand. It's dazzling and pure. The key to some great lock.

What's it made of, Clay?

I look closer. I lean in. The surface shimmers and swirls into shapes. I see stars. I see faces. I see people come and gone.

There's Pops on his horse.

Ash smiling behind a coffee cup.

Sage in her stilettos and Tuck stumbling in the night.

It's all right there in the stone. Everything. Everyone. The colors dance and the faces blur until there's only one left. Three-day beard and a black Cattleman. I know that look.

What's it made of, Clay?

I gaze at the stone and it stares back with my own eyes. It heats up in my hand. Warmer. Sizzling. Hot.

"Ouch!"

What's it made of, Clay?

"It burns!"

What's it made of, Clay?

"It's on fire!"

What's it made of, Clay?

Baxter barks and skin scalds but I can't release the stone. It's part of me. Always has been. I tip my head back and scream to the sky.

"It's made of me!"

Yes.

"It's made of you!"

Of course.

"It's made of God."

The stars and the stone and the pain all disappear. I'm all that's left. Just an ember in the void.

You see it now.

I see everything.

You feel it now.

I feel everything.

You started this.

And I can finish it.

Welcome home, Old Man. Welcome home.

Chapter 59

I come back to myself.

I open my eyes.

There's a face. There's a sneer. Black hair, high and tight.

"He's awake."

Sharp hands beneath my armpits. A grunting sportcoat hosits me to my feet.

"What was that bullshit?"

Oliver Hobbes glares at me from across the room. Drunk. Drooping. I ignore him and turn to my wife.

"What happened, Clay?"

Ashley looks worried. Coiled to rise but still rooted next to Claire. I flash a cowboy smile and her shoulders relax.

"I'm okay, Ash."

I take a deep breath and take stock. I'm perched between two sportcoats before an open closet door. The room tingles with uncertainty. Everyone seems to be waiting on me.

"Sorry for giving y'all a spook." I present my palms in atonement. "The Old Man sends his regards."

Arden perks up and catches my eye from the couch. Hobbes grumbles and polishes off his open beer.

I feel wonderfully serene. Transcendent. At peace. After all this time, I finally see what Del's been trying to show me:

I wrote this story.

Straight from the Old Man's almighty pen.

Now together we're gonna burn this motherfucker down.

I stand tall and smooth out my pants. There's a bulge in my pocket. Something round and firm. It's that fancy soap I grabbed when I took a piss. I reach down and pull it out and the Old Man plays his first Joker.

"What the hell?"

"Where'd you get that?"

Sat flush on my fingers is no lump of scented lard. It's a Voltstone. Shiny and true. Hobbes' eyes bulge as he storms over and screams at the sportcoat on my left.

"Why didn't you take this?"

"We frisked him boss, I swear."

"Well frisk him again!"

Two goons wrap me in a rubdown while Hobbes snatches the stone from my palm.

"Ow! What the fuck?"

He immediately drops it and shakes out his hand. The Voltstone rolls across the room and disappears beneath a couch.

"It's scalding hot!" Hobbes looks pained and confused. "Fucking burned me."

He shuffles to the sink and runs cold water over his wound. Sportcoats jostle my junk but find nothing else of note.

Everybody's quiet for a minute.

Then all hell breaks loose.

It's hard for me to tell what's happening at first. I hear a grunt and a thud and both sportcoats beside me hit the floor. There's a blur to my left and gunshots from my right. A shrouded form dives behind an armchair as bullets punch the wall beside my head.

I take cover in the closet.

Silence.

What the hell was that?

I have scant time to process before the specter moves again. A black robed figure vaults over the armchair and scissor kicks a goon on the other side. Both bodies drop and the hooded attacker rolls swiftly out of view.

Silence again.

I peek around the door frame.

The room is still, and I can't see Ashley or Claire.

Fuck.

I duck back as a pair of sportcoats pop out of a bedroom with pistols drawn. They creep cautiously past the big TV when it suddenly snaps on at full blast.

"...*pulled in the sixth inning after back-to-back doubles from Castillo and Jones but the bullpen held on for the...*"

One man turns to the sound just as a flying beer bottle hits him in the face. His cry draws attention from the second man who's bum rushed from his blind spot by a sexy elf.

Claire!

She sweeps both legs at the knee and the sportcoat's head cracks a table as he goes down. He's barely hit the floor before the TV topples over and Ashley stands glaring in its place.

Holy shit.

I want to call out, but my wife has this cold, crazy look in her eye. She grabs both guns off the groaning sportcoats and crouch-walks Claire through the open bedroom door.

Silence again.

I shake my head and try to process what I just saw.

The hooded figure. The beer bottle. The downed TV. By my count there are five sportcoats on the floor and my wife has two guns.

I suddenly feel better about our odds.

But what happened to Hobbes?

I peek slowly around the doorframe again. The suite is empty and still. Not a soul to be seen except...

Shit.

"Arden!"

He's still slumped heavily on the couch, a sitting duck amidst a hotel gunfight. The big man turns and smiles at me.

"You brought the cavalry after all, didn't you Clay?"

"Arden, get over here. Crawl to the closet. Stay low."

He shakes his head. "Not much for moving right now..." He shifts his weight and stretches a leg but makes no real effort to stand. "I'm molasses on the best of days, cowboy. We'll cuddle later."

I huff a frown but he's probably right. Injured and weak after days in a cell, poor Ard's had it worse than anyone else.

"Besides..." he goes on. "Looks like Ashley's got a piece now. We'll be out of this mess in no ti-"

Arden's cut off by another beer bottle smashing in the front of the room. In the same moment, our veiled savior bursts from hiding and sprints for the staircase leading to the loft. Gunshots follow from the kitchen as the fleeing figure climbs steps three at a time. I finally catch a glimpse inside the hood and it's fucking Sage.

Of course it is.

The stealthy assassin was her cosplay motif, and here she is live-acting the part. Black robes flutter and slugs splinter the banister, but Sage clears the threshold without a hit.

What a beast.

Craning up to follow her retreat, I see an open air duct in the ceiling above me. Is that how Sage got in? Am I living in a Hollywood flick? I take a deep breath and thank the Old Man.

This is your story, Clay.

Well, I'm glad I wrote in such capable women. Meanwhile I'm here cowering in the closet.

You'll get your chance to be brave.

I'm not sure I like the sound of that.

Just play lookout for now.

That much I can do. I've got good cover and a clear view of the suite. I figure half the sportcoats have been taken out, but there are still live guns out there. I whisper for Arden again.

"That ghost in the loft is Ashley's sister."

"Well, ain't she something."

"Wouldn't have come this far without her."

"Story of your life, Clay."

I grin at Arden's jibe. Ashley's carried me through thick and thin, and now Sage shows up to do the same. Old Man saw me married well.

"You got a read on any heavies?"

Arden tilts his head and speaks up so everyone can hear. "Trouble behind the bar, for sure. And that sounded like a .380 in the kitchen..." He leans forward and raises his voice another notch. "And don't think I can't see you two lovebirds in the john!"

Muffled curses from the bathroom as a sportcoat leans out and ducks back in.

"That's all I got, cowboy."

"Good work Ard." I glance at the door Ashley and Claire slipped through. It's open a crack, but dark beyond. I turn back to Arden. "Any guesses on Hobbes?"

"Fuck Hobbes."

"Amen, brother." I nod and pull back into the closet. "Keep your head down." Arden chuckles and coughs. I take a few deep breaths.

We're in a standoff now. Bodies tense in various hides around the suite, but who's going to make the next move? I pray it's not Ashley.

Just stay put, Boo. Anyone comes through that door you throw lead.

I wonder what Sage is plotting up in the loft. I don't think she's armed or she would have pulled it, but she's a lot smarter than me. Probably rigging up a pipe bomb out of pillows.

I smile at the thought as a funny smell hits my nose. Acrid and sharp. Like burning plastic. Shit, maybe Sage is going MacGyver up there. Or maybe...

My thoughts are interrupted by a break from the bathroom. Two sportcoats surge out and charge the staircase for the loft. I hear footfalls and brace for gunshots. After a few seconds of silence, someone behind the bar calls out.

"Status report?"

"There's nobody up here."

"Of course there is! Check everywhere!"

"He's in the ceiling or some shit."

"What are you talking ab-"

Right on cue, Sage reemerges from the ceiling just in front of my closet. She drops clean from the open vent, this time clutching a rope that runs back through the air duct and disappears out of sight. She freefalls for a moment - black cloak billowing - before the line catches her weight and jerks something heavy up in the loft. There's a crash and a scream and Sage swings through the open closet door like Tarzan.

"Holy shit."

"Stay down."

"What was that?"

"Big bookcase I rigged to tip over in the loft."

"How did you get into the vents?"

"Pickerington."

"Where'd you get that rope?"

"I brought the damn rope."

"You're amazing, Sage."

"Thank me later. We've still got problems in the kitchen and behind the bar."

"Did you see what happened to Hobbes?"

"Fuck Hobbes."

"Ashley's in the bedroom with Claire. Third door on the right."

"I saw that. What's that smell?"

"I think it might be-"

"Shhh."

Sage cuts me off as a fat scraping sound picks up across the room.

Schnnnk.... Schnnnk... Schnnnk...

She leans out the door for a moment then ducks back in.

"The refrigerator is moving."

"Huh?"

Schnnnk.... Schnnnk... Schnnnk...

"Someone's pushing the fridge. Using it for cover so Ashley can't get a shot."

"Well, where is it going?"

Sage leans out again.

Schnnnk.... Schnnnk... Schnnnk...

"Creeping around our left. We have to move."

"We have to what?"

"They're trying to flank us. Follow me on my mark."

"But we don't even-"

"Mark!"

Sage grabs my hand and pulls me out the closet door. I try to stay low, but have to leap over two unconscious sportcoats on the floor.

"This way!"

We pivot around a loveseat and sure enough there's a fridge looming on our left. A sportcoat leans out and levels his .380 but has to duck back as bullets ping the chrome facade. Cover fire from Ashley.

"Come on!"

We break toward the bedrooms, and I cast a hurried glance at Arden in the midst of all this heat. I give the big man credit. I'd be chin-deep in my own crack with all these bullets and bodies flying around, but he's got this queer kind of smile across his face. Almost peaceful.

He throws me a thumbs-up just as a lightbulb explodes above my head.

"Stay down!"

Sage jerks me to the floor. I go fetal while she throws herself on top of me and we roll together through the nearest door.

"Are you hit?"

"I don't think so."

I probe myself for holes but appear intact. We're slumped on the hard tile of a bathroom. Not the one I pissed in earlier, but an equally opulent washroom with a clear glass tub.

"Now what?"

"Lay low for a minute."

"I wish we could get to Ashley and Claire."

"Too risky. If we're all in the same room, Hobbes' men can concentrate their fire."

"Damn, you're good at this."

Sage shrugs and straightens her hood. "This costume really brings it out."

"I see that."

"Also, I want my fucking sister back."

"Amen."

I sit back and try to picture Ashley: Armed and sweaty and done with Hobbes' shit. We're so close now. Just a few layers of drywall and eggshell paint. I think about Del in his cell, and what Dixie said about getting out.

Master your mind.

I guess that's where the Old Man lives, after all.

Walk like a free man.

Could I pull that off? Just mosey across the suite like a Joe on holiday?

As if in response, another gunshot rings out and a sportcoat dives from the fridge to the closet we just left.

Musical cover.

"We need to finish these guys off." Sage keeps her voice low. "Before reinforcements show up."

"It's just the two left, I think."

"How about you take the closet and I take the bar?"

"What do you mean by 'take'?"

Sage frowns and pans her eyes around the bathroom. "There must be something in here we can use."

"Last time I grabbed a bar of soap, but it turned into a Voltstone in my pocket. Burned the shit out of Hobbes."

Sage gives me a queer look and I just shrug. No time to explain.

We both stand and rummage around the vanity. Egyptian hand towels. French cologne. Even the toothpaste looks high-end.

"I could kill a man with this..."

Sage admires an ivory toothbrush before slipping it into her cloak. She does the same with a sleek black hair dryer then turns to me.

"What do you want?"

"Ummmm..." I stare blankly at the toiletries. Nothing I'd bring to a gunfight. Sage sticks a bottle of mouthwash and a soap dish in my hands. The dish is solid marble and probably weighs ten pounds.

"I'll move first and draw most of the action," she says. "Ash should give us cover fire and you'll be safe if you stay tight to the wall."

I peek out and study the wainscot wall between me and the closet. It doesn't look all that safe.

"When I reach the bar, I'll cause a commotion and you jump your man. We drop these fuckers then get out of here."

I'm shaky and sore, but I nod my support. I'd follow Sage into Hades at this point. She's the one person who loves Ashley as much as me.

"Ready?"

"As I'll ever be."

She raises a gloved hand and counts down silently on her fingers, then drops into a crouch and crawls out of the room. I peek around the doorframe. The bar is about thirty feet away, a dark wooden counter with glass bottles shelved behind. You could throw a fucking rager with all that booze. I wonder if we spoiled Hobbes' post-convention party.

To my left is the closet where I woke up earlier with Ard. My route will take me past the loft stairs and a trio of closed doors. There's a couch and a coffee table I could use for cover, but Sage is probably right that the safest approach is to hug the wall. Assuming she keeps the barman occupied, the sportcoat in the closet shouldn't see me coming from out wide.

I watch Sage scuttle and pause behind a stout recliner. She's just outside Ashley's door, and I strain to spy shadows through the crack.

Sage turns back and waves to me. She counts down on her fingers again and I take that as my cue to move.

I channel my inner ninja. Sneaky. Stealthy. Spry. I take two steps out of the bathroom and immediately trip over my feet.

Fuck.

Sage bursts from cover and topples a porcelain table lamp. A head and a handgun pop up behind the bar, but before they can train on Sage she points the hair dryer like a pistol. The sportcoat flinches - just enough hesitation for Sage to find cover behind a couch. Ashley pops off a live round for good measure and the sportcoat drops back down behind the bar.

Now I'm the one exposed.

I scramble on all fours and struggle to hang on to the heavy soap dish. What am I supposed to do with this thing? I round the base of the stairs and slump hard into a corner.

Need some help here, Old Man.

You're a ghost, Clay. No one can see you.

I'm a ghost. I'm a ghost. I'm a ghost...

I clutch my mouthwash and do my best to blend into the wall. I can't see Sage from this angle, but she's probably covered half the distance to the bar. I slowly scoot toward the closet. Inch by inch like a kid on thin ice.

Suddenly a face pokes out of the doorway. A snarling sportcoat with a sloppy goatee. He pans around and looks right at me.

My heart stops.

My breath holds.

He swivels around again and pulls back inside.

Holy shit. Did he see me? How could he not?

You're a ghost.

I'm a sitting duck. All he has to do is lean out and blow me away. Can this soap dish stop a bullet?

I wait. Agonizing. Frozen. My heart starts back up and pounds like a piston in my chest. Seconds tick and moments pass and... nothing fucking happens.

Nothing happens!

He didn't see me!

It's your story, Clay.

While I drink the adrenaline of survival, Sage decides to make another move. This time she pops straight up, hands high and robe rippling. Ashley throws cover fire from the bedroom and Sage vaults across a table toward the bar.

What is she doing?

She's fully exposed, but no one takes a shot with Ashley winging lead. In one beautiful balletic move, Sage leaps from the table to the bartop. She lands with her palms down and swings a foot toward the rows of bottles on the wall. Dozens of fancy liquors cascade and crash onto the sportcoat below.

Move, Clay!

That's my cue. Muffled by the screams and shattering glass, I move quickly to the edge of the closet door. I've got a soap dish and some mouthwash and the element of surprise.

"Rinse this, asshole!"

Not the most heroic line, but a good holler gives me the courage to move. I lunge into the doorway and spot the sportcoat bracing on his knees. He looks up with a flash of recognition, but before he can raise his gun I spray a full quart of mouthwash into his face. Peppermint fresh.

"Ggggaaaaauuuuuuggghhh!"

I tell you what. You have not known pain until you've heard a man scream off an eyeball full of mouthwash. He drops his gun and goes writhing on the floor, tearing at his face like he's trying to rip it off. I could probably leave him like that, but this is no time for half measures. I heft my soap dish and clock him in the back of the head.

Out.

Poor guy should have shot me when he had the chance.

I stand there for a few seconds. A little shaky. A little shocked. I barely register when a hand slips around from behind and spins me into a kiss.

Chapter 60

You ever have one of those moments where you just shut down?
Like it's all too much and you can't process anymore?

That's what hits me when I finally embrace with Ash.

First, I'm kissing my wife. Something I've done a thousand times
before. It tastes familiar. Smells familiar. Her long hair tickles my face
like it always does.

Then it starts to hit me: I'm kissing my wife! After a week of chaos
and hell, she's actually here. In my arms.

I run a hand down her back, feeling out all the old dimples and
curves. She squeezes me tight but stays clear of my shoulder. Knows
her way around a busted cowboy.

It's intoxicating. Euphoric. Familiar, yet new.

Her lips are aggressive. Fingers probing and firm. It's like she's
trying to prove I'm real and I don't blame her. How long has it been?
The fucking Chaplain Hills? I left her underground at Del's with
armed mercenaries bearing down.

And now here we are. Fifty stories above Pittsburgh. Penthouse
suite surrounded by blood and broken glass. It's all too much.

"You found me..."

She whispers in my ear. Voice husky and soft. Waves of emotion
work me over and I go numb right there in her arms.

"Okay... easy Boo."

My body goes slack and Ashley has to hold me up. She's so fucking
strong. They've got her in some kind of roughspun jumpsuit, but I sink
into the softness of her chest.

She gives me a minute like that then pulls me back to reality.

"We need to collect the guns."

Of course. The fucking guns. I peel myself from Ashley's breast
and Sage steps in to embrace her sister. No words between them, just
the empathy of family.

Once we've had our little reunion, we round up the firearms and
herd the sportcoats into the closet. Guys are groggy and limping and

nobody puts up much of a fight. They eyeball Sage warily. Claire shuts the door on a dozen dusted goons and we shove a heavy love seat against the frame.

We did it.

It's over.

I step back to breathe a sigh of relief when Oliver Hobbes clears his throat from the couch.

"Ahem."

I turn. We all turn. Hobbes sits tall with a gun pressed to Arden's head. The big man looks nervous for the first time all day.

"Hobbes."

I want to run over there and punch him, but I'm not leaving Ashley's side. Where has he been hiding? Should be in the wind by now.

"Where did you come from?" Sage asks the question, but Hobbes just shrugs. Billionaire has earned a few secrets, I guess.

"Lay down your weapons."

Ashley and Sage each hold a pistol, and we stashed the rest in a tub. I see the girls clench, dying to take the shot, but that could be curtains for Ard. They drop their guns in unison.

"Good, good." Hobbes stands and gives Arden a kick. "Go join your friends."

Arden struggles to his feet and staggers over to our group. He's breathing heavy and it takes Ashley and I both to prop him up.

"Sorry to play the goat, cowboy. I left most of my fight in the hills."

"Arden, you're the only reason we got this far."

That's true enough. Ol' Kirby had us dead to rights with USAC minutes out. It was Arden and his wolf that bought Del and I time to slip. Even so, here we are at the wrong end of another standoff. I suppose this will be the end of it, one way or another.

"What do you want, Hobbes?" Claire takes a step forward and cocks a hip. The brazenness of youth.

Hobbes trains his gun but doesn't answer. He looks around the suite like he's calculating his next move.

"You've neutered my men, so I'll have to do this myself." He waves his hand to the glass doors on our left. "Everybody out on the balcony."

Nobody moves at first, then Hobbes puts a bullet in the wall above our heads.

"I'm not asking twice."

That gets everyone cowering for the exits. I strain to shepherd Arden along with one good arm.

"You fucking meddlers..." Hobbes snarls his words. "Trying to undo everything I've built." He holds the gun like a game controller. Not an expert, but no novice either. Wish I had another bottle of mouthwash to throw.

We herd through the sliding glass doors onto the penthouse balcony. It's a perfect summer evening in Pittsburgh. Balmy air. Popcorn clouds. Amber sunset paints the rivers below.

The balcony is a large enclosure framed in chest-high glass. There's a bar, a barbecue, and a cushy patio set. Ashley and I ease Arden into a wicker chair.

Now what?

Hobbes stands between us and the door. Arms folded. Gun dangling. Bit of crazy in his eye.

"Who wants to go first?"

Not sure I like the sound of that.

"What do you mean?" Claire asks.

"Over the top." Hobbes gestures to the glass-paned barrier surrounding the balcony. "Which one of you kids is ready to fly."

"Fuck off."

He slowly shakes his head. "We've reached an impasse. Your future is incompatible with mine."

"Who do you think we are?" Ashley steps forward and waves a finger. "Your plane landed on *our* land. Your bombs fell on *our* house. Your soldiers threatened *our* lives." She scoffs and gestures to our motley crew. "We're not some syndicate out to take you down. We're just trying to survive."

Hobbes shrugs. "You threatened to expose me. You put my name across the news. You've created more headaches that will cost me more money than you could ever imagine." He narrows his eyes and takes his own step toward Ash. "You're not the only one determined to survive."

That sets everyone quiet for a minute. Just the distant din of the city below. A bird lands on the empty barbecue and pecks at some charred remnant.

"Well, I ain't going off no building," Arden says.

"Me neither." Ashley stands protectively in front of the group. "If you want us dead, you'll have to do it yourself."

Hobbes frowns and clenches his jaw. He's thinking about it. Visualizing putting a bullet in each of our heads. His eyes glaze and fingers twitch on the butt of the gun...

Then an alarm goes off and shatters the spell.

"What the?" Hobbes turns to the sound then back to us with a devilish grin. Just over his shoulder, something flickers and glows. I lean out to get a better look and realize the couch is on fire.

"Looks like your little stunt with the Voltstone went too far." He sneers at me and rubs the blister on his palm.

"What's he talking about, Clay?"

"I don't really know."

It's true, I don't. Something happened when I went to find the Old Man. That stone turned up in my pocket, hot as a branding iron. Then it rolled under the couch and must have ignited the carpet.

"There's still one easy way down." Hobbes snickers and sticks the gun in his pants. "I'll leave you all to decide."

He slides open the glass doors and ducks back from the surge of heat.

"Wooooooo!"

Hobbes pulls his shirt over his mouth and slips inside without another word. He locks the door behind him with a *click.*

Chapter 61

"Bastard!"

Sage runs over and yanks at the door. She wrestles the handle then pulls back with a cry. "It's hot!"

Black smoke fills the suite behind her, obscuring everything but orange flames licking against the glass.

"What do we do?" Claire asks.

"We need to get inside."

"But it's on fire!"

"The whole building could go up. We'll die if we get stuck out here."

I turn to Ashley and she just nods. Arden frowns and shakes his head. Claire darts around the patio in a panic. "Help! Somebody help!" She runs to the rail and screams a desperate plea to Pittsburgh. "Hellllllllllp!"

No response but the wailing alarm. Claire sags to the floor and starts to cry. The rest of us contemplate mortality in silence.

This is still your story, Clay. Nobody needs to die out here.

Well then, we better act fast. I walk to the ledge and peek over. Certain death.

"Sage is right." I pull Claire to her feet as she wipes mascara off her cheeks. "We're too high up to be rescued. We need to get through that door."

Sage tries the handle again and growls in frustration.

"How thick is the glass?" Arden asks.

"At least half an inch." She tries a firm kick with her boot. "It's stout."

Arden nods and looks around the patio. "What about that grill?"

All eyes settle on the swanky barbecue set. Ard can burn a mean burger, but this obviously isn't the time. He wants a run at that glass. Ashley and Sage hustle over to check it out.

355

"Stainless steel... twenty-pound tank... four wheels... this could work!" Sage slams the hood a few times to confirm the strength of the unit. They wheel it opposite the door and eyeball the approach.

"We've got about fifteen feet."

"Everybody needs to push."

We each grab a corner of the grill while Arden stands by to count us down.

"On my mark..." He says. "Three... two... one... Go!"

We lurch like a drunk mule. The grill immediately turns crooked and Claire falls down. Ashley heaves to straighten us out and we roll headlong toward the door.

Boom!

Steel meets glass but nothing gives. Sage tumbles into me and the grill topples onto us both. Not our best effort.

"Again!"

Ashley barks orders and uprights the heavy grill. There's a spider web of cracks in the patio door. We wheel back to the starting point as Claire stands and brushes herself off. She's got blood on her knees and steel in her eyes.

"You all right?"

She just nods and sets herself in front of Ash. We arrange better this time: Sage and Claire nimble in the front, Ashley and I strong in the back.

"On my mark..." Arden counts down again. "Go! Go! Go!"

This time we break in unison, like a bobsled team sprinting down the cute. Everyone keeps their feet and the grill stays true as we aim for that tangle of cracks.

Boom!

No stopping it this time. The door explodes in a shower of glass and the grill goes tumbling into the suite. I'm hit with hot air and a face full of smoke.

"Back up!"

Somebody pulls me away from the door. Ashley or Sage, I'm not sure. I find myself coughing blind in Arden's arms while the big man pats me on the back. "Nice work, cowboy. Now we just need to walk through the flames."

The thought ties my nuts in a knot. Just standing by that door felt like a furnace on my skin. I get my breath back and blink away tears to see Ashley and Sage kicking glass shards from the frame. Claire stands next to Arden, shaking like a leaf.

"You can do this, sweetie." He offers a big bear paw and Claire dives in.

"I don't want to go in there." She sniffles against his breast.

"None of us do." Arden squeezes Claire tight and tries to wring out some of the fear.

Ashley and Sage jog back over, wincing from the smoke. Sage takes off her cloak and wraps it around Claire. "Protect your skin." Sexy Link straightens and nods, relieved to have some cover against the flames.

Ashley rips fabric from her own outfit and offers each of us a swath to cover our face. "There's a lot of smoke in there." She glances back and shakes her head. "Most important thing is *don't panic*. We move together. We stay together. It's going to be hard to see and hard to breathe." She pauses again, thinking through the layout in her mind. "Our exit is to the left, but we have to get around some furniture and flames. Stay low. Call out any obstacles you run into."

She stops and looks each of us in the eye. "Ready?" Solemn nods around the group. We link hands in a human chain. Sage takes the lead followed by Arden, Claire, Ashley and me. Before I can protest, I'm pulled to the precipice just outside the broken door.

Don't let me go, Boo.

I can hear the flames. A hissing, popping, pummeling sound. Sage takes one last look back, then disappears into the void.

This is really happening.

Arden ducks in gingerly behind, but Claire hesitates at the threshold. She shuts her eyes and recoils from the smoke. "It's so thick!"

Ashley leans forward and puts a hand on her back. "Stay low. Follow Arden. I'll be right behind you." Claire nods and drops into a squat, cinching her cloak and fighting every instinct to run. A moment more of indecision then she moves. Ashley follows quickly and I'm pulled headlong into hell.

My first awareness is the stench. Chemical and caustic. Hot smoke stings my nostrils even through the makeshift mask. I clear the door and drop to my knees as Ashley jerks me forward. We crawl a few feet until someone yells "Stop!"

357

I have no idea where I am. The airy suite from earlier has transformed into a smoky inferno. My instinct says to bear left, but half the furniture is on fire. I see a flaming couch and the big easy chair Sage vaulted over earlier. Large swaths of carpet glow orange like lava.

We crawl forward some more and I bang my head on a rigid edge. Table leg? A door? I feel polished metal and realize it's the fucking refrigerator. The surface is hot to the touch.

"Stay with me!"

Ashley guides me around the obstacle and toward the center of the suite. Hot sweat drips across my face. I feel like I'm melting. The heat is relentless as angry energy tries to tear me apart.

We stay low around a coffee table but then our path is blocked again. That mess of TV Ashley knocked down earlier. Sage reroutes toward the far side of the suite where the flames seem less intense.

"This way!"

I keep my nose in Ashley's butt. Something pops beside us and hot sparks shower my face. We roll hard to the right and lose contact with the rest of the group.

"What was that?"

"I don't know!"

I can barely hear her over the roar of the flames. Something flares across the room and a surge of hot air knocks us flat. The heat is unbearable. Knives and needles on my skin. I can smell my hair burning and feel my boots melting.

"Come on!"

Ashley yanks at me but I'm dead weight. Too frightened to move. Too suffocated to breathe. I press hard to the floor hoping it might just give way.

"Clayton Fucking Moore!"

Even Ashley's no match for this smoldering hell. We should have gone off the balcony like Hobbes suggested. At least I'd have died with clean air in my lungs.

I curl into a ball and prepare for the end. The inferno overwhelms me. Scorching. Smothering. Screaming like death. The flames themselves seem to whimper and wail. I close my eyes and cover my ears and-

Wait.

That sound.

358

Those screams.

It's not the fire.

It's not the flames.

The dawning horror snaps me out of my spell. I grope to my right and feel the firm frame of a loveseat, propped against a door confining twelve live men inside.

"The sportcoats!"

Ashley grabs my ears and pulls my face right up to hers.

"CLAY WE HAVE TO-"

"The sportcoats!"

"What?"

"Hobbes' men! They're still in the closet!"

"Oh God..."

Here we are burning to death beside a room full of people. Bad people. Lackeys for a madman. Do we try and help, or leave everyone to die?

Is that a real question?

Oh, come on. I don't owe these assholes anything.

It's your story, Clay.

Aaarrrgghhh! Fucking Old Man and your morals. Of course I have to save them. It might as well be me in there, after all.

Ashley yanks my arm again and this time I follow her lead. We stumble blind around the side of the love seat, clinging to each other like kids in a storm.

The screams turn hysterical. I've never heard such fear. Desperate men throw themselves against the door, but the heavy couch holds back any chance of escape.

I slip my fingers beneath the base of the seat. One good hand. I feel dizzy and faint and too weak to be much help. Hope Ashley still has her legs.

"Push!"

She grunts and strains next to me, but the couch doesn't even budge. Might as well weigh a million pounds. The door rattles as sportcoats pound in a panic. I sputter and gasp for breaths that won't come.

"Push, Clay!"

I am pushing. I think. So tired and weak. It feels like I'm drowning. All those years of smoking back to bite me in the lungs. I'm about to give up when a new voice hollers in my ear.

"What are you doing?"

Sage.

"The men in the closet!" Ashley yells back.

"We need to get out of here!"

"Help us push!"

Sage squeezes in next to Ashley and braces herself against the couch. She wastes no time counting off another effort.

"One. Two. Three!"

We all heave in unison and the love seat moves an inch. It's this damn extravagant carpet. So thick you need a plow to get through.

"New plan," I offer between coughs. "Lift and pivot."

The girls say nothing which I take as their assent. Every word wastes precious air. Sage just yells "Three!" and we go.

Go! Go! Go! Go!

We raise the edge of the love seat and work to swivel it wide. We open up six inches. Then a foot. Then two. My muscles scream for oxygen, but Sage and Ashley push on. Suddenly the door flies open and a horde of sportcoats knock me down.

"Fire!"

"The exit!"

"Which way?"

A chaotic stampede of bodies overwhelms us. I take a hard knee to the nose and my vision swims with stars. Two men tangle up with Ashley and she fights to get free.

"Move! Move! Bear right toward the door!"

Sage directs traffic as scared men scatter for survival. They scream and charge and one just keeps muttering: "He left us. He left us. He left us..."

I roll clear of the melee and try to get my bearings.

"Ashley!"

I call for my wife, but my voice is scratchy and weak. My throat is closing up.

"Ashley!"

I grope blindly as frantic footsteps trample past. Everyone for themselves in this boiling pit of death.

"Ashley..."

I crawl in the direction where I think she fell.

"Ashley..."

My brain turns soggy as blackness swallows me up. We're running out of time. Too much heat. Too much smoke. Too much distance from here to the door.

"Ash..."

My hand meets something solid. I feel the rough fabric of Ashley's jumpsuit.

"Ashley!"

Arms. Legs. Hair. A face. It's her, all right, but she's not moving.

"Ashley!"

I croak and plead but no response.

"Ashley..."

I collapse onto her chest. Faint heartbeat. Breathing slow. Oh fuck, we're fucked, oh fuck.

"Help... please..."

Does anyone hear? Has everyone left? At least Ashley and I are together now. That's all I really wanted in the end.

"I love you, Ash..." I whisper a prayer with the last of my breath. Hug her close with the last of my strength. Even through all the cinder and smoke, I catch a subtle whiff of rosehip. The faintest trace of better days.

"See you on the other side..."

I close my eyes and drift slowly toward the light. My soul skirts heaven and hell until a strong hand clamps around my arm.

"Up."

A voice I barely recognize. Sage, is that you? Someone lifts me off the ground like a limp doll.

All the fight is gone. All my strength is gone. I hang helpless as I'm carried through fire.

Old Man come to take me away.

Chapter 62

Sometime later, I find myself on a floor. It's hard and smooth and cool to the touch. My skin feels raw and my eyes are caked shut. I lay quiet for a moment taking staggered, painful breaths.

"Try not to move."

I peel open an eye and see a red-faced man with a sweaty goatee. I recognize the sportcoat as one of Hobbes' men. He nods down at me.

"Thank you for letting us out."

I try to formulate a response, but my tongue is like molasses in my mouth. He points to a spot next to me and I roll into the arms of my wife.

Ashley!

She's supine and sluggish, but coming around. Her hands squeeze mine softly and her eyes squint with a smile. I'd kiss her but we both need our breath. The sportcoat disappears and a new figure leans down.

"Take it slow."

Sage. Her voice is wheezy and hoarse. She helps me sit up and take a groggy look around. We're in a stairwell on the landing between floors.

"What happened?"

"That man carried you and Ashley out of the suite. We should be safe for now, but it's a long walk down."

The concrete stairs disappear in both directions. Emergency lights reveal a haze of smoke above.

"Did everyone get out?"

"As far as I know." Sage gestures to the descending steps below. "Arden and Claire are already on their way down."

Ashley sits up and puts an arm around my shoulders. She doesn't say anything, just holds me for a minute while we process that we're still alive.

I can't believe some sportcoat carried us out. The Old Man works in mysterious ways. If not for my decision to move the couch, we'd probably all be dead.

"Let's get out of here." Ashley stands and helps me to my feet. My whole body hurts, and my brain feels foggy from lack of oxygen. I take an unsteady step and completely lose my balance. Ashley holds me back from tumbling headlong down the stairs.

"Stay with me."

I lean against my wife and we start the long trek down. We march for what feels like twenty minutes when I catch the number on a passing floor.

Forty-four. We've covered six stories. Holy shit, this is going to be a slog.

We descend a few more levels before we run into Arden and Claire. They're moving slowly with a pack of sportcoats, hostilities forgotten as everyone navigates the endless steps.

"How you feeling, big man?"

"Wooo, Clay..." Arden eyeballs me with genuine relief. "It's good to see you breathing. Let's never do that again."

"It's off my list."

One of the sportcoats gives me a furtive nod then casts his eyes back down. I guess that's mercenary for "Thank you." Another limps badly on an injured leg, while a third keeps whispering to himself:

"He left us. He left us. He left us..."

Rude awakening when your boss abandons you to die. I wonder if any of these men will ever see Oliver Hobbes again.

We continue our interminable trek. Everyone's face is black with soot and Ashley's eyebrows have burned away. We start encountering other guests. A young girl clutching a stuffed giraffe. A fat man wearing a robe with no shoes. They join the flow as we march ever downward. Step after step. Flight after flight. Floor after excruciating floor.

"I'm not cut out for this."

Arden pauses on a landing, breathing heavy and sweating hard.

"Almost there, Ard." I look up to see we've reached floor twenty-nine. Not even halfway to the ground.

"You're full of shit, cowboy. Maybe y'all can just roll me the rest of the way."

My calves and quads are burning, so I can't imagine how poor Arden feels right now. You would think going down would be easier than going up, but you're still fighting gravity either way.

A commotion from below gets our attention as a pack of first responders come jogging up the stairs. I count four firemen, two police officers, and a paramedic.

"We've got reports of fire and gunshots."

I just point upward and the group continues on. Another pair of firemen come around the corner and stop to enquire about our state.

"Is anyone injured?"

"This man needs help getting down the stairs."

They take one look at Arden and move to hoist the big man beneath his arms.

"We can't carry you, but we can take some of the weight off."

"You'd need a whole brigade to carry me." Arden chuckles and coughs. "But I appreciate the support."

The trio sets off easing Arden down the stairs. We fall in behind and the journey continues. Twenty-eight. Twenty-seven. Twenty-six. Twenty-five. I try counting steps but give up around a hundred. I'd kill for a glass of water. My throat feels like it's full of sand.

"Where will we go from here?"

It takes me a moment to realize Ashley is talking. I march like a robot and point vaguely ahead.

"I mean after all this. Our whole valley was destroyed. I don't think I can go back to that."

It's a fair point. We're homeless now. I loved that land with all my heart, but there's no undoing what Hobbes and USAC did.

"You can stay with me as long as you like," Sage says.

"Always welcome at our hole in the hills," Arden puts in.

I squeeze Ashley's hand and she squeezes back. "All that matters is we're together now."

The descent goes on. Twenty-four. Twenty-three. Twenty-two. Twenty-one. More guests file down, and first responders file up. Round about floor fifteen we stop for another blow. Some passerby offers water and I give the guy a hug. We're all breathing hard. Knees scream with every step. My crotch is chafed like a bull rider without his chaps.

Reminds me of a time Pops and I got caught out crossing the ranch. I was eleven or twelve, familiar with a horse but far from seasoned. Pops asked me along to clear some Scotch thistle and had me on this ancient nag named Caroline. She was a smooth ride, but had a stubborn streak. More likely to give orders than to take 'em.

We got a few miles out when we ran into some weather. Hellfire and hailstones. Mean Texas squall. Pops turned us back, but Caroline spooked and took off. Ran me over three hills before she heeled up under a pecan tree. I could not for the life of me move her off the spot.

Pops caught up and we swapped mounts while he tried to coax old Caroline out. That put me on his horse, Donnybrook. This was young Donny, full of piss and eager to please. He'd go where I asked, but made a production out of getting there. Every step was full of bump, jostle, and buck.

So it was we humped back home through a downpour. Pops kept Caroline on a short rein while Donnybrook danced through puddles. Riding that horse was like straddling a clothes dryer. My ass turned into one big blister.

Not sure I ever would have made it without Pops talking me through.

"Just hold tight and keep moving," he said. "Only way to get there is to get there."

That was Pops. Practical and patient. Lead a couple of cattle drives and you learn some routes don't have shortcuts. Only way to get there is to get there.

"Ten floors left," Ashley declares as we round another landing. Can't tell if the group is encouraged by that or not.

"Nine." She starts the countdown, but nobody joins in.

"Eight." It's like those last miserable miles of a road trip.

"Seven." I'm never taking the fucking stairs again.

"Six." For the first time she gets a few more voices in the chorus.

"Five." Claire sticks her hand in the air while Arden takes a fortifying breath.

"Four." A little stronger now. A little more enthusiasm and hope.

"Three." Half the stairwell joins in. Folks can taste it. Almost there.

"Two." We round a corner, and the final flight comes into view. I fight the urge to just throw myself down the stairs.

"One!" Some cheers and huzzahs. Exhausted but grateful. We emerge through a fire door to a parking lot and flashing lights.

"This way." A man in uniform leads us away from the building. I hold tight to Ashley's hand as we walk shaky on solid ground.

I crane my neck and look up. Way up. Too far up. I see black smoke and blue helicopters circling in the evening sky.

There's a police cordon and a TV crew and a fire chief yelling into a phone. I spot our man Pickerington with a group of hotel brass. His suit is unruffled, and he gives me a professional nod.

Is it over? Did we win?

Ashley and I stagger toward a triage tent when she suddenly pulls me close.

"Over there." I follow her gaze to an idling entourage and meet the steely stare of Oliver Hobbes. He looks startled to see us. Even more so when a sportcoat stomps over and kicks him in the nuts.

That one's for you, Tuck.

We're almost to the medical tent when a body breaks the line and runs in our direction. Shirtless. Gauntlets. War paint. Del comes barreling into Arden and the two collapse in a pile of tears.

A young nurse leads me under the awning and helps me into a soft-backed chair. She checks my pulse and asks me questions, but all I can do is grimace and grunt. An oxygen mask slips over my mouth, and everything gets a little dreamy. I hear music but can't tell if it's a radio or in my head.

I doze.

I wake up.

Ashley's in a chair beside me. Her bandaged forehead leans against my arm.

Come and find me, Clay Moore.

We did it. Somehow. I kiss her hair and drift back into sleep.

I wake later to some commotion. Wave down one of the nurses and she calms me with a smile.

"We couldn't keep him out," she says.

What's that supposed to mean?

Almost too worn out to notice there's a bloodhound in my lap.

Chapter 63

Six months later.

"Watch your nose, boy."

Ol' Baxter's plugged into a pricker bush again. Every damn time.

"Easy out now. Back this way."

We're hiking up the back side of a craggy hill. Probably run this trail twice a week, but Bax always takes a swim in these brambles. Must smell an old gopher den.

"Boy you're in it now..."

I wait back and let him root his way through. No use scolding a bloodhound in a briar patch.

I sit on a stump and take in the sights. Crisp, clear evening. Bout an hour 'til sunset. We don't do night walks around here cause I ain't got the lay of the land yet. These slopes are treacherous enough when I can see my feet.

"You all right, Bax?"

He woofs an okay.

Something of a miracle he found me that day after the fire. We never figured out how, but that's a bloodhound for ya.

It took everyone some time to get right after all that. Ashley was dehydrated and spent two days in a hospital bed. I had surgery on my shoulder and need one more to clean out the scars. It's all right. We went to hell and came through it. It took me three showers to purge all that soot and I haven't touched a cigarette since.

After the hospital we spent a few weeks in Pittsburgh to get our bearings back. Rented a nice room - ground floor on a golf course. Not really my scene, but the food was on point. After that we bought a truck and started working our way west. No real schedule. No real plan. Eventually we reached Wyoming and shacked up with Arden and Del. Took one trip down to the valley and loaded everything we could salvage into the truck. It wasn't much. I've got a suit pending for damages against the *Cygneous Corp.* My lawyer says they'll settle, but it'll take a few years.

"Let's go, Bax. It's gettin' dark."

The three of us since settled down out here in Idaho. Bought a cabin in the hills overlooking some of the prettiest land you'll see. It's quiet out here. Skies are clear. Ashley hunts for venison and wants to start an herb garden in the spring.

Of course, we had to get away after all that Voltstone mess came down. Our little dead-man plea went live and suddenly everyone wanted a piece of Clay Moore.

I let Claire handle all the press requests. She's got this social media empire now. I laid low as long as I could, until we finally agreed to sit down with one of the national shows. It made for good TV, but I don't think folks really believed me. Hobbes denied it. *Cygneous* denied it. USAC didn't even seem to exist.

That might have been the end if not for something funny happening: Hobbes' men started turning on him. One by one these sportcoats came out of the woodwork like, "Yeah, it's all true." Started with those guys we sprung from the closet. Guess they didn't take too kindly being left behind to die.

Reporters chased the story and the snowball picked up speed. Once it hit Washington, the whole thing blew up. Hobbes lost all his friends. You know how politicians can be.

Round about then, Ashley and I slipped the scene. We weren't the story anymore. Of course, I still get phone calls, but service ain't that good out here. Ashley says I should write a book or something. I don't know.

"Clayyyytooon! Dinnnner!"

Ashley yells from the house and that gets Baxter moving. He scrambles out of the thicket and comes wagging to my feet. Couple of burrs on his snout, but no worse for wear.

"Let's go, boy."

We hike the last fifty yards back to the cabin. Our home sits on a hill with dense wood on three sides. The front porch overlooks a grassy meadow, and snow caps stand mighty to the east. We'll be under the white stuff before long.

"Get in here while it's hot."

I can smell the ginger stew before we're even in the door. Ashley's taken to all this preserve and canning stuff Del taught her. We've got a root cellar full of vegetables and two hundred pounds of frozen meat.

"And what have you boys been up to?"

Ashley stands tall behind a glazed oak table. Hair tied back. Smile in her eyes. Four months pregnant and already starting to show.

"Baxter walked me through an old deadfall across the ravine. I think there's an owl's nest over that way."

"I've been hearing them."

Ashley ladles hot soup into a couple of bowls and sets out meat scraps for the dog. Having a kid was never really our plan, but I wouldn't call it an accident either. After a few months to digest, I'd say we're downright excited. I just hope I can do as well as Pops did for me.

We slurp our dinner and cap the meal with a slice of cobbler from the fridge.

"Gosh those peaches are tasty."

"Lula says she puts cinnamon in the preserves."

Lula is our only neighbor. Old Paiute widow somewhere down the hill. She comes by once a week on horseback with a bag of provisions for Ash. Claims to be a midwife and a healer. Good people.

I clean the dishes while Ashley puts on a classical track. Tonight it's an Italian piece called *White Clouds*. Gentle piano warms the cabin while the sun dips down outside.

"You want to cuddle on the porch for a while?"

"You had me at cuddle, Boo."

"I'll get some blankets."

Ashley goes digging through the linen closet while I mix up a pot of decaf with cream.

A bunch of kids ended up finding Hobbes' Voltstone mine. Well not kids, but younger folks. Called themselves an "activist collective". They dug through sat data and eventually hiked in through the mountains of Pakistan. One day this crowd of Zoomers showed up with a bullhorn and a bunch of drones. There's a YouTube clip with like a billion views.

As for Hobbes, he flew the coop when all the heat got too much. Mr. "power rules the world" ran into a mess he couldn't buy out. Last I

369

heard he went underground somewhere in Belarus. Probably better than he deserves.

The rest of us mostly just went back to keeping on. Sage is on a tenure track with speaking gigs around the U.S. She said she'll take time off when the baby comes, and we promised to keep the guest room warm.

Claire helped me track down Tuck's brother Miles, and we all got together in Fresno for a beer. Well, a couple of beers. The man can throw 'em back. We swapped stories and raised toasts to the lost pilot. Miles and Claire had a thing for a while, but I think that's over now.

Arden was laid up pretty bad thanks to those slugs Kirby put in his arm. He had blood loss and bone fragments and fought off infection twice. Rough ride. Del kept vigil by his bedside until one day Arden popped up and walked out. I guess they'd both had enough. Now they're back home in the Chaplains, training up a wild wolf pup named Volt.

I'll miss those talks with Del. Blackfoot tells it so simple and true. We had a few more heart-to-hearts about the Old Man, and he said something that'll stay with me for a while.

"God is a partnership," he said. "The Old Man writes the story, and Clay Moore acts it out. But you can swap roles any time."

I'll raise a glass to that.

"You ready?"

"Let's do it."

Ashley, Baxter, and I fold ourselves into an oversized rocker on the porch. It's below freezing now, but we've got enough here to keep warm. Ashley kicks her feet up and nuzzles down into my chest.

"Do you think the baby will look more like you or me?"

"I don't know. Probably something in between."

"I hope it has your eyes."

Ashley's changed a lot these last few months. She's lighter somehow, like she let a bunch of old stuff go. She smiles more and sleeps better at night and talks more about the future than the past.

"Sage says mixed-race babies are better looking. Healthier too."

"Sage would know."

"It's the genes, I guess. They take the best of both sides."

"Well then our kid's gonna rule the world."

She grins and runs a gentle hand over her bump. An owl hoots in the distance and Baxter raises up an ear.

It's a perfect night. Full bellies. Full hearts.

High above, a plane tracks slow across the stars.

The End

Thank you for reading my novel. This was a special project for me, and I really hope you enjoyed it. As an independent author, I'm just out here slinging it on my own. You can show your support a few different ways:

1. Leave a review.
2. Tell a friend.
3. Visit my website. (**www.ericshoffman.com**)

Reviews and recommendations are the lifeblood of online sales, and it would mean the world if you took a few minutes to publicly profess your love for Clay Moore.

Scan to leave a review:

In addition to that, I'd love to hear from you. Email me directly at eric.s.hoffman.writer@gmail.com or visit my website where you can get updates on my life and future projects.

Acknowledgements

There's a little bit of everyone in this book. I started writing in the fall of 2019, shortly before my first child was born. I had this image of a man and his dog and a plane in the night, but had no idea where it would go or how to get there. I persisted through two kids and a pandemic to produce the manuscript you hold today. I'm very proud of it. I worked very hard.

Of course, nothing happens in a vacuum, and I have many to thank for their inspiration and their help. The title character is actually named after a beloved cat. Clay gave me fifteen years and followed me halfway around the world. When she passed, I made a vow to honor her with a story and this was the result.

I wrote the bulk of this book while living in Malaysia, and I'm grateful for the people that showed me so much love along the way. Thank you, Mak and Abah and the entire Kampung crew. I couldn't have done any of it without you. I wrote clips in coffee shops and hair salons and hospitals and hotels. Everywhere I went and everyone I met shaped the final work in some way.

Thank you to my beta readers, Andrew, Matt, and Ross. (But *especially* Ross.)

Thank you, nskvsky, for the amazing cover design.

Thank you, Mom. (Hi Mom! I wrote a book!)

Thank you, Su, my beautiful wife. We've been through so much together and our journey has only begun.

Finally, this book is dedicated to my late father: Bradley Arden Hoffman. Dad was a writer and a leader and my role model for life. I regret that he never got to see me publish, but just like Clay Moore and his Pops, I know he's with me always.

About the Author

Eric S. Hoffman is a writer and father of two. He's been all over the world, but currently resides at home with his family in Cleveland, Ohio. This is his first novel.

Also by Eric S. Hoffman: *Reverend and Raindrop* – a pulse-pounding horse adventure for young readers.

www.ericshoffman.com

Made in the USA
Middletown, DE
06 October 2022